THROUGH ANY WINDOW

DEB RICHARDSON-MOORE

Through Any Window
Red Adept Publishing, LLC
104 Bugenfield Court
Garner, NC 27529
https://RedAdeptPublishing.com/

Cover Art by Streetlight Graphics[1]

1. http://StreetlightGraphics.com

For Reid Lehman, Ryan Duerk, Lauren Stephens, Jeremy Huff, David Hanna, and all those who work to shelter our marginalized citizens

The Night Of

Riley never knew what woke her. A giggle, a sigh, a moan... someone else was in the pool house. She slipped from the bed that wasn't hers, clutching its lightweight comforter as a shield, and tiptoed to the closed bedroom door to listen.

Another giggle and a responding murmur—two people, and they weren't trying to be quiet. *Don't they know I'm here?*

Another thought occurred to her—she *wasn't* supposed to be here. For the first time all summer, she'd left the restaurant early.

Blood swooshed in her ears, making it hard to hear what was going on. The pair wasn't likely to be Mikala and Luke, who had the run of the expansive main house. Unless they were playing out—what, a cabana-pool-boy fantasy? She considered proper Mikala and her banker husband. Doubtful.

Then who?

The neighbors used the pool freely, but Riley had been living there for three months, and the pool house was her space, her home. For the moment, anyway.

Riley held her breath and turned the doorknob a quarter inch then another quarter and another. The knob was new enough that it rotated soundlessly. She pushed, and the door swung open, silent as absence. Outside, storm clouds blackened the sky, but pool lights gleamed through the glass doors and illuminated two people on the sofa, half-dressed, entwined. She could make out one but not the other. Scenes from the summer whirred and clicked into place, and she was pretty sure she knew the identity of the hidden one.

A flash of lightning and clap of thunder, all but simultaneous, made her jump. The long-awaited storm had arrived. A torrent of rain hammered the pool-house roof, causing a roar before the thunder crashed off to the east.

Movement across the living room caught her attention, and she lifted her eyes to the kitchen doorway some twenty feet away. Another figure stood watching the oblivious couple as they moaned and writhed. The figure's arm slowly rose and pointed.

Is that a gun? Riley started to cry out, but her throat locked. She swallowed and tried again, but before she could shout a warning, light and sound exploded. This time, it wasn't the storm.

She ducked back inside her bedroom and crouched on the floor, pulling the comforter over her head. She rocked back and forth, back and forth, shivering, her panicked breath too shallow to pull air into her lungs. She heard groans from the living room and a man's hoarse cry. A door slammed.

This couldn't be happening again. It simply couldn't. Riley closed her eyes and rocked and rocked and rocked.

Chapter 1

June—Three Months Earlier

Riley

Riley eased her dented black Beetle onto Gunter Avenue, a street that would occasion some serious jaw dropping back home. Her mama's best friend, Juanita, had once said she wanted to live on an *avenue* because it sounded so elegant. At the time, Juanita was under a hair dryer at Maisie's Beauty Saloon—yep, that was how Maisie spelled it—and Riley figured she was thinking Fifth Avenue or the Champs-Élysées. But these houses lining Gunter Avenue would have fit Juanita's fantasy just as well.

The neighborhood around Gunter was once a poverty-stricken extension of Greenbrier's dying downtown, or so Riley had read. But with the rebound of a lively city center, its old mill houses were being snapped up and torn down, replaced by these glitzy showplaces within walking distance of hot bars and restaurants. The original residents who had worked for Gunter Mill likely had whiplash from getting fifty-thousand-dollar windfalls only to find there was nothing else they could afford. Riley knew this because she'd been scouring the *Greenbrier Herald* archives, trying to decide if this was a place where she could disappear.

Her attention was especially drawn to number twenty-six, a stately three-story brick house with a glossy black door and brushed pewter lanterns—her cousin Mikala's house, where Riley was going to live.

But her hungry eyes had a hard time deciding where to land. Number twenty-four was a white Charleston-style beauty with side porches on both levels and pots of geraniums flanking a red door. She half expected a horse and carriage to clop by.

Number twenty-eight, on the other side of Mikala, was bigger than them both, though Riley had to peer along the side to appreciate how far the stucco and stone rambled into the rear of the lot. She wondered how many people lived in it.

Besides a tree-trimming crew on the next block, the street was empty in the late-afternoon heat, allowing her to continue her silent surveillance. Empty was good. Quiet was good. There had been precious little of either by the time she'd left Mobile.

She pulled into Mikala's drive, brick pavers giving way to concrete at the garage door. She breathed deeply and sneaked a look in the rearview mirror to check the new haircut—*Thanks, Maisie*—that grazed the bottom of her ears. After grimacing to check for lipstick on her teeth, she pasted on a smile and opened the car door.

"Dear God in heaven, don't let me blow this." Her sandals hit the pavement, and she tugged down her skirt, careful not to show any leg above the knee.

The front door of the house swung open, and bouncy blond Cousin Mikala rushed down the steps. "Riley!" she cried with more enthusiasm than was warranted. "You made it!"

Mikala was wearing an expensive blouse that strained across her bust, and her stomach protruded from a khaki-skirt prison. Riley recognized at once that Mikala was always dieting, kept a closet full of clothes in different sizes, and was currently losing the battle. *Or not losing.*

Okay, there it was—one of Riley's many flaws. Her cousin was kind enough to open her home, and Riley repaid her by harping on her weight. She clamped her lips to make sure the ugly words didn't burst past them.

"Mikala," she gushed, "you look fabulous."

Mikala grabbed her cousin in a bear hug. "You lovely liar." She drew back and squinted at Riley's face. "Aunt Crystal told us about that mess down in Mobile. You were right to leave."

Riley blinked back tears that pricked her eyes. *Oh, I sincerely doubt Mama told you everything. If she did, you'd never have let me come.*

Back at the car, Mikala wrestled Riley's suitcase from the back seat, sweat springing onto her forehead from the relentless sun. "Anything in the trunk?"

"No!" Riley answered a little too quickly.

Mikala's eyes narrowed—she had to know there was something in the elderly Beetle's front-end trunk. Riley wondered how much the family hotline had broadcast.

Mikala gazed at her for a moment then turned on the megawatt smile Riley remembered from the Miss Alabama preliminaries. "Too hot to stand out here. Come on in the house, and let's get you settled."

"I... I thought I was staying in a pool house."

"You are." Mikala patted her arm. "But I'm not going to make you walk around the yard to get there, silly."

Mikala led the way up wide brick steps with pots of English ivy and gold lantana flanking every other one. The entrance hall was dim and cool, a welcome relief from the fiery June sun. She flung a casual hand at a formal living room on the right and a dining room for twelve on the left before continuing down a hallway to a cavernous kitchen and sunroom that stretched across the back of the house.

Riley tried not to gawk, but this was truly gawk worthy. She recalled her shabby rental on Dauphin Island and her parents' tired clapboard home in Mobile and felt a twinge of guilt. She didn't deserve this splendor.

Mikala skirted a curved marble-topped island with six upholstered stools and exited through French doors. Riley followed, emerging onto a patio with umbrella tables at either end. An impossibly blue pool glittered beyond it, and to one side stood a low-slung brick pool house with a wide terrace.

Her new home. She immediately looked for the windows. She'd learned the hard way that privacy was an illusion. Riley was so busy scouring the lines of sight into the charming structure that she missed Mikala's first words. Something about Luke's mama getting sick as they were building the pool house.

"It became a sort of mother-in-law suite instead," Mikala explained, "with an honest-to-goodness kitchen and bedroom we hadn't planned. Now it's more like a guesthouse with a pool."

"And Luke's mama died?" Riley knew this from her own mother.

"Yep. We had hospice come right here. From beginning to end, she didn't last a year."

Riley looked up at the towering trees along the yard's perimeter. Even before the official start of summer, they'd cast off a few yellow leaves that floated on the pool's surface. The fence was black iron separated by brick pillars, and beyond it were the backs of similarly grand houses—except the one directly behind Mikala's. That three-story structure seemed to be leaning, and its paint had peeled so that it appeared two-toned—dirty blue and dirtier cream. Through the foliage, Riley could make out torn screens on the back porch and a rusted washing machine in the yard.

"Can you believe that?" Mikala asked. "Our builder assured us it would be gone in six months. Three years later, here we are."

"Who lives there?"

"Who knows? The owner runs it as a boarding house, so it's whoever can afford to live there this week." Mikala pointed to the immaculate Charleston-style house. "Savannah, next door, has offered triple what other houses went for. But this guy won't let go." She shrugged.

"It's just a matter of time. Sooner or later, he'll be taxed out of the neighborhood."

Riley heard a swishing from Savannah's yard and jumped. "What was that?"

Mikala laughed. "The neighborhood cat, I suspect. He's always creeping around. I think he sleeps on the porch of Savannah and Cate's potting shed."

She pointed to a quaint structure painted the same white as the main house, with a porch and antique milk cans filled with more red geraniums. It looked too pretty to be a potting shed.

"That's not a playhouse?" Riley asked.

"No. They have a teenage son, Isaiah. I don't think he's into playhouses." Mikala laughed again. "But Cate is a master gardener. Well, more than that. A landscape designer. Very high-end."

The shed's uncovered side window faced the back of the pool house. Riley would have to remember that. "Do they keep it locked?" She tried to sound conversational rather than paranoid.

"Why would you lock a potting shed?" Mikala peered at Riley and seemed to sense her nervousness. "It's super private back here."

Riley tore her eyes from the potting shed and the dilapidated boarding house. "Isn't there a homeless shelter nearby?"

The newspaper archives were filled with stories about a popular bike trail and park and the resulting breweries jostling for adjacent property. The Greenbrier Gospel Mission was in a perpetual uproar because its residents, most of them fighting addiction, were faced with open-air beer gardens every time they left the shelter.

"Oh, yes. The mission is two blocks down, where Gunter crosses West Roosevelt." Mikala waved vaguely in its direction. "You'll see men walking up Gunter to the public library. It's their cut through." She smiled and shrugged again. "Urban living."

Riley exhaled and rolled her shoulders. Homeless men were no threat to her. Boarding houses were no threat to her. Any threat would come from *inside* the pool house.

As Riley's mama had told her many times, she was her own worst enemy.

Chapter 2

Mikala

Mikala left Riley to settle in and maybe even nap after the five-hundred-mile drive. She was starving and sidled up to the refrigerator. Seeing the baby carrots front and center made her irritable. She'd eaten enough of them this spring to grow bunny ears and hadn't lost a pound.

She checked her watch. *Close enough to five o'clock.* She grabbed a bottle of chardonnay, poured a generous amount into a wineglass, and carried it to her favorite seat in the sunroom. The room sported a stone floor and black wicker furniture covered in cheery yellow-checked fabric, with black-and-white accent pillows. It was a fun spot for guests to gather as Mikala put finishing touches on hors d'oeuvres or dinner.

She'd enjoyed choosing materials and furnishings as they were building the house and showing the place to friends from the suburbs, who couldn't believe she and Luke were moving downtown. Luke was a banker and had enough developer clients to know that these houses were great investments. He estimated that theirs had already increased in value by twenty percent.

Mikala gazed out the uncovered windows to the perfectly tended yard. Seeing her cousin reminded her of her glory days back home, where she'd been Miss Mobile and third runner-up to Miss Alabama. Anyone who knew the strength of the Southern states understood that was as good as winning Miss Idaho or Miss Montana or Miss

Rhode Island. It had been her misfortune to be a beauty in a land of beauties.

Snaggle-toothed Riley had begged to watch Mikala practice her tap dancing in a studio that had turned out two state queens and try on pageant gowns in a shop that drew competitors from all over south Alabama. That little kid was nowhere to be found in the stunning twenty-five-year-old who'd shown up that afternoon.

But brunette, mocha-eyed Riley wasn't exploiting her attributes. *For goodness' sake, what is she thinking with that dowdy skirt and those flat sandals?*

She even had tattoos—a lily on one forearm and, on the other, lettering that Mikala couldn't make out. The Miss America pageant wouldn't put up with *that* no matter how much it bragged about keeping up with the times.

She hadn't seen Riley in at least fourteen years, since Mikala graduated from Auburn University and her parents moved to South Carolina. But her mother had passed along news of Aunt Crystal's wild child and her even wilder sibling. This latest incident with Riley had been hushed up even along the family gossip line. Mikala was forced to go online to the *Mobile Press-Register* and *Pensacola News Journal* sites. Even then, the story was murky. The papers had been remarkably restrained about the young woman at the center of the high-profile murder.

Mikala swung her legs to the floor and inched her skirt zipper down so she could breathe more easily. She was famished, and Luke was taking his sweet time getting home. She considered eating those damn carrots so her irritability wouldn't get the best of her. Then the three of them would walk to Pizza by the Park, where Luke had already inquired about a job for Riley. Mikala was eager for her husband to meet her cousin. Oh yes, very eager.

Chapter 3

Cate

Cate stepped away from the window of the second-floor bedroom she shared with her wife, Savannah. The plantation shutters were folded back, since a narrow porch on the other side blocked anyone from peering in. Not that there was anyone in the backyard to peer in.

She'd been watching her neighbor Mikala Hardy. The young woman with her had to be the cousin Mikala had mentioned. Something was going on with the cousin—Cate could tell that much from Mikala's manner. She'd never said expressly what it was, but Cate now had an inkling.

Once Mikala had entered the main house, the cousin slipped around to the driveway. Cate waited until she returned with a cardboard box, staggering under its weight. Even from a distance, Cate was able to make out the logo of the liquor superstore near the interstate. *Interesting.*

The cousin disappeared into the pool house, so Cate wandered down to her first-floor office and looked at the open Day-Timer on her desk. She preferred this old-fashioned method of marking appointments. Her landscaping jobs were penned neatly in the spiral-bound book, and she could see at a glance what a week held—this time of year, not much. She'd had a busy fall and winter and an even busier spring. At last, the June heat dictated no more planting. The next three months were set aside for meetings with clients and design work. Cate was ready to give her sunburned skin a respite.

She thought about starting supper then remembered it was Monday, Trivia Night at

Pizza by the Park. She and Savannah always joined their neighbors at the popular bar and restaurant on the edge of Roosevelt Park. Cate grappled with her feelings about the new park and the pulsating restaurant scene sprouting around it. After years of planning and citizen input, City Council had named the fifty-acre green space Roosevelt in honor of the Black high school that once occupied a corner of the property. The school had mysteriously burned in 1961, but its presidential name still held meaning for the city's Black community.

Cate wasn't sure the name was enough to offset the gentrification that had forced many residents—Black, white, and Hispanic—from the formerly low-income neighborhoods that surrounded the park. She was uncomfortably aware that she and Savannah and Isaiah occupied a site that had once held a decrepit mill house. Savannah made arguments—good ones—that a redeveloped Gunter Avenue raised the city's tax base, contributed to a vibrant city core, and promoted infill over sprawl. She even sent spirited letters to the editor protesting the newspaper's use of the word *gentrification*—it was *urban renewal*, she'd written. *And urban renewal creates racial diversity among formerly minority neighborhoods. Isn't that what we want?*

Cate cringed when she read those letters. It wasn't that Savannah had been wrong exactly. Just tone-deaf.

Cate felt on more solid ground when she and Savannah supported local businesses and the Greenbrier Gospel Mission and stood up to neighbors who complained about homeless men tramping up their street. But though she'd been comfortably removed from the negotiations, Cate knew that whoever had resided in the vanished mill house on their property could no longer afford to live in the vicinity.

Sometimes, she feared that she'd given in too readily to Savannah's decision to move here. It was easy to do. Savannah, their friends agreed, was a force of nature, a land developer in an industry inimical to women. She'd been honored repeatedly by professional women's groups for her "groundbreaking" work. Reporters used the pun in every story as if they were discovering it anew each time.

Cate wasn't the kind of person who made headlines. In fact, she was surprised to be *married* to the kind of person who made headlines. It was not what anyone would have imagined for Cate Rosemond in high school. She'd known she was gay and had spent a lot of energy making sure no one else knew it. Looking back, she believed she'd overestimated her classmates' interest.

She'd come out at Clemson University, surrounded by fellow outdoor lovers in her horticulture program. In taming the Carolina red clay, she found a contentment she'd never known, working alongside her professors and fellow students, digging, planting, watering, learning irrigation and hardscape and soil makeup. She was never sure which feeling dominated—the relief over being honest about her sexuality or the rapture of finding her vocational passion. Whichever it was, Cate was happy for the first time in her life. Dirty, sweaty, sore, and happy.

She met Savannah while in the blush of that discovery, when both were starting their careers, she in landscaping and Savannah in construction. It was a dizzying development that took them both by surprise, partially because Savannah was already in a relationship. At another time, Cate would not have had the courage to pursue the glamorous Savannah. But Cate's confidence was at an apex, and Savannah was attracted to it.

Their friends suspected it would be a fling, but the couple had been together for nearly two decades. Decades, Cate now realized, in which her confidence had been leaking away. She wondered how and when that had happened. Surely, she hadn't woken one morning uncertain of her spouse, needy of affirmation. No, it was more a slow erosion of her self-assurance, an erasing of her reflection in Savannah's eyes.

Cate drifted from her office, wondering if Isaiah had come in while she was upstairs. Sometimes he accompanied them to Trivia Night, adding value in the pop-culture category. She called up the stairwell. There was no answer, and the house had that empty feeling it got when Savannah was at her downtown office and Isaiah at his lifeguarding job. Then she remembered that he was working a party at the city's indoor pool that night. At sixteen, he was too young to get hired full-time, but the city used him when the pool had large groups.

Maybe it was Isaiah's age that made Cate anxious about their move. For all they knew, he'd been born right in this neighborhood, back when crack houses and bootleg stores were camouflaged among the residences. They knew he was from Greenbrier, the son of a Black father and a white mother with addiction issues. The couple had been homeless, and when the mother tested positive for cocaine at delivery, the county's Department of Social Services bundled the baby into custody. He'd been in foster care for nine months when Cate and Savannah adopted him.

Some days, Cate looked out the window of her home office and wondered if a man trudging from the Gospel Mission could be his father or a woman panhandling in front of the liquor store on West Roosevelt could be his mother. Some days, it felt too dangerous to live here, as if they were testing fate by showing Isaiah's sculpted bronze face to anyone who happened by.

Savannah scoffed that she was being ridiculous, saying Greenbrier was a big place and Isaiah's parents were dead or long gone. But Savannah didn't know about the woman Cate had run into yesterday. Cate had been jogging, and the woman stood in front of the main post office on West Roosevelt, fat and sweating and reeking of body odor.

At first, her wheedling voice was set on automatic. "Lady, I need some food." But then she raised the eyes in her bloated face and looked directly at Cate. Her blank expression changed. She scowled, got more aggressive. "Lady, I know you can help me. I need medicine."

Cate scrabbled toward the street that abutted the sidewalk, holding her palms out. "No cash in my running clothes," she apologized, her rhythm broken.

The woman sneered and said, "You could come back. I'll wait," as if she knew that Cate lived nearby.

"No, sorry. We support the Gospel Mission." Cate pointed to the building across the street.

"They don't help no women."

God. Cate didn't want to argue with this woman. She looked longingly up the street. "No," she said more emphatically, inching away. "Not today." She resumed jogging.

The woman yelled after her. "I know your kid spends a hunnerd dollars on tennis shoes!"

Cate froze, wondering if she should turn back and ask the woman how she knew. *Or is it a guess, something she assumes teens in this neighborhood do?*

The woman sensed her hesitance. "And five hunnerd on a bike!"

No, Cate wouldn't engage. She'd cranked up her speed until she was three blocks away, gasping for breath. *Does the woman know I have a teen? Does she know about Isaiah?*

Cate heard the crazy paranoia in that thought, but her heart ratcheted up even at the memory. Savannah would roll her eyes and say Cate was letting her imagination run away with her, and she would be right. *Or would she?* Perhaps Savannah had been cavalier in moving them to the neighborhood where Isaiah was likely conceived. If push came to shove, Isaiah would choose them over his biological parents, surely, but why risk the ensuing acrimony?

Cate shook her beautiful silver hair, and it fell smoothly into place around her tanned face. Not working was detrimental to her mental health. She glanced down at her cargo shorts and ripped T-shirt. She needed to shower and change. On second thought, she was glad Isaiah wouldn't be going with them that night. He was at his job at the city pool, safe from the prying eyes of the street.

Chapter 4

Riley

The flimsy comforter slid to the floor as Riley struggled awake. The air-conditioning in the pool house had felt chilly when she arrived, but she was sweating now and groggy from the deep sleep that had overwhelmed her. Mikala and Luke were expecting her for dinner in half an hour.

Before showering, she padded through the space to more fully appreciate the watery greens, blues, and whites that permeated Mikala's decor. The wide living room was tiled in mint green and anchored by a pool-facing floral sofa and two striped wing chairs. Riley pinched herself. She could be in a pricey villa on the Gulf Coast.

Upon reaching the aquamarine kitchen, Riley pulled a bottle of vodka from its cardboard box. *Briar Patch Liquors* was printed in huge letters on the container's sides. She needed to get rid of the box and hide the contents in case Mikala and Luke were the kind of hosts who walked in unannounced.

Her bedroom closet was her first choice. Bottles of vodka, rum, and tequila went behind her jumble of shoes. Fortunately, she owned lots of shoes.

The bathroom linen closet was next, and she placed six bottles of wine behind stacks of colorful bath and beach towels. Then she hesitated. *Will Mikala's pool guests use these towels?* She hauled the bottles back out and placed them under the bathroom sink, where toilet paper and cleaning supplies could hide them.

Returning to the kitchen, she left a respectable couple of bottles in plain sight. She poured a hefty slug of vodka into a glass and added ice. The refrigerator held a six-pack of Diet Pepsi, a six-pack of Corona Light, and a case of bottled water, presumably for pool goers. In an attempt to pace herself for the evening ahead, she grabbed a Diet Pepsi and added a splash to her glass.

Thirty minutes and two drinks later, she was freshly showered and dressed in jeans and a white tank top. She thought about adding a shirt to cover her tattoos and chest, but she'd spent the past year in long sleeves, baggy pants, and ugly skirts, trying to fight the image held by detectives of the Mobile County Sheriff's Office. She was tired of that frumpy girl.

Riley was steely eyed about her situation. She was twenty-five years old. One-third of her life was over, and all she had to show for it was a dead boyfriend. Not by her hand, exactly, but it might as well have been.

She locked the pool-house door and crossed the patio. When she reached the kitchen, Mikala threw open the door. Riley could tell she'd been drinking too.

"Riley," she trilled too brightly, "meet my husband. Luke, this is Riley, the cousin I've been telling you about."

At first glance, Luke was not the husband she would have expected for Mikala. Riley recalled a string of square-jawed blond jocks from Mikala's high school years, one indistinguishable from the next. Luke was tall, slim, and muscular, and Riley immediately thought *runner* or *swimmer*. He had dark—almost black—hair and horn-rimmed glasses that made him look approachable.

He grinned widely and held out a hand for her to shake. "Cousin Riley," he said with a mock bow. "I am so glad to meet you. Welcome to Greenbrier."

She warmed to his friendliness. "I very much appreciate your hospitality," she said, careful to include Mikala in her smile. She would not give her cousin a reason to question her loyalty.

"The place we're going for dinner," Mikala said, "needs a waitress. Luke knows the owner, and he said the job is yours if you want it."

Riley glanced down at her clothes. "Do I need to change? Is it a job interview?"

"Goodness, no," Mikala said. "You're dressed exactly like everyone else will be."

Riley noticed that Mikala was wearing tailored slacks, an eyelet blouse, and wedge heels. But maybe the banker's wife needed to dress a little better than everyone else.

With the sun behind the trees, the afternoon was comfortable as the three set out. With Luke leading the way down Gunter Avenue, they passed houses as big and impressive as theirs, in an array of styles. The one recurring feature was a relatively narrow street presence, so the houses rose several stories and rambled deep into their lots. As they approached West Roosevelt, the older, smaller houses that remained looked sad and out of place.

Luke pointed them out. "I guarantee you the owners get an offer a week for those properties. They won't last long."

Riley murmured something noncommittal, uneasy with the stark differences in houses and unsure why.

"The problem," he continued, "is multiple owners. These mill houses have been passed down for generations and are often owned by several family members who haven't lived in Greenbrier for decades. The developers have a heck of a time tracking them down to arrange a sale."

They reached the Greenbrier Gospel Mission, where two men in wheelchairs sat on the sidewalk and another dozen lounged at picnic tables on a concrete slab. They watched the trio pass, and several acknowledged Luke's wave. Riley studied the sidewalk beneath her feet. She'd encountered shelter residents in Alcoholics Anonymous meetings in Mobile and didn't want a reminder of that time or that place.

"Right behind the mission," Luke pointed out, "is the Crescent Trail for biking and running and skating or whatever. It's named for the Textile Crescent, the semicircle of textile-mill villages that Greenbrier grew from."

After another three blocks, Riley heard the unmistakable clink of glasses and hum of summer voices, backed by a Motown soundtrack. Pizza by the Park was in full swing, with every outside table filled. A woman with pale skin and beautiful red-and-blond-streaked curls waved them over.

"There's Savannah," Mikala said. "Our team saved us seats."

"Team?" Riley asked.

"We Drink and We Know Things," she said solemnly.

Riley caught the *Game of Thrones* reference and laughed. *How long has it been since I found anything funny? Too long.* She took a deep breath and vowed to blend into this community so unlike the one she'd run from. Greenbrier was a chance for a much-needed do-over, and she intended to grab it.

A stocky woman with toned arms and shoulder-length silver hair rose to shake her hand. "I'm Cate." She smiled. "And this is my wife, Savannah. Welcome to Greenbrier."

"Where's Isaiah?" asked Luke. "We need him to cover the unfathomable teen subjects."

"Sorry," said Cate, "he's working a pool party. He said to tell you to answer 'Trampled by Turtles' no matter what the question is."

Savannah and Cate had beers in front of them, and Riley eyed them thirstily. Luke asked what she wanted.

"I'll have whatever Mikala's having," she said, "but should I meet the owner first?"

"Sure thing. Come with me."

"Chardonnay for me!" Mikala called as she sat down.

Luke placed his hand on Riley's back to steer her through the crowd, and her spine went rigid. She turned in time to see a puzzled look cross his face. He quickly found Roman Baxter working the bar and introduced Riley.

Roman was in his sixties and short, with a military buzz cut and a rugby player's square build. Riley noticed sports physiques when she met people, maybe from her soccer days in Mobile, when even with all their running, she could tell a soccer player from a cross-country runner. At the thought of high school, her heart twisted. She wouldn't think about it. She didn't have time to go there.

"Roman is into beach music!" Luke shouted over the Temptations. "Can you tell?"

She could tell. Her mama had taught her to dance to this music during weekends on Dauphin Island. Riley had always been a little out of touch with her own age group, so this was the music of her childhood. It was familiar, soothing.

"You've had waitressing experience?" Roman asked loudly.

She nodded. "And bartending."

"Ah, really?" He looked pleased. "That would help, as you can see." He poured a frothy pink concoction from a blender into two glasses and handed them to a petite waitress. "Ordinarily, I'd ask you to come in for an interview, but we're shorthanded, and Luke vouches for you. If you want the job, come in Thursday at four."

"Will do," Riley said. "But I'm available earlier if you need me."

The waitress opened her eyes wide and nodded at Roman.

"Okay," Roman said. "Make it tomorrow at four."

Riley exhaled in relief. "Thank you, Mr. Baxter. You won't regret it." Had she said those same words to her last employer? If so, they would have been a lie.

"Roman," he corrected, turning to Luke. "Your usual?"

"Yeah. Plus two chardonnays." Luke flipped his hand to high-five Riley then held onto her hand for a moment. "Well done."

The blond waitress passed her and winked. "Welcome aboard. I'm Farrah. I can sure use the help."

Riley thanked her and turned to drink greedily from her wine, only to find a busboy staring at her. He didn't smile but nodded slightly. He wasn't a teenager working a summer job. He was close to her age, thin and awkward, with too-long blondish hair flopping over his ears and forehead.

Busboys were important to turning over tables, so she smiled at him. He ducked his head and shoved more dishes into his carrier.

Chapter 5

Caleb

Caleb got off from his dishwashing job at eleven o'clock and headed straight for his boarding house. He couldn't believe that the young woman he'd seen that very afternoon from his bedroom window was going to be the new waitress. *Sweet.* Not that Caleb would ever have a chance with a chick like that.

Caleb had too many bad decisions in his past. He'd be paying for them for a long time to come. Maybe for the rest of his life.

Bad decision number one: leaving high school his senior year. He had a temper, and he'd let his literature teacher, Mrs. Prescott, get to him. As his counselor at the Gospel Mission helpfully pointed out, "And did your dropping out teach her a lesson?"

Mrs. Prescott was probably sitting on a beach in retirement, and he hadn't had a job interview yet in which the interviewer didn't flinch at his lack of a diploma.

Bad decision number two: Becca Ragsdale. He was eighteen. She was sixteen. Her daddy had caught them. Goodbye, Becca. Hello, Sex Offender Registry. He'd thought the lack of a high school diploma had hurt his chances for a job—now he got to watch interviewers' eyebrows shoot up even higher when they heard he was on "the registry."

Bad decision number three: methamphetamine. Figuring he had nothing to lose, he'd moved from booze to crack to meth. Old Crow Medicine Show had it right—he'd crouched behind his share of trailer doors, waiting for the drug to hit him like a hurricane and send him reeling into the streets.

Though Caleb was willing to accept responsibility for his bad choices, he knew the worst choice of all was beyond his control—being born to a worthless meth-head mother. He recalled the creaky, impossible-to-heat house in northern Greenbrier County and the days she'd lain strung out on its stained, sagging couch while he foraged through food boxes provided by the nearby Baptist church. Luckily, he hadn't particularly stood out in his semirural schools as he scarfed down free breakfasts and lunches and accepted leftovers from dieting girls.

He'd despised his mother for as long as he could remember. Unlike books that depicted children anxiously awaiting a glimpse of a drug-free parent, Caleb's memories of Doreen March held no warm fuzzies. Drug-free Doreen had been no better than drugged Doreen. He remembered only brittle black hair, decayed teeth, screeching demands, and infuriated slaps. He'd left home the same day he left school.

That was the ironic thing. He had seen what life as an addict entailed and sworn he'd never, ever be like her. Then, safely away from her, he turned to the drug anyway. He was living in a tent in the woods, waiting for the overdose that would kill him, when Greenbrier's interagency outreach team found him. The social workers were quiet and respectful and not pushy. They brought granola bars and bottled water and those vile Vienna sausages they thought homeless people liked. He talked to them six or eight times before he agreed to try a few nights in the Greenbrier Gospel Mission.

His counselor there was also respectful but no-nonsense. He challenged Caleb to look to his future and set goals. He made him look at his assets—his youth, his health, his mental acuity. He got Caleb to see that most of his homeless cohorts couldn't claim all three.

That had been two years ago. Caleb had lived in the mission for a year, watching young men with the same bad decision-making and lack of parenting get on their feet—or not. He figured he'd tried it his way long enough. Time to listen to somebody else.

He landed a job as a dishwasher-slash-busboy and saved money. Then his counselor helped him rent a room in a boarding house by explaining to the landlord the consensual nature of his registry offense. Persuaded that Caleb wasn't a raging pedophile, the landlord offered him a room on the third floor.

From his window, Caleb spent days looking over the boarding house's weed-choked yard to the manicured property beyond a brick-and-black-iron fence. He noted the odd familiarity of a giant sycamore and, with growing certainty, realized it was a yard he'd once known, back when it was bare earth with three run-down doghouses and three pit bulls that dragged chains in circles where no grass could grow.

The current yard with pool and pool house was unrecognizable. Caleb had finally walked around to Gunter Avenue to assure himself that he was looking at the right property. Indeed, he was, though it took the *26* on the shiny door to confirm a distant memory.

He'd learned that number twenty-six belonged to Luke and Mikala Hardy, Greenbrier bigwigs. In this neighborhood, lots of people were bigwigs—the newcomers, anyway, if not the bent old-timers in their tired mill houses. And maybe not the new woman either. Riley. He'd heard Roman say her name and mention that she was a cousin of one of the Hardys.

Caleb could see she was living in the pool house, not the main house, and he was curious. *Poor relation? Country mouse come to visit city mouse? Or does she simply desire privacy?*

She was a looker—that was for sure. Her sleek dark hair cupped the back of her head, and her light-brown eyes glinted with gold sparks. Her full lips curved into a heart-stopping smile, and the milky inside of her forearms bore tattoos. He managed to read the cursive lettering on one: *We know what we are but know not what we may be.* Caleb had recognized the quote from *Hamlet,* thanks not to Mrs. Prescott but to the high school counselor's penchant for hanging inspirational posters in his office.

He moved his threadbare curtain with a single finger. Peering into the Hardys' yard, he remembered a little boy swinging on a tire placed well away from those ghost doghouses. "Look at me, Granddaddy! Look at me!"

Lights were on in the pool house but not in the room closest to him. He knew that was the bedroom from the afternoons he'd watched Mikala Hardy's pool guests tromp in and out.Now the lovely Riley would sleep there. *Sweet.*

Chapter 6

Riley

She had the dream. Of course, she had the dream. Whether it was from too much wine or too many new people or the pool lapping outside her door, Riley dreamed of the shrimp boat on the Gulf.

It started the way it always did—with Silas, baseball cap pushed high enough to reveal his tanned face and sparkling green eyes. Even in this early scene, she felt uneasy. Something was wrong about her presence on his boat. Her mind fought to catalog the feeling in that way of dreams. *Are we lovers? Am I married to someone else? Is he?*

"Riley!" he yelled, the grin never leaving his face because he was always smiling in those early days. "I think we've caught a shark!"

She peered into the shrimp nets and saw them jerking powerfully alongside the boat. Silas waved and, in a flash, disappeared over the side. She didn't see what happened next, but she heard his young Vietnamese crew shriek in terror.

"Boss! No, boss!" They rushed to the side of the boat, causing it to pitch and roll.

The boys pointed to the water, and she saw it then—the gash of red. Her screams joined their clamor until all was red noise inside her head.

Her screams woke her. She was thrashing, her pillow wet with sweat and tears. She scanned the bedroom frantically, grounding herself in who she was, where she was. The sight of blood in the water gradually faded. *That wasn't what happened*, she told herself. *That wasn't what happened at all.*

And it wasn't. Her subconscious got the details all wrong. But the result—that part was right.

She rose from bed and slipped into last night's jeans, a loose T-shirt, and flip-flops then headed to the kitchen to undergo her daily ritual. Some people stepped on bathroom scales. Riley checked alcohol levels.

She was relieved to find the vodka as she'd left it before dinner. Sometimes she woke and found way too much gone. She opened the refrigerator and saw the bottle of chardonnay she'd uncorked when she got home. She'd stopped at three glasses during Trivia Night, which didn't cause anyone to blink. Three glasses, at most, were gone from this bottle. *Good.* She didn't even have a headache. *Doubly good.*

But she was hungry and needed groceries. She snatched her purse and headed out into the June morning, which was bright and hot but humidity free in a way Mobile seldom was. Mikala was seated beneath a blue-and-white-striped umbrella, reading the *Greenbrier Herald* and drinking coffee. She was dressed in a purple sleeveless blouse that did not flatter her upper arms and white capris that Riley suspected did not flatter her butt.

"I brought you bagels and coffee for your first day," Mikala called.

"How nice." Riley poured a cup from a coffee maker on a rolling cart and selected a bagel. After slathering it with walnut cream cheese, she gulped down a bite.

Mikala turned on her sunny smile. "Think you'll like working at Pizza by the Park?"

"It looks like a fun bar. I'm assuming most weeknights aren't as busy as Trivia Night?"

Mikala wagged her hand. "It's getting there, especially during the summer. People are so glad to be out after that coronavirus mess."

Riley recognized that *mess* was Mikala's word for anything unpleasant and wondered what it was like to be her—married to a good guy, living way beyond anything they'd known in Alabama, dabbling in volunteer work because she didn't need a paycheck.

"What did you think of the neighbors?" Mikala asked.

"They seem nice." Riley was taking care to avoid any conflict, any traps. Meek, unobtrusive Riley. *Please don't take notice of me.*

"Oh, come on," Mikala teased. "You can tell me."

Riley didn't know what to say. Trust was something she no longer understood. "Well, um... I liked Cate."

Mikala leaned in as if she had some juicy gossip. "She keeps an eye on Savannah—I can tell you that."

Savannah was unequivocally the extrovert in that relationship. She'd been all in on the trivia game, rounding up guesses and answering for the team. Between rounds, Savannah had worked the patio, her red mane streaming behind her, seeming to know someone at every table.

"What do you mean?" Riley asked.

"I suppose it's like any marriage. There's always the fear of straying, isn't there?" Mikala paused. Clearly, Riley wasn't giving her what she wanted.

Riley desperately changed the subject. "I hope you're not missing your museum work because of me." She'd caught enough conversation the previous night to learn that Mikala sat on the board of the county art museum and was in the middle of planning a fundraiser.

"I'm going, I'm going." Mikala laughed. "My committee doesn't meet until ten. I should use the time in the gym or at least walking. You see what I'm doing instead." She popped a last bite of bagel into her mouth.

Riley relented at her cousin's openness. "I'll be glad to walk with you if you like. Before work."

"Ugh, in this heat?" Mikala stood and wiped crumbs from her hands. "We'll see." She grabbed her coffee mug for one last gulp and, almost as an afterthought, asked, "And Luke?"

Riley was confused. *Luke what? Luke walks? Luke works?*

Mikala spoke as if addressing a recalcitrant child. "What did you think of Luke?"

"Oh, he's nice." Riley knew she sounded like a robot, but she'd learned her lesson about married men. She added weakly, "That was very nice of him to get me the job."

Mikala smiled, but the friendliness didn't reach her eyes. "Yeah, Luke is nothing if not nice." She turned to leave. "Have a great first day at work."

Chapter 7

Mikala

Mikala backed her silver BMW out of the garage and clicked the remote to slide the door shut. Theoretically, she could walk to the art museum. After all, that was the selling point of this neighborhood. *Walk to Roosevelt Park! Walk to dinner! Walk to the art museum!* But under South Carolina's blistering sun, people with air-conditioned cars drove them.

She parked and adjusted the waistband of her capris, wondering if they made her look fat. White could do that, she knew. They were designed to flatten her stomach, but she felt a muffin top bulge under her blouse.

She sighed and entered the museum through its gargantuan back doors to access the basement-level conference room. Mikala hadn't been in the galleries since the last gala. All that Important Art. She liked the idea of it, but the mad swirls and grotesque images sailed past her. She could talk parties and funds and purchase prices but had learned to keep her mouth shut when the conversation turned to the paintings themselves.

Luke, on the other hand, went on and on about brushstrokes and influences and light and shadow. Somewhat pretentiously, in her opinion. He'd even formed a committee at his bank to buy local art. Those pieces weren't *important* enough for the Greenbrier County Art Museum, but he had wisely sought the advice of the museum's director and curator before making purchases. Thus was born a friendly partnership that served both bank and museum. It had the added advantage of bringing Mikala into the inner circle of museum volunteers, which was not easy in an old Southern town with an invisible web of relationships and alliances. Mikala's hard work and attention to detail had paid off—she'd been tapped to stage the institution's frequent fundraisers.

Her cohorts were unanimous in their praise of native-son Luke. "Isn't it wonderful how First State Bank supports local artists? Have you seen the new Diane Coltrane in his lobby? The bank raised its sponsorship level for next month's gala!"

Luke, Luke, Luke. He was practically a standing member of *GreenB Magazine*'s Forty under Forty. At first, Mikala had enjoyed basking in his reflected glory. She'd enjoyed the status of being Mrs. Luke Hardy... right up until the moment last summer when she walked into the museum curator's office and found a red-faced Luke stooped and nervously tying his shoe. Curator Emily Ravine, not too many years out of grad school, was similarly flushed and fiddled with her necklace. For some reason, Mikala zeroed in on that necklace, which brought her eye to something she might have otherwise missed—Emily's blouse was buttoned wrong.

Mikala didn't let on that she'd noticed anything. Luke kissed her chastely and departed, and she calmly asked Emily about display pieces for the upcoming event. Then she walked into the employees' restroom. Leaning against a bolted stall door, Mikala drew a ragged breath and took stock. She was surprised to find that she wasn't so much hurt as outraged.

She considered her options. She could divorce Luke and come away with a decent financial settlement. But did she want to cease being Mrs. Luke Hardy? No, she did not.

She could pitch a fit and bully Luke into line with the threat of exposure. Greenbrier was still conservative enough that an affair on the part of a bank president would cause waves. But was she willing to face the embarrassment of being the cheated-upon wife? No, she was not.

So Mikala chose a third option—get rid of Emily Ravine. It turned out to be laughably easy. She started with a whisper campaign about the curator flirting with members of the Up-and-Comers, the museum's targeted young donors. She hinted separately to two long-time supporters that Emily was having an affair, wringing her hands over what that might do to the museum's reputation. She was careful not to name anyone who would be able to deny it—just whispers and innuendo and suspicion.

The director got wind of his donors' unhappiness, and Emily was dispatched to a museum in Davenport, Iowa. Mikala offered to give her a poolside going-away party, but Luke had nixed the idea. Problem solved. But now Mikala knew her husband was a cheater.

After the Emily episode, Mikala had watched Luke carefully. There was no perfume on his business suits and no obvious flirting at parties. There were no late nights at work. All was calm.

Until that spring. It was a small thing and might have passed unnoticed had Mikala been less alert. One night in late April, Luke had gone for a run. Standing in the kitchen an hour and a half later, he pulled off his sweat-soaked T-shirt, exposing the long, lean physique that had first attracted her when they were classmates at Auburn. He tossed the shirt into the dirty clothes basket in the adjoining laundry room.

Ordinarily, clothes might sit for three or four days. But the basket was full, and the housekeeper wasn't scheduled until the end of the week. Mikala thought she might as well start a load.

She clutched an armful of clothes, which brought the wet T-shirt close to her nose. An unexpected smell assailed her—chlorine. She brought the shirt closer. Yes, definitely chlorine. *Did Luke jump in the pool after his run?*

She started to call up the stairs to ask him but stopped. Something niggled at her. Luke had always enjoyed running, often during his lunch hour before showering at the YMCA. But lately, his evening runs had picked up.

She washed the laundry, holding her counsel. A few nights later, Luke announced he was going for a run. After he left, Mikala turned off the lights in the sunroom and kitchen and turned them on in the street-facing living room so Luke would think she was at the front of the house. Then she waited in their darkened second-floor bedroom, careful to hide behind the voluminous drapery.

An hour later, she spied him, hands on hips, in the backyard. *Where did he come from—the driveway? The side yard? The pool house?*

He knelt on the concrete deck beside the pool and dribbled water down his shirt. Then he splashed another handful onto his neck, letting it wet his hair and drip down his back.

She ran down the stairs and was pouring a glass of water when he walked into the kitchen. "Good run?" she asked.

"If sweating like a pig makes it good," he'd said, pulling off the shirt and tossing it into the laundry room hamper. "Whew, I'm beat. I'm going to take a shower."

This wasn't proof—she knew it wasn't. If she asked him, he'd act shocked and say he'd used the pool water to cool down, not to make a dry T-shirt appear sweat soaked. But Mikala knew in her bones that Luke was at it again.

And that incensed her. She recognized a swell of temper she hadn't felt in a long time, not even over young Emily Ravine. Luke's wandering refused to be *fixed* in the way Mikala wanted. Possibly, she was as infuriated as she'd been the last time someone threatened to deprive her of something she wanted. *No, not wanted. Deserved.*

She'd been aging out of the pageant system and had one more shot at Miss Mobile and then the real prize, Miss Alabama. But during the week of the Miss Mobile pageant, she learned that Magdala what's-her-name had chosen the same song for her tap dance routine that Mikala was using. It was bad enough that they were both blond and their names—Mikala, Magdala—were similar. Now the judges would see them tapping away to "Puttin' on the Ritz," and the girls would blur indistinguishably in their minds. Mikala hadn't put in years as Miss Watermelon Queen and Miss Shrimp Festival for that to happen.

As the televised final night neared, the girls practiced entrances and exits, evening-gown and swimsuit competitions, and a rousing musical number. And of course, their individual talents. From the darkened auditorium of Mobile's civic center, Mikala watched Magdala rehearse with her silver cane and sequined top hat, tapping and spinning and wiggling her tight bottom. Grudgingly, Mikala admitted that Magdala was good, possibly as good as Mikala. But worse, the girl had recorded herself singing "Puttin' on the Ritz" to accompany her dance. How blatantly unfair to show the judges she was a double-talent threat. Mikala couldn't believe the pageant allowed it.

It was the unfairness, Mikala told herself, that had provoked her to do what she did. Backstage was a mess of cameras and sound equipment and thick cables taped to the floor. Contestants knew to step gingerly until they made it to the open expanse facing the audience. During the lunch break before Magdala's final rehearsal, Mikala slipped backstage and removed the tape from the snaked cables. She then hid behind the thirty-foot curtain for Magdala to make her way through the murky obstacle course. Her goal was a simple twisted ankle, maybe a sprain, for her rival—just enough to clear the way for Mikala's dance routine to shine alone.

But at the last minute, Mikala left nothing to chance. As Magdala stepped over a thick cable, Mikala grabbed the cord twenty feet away and whipped savagely. It rose in a wave and threw Magdala off-balance. She cried out and crashed to the floor, shattering a kneecap.

In the ensuing pandemonium, Mikala had slipped away then circled back to express the same shock and horror as the other contestants. The next night, she'd been crowned Miss Mobile.

The thought of Luke cheating—for a second time—awakened a latent ferocity. Mikala was a good wife—damn close to a perfect one. *Is it so hard to let me have what I deserve—what I've earned?*

So the morning after watching Luke douse his shirt with pool water, she called her mother. She needed a repeat of the story her mother had whispered about Cousin Riley being questioned in a murder on that godforsaken island south of Mobile. The victim had been a married man, *right*?

Mikala wasn't sure what her plan was. And if she admitted to herself that she had a plan, she might not have the nerve to carry it out. But a cheating homewrecker in her own family—better yet, one accused of murder? That was worth exploring.

Chapter 8

Riley

Riley wasn't sure about the parking situation at Pizza by the Park, so she left the Beetle at Mikala's house and walked. She was curious, anyway, to look over the neighborhood. Many of the houses were Craftsman style, which meant they looked like oversized cottages with wooden pillars mounted on stacks of stone across the front. Adirondack chairs, round tables, and earth-toned rugs were plentiful. She pondered whether the neighbors used those porches. Clearly, they didn't at three thirty on a June afternoon. As the sun baked her head and sweat prickled under her arms, she understood why.

She looped between blocks so she could see sections she'd missed the previous night. On Parker Street, redevelopment hadn't reached the level of Gunter, and there were equal numbers of large new houses and small older ones. The owners of a staggering glass-and-stone house must have been betting on the elimination of the boarded-up shack across the street.

Riley continued to the corner of Parker and Montreat, where two older houses nestled in untamed vegetation. One was a mill house with sickly green siding, the other an orange brick rectangle. She froze.

Riley resolutely studied the mill house, which appeared to have the classic four rooms with a bathroom added to the back. Its lawn was patchy, and its porch bloomed with orange, red, and yellow zinnias in coffee cans. An overweight white-haired lady was seated on the porch, support hose rolled down to her knees, fanning herself with a magazine.

Then Riley was in front of the brick house, and she could no longer ignore the crash of memories. She halted in the middle of the sidewalk and stared at its blank windows. If you moved this building five hundred miles south, it could sit on the inlet that wound through Dauphin Island. This was Silas's house, and though there was nothing charming or welcoming or even Southern about it, it held some of her best memories. And most of her worst.

She'd been twenty-three and a college dropout when she fled Mobile for nearby Dauphin, where her family vacationed when she was a kid. Riley was growing uncomfortably aware that she was a screwup who was using booze to postpone any decision-making. She came by it honestly. Her daddy had warned her that he'd had a drinking problem before she was born and that his dad was a lifelong alcoholic.

Her questionable response was to get a job as a bartender at Dino's, a ramshackle seaside bar and grill that appealed to locals and savvy tourists. She promised herself it was a temporary reprieve, a time to decide whether this was an extended gap year or if she was done with college. But as the customers bought her beers during happy hour and shots at night, she was getting little thinking done.

Like most of the island's restaurants, Dino's specialized in shrimp, scallops, and fish pulled fresh from the bay. Silas Hightower was a shrimper who made deliveries and stayed for lunch and a beer. And stayed. There was nothing about Silas in those first days that gave her any clue what was to come. For one thing, he was nearing forty. He was handsome in the outdoorsy way of people who'd grown up on the ocean, with too much sun and wind. All that sun-darkened skin set off his light-green eyes, making them eerily captivating.

He had funny tan lines she could see when he reached across the table and his short sleeves rose to reveal white upper arms. Back in

Mobile, they'd called it a farmer's tan, but fishermen had a version, too, and it was one of Riley's turnoffs.

"Why don't they take off their shirts and get tan all over?" she'd asked her mama when she was in middle school. "Like lifeguards?"

Her mama had shaken her head and laughed. "Girl, you're never gonna get married. You've got too many boxes to check."

Riley wasn't looking at Silas that way, though he was friendly and a big daytime tipper. She usually didn't get tips that size until after ten o'clock at night, when drunks thought they had a chance with the bartender. But Silas lingered and talked as she shuttled back and forth with his burger, fries, and beer.

On the first day of November, about two weeks after Silas started coming in, she overheard him talking to Dino. "Aren't you usually gone by now?" Dino asked.

"Yeah," Silas answered. "But the weather and the runs have stayed so good I'm playing hooky."

Business was slow as Silas ordered a rare third beer and invited Riley to join him. She wasn't sure how Dino would feel about her sitting at a table, so she suggested he sit at the bar. He immediately moved to a stool.

"You'll be heading out soon?" she asked, wiping down the bar.

He twisted his beer bottle in his hands. "Not sure."

"I assumed you were a local."

"My family *is* from here," he said. "Third generation. But I moved to Mobile and run a fleet of boats in a lot of these waters."

"So you *are* a shrimper. Sometimes."

He laughed. "On my best days. My brother and I run the business, and neither of us wants to forget the hands-on part. We take turns visiting and working the boats."

"Did you grow up on the beach?"

"No—a little hole-in-the-wall on the inlet. My grandfather built it and lived there, and then our family did. But my mother was adamant that my brother and I go to the University of Alabama and study business if we were going to stay in the family company." He peeled the label off his beer in ragged pieces. "She was right, economically. But there are days in that office when I wonder if I woulda been happier staying on the boats." He smiled. "Enough about me. Do you ever have a night off? Or a day off?"

Is he asking me out? She'd been surprised and then even more surprised to realize she was pleased at the prospect.

"Riley!"

She was confused for an instant as she looked around for Silas or Dino. But there was no inlet behind this orange brick house, no swampy smell of muck, only a pair of unpruned maples. Riley recognized the busboy from the previous night, jogging down the sidewalk. She was unnerved by how completely she'd been transported from this place.

"Riley, right?" he asked. "We must be working the same shift."

She produced a shaky smile. "I'm sorry. I didn't catch your name."

"Caleb. Caleb March."

They were both dressed head to toe in black, Roman's suggestion for hiding pizza sauce. Caleb fell into step beside her but said nothing further. Their rubber-soled shoes were silent on the sidewalk.

"Anything I need to know or watch out for?" Riley had worked enough bars to know there were undercurrents and personalities that could sink you before you got a proper start.

Caleb was forthcoming. "Roman's a yeller, but he's harmless. Gus is the big guy behind the bar. You want him on your side if you get in a fight." He flashed a smile. "Not that I expect you'll be getting in fights." He laughed at his own joke. "The waitresses are mostly good about sharing tips, especially Farrah. She's rich, a college girl slumming for the summer." He regarded her sideways.

"I wouldn't cut anyone out of tips," Riley assured him, which was true. That was a good way to get on the wrong side of her colleagues so that when there was an incident—and there was always an incident—they wouldn't have her back.

Chapter 9

Cate

Cate and Isaiah settled into an outdoor table at Pizza by the Park. "You sure you don't mind eating here two nights in a row?" he asked.

She smiled. "I'd eat anywhere to spend time with you."

He laughed. "You are such a doofus." He glanced around at the other diners. "Where's Savannah Mom tonight, anyway?" That was what he'd called them since he was a toddler—Cate Mom and Savannah Mom, though in the early years, the latter had sounded more like "Santa Mom."

Cate looked up from her menu. "Working late."

"Plotting to get some poor family out of their house?"

"Isaiah!" Cate was shocked.

"What? You don't agree?"

Cate didn't know how to answer because his sentiment was precariously close to her own. "It's just... I don't think I've ever heard you express that."

He shrugged. "Our summer reading list."

Cate stared at him. Teens could be so cryptic. "What about it?"

"We're reading *Evicted* by Matthew Desmond."

"Ah, I see."

Her book club had read the nonfiction book about the role of evictions in a handful of poverty-stricken families in Milwaukee. Obviously, eviction and poverty went hand in hand, but Desmond's book showed that evictions not only exacerbated the problem but, in many cases, *caused* lifelong poverty. Before she could think of what to say next, they were interrupted by their new neighbor.

"Hello, Riley. I didn't realize you were starting work so soon," Cate said with some relief. "This is my son, Isaiah."

Isaiah's brown eyes widened. "Hi," he muttered, staring at the wrapped cutlery Riley handed him.

Cate smiled to herself. Normally, he'd chat up a waitperson, seeking a life story. She could tell he was stunned into silence by Riley's beauty.

"It's nice to meet you," said Riley. "What can I get you to drink?"

Cate ordered water with lemon, and Isaiah asked for Dr. Pepper. As he stared after Riley, Cate remembered the problem Mikala had hinted at and the liquor box she'd seen Riley lug into the pool house.

"She's in her twenties, Isaiah," she murmured.

He snapped out of his daze and grinned at her. "So?"

"A little old for you."

"A little young for you."

She punched his shoulder. "Cheeky boy."

He laughed and rubbed his arm. "I'm kidding, Mom. I'm kidding."

She hid a smile. "So, tell me more about your reading. I'm sorry I haven't thought to ask about your summer list."

Isaiah attended a private school with high academic standards and community-service requirements. He had collected toiletries and served meals and built shelves for the Gospel Mission. In the upcoming school year, he would tutor its residents.

"Well, after reading *Evicted,* we had to access a bunch of newspaper articles from around the state," he said, tipping back in his chair. "South Carolina has one of the highest eviction rates in the whole country. Disproportionately Black people. It got me to thinking about Savannah Mom's work. I mean, I've even heard you ask about the people who used to live on our street."

Cate sighed. "Well, I don't think they were evicted. They got bought out."

"*If* they owned. But if they rented, it would be the owner who got bought out, and the renters would have to leave. They might be paying their rent just fine and get evicted all the same."

"I see what you mean," she said.

Her son was putting into words the thing she'd tried to avoid. She had worked so hard to create a family out of three disparate people. She didn't want a rift.

"Just look at the houses close to West Roosevelt and on Parker and that one behind the Hardys on Montreat. Savannah Mom is making offers on them constantly."

Cate squirmed under her son's gaze. "I can't answer for her," she said finally. "This is a conversation you and she, or the three of us, need to have."

Riley returned with their drinks and took their orders. Cate relaxed into her seat as Isaiah talked about the previous night's pool party. A lanky busboy was clearing the table beside theirs. Cate caught his eye and smiled. He looked surprised, as if he was not accustomed to being noticed.

Chapter 10

Riley

Riley and Farrah cashed out at eleven o'clock, counting out money for the busboys. The good thing about a yuppie bar was that customers tipped decently *and* got up early, so they didn't stay out all night drinking. It was almost worth the douchebag nature of some of them. Clearly, Farrah had taken the brunt of the leering until Riley arrived. With some of the attention diverted, she was Riley's instant fan.

"You gotta stay through the summer," the pretty blonde told her as they pocketed their remaining tips. "At least until I leave in August."

"Deal. I can make it that long." Riley smiled shyly. "Where do you go in August?"

"University of South Carolina in Columbia. I'll be a junior." She stuck another twenty-dollar bill into the communal jar. Riley noted that Farrah had shared way more than a third of her tips. "How about you? Are you a student?"

"Still trying to decide. I was at the University of South Alabama but dropped out."

"Long way from home." Farrah flashed a warm smile and zipped her wallet. "If there's anything I can do to help you get settled in Greenbrier, let me know. I'm a lifer."

They parted on the terrace, and Farrah headed into Roosevelt Park. Caleb stood waiting to walk Riley home in the opposite direction.

"You didn't have to do that," she said.

He shrugged. "This isn't the safest neighborhood in the world." He motioned toward the Gospel Mission. "Anybody who missed curfew at the mission is out here. Plus, there are camps hidden in these woods."

She looked around, but all she could see were hulking trees.

"Believe me," he said. "I've heard stories."

"Did you ever live in the mission?"

"Yeah, for a year."

"Will you be far from your place after you drop me off?"

He grinned. "Not really. I stay in the boarding house right behind you."

A cold sense of dread clutched her stomach. "How do you know where I live?"

"I saw you from my window." Caleb must have felt her stiffen because he tried to reel his words back. "I mean, I wasn't spying or anything. I happened to see you and your cousin back there."

She whirled on him, suddenly livid. "How do you know she's my cousin?"

He held up his hands, looking embarrassed. "Roman said he was giving a job to a cousin of the Hardys. Hey, I'm sorry if I wasn't supposed to know. I didn't think it was a state secret."

Now Riley was embarrassed. "It's... it's not. I'm just a little..." *What? A little paranoid? A little insane?* "I'm sorry," she said lamely. "It's been a long day."

She and Caleb walked on in silence. When they reached the intersection of Parker and Gunter, he veered up Parker without looking at her. "This is my cut through. See you later." He disappeared from the pool of streetlight and into the darkness.

Riley stood beneath the light pole, imagining the orange brick house in the next block. She would not pass it again, but it had awakened memories she would have to face. She hurried to the pool house and locked herself in, wishing there were draperies on the pool-facing French doors. She'd known Roman would be watching the new girl, so she'd downed only two shots during her shift—not nearly enough to allow her to sleep. She poured a generous vodka on the rocks and moved to the sofa, trying to calm down. *Caleb saw me through his window.*

These houses were too close, she realized. They were huge and gracious and luxurious, but they were too damn close. She switched off the lights and tiptoed to the uncovered window over the kitchen sink. She could see into Mikala's sunroom and kitchen. A single pendant light over her sink suffused both rooms with a soft yellow glow. None of the windows or back doors were covered.

Doesn't Mikala know that people in the boarding house can see in? Maybe she didn't care. Maybe she and Luke didn't keep the kind of secrets that could be seen through windows.

The pool house also had a kitchen door that opened onto a small concrete pad in the side yard. Its top half was glass, which was covered by a Roman shade. Riley lifted it to gaze at Cate and Savannah's house. Their Charleston-style porches ran along the entire side that faced her. Through the lower level, she could see into their kitchen and, through the upper level, their master bedroom. The porches must have provided them a false sense of privacy, because no draperies or shutters were closed.

She hurried across the cool tiles to the rear of the living room, where a small window was covered by floor-length sheers. Through them, she could see only the fence, Cate's potting shed, and the impenetrable darkness beyond. She was satisfied that the empty shed blocked anyone from seeing in.

One more room to check. In her bedroom, a second Roman shade covered the lower half of the window, leaving the upper part exposed. Wriggling between her bed and nightstand, she could see through the trees and into two rooms of the boarding house. In the winter, when those trees were bare, it would be worse.

She threw open the linen closet and found a beach towel. She couldn't locate a hammer and tacks, so she draped the towel over the top of the window frame. It was too heavy and slipped off. She tried a sheet, a pillowcase, a blouse, but nothing would stay.

Well, there was nothing to see that night anyway. And if she was careful, there wouldn't be on any other night. *But that's the thing—can I be careful enough?*

Riley poured a second vodka, then a third, and her fear receded. She stumbled to her bedroom and lay under the ceiling fan, allowing her mind to go where it wanted to go—to the orange brick house. Blocky and squat and lacking in architectural beauty, the house sat on the saltwater inlet that ebbed and flowed through pokey little Dauphin Island. Riley had encountered it when Silas invited her for an evening on his shrimp boat. She left her black Beetle—the same one currently parked in Mikala's driveway—at the unprepossessing house, and they drove his truck to the docks.

Four Vietnamese teenagers fought to help her board then hurried to appear busy when Silas looked their way. They chugged into Dauphin Bay, the five men speaking in Vietnamese. After setting the flattened cone-style nets to skim the ocean bottom, Silas pulled two beers out of a cooler.

"With a beautiful lady on board," he said, "I'm going to let my crew do the work." They clinked bottles.

It was a clear, cool night on the water, with the lights of two other shrimp boats off in the bay and the island lights twinkling in the distance. Silas wrapped her shoulders in a sweet-smelling blanket that she suspected he'd bought for the occasion.

"I can see why this is your favorite part of the job," she said, snuggling into the blanket's lavender scent. "It's magical out here."

They talked as the boat trawled, scooping up the bottom-dwelling shrimp that popped out after a day buried in the ocean floor. Silas talked about growing up on the water, and Riley told him about her parents in Mobile.

"No siblings?" he asked.

"One younger sister. Rayanne."

"Are you close?"

Thorny question. She remembered Rayanne of the days on Dauphin Island when she and Daddy and Riley would hurl a skimboard into the shallows and run shrieking to jump aboard. Skinny little Rayanne had to do everything Riley did, from Vacation Bible School to peewee soccer, and wear everything she wore, from two-piece swimsuits to sneakers. She made their mama style their hair the same, decorate their rooms the same, and give out the same favors at their birthday parties. Riley could see her scrawny sister, hair in pigtails, darting out their front door if Riley dared leave without her. "Wait up, Riley! Wait for me!"

"When we were little, we were close," Riley said, hedging.

But even then, there'd been something about Rayanne that was not quite... right. Another image of an early vacation on Dauphin Island rose. Riley had been maybe eight, Rayanne seven. The family stopped at a beachside bar for lunch, and Mama ordered a frozen blue drink with a paper umbrella. She was relaxed and laughing in a way that made Riley happy for her.

They stayed after lunch because the restaurant was holding hermit-crab races on a table outside on the sand. Daddy paid a dollar each for the girls to race painted crabs. Riley's sported an orange flower, Rayanne's a blue spiral.

It was a bright, hot day, and six kids hopped around excitedly, their parents cheering as the crabs tottered off in their makeshift lanes. Riley was focused on her crab—Orangie, she'd named him—and didn't pay much attention to Rayanne until the crab of a chubby preschooler crossed the finish line. It had a red star on its shell and skittered away from the pack as if it really understood the concept of racing. She glanced up and saw Rayanne watching her blue-spiraled crab spin in circles. Her pointy little face bore no expression as she raised a clenched fist.

Riley frantically looked for their daddy, crying out, "No!"

But it was too late. Rayanne's fist landed on the boy's star-bedecked crab, crushing its fragile shell and splattering the tiny body onto the table. There was a moment's hush—the boy wide-eyed, the mothers' mouths open in silent *O*s, the fathers staring incredulously. The bartender pushed into the crowd, glaring at Rayanne and scooping the remaining crabs to safety.

They didn't wait for the outrage, the pointed fingers. Mama, her face drawn, her ebullient mood extinguished, shoved the girls toward the car. Daddy stayed behind, Riley assumed, to apologize and pay for damages. On the drive home, Daddy had yelled at Rayanne, demanding to know what she had been thinking.

"My crab wouldn't run," she'd said. "You shoulda bought me the star crab."

Riley hadn't wanted to bring the specter of her sister onto Silas's boat or to think about later, when Rayanne's emulation had become obsessive and she raided Riley's closet so often that their daddy put a padlock on Riley's bedroom door. She demanded to play soccer, like Riley, despite the coach's insistence that Rayanne's sport was cross-country. Then she'd extended her covetousness to Riley's friends.

Mama and Daddy called Rayanne difficult, high-spirited, unruly. Mama told Riley that Rayanne was simply jealous of her. Whatever the cause, whatever their amateur diagnoses, none of them had recognized the danger.

But Riley didn't want to talk about all that on this glorious night, so she hurriedly said, "When we came to this beach, we'd see shrimp boat lights at night. I always wondered about the people on board."

"Now you know." Silas's light eyes and white teeth shone in the dark. "Have you ever eaten at High's in Mobile?"

"Of course! World's best she-crab soup."

"That's us."

"*What?* You're kidding." She was astounded that his shrimping business included the ritzy restaurant chain. "Oh, High's. Silas *Hightower.* I get it."

Riley could see his smile gleaming as she finished the beer and reached for another. So Silas Hightower was the owner of the High's chain of seafood restaurants. *A rich guy. How about that?* She would never tell Rayanne.

Perhaps Silas's revelation had no bearing on her decision to enter the bedroom of the orange brick house a few hours later. Maybe she'd had so much to drink by then that she would have gone anyway, whether Silas Hightower was rich or poor. She'd awakened more than once in a bed where she had no business being.

She'd giggled as she pulled Silas's shirt over his head and saw the fisherman's tan—sun-scorched neck and forearms and a V on his chest, contrasting with white shoulders and upper arms. "Redneck," she whispered, nuzzling him there.

He picked her up easily in his work-hardened arms and carried her into the bedroom, where fresh flowers and scented candles battled the mustiness of the seldom-used house. The bedspread was old, but the sheets were fresh and soft. Even in her impaired state, she could tell that he'd taken care with these touches. But he'd forgotten the curtains. In all their time in that house, they'd never once thought of what someone might see through those windows.

The dream that plagued Riley during her second night in the pool house was a little different from the others. Her overtaxed subconscious was trying to work through too many things. Shrimp boat—check. Silas—check. Vietnamese boys—check.

But this dream had a shadowy figure that grew and blocked the full moon and created a trepidation separate from the sharks that raced alongside the boat. She cowered in the darkness cast by the shadow, only gradually realizing that Silas was gone. *Did he fall overboard? Did the shadow overtake him?*

A sound rose—a murmur at first, then a shout, then a roar of fury. The shadow shrank until it was a huge man with a bristle haircut, broad shoulders, and tight muscles, angry muscles. Detective Miller Washburn. With one meaty hand, he shoved a slight, familiar figure toward Riley—her sister, Rayanne. Riley was stricken with fear. He had Rayanne. He *knew.*

Riley woke in utter confusion. At first, she thought her mind had fused two different scenarios on Dauphin Island—childhood vacations and her more recent time with Silas. But as she watched the ceiling fan spinning slowly, the details clicked into place, and she remembered how the two had meshed.

When she entered the kitchen, she cringed to see the vodka bottle, two-thirds empty. She slid the garbage pail from its built-in cabinet and found an empty wine bottle. Nervously, she peeked at the half gallon of rum shoved behind the coffee maker and was relieved to find it unopened.

Her head pounded, and she felt nauseated, but it was nothing that two Excedrin and toast and coffee wouldn't cure. Rayanne favored a mimosa or a screwdriver to wipe away a "night before," but that was one practice Riley avoided. Her sister was eleven months younger, and Riley felt a certain amount of guilt about Rayanne's drinking. Riley was the one who'd bought liquor for Rayanne and her friends in the short time when Riley was legal and they weren't.

Her AA acquaintances assured her that Rayanne would have gotten it one way or another, and Riley knew that Rayanne had a fake ID. But guilt was an insidious thing, easily triggered.Take, for example, the fact that she'd ditched AA and ignored all the checkup phone calls until members finally gave up.

She ate a piece of wheat toast with a cheese slice then took a second cup of coffee onto the patio. Luke was scooping leaves out of the pool. She tried to step back inside, but he'd already seen her and smiled a welcome.

"I didn't know you were out here," she said, embarrassed for coming out in pajama pants and a sleeveless T-shirt with no bra.

"Good morning!" he said. "How'd your first day of work go?"

"Great." She crossed an arm awkwardly across her chest. "Cate and Isaiah came in."

"He's a good kid." Luke netted the last leaf out of the pool. "Mikala insisted I get these leaves out. Immediately. I'm not sure who's swimming, but aye, aye, Captain." His amused eyes raked over Riley's body—or maybe she was imagining it. "Got any more of that coffee?"

"Um, sure. I'll be right back." She hurried to her bedroom and slipped on a bra before running to the kitchen and pouring him a cup. When she opened the door, he'd put away the pool net and was seated at an umbrella table, his long legs stretched out. He was dressed for work, minus a suit jacket.

"Ah, thank you," he said, taking the mug. "Join me. Please."

She glanced at their kitchen window and saw Mikala at the sink, waving gaily. Riley sank into a chair across from him.

"Tell me about Riley Masterson from Mobile, Alabama."

"Not a lot to tell. I played soccer in high school. Went to the University of South Alabama because I thought I wanted to be a nurse. But when I hit clinicals, I decided, oops, no, not for me."

Luke laughed. "I can understand that." His open face invited her to continue.

"I dropped out junior year. My gap year turned into two, three, and then, um..." She wondered how much he already knew.

"Never too late to go back. If that's what you want."

Riley couldn't tell if he was being polite or if Mikala hadn't told him about "that mess down in Mobile." Maybe Mikala was embarrassed by her family. Riley wouldn't blame her.

When she didn't respond, Luke said, "Clemson is right up the road, and USC in Columbia is only two hours away."

She smiled weakly.

"I think sometimes about going back to school myself," he mused. "I'm not sure if I can handle forty years of banking."

Riley was surprised. "Really? I guess I thought with a career like that—well, any professional career—you'd be set for life."

"Yeah, you'd think that, wouldn't you?" Luke gazed over his pool, lush lawn, exquisite flower beds. "But I suppose you can discover that anything is empty once you get there."

Riley sensed he was talking to himself more than to her, so she remained silent. He appeared to study Greenbrier's skyline in the distance. Then he slapped the table, and the striped umbrella quivered.

"But I'm not the one to advise you. It's your life. We're glad to have you here." He stood to leave. "See you later." He gave her shoulder a squeeze as he passed, and Riley noted that his body blocked Mikala from seeing it.

Or am I hopelessly distrustful about the most innocent gesture?

Chapter 11

Cate

Cate had looked forward to some downtime but now found herself at loose ends. Savannah was at work, and Isaiah was sleeping in. From her bedroom window, she idly gazed into the Hardys' backyard. Seeing Luke leave, she decided to take Mikala up on her frequent invitations to use the pool. She gathered sunscreen, sunglasses, a towel, and a novel and placed a Coke and ice in an insulated tote.

Savannah made fun of Cate's tan lines—bronzed arms, face, and shins combined with pasty feet and thighs. Determined to even things up a bit, she slathered sunscreen on the tanned places and dragged a lounge chair across the terrace so her legs could be exposed to the sun while her torso stayed in the shade.

She hesitated before sitting down. *Am I intruding on Riley's space?* Mikala had invited her to use the pool, but this was Riley's home for the moment. She knocked on the pool-house door.

Riley seemed pleased and waved her in. "Can I get you some coffee?"

"Well, sure," Cate said. "I wanted you to know I'm using the pool so you wouldn't be startled when you came out."

Riley poured a mug of coffee and brought it to her. "I'm glad I'm not preventing people from using it."

Cate looked around the expansive living room with a view of the pool through double glass doors. "I've never been in here since we can change clothes at our house. This is beautiful." Her eyes landed on a table beside the sofa, and she recognized a novel by South Carolina author Paulette Alden. "Oh, I've read this. We went to her book signing."

She flipped to the book's dedication page and found a handwritten note from the author. *To Savannah and Cate.* She frowned. "This is ours. How did it get here?"

Riley shrugged. "Maybe Mikala borrowed it?"

"Yeah, maybe."

Cate and Savannah were big readers. Savannah always carried a book with her in case she had a few minutes between appointments. *So why is this one in the Hardys' pool house?* As far as she knew, Savannah hadn't been swimming that spring—she'd been too busy working.

Cate shook her head. Maybe Riley was right. Mikala could have borrowed it. She thanked Riley for the coffee and carried the mug outside to settle between the sun and shade.

But she couldn't concentrate on her book. She'd devoured Alden's *The Empty Cell* when it came out but wasn't sure Savannah had read it. She couldn't remember them discussing the story, which was based on a real-life lynching in the 1940s. She'd have to ask.

She laid her head back and closed her eyes. There had been a time when she'd thought of her life as an empty canvas on which other people painted their stories—she was a human backdrop. She still saw truth in that old image, and she knew what had shattered it—adopting Isaiah. Savannah had gone along with the adoption because Cate wanted it so badly, but in their most private places, the women knew that Isaiah was Cate's baby. Being his mother had brought her a joy that eclipsed even working her beloved Carolina dirt.

It also brought out a fierceness she hadn't known she possessed. She would protect Isaiah at all costs. That was why a public school supporter like her had enrolled him in a progressive private school, where having two mothers didn't cause a stir.

And that was why she would continue to make a stable home with two parents. *At all costs.* She put her book aside and dove into the pool.

Chapter 12

Caleb

Caleb shut the borrowed laptop of a third-floor hall mate who worked the day shift. The young man was glad to let him use the device as long as he locked it inside his room afterward. Caleb tried not to take advantage by using it too often, but his friend's generosity had saved him a walk to the library.

Tracing the history of Twenty-Six Gunter Avenue had been easier than he'd imagined. Sure enough, his granddaddy's name, Henry March, surfaced quickly, first listed as owner in the 1950s. Caleb had the vaguest memory of a dark, cramped mill house stuffed with newspapers, its tables filled with photos in cheap frames. And some kind of cabinet crammed with knives and hooks with funny feathers.

Apparently, his uncles Roger and Alan had sold the house to a Savannah Darwin five years earlier, and she tore it down. Fast. She then built that three-story brick fantasy and sold it to Luke and Mikala Hardy. The value had increased exponentially since his grandfather's day.

Caleb wondered where his mother was in all this and why she hadn't inherited the property along with his uncles. He went next on an obituary search and discovered that his grandfather had died in 2010. Caleb would have been nine at the time. He had no memory of a funeral. Maybe that was part of the problem. If his mother hadn't bothered to attend her own father's service, there must have been a breach.

Damn her. One more way she'd screwed up her life. And his.

Caleb walked to his window and stared into what had been his grandfather's hard-packed yard, visualizing the scary pit bulls lying in the red dust. He closed his eyes and remembered tiptoeing along the fence line farthest from the dogs to reach the tire swing. He hadn't trusted them not to lunge and didn't trust those rusty chains to hold them if they decided they wanted a piece of him.

Once again, he heard his gleeful cries. "Look at me, Granddaddy! Look at me!" *But who was I calling to?* He couldn't picture the old man.

He opened his eyes and took in the lush lawn, flower beds, brick patio, and shimmering pool. There was a woman out there, wet from a swim, settling onto a lounge chair. He recognized her from Pizza by the Park, an outdoorsy woman with muscular arms and silver hair that swung when it was dry. He'd seen her with that flashy redhead and their biracial son. Isaiah, she'd called him. Now, there was a boy who'd landed in high cotton. Caleb could hear what his mother would say about Isaiah's good luck, her tone whiny and self-pitying.

Caleb was seized by a familiar smoking-black anger at the thought that he'd spent his first seventeen years with that self-absorbed, neglectful woman in a run-down house on a run-down road north of town. He would spend the next seventeen in this shitty boarding house that he shared with eight slobs when that property *right there*, that million-dollar property, was rightfully his.

He looked out again and caught the wisp of a memory—an overweight man in a recliner, offering him ginger ale for breakfast. Dragging a frayed lawn chair across the weedy yard to watch him swing. "Look at me, Granddaddy!"

On its heels, he remembered the woman who'd passed Pizza by the Park the night before as he'd waited in the shadows for Riley. A baseball hat hid her hair, but there was something about the way she scuttled, shoulders hunched, back bent, as if cringing for a blow...

But no, he couldn't imagine his mother anywhere but in that ratty old house in the sticks. She'd have no reason to leave. Maybe he'd track down his uncles, who lived in Raleigh, North Carolina, according to the sales record. He'd ask why they had cheated their sister out of her inheritance.

Then he recalled the price his uncles had gotten for their father's house—sixty-one thousand dollars. His anger fizzled. While a third of that could change *his* life, his mother would have smoked and gambled it away before he ever saw a penny.

Unexpectedly, he heard his counselor's voice in his mind. "There are things we can do something about. There are things we cannot. Wisdom is knowing the difference and acting on it."

Caleb had recognized that his counselor was paraphrasing the Serenity Prayer. Heck, the words were hanging on a poster above the man's desk. But sometimes, you needed to hear things in different words for them to sink in.

He couldn't do anything about a sale that had taken place five years ago, but maybe he could step up his own savings if he wasn't paying a hundred twenty-five dollars a week for this crappy room. He eyed the Hardys' pool house. Riley had staked that out. But beyond the pool house, in the next yard, was a pristine white structure. From what he'd seen, the woman who was currently at the Hardys' pool was the only one who went in it, and even she might go weeks at a time without entering.

The place looked like one of those tiny houses the Gospel Mission volunteers talked about, but it was fancier than any he'd seen. With its windows and porch and geraniums, it looked like a perfect little house, only in miniature. It would be perfect, anyway, for him to stay in for a while. Just long enough to save that hundred twenty-five dollars a week until he could buy a car and get out of here. Maybe go to Raleigh and appeal to his uncles' sense of fairness.

He let the curtain drop. *Do I dare?*

Chapter 13

Riley

Riley's hangover wasn't responding to the coffee and Excedrin as it usually did, so she sank onto the sofa with a groan. *What is up with all the visitors, anyway?* First Luke then Cate. She'd expected more privacy. But to be fair, it *was* June. If she was still here this fall, the situation would be different. She hoped.

She contemplated Rayanne's hangover remedy and wondered if that was what she needed. Just this once. When she stood, she glimpsed a long hair hanging from her T-shirt. She held it up to the light, watching the sun catch its red-gold gleam, and recalled Cate's surprise at seeing Savannah's book in the pool house.

Riley grabbed the cushion at one end of the sofa and turned it over. Another long red-blond hair, not Cousin Mikala's whitish blond. Savannah had been in the pool house. *But when? Could she have been swimming while I was at work?*

Uneasiness crept over her. Riley didn't like that other people were in the pool house while she was away. They might poke in her closets. She sighed. Beggars couldn't be choosers, and unfortunately, she was a beggar.

Her head ached too much to think about it. Under the bathroom sink, she rummaged for a bottle of Prosecco. In the kitchen, she poured it into a tall glass then topped it with orange juice. A sissy drink with hardly any alcohol at all but maybe just enough to stop the hammering.

She stretched out on the luxurious living room sofa, propping a second cushion on the armrest so she could sit up enough to drink the mimosa. Rayanne's drink. She recalled the first time her sister had drunk one. Well, the first time that Riley knew of.

Mama's sister, Eileen, and her husband, Foster—Mikala's parents—had planned to drive through Mobile while on vacation. Daddy complained that they weren't going "to their own damn beaches," but Riley thought he just didn't like the way Eileen made Mama feel. Eileen and Foster had made quite a bit of money in South Carolina, and Daddy felt they lorded it over their Alabama relatives. Riley wasn't sure that was true.

What she did know was that her mama had worked for weeks to get the house ready for Eileen's visit. She scrubbed floors and washed curtains and even repainted the dining room. Mama had splurged for Prosecco and an expensive brand of orange juice to make the mimosas she'd read about in *Southern Living.* During brunch with Eileen and Foster, Rayanne, thirteen at the time, sneaked several drinks, telling Mama they were pure juice. That was what they blamed her subsequent actions on, anyway.

After eating, Daddy and Foster walked out to their car, and Rayanne whispered to Aunt Eileen that she wanted to show her something in her bedroom. They'd been gone for some time when Mama asked Riley where they were.

"Rayanne's room, I think."

Mama cringed, and Riley knew she hadn't wanted Eileen to see the worn rooms on the second floor. Riley followed her mama up the stairs. Rayanne's door wasn't closed, and they could hear her inside, her voice wheedling.

"It's just that I'll never be anything down here, Aunt Eileen. You see how they live. Hicksville."

Eileen murmured something they couldn't make out.

There was a squeaking sound, and Riley pictured Rayanne flouncing dramatically on her bed. She couldn't make out what she said next, but certain words punched through with devastating clarity. "Rednecks! Those mimosas! She's pathetic!" And then Rayanne raised her voice. "Please, Aunt Eileen, let me live with you and Uncle Foster."

Mama's face flooded with embarrassment. She grabbed Riley's arm and jerked her down the stairs, stumbling in her haste to get outside. She swiped her face with vicious jabs and muttered in Riley's ear, "Don't say a word."

Within a few minutes, Eileen came down and, with a forced smile, said, "Rayanne wanted to show me a picture of her soccer team." She hugged Mama—overlong, Riley thought—and got into the car. And they were gone.

Mama and Riley talked about the incident only once. "It turns out your sister got into those mimosas," Mama whispered when she entered Riley's room late that night. "I guess they made her speak like that."

Still, her eyes were red. She looked sad and smaller somehow. That was the moment Riley had realized her feelings about her sister had changed. It was one thing to raid Riley's bedroom, copy her obsessively, and horn in on her friendships. It was another to hurt their mama.

Riley took another sip, finding the mimosa too sweet. Or maybe it simply carried too many memories.

The last time she'd seen her sister, Rayanne was packing her pickup truck and heading to Panama City. Riley threw pillows and blankets into the truck bed and anchored them with hastily packed boxes, urging Rayanne to move faster, faster. Detectives had made Riley's life on Dauphin Island a living hell and were about to do the same in Mobile. There wasn't much she could do to spare her parents, since she'd had to tuck tail and run to their house, but she could urge

Rayanne to get out. Riley was never sure how much of her rush had been about protecting Rayanne—for their parents' sake—and how much was about ensuring she didn't have to see her sister again.

It all went back to that orange brick house on the island. After the first night with Silas, they hadn't been able to get enough of each other. November and December flew by in a flurry of drinking and sex, one of those out-of-time stretches that didn't even feel like her life but maybe a movie version of it. A Crayola-colored, improved version.

Silas would pick her up after her shift at Dino's. If it was early, they'd go out on the shrimp boat or to the Sand Box, a beachside bar favored by locals, with plastic sheeting mounted around the deck and a jukebox rocking with old beach music. If it was late, they'd head to his house and drink red wine in the cozy bedroom he'd set up.

Riley had enjoyed her share of boyfriends and would have said she'd even loved one or two of them. But her time with Silas was different. He was more experienced, more worldly, more generous than anyone she'd ever been with. In the house's tight little kitchen, he made incredible meals of scallops and shrimp pulled fresh from the bay. He introduced her to wine from High's private stock. He even once made his restaurant's famous she-crab soup. That was the night, in fact, that they hit their first glitch. Riley took a picture of the soup and was posting it on Instagram when Silas stopped her.

"I want to let everyone know I'm eating High's famous soup made by High himself," she protested.

"No, Riley," he said quietly, taking her phone.

"Bad for business?" she asked.

He sighed. "Bad for my marriage."

"Oh." Her shoulders slumped, and then just as quickly, she was angry—red-hot, bitingly angry. "Just down here for a little slumming, are you?"

"No," he said, grabbing her hand. "No, Riley, not at all." His green eyes never left her face. "And I think you know I'm not that good an actor."

"Then what? What is all this?" She flung an arm to indicate the meal, the wine, the bedroom he'd gone to such trouble to make inviting.

"This surprised me as much as it did you," he said, his voice catching. "I've been down here a dozen times to work our boats. I'd stay ten days then go home." He held out his palms helplessly. "And then I saw you. Got to know you." He halted, his eyes pleading. "I can't explain it. I am so sorry."

"I'd better go." She got up, hoping he would stop her.

He didn't. She drove back to her scruffy rental house in a blur of unshed tears and was both surprised and irritated to find a rusted white pickup truck parked in front, with four young people crammed onto its tailgate.

"Rii-ley!"

She registered her sister's high-pitched squeal seconds before Rayanne hopped onto the pitted road. The yellow porchlight showed Rayanne's brunette hair curling past her shoulders, just as Riley's did.

"Man, you weren't kidding," came a male voice. "You could be twins."

Rayanne slipped an arm around Riley's waist, showing her friends their similar build. They were even dressed alike in tight jeans and tank tops. Riley shivered, the tank top not warm enough in the breeze that came off the bay.

"Ta-da! I told you!"

Riley wriggled from her grasp. "Rayanne, what are you doing here?"

"Mama hadn't heard from you, so I volunteered to drive down and see what's up. These friends kindly came with me."

Riley looked more closely and saw Rayanne's friend Cheri but didn't recognize the two young men.

"Can I come in and pee?" asked Cheri.

"Can we, Riley? We brought beer." Rayanne held up two six-packs, though it was clear the four of them had already been well into the booze.

She didn't want Rayanne in her house. She didn't trust her and didn't want her fake cheeriness or her false friendship. But neither did she want a scene in front of Rayanne's friends. Four faces turned to her expectantly. She had nothing else to do that night but agonize over Silas.

"Come on in." She sighed, taking a bottle from Rayanne.

"Whoo-hoo!" Rayanne yelled. "Let's party!

Silas showed up an hour later. His unnerving green eyes scarcely registered the four young people sprawled in varying states of inebriation across Riley's living room couch and floor. Riley had been trying to get there, too, but the alcohol had yet to penetrate the hole in her chest.

His eyes zeroed in on hers. "Riley, can you come back with me? Can we talk? Please?"

Rayanne stood, swaying. "Well, who is this? Riley, what have you been hiding?"

Silas looked confused as his eyes swung between the sisters. Then understanding dawned. "You must be Rayanne," he said politely. "It's nice to meet you. I'm Silas."

Riley noticed that he didn't give his last name, and the continued deception added to her wrath. But even in her anger, she had enough presence of mind not to bring his world crashing down. She held herself stiffly and met his eyes.

"No, I don't think so," she said. "I have work in the morning, so I was going to bed."

Silas's eyes were imploring, and for a moment, she was tempted to go back to the little house on the inlet where he would build a fire and hold her as they talked. She could tell he wanted to say more but couldn't, or wouldn't, with Rayanne and her friends present.

He turned to go. "I'll call you tomorrow," he said, letting himself out.

Rayanne hardly waited until the door closed before hooting, "Who in the hell was that?"

That was the moment. Right there. That was the moment Riley could have changed things, stopped the train, avoided disaster. But she was too upset to recognize it.

"A friend," she said to Rayanne.

"A friend? Riley, he's Dad's age."

"No, he's not."

"I mean, he's a hunk. I'll give you that. Are you *dating* him?"

"No," Riley had said. "He's a friend from work."

Had a wisp of warning grazed her? Had she thought of Chad Evers? She honestly couldn't remember. She'd walked into her bedroom and shut the door, hiding from her sister's curiosity and her own screaming questions. When she'd woken the next morning, Rayanne and her friends had gone.

Riley blinked drowsily and registered the few ounces remaining in her glass. Drinking the mimosa hangover remedy made her think of Rayanne, and she didn't want to do that. Sisterhood carried a certain weight of responsibility. That weight that had nearly killed her once. At the very least, it had sent her fleeing Alabama for South Carolina.

She got up and poured the rest of the drink into the sink. No more mimosas. No more memories of Rayanne.

Chapter 14

July
Mikala

Luke straightened the hem of Mikala's slinky red blouse and lightly tapped her bottom. "Looking good, Mrs. Hardy."

She patted her shrinking stomach with satisfaction. After a year of yo-yo dieting, she'd lost four pounds in the past month. She suspected it was the thrill of putting her plan into action.

"Tell me about tonight's shindig," said Luke as he stepped into freshly polished wing tips.

"I already have," she snapped. "Were you not listening?"

He paused. "Well, I know it's a fundraiser for the museum. But are you raising money for a particular purchase or exhibit? Who can keep up?"

"I would think the great Luke Hardy, Greenbrier's foremost art connoisseur, could keep up." She sounded bitchy even to her own ears.

Luke looked at her in puzzlement. "Okaaay. I'll wait for you downstairs."

Mikala made a face in the mirror as she attached dangling diamond earrings. She would need to be more careful. As she tottered down the curving staircase in high heels, she resolved to play all her roles perfectly that night. Charity queen. Adoring wife. Savior of wayward cousin.

She smiled as she reached the kitchen. "Sorry. I'm probably hungry. Tonight's event is—drumroll, please—to purchase a Faith Ringgold. We want to bring a taste of Harlem to our textile collection." She had memorized that much for her elevator speech.

"Ah, I know Ringgold. *Tar Beach*, right?"

"Well, we're not buying *Tar Beach*, but yes, that's her."

"Got it. Is Riley coming?" he asked.

Mikala searched Luke's face for some emotion—excitement or lust maybe. He appeared guileless, but he was practiced at deception.

"Of course. Here she is now," Mikala said.

Riley was an apparition at the patio door, dressed in a simple white sundress that showed off her dark hair and newly golden tan. Luke threw open the door and bowed. "Wow, two gorgeous women on my arm tonight. How'd I get so lucky?"

Mikala beamed at her cousin, but Riley's eyes darted between her hosts. "Are we walking?" Riley asked.

"Ha. In these shoes? I think not." Mikala paused. "Unless you and Luke would like to. I can drive so we'll have the car for the ride back."

Luke looked puzzled again. "No, we'll all go together."

When Mikala turned toward the garage, he mimed a shrug at Riley. Mikala caught it out of the corner of her eye but pretended not to.

The fundraiser was held in the museum's galleries on the floor where the Southern textiles were displayed. In the place where the Ringgold would eventually hang was a graphic of a giant thermometer, its red "mercury" halfway to the top. Mikala expected it to reach its zenith by the end of the evening. If it didn't, she would lean on Luke for another donation.

She glided through the crowd, smiling and accepting compliments on everything from the catering to the flowers to the swing band in one corner. They usually hired string quartets for these events, but Mikala had spiced things up with a nod to Harlem in the 1940s. She made sure the band was heavy on Black musicians.

As she mingled, she kept an eye on Riley, who was studying the art. After a half hour of backslapping and glad-handing, Luke approached her cousin, a glass of white wine in his hand. Mikala watched as Riley accepted the wine but subtly moved away from Luke.

That was all right. Mikala had every confidence in her husband's charm. She caught sight of Savannah Darwin sidling toward Luke, undoubtedly to talk real estate. That wouldn't do.

Mikala cut smoothly into Savannah's path and grasped her arm, steering her to the nearest food station. "Hey, neighbor, have you tried these stuffed mushrooms?" she said brightly. "Crab straight from the coast. They're the best."

Chapter 15

Riley

I*s there anything worse than a party where you know hardly anyone?* Riley talked to Mikala's neighbor Cate for a bit. And to Luke, of course. But something was off there. He was nice enough and offered to run her home if she was bored, but somehow, she didn't think that was a good idea.

When they were interrupted by a colleague from his bank, Riley escaped. On her way out, she whispered to Cate that she would walk home and to please let Mikala know. Out in the balmy July evening, Riley relaxed against the side of the museum and removed her low heels. She was homesick—for Mama, for Daddy, for Mobile. Even for Silas and Dauphin Island, though she knew she'd never go back there. Riley gazed down at her favorite sundress and thought about the last time she'd worn it.

The morning Rayanne and her friends left, Silas had shown up at her island house with raspberry-filled croissants and coffee. She'd crumbled in the face of his apologies and the sincerity of his pain. She tamped down thoughts of his wife in Mobile, and they had a delicious week of makeup sex, leading to the unseasonably warm night that she pulled this sundress from the back of her closet. They were going to the Sand Box to drink and dance, but she knew how Silas would remove the dress later, sliding its spaghetti straps down her arms slowly, slowly, before kissing her breasts almost reverently. That was how Silas made love—with aching gentleness. Until she had ruined it.

Riley shoved her weight from the side of the museum and set off, enjoying the feel of the smooth concrete under her bare feet. Even when she hit the rougher sidewalk, she kept going. Her feet knew they were headed to the square brick house on Parker Street before her conscious mind caught up.

She slid through quiet streets lit by Dickensian streetlights. Two men on bicycles passed her, and a woman jogged by with a German shepherd. She arrived at the squat house and stopped as the memories rushed her like a rogue wave. She hadn't noticed before, but the house appeared vacant—no lights, no porch furniture, no yard detritus. It had probably been sold and was awaiting demolition. She shuddered against the tightness in her chest.

That night at the Sand Box, Silas had confided that the manager at High's had quit unexpectedly, and he had to return to Mobile the next day. He promised to work something out—revisit Dauphin, set up a meeting place for them in Mobile, or *something.* He wasn't going to give her up.

Riley did what she usually did when faced with bad news. She drank. She drank white wine, red wine, then tequila shots. Silas begged her to slow down. When she didn't, he paid the bill and insisted they go back to his house. He wanted to make love, but she was spoiling for a fight.

When he slid her dress straps down, she stood trembling, her emotions at war. Part of her wanted the tenderness that would follow his reverent caresses. The darker part—the part that knew how wrong the relationship was—wanted to blow things up.

The darkness won, and Riley yanked the straps back onto her shoulders. She accused him again of slumming. Finally, she banged out of his house, slamming the screen door. She had no memory of the drive back to her rental, but she remembered opening another bottle of tequila when she got home and taking it to her bedroom.

And that was all she remembered until the Dauphin Island Police woke her the next day.

The evidence against her was damning. A fisherman in the house beside Silas's—a place she had literally never seen through the scrub oak and tangled vegetation and her own self-absorption—knew them well. He identified Riley as the girl who had spent the past eight weeks coming and going from Silas's homeplace.

"They didn't bother to cover their windows," he told the officers. "I saw her there a bunch of times."

And on that last night, he saw her, same as usual. She was wearing a white sundress. She'd crashed out of the house, making enough noise to silence the tree frogs.

The fisherman hadn't heard her return, he admitted. But a couple of hours later, he glanced through the window again and saw her standing in the kitchen, staring down at the floor. That was when the officers decided Riley was the one who had stabbed Silas Hightower with his own fishing knife.

Sadness and revulsion engulfed Riley in a way they hadn't in a while. She doubled over and spewed the wine and crab she had consumed at the museum. Embarrassed, she wiped her streaming eyes, but no one was around to notice. Unless they were watching from their windows. She crawled away from the streetlight and into the darkness. Only then did she feel safe.

She lay back in the scraggly yard and recalled those dark and frightening days after Silas's death. She'd spent a sixteen-hour stretch being questioned in the Dauphin Island police station, which resembled a marina outpost. She'd watched enough *Law and Order* to feel eyes through the mirror in the small room where she drank endless Cokes in an attempt to calm her stomach. Despite the witness's account that placed her in Silas's house at the time of the murder, none of the fingerprints on the knife were hers.

The police searched Silas's house and the inlet out back, Riley's street and house, and the road to Dino's as well as the entire restaurant. Nowhere could they find the gloves they were sure she'd worn. They interviewed the two Vietnamese youth, whose fingerprints *were* on the knife. Both explained—with great terror, she imagined—that they'd borrowed their boss's knife while on the boat. And of course, there'd been Silas's prints. And a thumbprint from an unidentified person.

That thumbprint stood between Riley and prison. She wasn't a praying gal, but she thanked the Lord she'd never touched that knife, not even to move it off the kitchen table.

The police had insisted she stay on the island for the next two weeks while they investigated—two weeks with no income since Dino had fired her. She huddled in her house, wondering if she could have done what everybody said she'd done. For it came down to two options. Option one: after consuming half a bottle of tequila, she'd driven back to Silas's house during a blackout and, with the foresight to wear gloves, stabbed him to death with his fishing knife. Option two: for some reason, Silas's elderly neighbor was lying. Or confused.

She wasn't sure why it took her so long to arrive at option three—perhaps she'd had an emotional blackout rather than an alcoholic one. The police had released her to her parents' custody after her island landlord raised hell because she could no longer pay rent. She was pulling into the driveway of her childhood home in Mobile when she glanced past its peeling clapboard to her second-story bedroom. A figure stood in the window, watching, and suddenly, Riley understood who had killed Silas.

Chapter 16

Caleb

Living in the potting shed behind Twenty-Four Gunter Avenue was working well. *A freakin' potting shed.* That was what the tiny white house had turned out to be. Caleb didn't know until he got inside and found the neat array of pots, landscape tools, stacks of bagged soil, and manure.

He almost laughed when he thought about people building homes for stuff and not humans. Almost. He'd met men who had lived for weeks, even months, in commercial storage units. There was profit in providing shelter for stuff. For humans, not so much.

Before he moved, he had nabbed an abandoned sleeping bag from the boarding house and helped himself to canned ravioli and tuna left by previous tenants. Once he was living in the shed, he gathered apples and oranges and raisins from a food pantry, sandwiches from Trinity Faith Center's soup kitchen, and discarded pizza and calzones from Pizza by the Park. Finding food was not a problem in Greenbrier.

He was careful not to leave leftovers that might attract squirrels and raccoons or even the cat that frequented the yard of number twenty-four. When he went to work, he carefully stowed his sleeping bag, library books, and flashlight in an unkempt thicket behind the boarding house. He hadn't seen the silver-haired woman—Cate, he'd learned—enter the shed that summer, but he didn't want to take any chances.

Already, he had saved the entire five hundred dollars he would have spent on a month's rent at the boarding house. For his few needs—laundry, flashlight batteries, the occasional Coke—he used tips that the waitstaff sent his way. To Caleb's surprise, Riley had let him shower in the pool house after he lied about the third-floor shower at the boarding house not working. Once she'd seen he was no threat, she seemed to welcome his company. She didn't even mind when he used her soap and floral-scented shampoo.

He didn't want her to know that he was staying in the shed less than ten feet from her, separated only by the iron fence. The most obvious reason was that he feared she would tell the Hardys or even Cate or Cate's wife, who turned out to be the developer Savannah Darwin. The less obvious reason—and he wasn't proud of this—was that he enjoyed the view.

The window on the side of his potting shed faced a window at the rear of Riley's living room. Her window was covered with sheers because Mikala—and probably Riley—assumed the empty potting shed blocked the need for more coverage. After work, he would watch Riley pour herself a glass of wine or a tumbler of liquor and tuck her legs beneath her, staring out at the pool lights.

She was never naked, nothing like that. Sex Offender Registry notwithstanding, he was no pervert. He just liked watching her. Riley was sad and lonely—that much was clear. When he showered at her place, she offered him a beer and encouraged him to stay and talk. After learning that he was twenty-one, she'd seemed to relax and accept him as a buddy or even a younger brother. In turn, Caleb accepted life in the friend zone, understanding that it was the best he was going to do with someone so clearly out of his league.

On Caleb's day off, he walked to the bus stop in front of the library. He didn't really want the day off. As his bank account grew, he preferred to pad it rather than spend the tips he'd hidden in a cracked flowerpot. But Roman had made the schedule and hadn't responded when Caleb offered to cover another shift.

He caught a bus to the car lot run by the Greenbrier Gospel Mission. Donors gave the mission their old cars to sell, and Caleb had his eye on a 2005 Honda Civic with one hundred eighty thousand miles. It was listed for fourteen hundred dollars, but he planned to offer a thousand as soon as he had the money. As a graduate of the mission, he thought they would help him. Then he could drive to Raleigh to find his uncles and wouldn't arrive on a bus, all rumpled and pitiful. *Deal from a position of strength,* his mother used to say. Though she'd done no such thing.

He stopped by the maroon Honda to pat its hood and whisper a plea to wait for him. Then he entered the thrift store adjacent to the car lot. Standing at the checkout counter was an older woman in cargo shorts and a faded T-shirt, her witchy black hair tangled in the straps of her backpack. She was turned away from Caleb, but he slammed to a halt nonetheless. Then he backed out of the store.

On the sidewalk he breathed heavily. He had to know. Greenbrier wasn't big enough for him to avoid his mother if she was indeed homeless. He would run into her somewhere—the church soup kitchen, the mission store, the streets.

Hastily deciding, he returned to the bus stop and waited twenty minutes for the bus heading north to the hardscrabble community of Bender, on the far side of Greenbrier County. He snatched a discarded newspaper in case he needed to hide his face, but the woman never emerged from the thrift store.

After the bus ride, Caleb faced a two-mile walk from Bender's tiny post office to his old house on Fish Trap Road. The familiar pockmarked road wound through scrubby fields dotted with rundown trailers. If there were any ponds or lakes or fish, they were farther down this road than he'd ever gone. Dry dust mixed with his sweat so that when he wiped his brow, his hand came away with brown stains.

As soon as he glimpsed the shack, he saw the tape across the door. *Condemned.* He didn't know what he'd expected, but he was shocked.

He ripped off the tape and pushed through the door, which swung crookedly from a single hinge. Inside, trash covered the floor along with mouse pellets and the gnawed remnants of other animal visits. A three-legged sofa slumped to one side, and the stuffing flowed from a wing chair. The tables and lamps that Caleb remembered were gone, possibly inside some of the trailers he'd passed.

Entering the sole bathroom, Caleb saw that the tub and toilet had crashed through to the ground below. That explained the condemnation. He walked into his mother's bedroom, stepping carefully to avoid another hole in the planking. A few bedraggled dresses hung in the closet, but he could tell she'd taken at least some of her clothes. He wondered about the secret she thought she'd kept but that he'd discovered before he was eight. He lifted the stained mattress and shoved it aside to reveal sagging box springs. *Deal from a position of strength,* indeed. To his surprise, the gun was still there. He stuffed it into his jeans pocket.

Caleb debated whether to enter his old bedroom and decided there was nothing to be gained. But as he walked past the door, something drew him in. The table where he had done his homework was gone. He'd dragged it from an abandoned trailer when he was in elementary school, so it had probably returned to a similar home. He shuffled tentatively across the old floorboards, testing for rot that could send him plunging to the ground like the bathtub. His NASCAR posters hung on the walls, tattered but celebrating the valiant efforts of Jimmie Johnson and Dale Earnhardt Jr.

His soiled twin mattress was on the floor—someone had taken the bed frame. He recalled waking in here to a rooster-shaped alarm clock given to him by his third-grade teacher when she learned his mother couldn't be trusted to wake him. He had set it fastidiously every school night. When its raucous *cock-a-doodle-doo!* sounded in the morning, he'd splashed some water around, dressed, and made the bus in time for breakfast in the school cafeteria.

Where is that rooster? He'd packed it when he moved out, but it had been lost, or stolen, somewhere between the encampment and the mission.

His third-grade teacher had been Miss Nelson—like the book she'd read aloud to the class, *Miss Nelson Is Missing*. How they'd screamed with laughter when scary Miss Viola Swamp replaced the pretty teacher in room 207. Caleb wondered what it would be like to have Miss Nelson—the real one—as his mother. He wished for it every single night of third grade, huddled in his room, hearing his mother stumbling around the living room with her user-loser friends, hearing the fake moans from her bedroom as she paid her dealer with more than money.

He hadn't understood what was going on at the time, only that it made him feel empty and hopeless. He hated the men who cuffed him on the back of the head, or worse, asked about his schoolwork or his NASCAR heroes. He didn't want to share with them. He knew they'd never come back, like the dad who never came back. He wasn't the kind of kid who asked about his dad or went looking for him. By the time he was ten, he suspected that his mother didn't even know who he was.

He had placed all his hopes and dreams on Miss Nelson's oft-repeated mantra: "If you don't like where you are in life, education is the way out." He always felt she was looking at him when she said it. Education. That was why he'd gone scavenging for a table to do his homework on. That was why he'd gotten up and out of this shack in a wet South Carolina January when it was thirty-three degrees out, just shy of the iciness they would need to call off school. And that was why he'd jolted awake every day to that damn *cock-a-doodle-doo!*

Early on, his mission had been concrete—if he could make himself smart enough, quiet enough, good enough, maybe Miss Nelson would adopt him. By the end of the third grade, he realized that was a childish dream. But he clung to her promise about the power of education, like a drowning man in the trash-strewn currents of his home life.

Then he'd thrown it all away because of another teacher. Mrs. Prescott was a Viola Swamp, sure, with her dyed-black hair and her grating voice. But why had he let her force him off his road to an education?

He scanned the room, recalling his mother's jeering voice when she found him studying. "You think you're better than me, doncha?" she would rave, falling heavily onto his bed while he worked at his table.

Well, yeah, who isn't? Had he said that out loud? He couldn't remember.

When he'd expressed ambivalence about *The Great Gatsby,* Mrs. Prescott had said, "So, Mr. March, you think you can write better than F. Scott Fitzgerald?" Condescending. Sneering.

Why, oh why, did I let her get to me? She'd made comments like that all the time, but the night before that particular remark, there had been more than the usual number of dopers in his living room, and he'd been groggy when the mechanical rooster crowed. So when he looked at her thin lips disappearing into a tight pucker and her beaky nose flaring and her dyed hair coarse and brittle like his mother's, he swept up his books and stomped out of the classroom, screaming, "You bitch!"

The same afternoon, he moved out of his mother's house, relocating to an abandoned trailer on Fish Trap Road. He refused outreach efforts from the principal and even a county-wide task force for dropout prevention. In his mind, Doreen March and Mrs. Prescott were one and the same, and he reviled both with a bottomless black hatred. But within weeks, he'd known what his counselor at the Gospel Mission eventually voiced—he had hurt no one but himself.

Sighing, Caleb pivoted from Jimmie and Dale and all thoughts of Miss Nelson. He'd learned what he needed to know—his old house was vacant, and it was indeed possible that his mother was homeless in Greenbrier.

Chapter 17

Riley

Riley was trying to save money, but she needed more of the black pants and black T-shirts they wore at Pizza by the Park. She'd been doing laundry every other day in Mikala's house and feared that she, or her housekeeper, Maria, would eventually complain.

Walmart had exactly what she needed, so she bought three more of each item and avoided a trip to the mall. She also picked up a sixty-four-ounce container of the high-end detergent Mikala used, cringing at the cost. She contemplated going to a matinee, since she'd told Mikala she would be out most of the day. But she was in the middle of reading a great domestic thriller, so she returned to the pool house. Deliberately pouring a Diet Pepsi and no alcohol, she settled into the comfy sofa.

She'd devoured two chapters before she heard the side door to the kitchen open. She knew she'd locked it. *Was Mikala planning to search my things while I was out?* Riley contemplated hiding to see what her cousin would do, but that would be too embarrassing for both of them. So instead, she strode into the kitchen.

To her surprise, Savannah Darwin stood there, a key in her hand. A blush crept up the woman's neck, but she recovered quickly. "Riley! I'm so sorry. I was coming over for a swim. I thought you were at work."

She was dressed for the office and clearly had no bathing suit, but Riley pretended not to notice. "No, I don't go to work until four o'clock. But you're welcome to come in. I'm having a Pepsi if you'd like one."

"Yes. Sure. Th-That's fine," Savannah stammered. "I just need to visit the ladies' first."

She fled into the bathroom situated between the kitchen and living room, and Riley heard murmurs as she made a phone call. Then came the running of tap water, and she emerged, hair and makeup impeccable, all fluster gone. Savannah was stunning, with dark-green eyes set in a lightly freckled face framed by a tumble of red-gold curls. She sat in a wing chair next to the table where Riley had placed her drink.

"You're welcome to go swimming," Riley said, "whether I'm here or not."

"Ah, no, no, that's all right." Savannah grinned conspiratorially. "I'm not really much of a swimmer."

Riley was unsure if she was acknowledging what was going on, so she searched for a neutral topic. "The Roosevelt Park neighborhood must keep you hopping."

Savannah's face grew animated. "You have no idea! If you could've seen what was here before, you wouldn't have believed it. Crack houses, trash piles, broken bottles, men standing idle on corners. We've had power lines buried, streets repaved, streetlights added. People take pride in the neighborhood now." She sat back, her face glowing. "This is your first trip to Greenbrier, isn't it?"

Riley nodded.

"Then you'd have no way of knowing. But it truly is a renaissance." She gestured at the boarding house behind Mikala's back fence. "There are a few holdouts, like the crabby old codger who owns that. But I don't blame them. They see how values are going up and want to get in on it. That's natural."

"But I guess it causes you problems with the people who've already bought here."

Savannah nodded vigorously. "Absolutely. The Hardys want that boarding house gone, as do the Garlingtons and McAlisters on either side of it. As do Cate and I, for that matter. But as I try to explain to newcomers, that's the cost of getting in early. You pay less than the last ones in, but you may be inconvenienced for a while."

So people like Caleb were an inconvenience to her. If not for Mikala and Luke, Riley would be an inconvenience too.

"Not that I'm unsympathetic to the people who lived here before," Savannah said as though realizing how her previous statement sounded. She looked at Riley earnestly, and Riley could imagine how well she played to Greenbrier's City Council. "My company is paying three times what these properties sold for in the past. But frankly, they were a drain on city coffers. You had abandoned houses where homeless people burrowed. Endless calls for police and emergency services. We are raising the tax base for all sorts of city services, including the park itself, which draws people from all over the county."

Savannah sat back, confident in her well-rehearsed arguments.

"I read the *Herald* a good bit before I came," Riley said tentatively. "There was a lot about the Gospel Mission being unhappy with all the bars and breweries moving in."

"Yeah, I get that," Savannah admitted. "Cate and I are supporters of the mission. But that's the free market at work. The city could have rezoned to prohibit certain types of businesses, and it didn't." She shimmied to the front of her seat and directed her laser focus on Riley. "The thing is, Riley, I love Greenbrier. I grew up here. My grandparents lived in the poorest textile village in the Crescent. But they worked hard and sent my dad and uncle to college. Dad and Uncle Robert were developers and taught me the business. Now they're off building golf course communities, but I came back to the inner city."

Savannah turned to indicate the downtown skyline visible beyond the Hardys' trees. "If you want the museum and the performing arts center and the good restaurants and energetic nightlife, you need safe neighborhoods nearby. Frankly, what was here before was a drag on the city. I know that's not politically correct, but it's true." She stood and laughed. "But you don't need a civics lesson from me, do you?" She carried her Diet Pepsi can to the recycling bin, saying over her shoulder, "Isaiah mentioned that he'd met you at Pizza by the Park."

"Yeah, he seems like a nice kid."

"I just wish..." Savannah paused. "I'd hoped he would follow me into the business. Smart, good-looking kid like that. Heck, he could be mayor of Greenbrier one day. But he doesn't seem to value urban renewal." She squared her shoulders. "Anyway, thanks for the soda."

Riley expected Savannah to ask her not to say anything to Cate or... *Wait a minute. Who did she plan to meet here—Mikala or Luke? Or someone else?* Riley tried to envision each possibility and couldn't.

But Savannah didn't ask for Riley's discretion. She simply winked and slipped out the door and around to her driveway.

Chapter 18

Cate

Cate smiled at her neighbors and hoped it didn't come across as a grimace. Parties were not her thing. She was an introvert, happiest when she was alone with her wife or son or, if she was honest, her plants. But Savannah insisted that these block parties were her greatest sales tools, so here they were at a pre–Fourth of July party along blocked-off Gunter Avenue, not to be confused with the city's upcoming Fourth of July party, which would be along blocked-off West Roosevelt.

Dozens of people milled around tables laden with barbecued pork, chips, brownies, soft drinks, beer, and wine. A banjo-and-mandolin duo were set up at the end of the block under a white tarp. These houses had plenty of shade trees behind them, but much of their street shade had been sacrificed when the houses went in. As a result, the late-afternoon heat was intense.

Cate wiped sweat from her top lip. She didn't recognize many of the guests, because Savannah had encouraged residents to bring family and friends. They considered it a sign of Savannah's generosity, but Cate knew the invitations were bait for Savannah's hook—she wanted to land potential buyers.

Obviously, the block-party invitations had to include residents in the small mill houses and boarding houses, but Cate didn't see a single person she suspected of living there. No, it was understood that these events were by and for the excited new residents of Greenbrier's rejuvenated park neighborhood, who even now gathered around

Savannah to hear the latest plans for Roosevelt Park. Cate could tell what the topic was by the way Savannah waved an arm toward the park every few seconds. She could almost hear her—"More trail spurs! A water feature! A wine-tasting room!"

Cate sighed and grabbed a Dixie cup filled with white wine. She was no wine snob, but really, she would have to sneak into her kitchen for a real glass. She imagined the taste of wax even if it was a memory more than reality.

Before she could move, Luke slid up beside her, hoisting his cup in a mock toast. "How's your summer going?"

"Fine. Relaxing. How about yours? Any vacation plans?"

"Nah. We went to Litchfield in May, and I ended up on the phone half the week. Things at the bank are too busy for me to get away. Thanks to your wife, by the way."

Cate laughed. "Really? She can impact an entire bank?"

Luke raised his eyebrows. "It seems that way sometimes. She's selling more than anybody in town. Or at least, any other developers who are using First State."

"She's a fireball all right."

They watched Savannah as she talked, touched arms, and laughed uproariously. Cate sneaked a sideways glance at Luke. *Does he see Savannah as his unattainable gay neighbor, or does he know more?*

His eyes flicked away, and she followed his gaze. Riley was walking down his driveway, dressed in no-nonsense black pants and shirt, ready for work. But the drab clothes couldn't hide the girl's dazzle. She looked up and waved at Luke and Cate before turning onto Gunter Avenue and pushing through the partygoers. She spoke to a few, probably her customers, but didn't stop. Riley quickly exited the party zone and continued toward the park.

Cate excused herself and headed toward her front door, nominally to switch out cups but also to grab a few minutes of blessed quiet. She swerved by her mailbox, which swung from a handsome black post and was covered by a red trumpet vine. Inside were a stack of bills and a slick card advertising a new dental practice. An envelope fell out of the pile and landed at her feet. There was no stamp, only hand-printed names, which were misspelled: *Savana Darwin and Kate Rosemund.*

Something in the handwriting—scratchy, childlike—caused Cate to blanch. Her heart began to hammer. She tore into the envelope as she hurried up the driveway.

Inside the cool house, she let the rest of the mail drop to the floor and snatched the single sheet from the offending envelope. It was the message some part of her had been expecting for nearly three years.

That's a handsum boy you have, but he arent really yours, is he. If you don't wont him to meet his real mother, leave $5,000 in unmocked bills under the center bush in your back hege by midnite Sundy.

Cate teared up in frustration. This was every adopting parent's nightmare. She let out a shriek of rage. "'Unmocked bills,' you idiot? I'll be sure to unmock them."

It didn't cross her mind to doubt the letter's authenticity. The low ask—she had more than that in her checking account—told her the writer was no financial genius. Plus, the writer had undoubtedly gotten the idea of *unmarked* bills from TV. *What the hell is a marked bill, anyway?*

Fear was causing Cate's mind to fracture. She focused on the money drop in her own backyard. The writer was familiar with this neighborhood.

She peeked through the plantation shutters at the party outside. All those neighbors. She searched for someone out of place, someone with no grasp of spelling or grammar, as if she could tell by looking. She recalled the fat woman in front of the post office and pictured her circling their block, creeping up to their mailbox. Cate had deliberately changed her jogging route so she wouldn't pass the woman again. But that didn't mean the woman hadn't seen Cate.

She slipped through her high-ceilinged hallway to the elegant black-and-white kitchen. Through double glass doors, she could see past the potting shed to the waist-high hedge that created a back border. That was where she was to leave the money.

The Garlingtons lived in the yellow Victorian directly behind her house. They'd left the hedge to her for upkeep and seldom used their backyard. But next to them was the boarding house that Savannah had tried—repeatedly—to purchase. *Does the fat woman stay there?*

Cate whirled and ran up the stairs to her bedroom then spun the dial on the safe in her closet. Inside, she found the small pistol that she occasionally took on design jobs. She'd only used it once—on a copperhead—but she never knew when she might need it. Rotting logs and creek beds and tangled vegetation were hideouts for the venomous snakes, and her worksites often abutted such places.

Cate grabbed the gun, wondering about the legality of shooting an intruder in her yard. She could claim she feared for her life. Maybe she could even lure the woman into the house and say she'd broken in. That would be a slam dunk.

She sank to her bedroom floor, her heart pounding in a mixture of wrath and panic over the frightened and vengeful person she had become. *What is wrong with me?* Somewhere deep inside, she must have been afraid of losing Isaiah. But that couldn't happen. *Could it?*

She was furious that she hadn't spoken up more forcefully when Savannah wanted to move to Roosevelt Park. Cate's wife had been so money hungry that she didn't seem to recognize the danger.

"Are you happy, Savannah?" Cate hissed into the empty house.

Chapter 19

Mikala

Mikala had tried to talk Riley into begging off work so she could attend the block party, but her cousin was proving committed to her silly little waitressing job. Mikala watched her walk down Gunter and meet up with the dishwasher kid in the next block. She pursed her lips and exhaled in exasperation. He seemed to be around all the time. Mikala was fairly sure there was nothing going on between them, but his frequent presence at the pool house was irritating. She wasn't running a damn hotel.

Her gaze flickered to her cobalt blue cropped top and matching capri pants. Did they make her look fat? She stood straighter and tossed her hair over one shoulder. Her thick blond hair had always been her best feature. She had been complimented on it all her life. It was just her luck that Savannah Darwin—the only woman in their circle with similarly spectacular locks—lived next door.

Mikala sipped her white wine and looked around. *Where is Luke?* If he was seeing someone in the neighborhood, maybe he would be careless enough to show his hand. Her narrowed eyes raked the crowd. He was making his way toward Savannah, who was holding court. No danger there, but Lord, if Mikala's neighbor hadn't been gay, Mikala would be in a funk. She shook her head dismissively. Savannah and Luke would simply talk real estate until dusk.

Mikala pivoted to find a museum supporter headed her way. *Time to bask in more praise for the Ringgold fundraiser.* She could never get too much of that.

The block party broke up as the summer evening fell and the cicadas launched their nightly cacophony. There had been news this year of thirteen- and seventeen-year super cycles of the underground insects, but in South Carolina, their reverberations accompanied every summer. As her neighbors cleared away tables and dirty dishes, Mikala lifted a bottle of pinot grigio and carried it inside. She wandered the house until she found Luke asleep in the recliner of his third-floor man cave, with a decades-old golf match turned low on his wide-screen TV. She huffed in irritation. *As if live matches weren't boring enough.*

She headed downstairs to the sunroom to enjoy a final glass of wine. Mikala had a nice buzz going and didn't want to lose it. She gazed out at the pool house, which was faintly aglow in the reflection of the underwater lights. With Luke asleep and Riley at work, it would be a good time to investigate what Riley had brought with her from Mobile. For there was no question that Riley owned a gun. Every Alabama girl did. Well, every Alabama girl with a worried daddy. And Uncle Ed was one worried daddy.

From whispered conversations she'd heard over the years, Mikala knew that her aunt Crystal had married a wild boy from a large, roughneck Louisiana family. Supposedly one brother had disappeared into the swamps, never to be seen again, and a sister ran off and got married at fifteen. Ed's mama had committed suicide.

Of course, no one ever told Mikala such things directly. Her mother's summary of Ed was that he drank hard and "carried on." For the first time, Mikala contemplated exactly what the euphemism might cover, wondering if Riley had inherited a propensity for "carrying on." She'd had an affair with a married man and then killed him. Possibly. Probably. The only mystery was why she'd used a knife rather than the gun Uncle Ed undoubtedly had sent with her into the world. And the only question Mikala had now was whether she'd brought that gun to Greenbrier.

Mikala grabbed the pool-house key from a hook beside the patio door. She walked barefoot across the rough brick to the stamped-concrete terrace and let herself in. She started with Riley's bedroom, opening drawers and closets and checking under the bed. No gun, but she did find unopened bottles of rum and tequila behind a jumble of shoes. *Ah, Riley, are you hiding them from me or from yourself?*

She moved into the adjoining bathroom and groped blindly behind the sheets and towels in the linen closet before looking under the bathroom sink. No gun, but several unopened bottles of wine. *My, my, little Riley. I believe you may have your daddy's problem.*

Mikala straightened, hands on hips, and surveyed the two rooms. She spied Riley's suitcase in a corner and quickly unzipped it. Empty.

She entered the living room and conducted a methodical search of its drawers then moved to the kitchen. She doubted Riley would hide a gun in those rooms, but where else could it be? Her eyes fell on Riley's car keys on the kitchen counter. She swept them up and headed across the yard to the driveway.

After clicking open the ancient Beetle's passenger door, she popped the glove compartment. And there in a velvet Crown Royal bag—*classy, Riley*—was the expected pistol. But no magazine. Careful to avoid touching the grip, Mikala replaced it as she'd found it. Then she walked around to the Beetle's trunk and popped it.

Ah, there was the magazine. She closed the trunk. No need to remove either just yet.

Chapter 20

Riley

Amazingly, the block party had done nothing to cut into the business of Pizza by the Park. Riley's daddy used to talk about how Southern mills from Alabama to the Carolinas shut down for the Fourth of July week. Mill families rushed to Myrtle Beach or Dauphin Island or Panama City or Daytona. Now that the mills were shuttered, the residents of Greenbrier apparently didn't go anywhere. Instead, they clogged the terraces of every downtown restaurant.

Pizza by the Park drew customers from far beyond Roosevelt Park. Walkers and bicyclists chugged up from the trail behind the building, and a nearby warehouse lot held the SUVs of suburbanites. This evening, there was a line up the sidewalk for patio seating. Eight waiters and waitresses rushed to fill orders, keep up with refills, deliver bills, run credit cards, and smile, smile, smile.

Roman was handing Riley four margaritas for one of her tables when he motioned toward Luke's colleague from the bank, who was sitting at the bar. Riley hadn't even noticed the man come in. "Mr. Yuppie over there wants you to wait on him."

"Does anyone still say yuppie?" she asked.

She and Roman had fallen into an easy banter. He'd moved the jukebox and speakers to the patio, so it was easier to hear conversation inside the restaurant. The accuracy of their drink orders had improved dramatically.

Roman rolled his eyes. "I told him you were serving food tonight, not bartending. He's going to order dinner."

"Okay, boss." She glanced at Luke's junior associate, who had been in the restaurant before. He was staring in a way that made her uneasy. *Richard? Rick? No, Rich. How appropriate.*

"Hello, Mr. Rich," she said, attempting joviality. "What can I get for you?"

He wasn't bad looking, with an expensive haircut, white dress shirt with rolled-up sleeves, khakis, and boat shoes with no socks. She'd seen enough of Luke's management trainees to recognize the off-the-clock-banker look. It must have been in their manual.

He eyed her from head to toe, giving her a creepy vibe. "Hey, doll. Scotch on the rocks, please."

Honestly, he was a little young for the wise-guy schtick. Plus, Riley could tell from his breath that he'd already been into the Scotch. "Coming right up."

She added his drink to an order she was filling for a large table and dropped it off quickly. He attempted to speak, but she displayed her full tray and didn't stop. Roman said he wanted dinner, however, so eventually, she had to return. She was surprised to find his glass empty.

"I believe you wanted to order dinner?"

"Another one of these first," he said, shaking the glass.

She dutifully got him another Scotch and asked again for his dinner order.

"Any chance of you joining me?"

She laughed in disbelief, throwing out an arm to indicate the crowd. "No, we're pretty busy." *You can't see that, dickhead?*

He took a deep swallow. "Then what time do you get off?"

His arrogance was beginning to irritate her. "Not for hours and hours."

"I can come back and pick you up."

What is it with this guy? He acted as if she'd already accepted his invitation and he was working out the details.

"Thank you," she said firmly. "But no."

He finished his drink, holding her eyes over the rim. "I know who you are, you know."

Her body went still and cold. *What does he mean?*

She attempted to laugh it off. "Well, Luke Hardy introduced us. My cousin's husband." She hoped the mention of his boss would persuade him to back off.

"No," he said, all friendliness leaving his face. "I guess I should say I know who you *were*. When you lived on Dauphin Island."

Riley felt her face flush and glanced around to see if anyone had heard him. Caleb was clearing a nearby table and staring straight at her. He picked up his dish carrier, but instead of heading to the kitchen, he walked behind the bar to where Gus, the burly Black bartender, was working.

She turned back to Rich. "Did you want to order?" Even to her own ears, her voice sounded tinny.

He ignored the question. "But I don't have to tell Luke." He clutched her arm and leaned in close. Too close. "Or Roman. Or anyone else. Can I pick you up when you get off?"

For a moment, she was dizzy. If he told Roman, she might lose her job. Her former boss, Dino, had gotten rid of her the minute she was questioned in Silas's murder. It might be worth meeting Rich to avoid that. She tried to tug her arm away, but he had an iron grip. His eyes were bloodshot, and his boozy breath brushed her face.

"No," she repeated, looking around wildly. "I think I ought to get you another waitress."

"Now, Riley Masterson, why would you want to do that? You're all the waitress I need." He lurched into her space.

She backed up and collided with someone. Farrah bobbled her tray but righted it before the plates slid off. "You all right?" Farrah murmured.

"Sor-Sorry," Riley stammered.

Rich laughed and ogled her breasts. "You need to get a grip. Maybe get a few things off your chest."

"I-I'll find you another waitress."

"That won't be necessary," said a voice over her shoulder. "The gentleman is leaving." Roman nudged her aside and seized Rich by his shirt collar and waistband. Gus crowded him from the other side.

Rich held up his hands. "Hey, hey, what's going on? I'm trying to order a drink here."

"You'll have to get it somewhere else, bud," Roman said. "We don't want your business."

Rich continued to protest, but Roman and Gus half shoved and half carried him through the kitchen to the grassy area out back. Riley followed them into the kitchen, and when they returned, Roman pointed to his office.

"Take five if you want," he said. "Then we need you on the floor if you're up to it."

She nodded shakily and sat down at his desk. Caleb walked by, and she mouthed, "Thank you."

Farrah rushed in a moment later. "You okay?"

Riley exhaled and nodded. "Sorry if you have to cover for me."

"Don't mention it. Take all the time you need." She smiled. "Up to ten minutes, anyway."

Riley smiled, too, and stood to rejoin her, blowing a shuddering breath from her tight chest. Apparently, five hundred miles wasn't distance enough from her past.

Chapter 21

Cate

It was midmorning on Saturday, July 4, and Cate had changed her mind a dozen times. She'd placed five thousand dollars in cash in her bedroom safe in case she decided to leave the money under a shrub the next night like some damn Easter egg. And she'd picked up her phone a half dozen times to call the police. She was sure they could pick up the woman when she ventured into Cate's yard.

But then Isaiah would meet his real mother. *Would that be a terrible thing? It would be if he wants her in our lives.*

Cate could not decide. She knew what Savannah would do—tell the police immediately, shut the woman down. That was why she hadn't told her. She didn't want Savannah snatching the decision from her.

Besides, the police would have their hands full that day. Between the heat and the drinking, bad actors would act badly. She'd heard that line from Gospel Mission staff, who dreaded the summer holiday.

Cate paced her professionally equipped kitchen, coffee mug in hand, stopping occasionally to stare at her yard. Her crew had mowed the grass the previous day, so it was manicured and lovely. Lantana, geraniums, salvia, and lavender bloomed riotously in the sunny spots. Hostas and ferns and impatiens thrived in the shade. The sight momentarily soothed her.

She heard the ring of her cell phone, which was set to mimic the ice cream truck of her youth. But since the threatening letter had arrived, the ring no longer elicited a childhood memory, only fear. She closed her eyes and grabbed the phone.

Mikala was breathless. "Did you hear?" Without waiting for an answer, she blurted, "A girl was assaulted last night. On the Crescent Trail."

"Assaulted?" Cate repeated. "Sexually?"

"Yes, raped and beaten pretty badly."

"Oh my God. Do you know who it was?"

"A waitress at Pizza by the Park. Farrah Newell."

Cate gasped as she pictured the petite blond college student. "Oh no!"

"Anyway, there's a meeting of all the park neighbors tomorrow afternoon."

"About the assault?"

"Yes. The phone tree has been going crazy all morning. People are up in arms."

"I'm not sure I understand," Cate said.

Mikala cleared her throat.

"Mikala, what?"

"People want Savannah there. They say she promised them the park was safe from homeless guys."

"A homeless guy attacked Farrah?" Cate asked.

Mikala paused again. "I don't think they know yet."

Cate was beginning to understand. "But they will jump to the conclusion that it was a homeless man. And they're going to blame Savannah for luring them to a neighborhood near a homeless shelter."

"Yes, they are." The voice came not from Cate's phone but from behind her. She whirled to find Savannah standing in the hall, her face tight, her own phone held aloft.

"Fifteen messages," Savannah said.

Cate spoke into her phone. "Mikala, I'll talk to you later."

Savannah heaved herself onto a high-backed stool at the island and pushed strawberry curls off her face. "Can you believe this?"

"That poor girl," agreed Cate, though she wasn't sure she and Savannah were talking about the same thing. "I think her family lives in that gated section near Pizza by the Park."

"Oh, great. I guess they'll come after me too."

Cate was taken aback. "What do you mean?"

"As the phone tree callers so kindly inform me, I am the boogie man. They say they asked about those homeless people in the woods. They even point to that award the mission gave us."

Cate recalled the Greenbrier Gospel Mission's annual fundraiser two years back, when she and Savannah had been named Angels of the Year for their significant gift toward a kitchen renovation. "You're kidding."

"I kid you not," Savannah said wearily. "Two callers mentioned that plaque with our names beside the cafeteria door."

"I'm proud of that plaque! And of how Isaiah volunteers there."

"Yeah, well, tell that to these callers."

"What exactly are they accusing you of?" Cate asked.

"The gist is that I lied about the safety of this neighborhood so people would buy these expensive houses. And now their safety is compromised by the homeless people in the park encampments and in the shelter."

"That's insane," Cate said. "Do they even know it was a homeless person who attacked Farrah?"

Savannah shrugged. "No, but it probably was."

"Savannah! What's gotten into you?"

Savannah hopped off the chair and buried her face in Cate's hair. "I don't know. I guess I don't take criticism well." She raised her face, and Cate was struck, as she often was, by her wife's pale beauty. "It's just that I—we—have worked so hard, you know? And to have it all endangered by one incident... It makes me think these people were just waiting to pounce."

Cate stroked the tangled waves of Savannah's morning hair. "Could be. But the mission was here long before these new residents. They have to remember that. We all have to remember that."

"Yes, ma'am." Savannah sighed and picked up her ringing cell phone.

Chapter 22

Riley

Caleb and Riley slid into the pew behind Cate and Isaiah at Trinity Faith Center, the church that had offered its sanctuary for a hastily called neighborhood meeting. Like the Gospel Mission, the church had an active outreach to homeless citizens, but it sat several blocks away and wasn't viewed in quite the same light as the shelter. From conversations Riley had gleaned from Luke and Mikala, this meeting could devolve into a fight between moneyed new residents and those serving the homeless population. The city had four police officers in attendance. Savannah sat on the front pew because she would be expected to speak.

First up was the police department's public information officer, who explained that a woman had been assaulted on the Crescent Trail at eleven thirty the night of July 3. Riley's heart pinched as she pictured Farrah checking on her after her encounter with Rich. It was later that same night, in fact, that Farrah had been attacked on her way home.

Riley imagined Rich, unceremoniously removed by Roman and Gus, lying in wait on the trail and nursing his rage until Farrah walked by. *What if I provoked a temper tantrum that he then took out on her? But Farrah would have recognized him, wouldn't she?*

Riley shoved the thought away. Like so many of her imaginings, it threatened to cripple her. She jerked her attention back to the officer, who was encouraging anyone with information to come forward. He'd hardly finished speaking before a man rose from the audience.

"Here's some information for you," the man said loudly. "It's a transient from the Gospel Mission. Or from one of those camps off the trail. That's only common sense."

"Actually, we don't know that, sir," the officer responded. "We do not have a suspect at this time."

A woman stood. "Savannah, you assured us the trail was safe," she said stridently. "I asked that specifically before we bought our house. You said there was a constant police presence. Our children ride that trail. We walk that trail. And now this!"

Her voice was nearly a shriek by the end, and the audience murmured their agreement. Shouts of "Yeah!" and "That's right!" and "You told us that too!" floated from different directions. Riley saw Cate reach for her son's hand.

Savannah rose slowly and took her time to look over the audience. She waited for the rumbling to quiet. "You're right. I said all of that, and I stand by everything I told you."

Derisive laughter filled the sanctuary. Again, she waited for the noise to subside.

"Urban living—or living anywhere, for that matter—carries risks," Savannah said. "The police *do* have a presence on the trail. I know you've seen them on bikes. I'm as upset by this attack as anyone. I, too, have a son who rides the trail. My family walks the trail." She paused and made eye contact with the man and woman who'd spoken. "But criminality knows no bounds. This assault could just as easily have happened in my old east-side neighborhood. We cannot promise one hundred percent protection against crime. No one can."

Another man stood, his face contorted with anger. "Yeah, but we can lower the danger by eliminating certain risks. And yes, I'm talking about the Gospel Mission and the lowlifes it attracts. I think it's time for the mission to move outside the city limits."

A startled silence descended. Everyone seemed surprised that the conversation had spiraled so quickly into an attack on the mission. A man from the front row joined Savannah and the police officer.

Caleb elbowed Riley. "That's the mission director," he whispered.

"I'm Russ Denton, and I know many of you from your support of the Greenbrier Gospel Mission." The director spoke with the same measured calm that Savannah had shown. "I would simply remind you that the mission has been at its current location for sixty-plus years." He looked as if he was considering his words. "Roosevelt Park and the new housing and businesses around it have come about only in the past five or six years. We are certainly willing to welcome you to the area. But we'd ask the same in return."

A good many in the audience applauded. A woman Riley recognized as a restaurant customer stood. "Mr. Denton, isn't there land out in the county where you could do your work with more privacy? I'm sure you could sell your property for much more than you paid for it and buy double or triple the amount of land somewhere else."

Those who had not applauded Russ Denton clapped now.

The shelter director clasped his hands so tightly his knuckles turned white. He waited for quiet to return. "Our men walk to work in downtown restaurants. If they don't worship with us, they worship here at Trinity Faith. They have access to the public library and homeless service providers who help them get on their feet. None of those things are available 'out in the county.'"

Savannah had shifted subtly away from Russ Denton, and her eyes were on the floor. It occurred to Riley that Savannah's job would be easier if the mission *were* to leave.

The same thing must have occurred to Isaiah because he hissed to Cate, "Why isn't she defending him?"

Cate turned to her son with stricken eyes.

Isaiah shot to his feet. "I think we are confusing the issues here. There are homeless people, and there are criminals. Homeless people are no more likely to commit crimes than anyone else."

Mutters of disagreement greeted his comments.

"I volunteer at the mission," Isaiah continued, "and the work they do is nothing short of miraculous. Everyone in this room moved to this neighborhood knowing the mission was here. It is unfair to turn around now and try to remove it."

Isaiah's articulation and passion surprised Riley. He must have gotten his speaking ability, if not his politics, from Savannah, who was gazing at her son coolly, a strained smile on her lips.

An older man and woman helped each other to their feet, looking uncomfortable and out of place in this crowd. His gray hair was sorely in need of cutting, and he wore threadbare pants and a faded work shirt. Her floral dress was belted at an ample waist. She looked familiar, and Riley realized she was the woman on the flower-filled porch on Parker Street, next door to the orange brick house so like Silas's.

"Speaking of confusing the issues, there's something else going on here." The man pointed a gnarled finger at Savannah. "And that is all you newcomers who think you can take over a neighborhood that's been here a hunnerd years, because you have money."

An awkward silence fell over the crowd.

"I ain't no fan of these homeless guys neither," he continued, "but they're a damn sight better than all of you coming in like carpetbaggers to take advantage of retired mill workers." He stared at Savannah in disgust. "You come to my house and offer a pittance for my properties so you can turn around and build your mansions. You oughta be ashamed."

Another smattering of applause broke out. Luke and Mikala exchanged befuddled glances. Riley could tell they were surprised that residents of the old mill community had come out. She imagined Mikala and her husband had not seen these people before.

Caleb whispered in Riley's ear, "That's the owner of my boarding house. Earle Meadows."

She turned to him in surprise. "Really?"

"Yeah. Apparently, he inherited it from his mother. She ran it as a boarding house, and he kept it going after she died."

"But he lives over on— "

"We're getting too far afield!" The first man who had spoken pointed to Russ Denton. "Obviously, you don't care what your guys do to decent human beings. But I want to know what you... and you"—he gestured toward Savannah and the police officer—"are going to do about crime on the trail."

The crowd erupted into scores of conversations at once. The police officer tried to speak, but he'd lost control of the room. A dozen or more people surged forward to talk to him and the Gospel Mission director in smaller exchanges.

Riley quickly lost sight of them. Only Savannah remained visible for another instant, her face drawn and white, her jaw set, before she, too, was lost in the heaving crowd. It was clear that many issues were roiling through this neighborhood. And at the angry center of more than one was Savannah Darwin.

Chapter 23

Cate

Savannah and Isaiah were asleep, though Cate didn't see how. The meeting that afternoon had shaken her. She had been surprised by the extent of her neighbors' ire at Savannah over the trail attack, which struck her as unfair. Savannah might have been a little unfeeling about the people being displaced in the park neighborhood, sure, but she couldn't be blamed for random crimes.

More worrisome, Cate had not been aware of the fissure growing between her wife and son until Isaiah stood up to defend the Gospel Mission. Cate had realized then that Savannah was moving away from her support of the homeless shelter. Savannah was willing to sacrifice the mission if it meant more sales. It was all about sales.

Cate ran a hand through her hair, wondering if the money had always mattered this much to Savannah. *Has Savannah changed, or have I?*

Their former house on Greenbrier's east side had been charming if undistinguished, surrounded by flower beds bursting with three seasons of color. Cate had loved the updated brick ranch with its elaborate swing set and tree house installed in Isaiah's younger years. But Savannah, when she started developing Roosevelt Park, became dissatisfied with their subdivision. Cate didn't remember agreeing to a move. It had suddenly become an accomplished fact.

But that was unfair, Cate knew. She couldn't just drift along, passively allowing Savannah to make decisions then deciding after the fact that she disagreed. She owed it to Isaiah—hell, she owed it to herself—to stand up for what she wanted. They hadn't talked about all this as a family, but that discussion was coming.

Cate had a more immediate concern. It was Sunday night, and she had not placed the money under the hedge as instructed. She hovered on her dark porch, staring into the backyard. It was almost midnight, and she hadn't seen any movement.

She glanced into the lighted kitchen of the Hardys' pool house, where she could see Riley and that friend of hers—Caleb, the skinny kid from Pizza by the Park—passing in front of the sink. He was over there a lot. Cate idly wondered what was going on between them. She never would have pegged them as a couple. Maybe they were *hooking up*, as their generation termed it.

She looked again at the hedge and thought she saw the bushes move. But it was so dark she couldn't be certain. Fat woman or skinny, possum or raccoon—she couldn't tell. She might as well go to bed and pretend to sleep. After agonizing for four days, she hadn't told the police, and she hadn't left the money out. Cate had done nothing at all.

Chapter 24

August
Riley

The morning was the first in a while that Riley suffered no headache. Not coincidentally, she found the liquor levels within reason. She had plausibly clear memories of the previous night, too, which hadn't always been the case in the wake of the July attack on Farrah.

Farrah had quit her job at Pizza by the Park. According to Roman, she was healing at home until college resumed in late August. Out of Roman's hearing, rumors careened around the restaurant and the neighborhood. The culprit was a mentally ill homeless man who'd caught Farrah on the short trail walk from the restaurant to her town house. Or he was a former boyfriend. Or a customer she'd refused to date. Or an entire gang of homeless teens living in a camp near the trail. Caleb told Riley that summertime brought out kids who might otherwise stay with an aunt, friend, or grandmother.

The only thing she was sure of was that the police hadn't made an arrest. Every day, she thought about calling Farrah. But then she would try to imagine what she would say. Riley still hadn't made the call.

With no hangover to nurse, Riley grew restless. She walked onto her terrace, and the suffocating heat of August hit her like a wall. The air was heavy, oppressive, a physical barrier. She glanced around at the unmoving trees—no breath of a breeze stirring. It felt like something was off—or, perhaps, like something was coming.

She didn't want to stay in the pool house, so she dressed and headed for the cool of the Greenbrier Mall, off the interstate. She'd promised Roman she would come in early, but she still had three hours. Riley entered the rambling mall and sought out a bagel shop, where she hunched over an egg sandwich, two cups of steaming black coffee, and a discarded *Greenbrier Herald.* On an inside page was a follow-up to the investigation into Farrah's attack. As a rape victim, Farrah was unnamed, but the story referred to the July 3 assault on the Crescent Trail. Riley read it slowly.

The new detail was that police were seeking a former resident of a Roosevelt Park encampment as a person of interest. The article described him as *white, shaved head, midtwenties, powerfully built.* An artist's sketch was included, showing a menacing man with hooded eyes. Apparently, he'd lived in a camp near the trail until the Fourth of July then disappeared.

Poor Farrah. Riley hoped the assault wouldn't affect her outgoing personality or her studies in premed, but how could it not? She felt a pang for not reaching out to her colleague. Before she could change her mind, she whipped out her cell phone and punched the number Farrah had given her on her first day. It was another reminder of how welcoming Farrah had been.

When Farrah answered, Riley stumbled around, apologizing for her silence.

Farrah interrupted. "It's okay, Riley. No one knows what to say. I'm packing for school if you'd like to stop by."

Riley immediately agreed.

"Give me an hour to shower and dress," Farrah said.

Riley threw her trash in a receptacle and set out to fill the intervening hour with end-of-summer sales. She found a sundress at half price, its red and pink swirls setting off her tan nicely, its hemline higher than anything she'd worn in two years. Maybe a day would come when she'd enjoy dressing up again.

At noon, she drove to Farrah's address in a complex of elegant townhomes two blocks down Gunter Avenue from Pizza by the Park. Riley passed through a gatehouse complete with a security guard who had her name. Farrah greeted her at the front door, wearing shorts and a tank top. Her shiny blond hair was pulled into a ponytail, and her makeup-free forehead showed a fading yellow bruise. She was paler than before and slimmer. She tugged at her shorts to keep them up. Riley started to hug her, but Farrah recoiled almost imperceptibly.

"How nice of you to come," Farrah said. "My parents have finally gone back to work, so I'm glad to have company."

As Riley moved into the foyer, Farrah locked and bolted the door behind them. She led her friend into a bright white kitchen, where she had tomato soup on the stove.

"I know soup isn't the best lunch in August, but it's about all I know how to cook." Her smile looked forced.

Farrah's newfound reticence increased Riley's nervousness. "It's okay. I had a late breakfast at the mall." Riley paused then apologized again for not coming sooner, but Farrah waved her words away.

"Truthfully, I wasn't in the greatest shape to see anyone."

Riley indicated the *Herald* lying open on the table. "I saw the story about you. Was that the guy? The one in the artist's sketch?"

"Maybe," Farrah said with a grimace. "He kept... he kept me face down the whole time. All I was able to tell the police was that he was white—I saw his hands—and that he smelled like smoke. Not like cigarettes but on his clothes. Like a campfire. Which makes me think he lived in one of those camps. That's why they think it may be that guy who left town."

"You know what I keep thinking?" Riley asked. "It was the same night that guy Rich was in the bar. The one who hassled me, who Gus and Roman threw out. It couldn't have been him, could it?"

"Nah. He would've smelled like Old Spice, not a campfire." Again, Farrah attempted a smile. "This guy's fingernails were filthy. Nothing like Mr. Wannabe-Bank-President."

Riley was oddly relieved. "So, how are you doing? Really?"

"Better than I was. I won't lie—I was undone those first few weeks. Not sleeping. Jumpy." She made a face. "I still haven't left the house."

"But you're packing for school?"

"I'm gonna try. I hope that getting away from the trail, getting out of Greenbrier, will help. Mom and Dad plan to put this place on the market once I'm gone so I won't have to come back to the park." Farrah poured the soup into two bowls and brought them to the table, where glasses of iced tea and a plate of crackers and cheese waited.

"I hear a *but* in there."

"But that assumes I can manage school. I've had enough therapy to know the real trauma is inside my head, not in my location."

"You've been seeing a therapist?" Riley asked.

"By teleconference. She's been good. I think."

Riley sat back. "Farrah, I am so sorry this happened to you."

"I know." Farrah toyed with her soup, stirring but not eating. "If you can believe it, those neighbors who want to get the homeless out of the park called my dad. They want me to speak at a meeting."

"What did he tell them?"

"Well, he left it up to me. But the idea makes me uncomfortable." She continued to twirl her spoon in the soup. "I do think the guy was homeless, and believe me, nothing would suit me better than to see him in prison. But to spread the net to include all homeless people is like saying, 'That mass shooter lived in a house, so we need to go after all the people who live in houses.'"

Riley smiled. "You have a quirky mind."

"So I've been told. But where you live has nothing to do with whether you're a criminal or not. If I *were* able to speak at a meeting—and I doubt I can—I'm afraid the organizers would get a nasty surprise." She raised her eyes, and a flash of the old Farrah emerged. "That might be reason enough to do it." She finally sipped from her soup spoon. "But enough about me. Tell me what's going on at Pizza by the Park. Roman sent flowers. Twice."

"He's such a nice guy. Let's see. Not much happening. We're busy. The patio is stiflingly hot, but that doesn't keep anyone away. Everybody misses you terribly."

"And with you? How are things?"

Farrah's simple question caught Riley off guard, and tears unexpectedly burned her eyes. She hadn't had a friend in so long.

Watching her, Farrah stopped eating. "Riley? I'd seriously love to hear about something outside these walls if you need to talk."

"I feel silly complaining about anything after what you've been through."

"It's not a contest," Farrah said with a sad smile.

Riley thought of the nightmares that left her exhausted most mornings. The shadow on Silas's boat that threatened her sister and made Riley instinctively want to protect her, though when she woke, she wondered why, and the old, tired anger returned. Maybe it would help to talk. Maybe she could share not *the big thing* but, instead, a thousand little things.

"Well," Riley said, "my sister, my younger sister, has been on my mind. She's kind of the reason I'm in Greenbrier." *Careful, careful.*

"From your tone, I take it the relationship is not good."

"No, it's definitely not."

Farrah would never meet Rayanne. Riley could share a few things. In fact, suddenly she was eager to talk.

Riley drew a deep breath. "We haven't gotten along since our early teens. She tended to lie. And steal. And cheat."

Farrah ate her soup, unfazed. She nodded for Riley to continue.

"I know all sisters fight. But I saw my friends' relationships with their sisters. You know, they'd have out-and-out hair-pulling screaming matches, but then they were friends again. Rayanne was different."

Farrah cocked her head. "How so?"

Riley had never told anyone about her sister, not even in AA meetings when she'd shared her guilt about providing Rayanne with alcohol. She hadn't spoken about Rayanne's behavior or about how she'd grown to distrust her then dislike her, especially after her petty betrayal of Mama to Aunt Eileen. Maybe Riley was ashamed of her. Maybe Riley was ashamed of herself.

"She wanted everything I had," Riley said tentatively. "And I mean, everything. Toys. Clothes. Shoes. Bedroom decor. Jewelry. Soccer team. Money. Then, um... friends."

"She wanted your friends?"

"Yeah. Yeah, she did. She'd tell them things I supposedly said about them so they would drop me and be her friend. God, that sounds so middle-school mean girl, doesn't it? But she did that." Riley shook her head, thinking of Glenna, Maxie, and Jannelle. "But it wasn't a big school, and people caught on. She gave it up only because it stopped working."

"She sounds horrible."

"To put it mildly," Riley said.

She wasn't sure whether to tell this next part, but it felt so good to get her feelings about Rayanne out of her system. She could never tell Mama or Daddy, and she hadn't wanted to stoop to Rayanne's level back in Mobile. But Farrah would never meet Rayanne, so she plunged ahead.

"When I was sixteen, I had my first boyfriend. Chad Evers. He was a year ahead of me in high school. He was a soccer player on the boys' team, and I was a forward on the girls' team. Mama and Daddy knew his parents and trusted Chad, so they extended my curfew an extra hour on weekends. Rayanne hit the ceiling. Screamed about how unfair it was, how 'Riley gets everything.' Which was completely untrue. She was the one they made exceptions for. But this time, my parents didn't cave in." Even now, the memory curdled in Riley's stomach. "Anyway, Chad and I had been dating about six months, and I was..." She felt herself blush.

Farrah questioned her with her eyes but didn't say anything.

"I was a virgin," Riley said hurriedly. "Like I said, Chad was older and starting to pressure me a little bit. Not bad, but you know, typical guy stuff. One Saturday night, he brought me home, same as usual. We went in, watched TV for about an hour. Meanwhile, Rayanne sneaked out and hid in his back seat."

"She did not!"

"I didn't learn this until later, but as he was driving home, she popped up and offered 'to do what my sister won't.' Chad turned his car around and put her out at our driveway. But Rayanne told people at school they'd gone to our town's make-out point and 'done it.'" Riley took another deep breath. To this day, the humiliation rankled. "Sure enough, I started hearing the rumors from Chad's teammates. A few days later, he literally had to stand up in a locker-room meeting and tell them the truth. After that, the rumors petered out."

Farrah widened her eyes.

Riley plowed ahead. "Some people started avoiding Rayanne, so she took up with a rougher crowd. Bikers, druggies, those types. But it was so uncomfortable for Chad to run into her at my house that we broke up."

"That is positively sickening," Farrah said. "Did you confront her?"

"Sure. She denied getting in his car at our house and said that Chad came on to her at school. Then they went for sex in his car." Riley affected a simpering tone. "Surely I could understand if he preferred her to me, couldn't I?" She stood and took her soup bowl to the sink, marveling at how she could still get upset at this incident in light of Rayanne's far more egregious sin.

Farrah joined her at the sink. "Well, congratulations, Riley Masterson. You've managed to do what no one else has done—you made me forget about *me* for five minutes."

The young women laughed without joy, bonding over the awfulness of their experiences.

"Well, it was worth revealing my most mortifying secret, then." Riley gave her a hug, and this time, Farrah accepted it. "Glad my shitty life is good for something."

Minutes later, Riley exited Farrah's parking lot and crossed Gunter to the warehouse parking lot where she'd leave the Beetle for her restaurant shift. A fluttering orange flier taped to a streetlight caught her attention. On it was the artist's sketch of Farrah's attacker from that day's newspaper, but the text indicated more than the *Herald*'s reporting:

Is this the kind of person we want in our community? Join your neighbors for a meeting at 3 PM August 15 on Gunter Avenue to discuss moving the Greenbrier Gospel Mission out of Roosevelt Park.

Riley gazed up Gunter and saw the orange sheets flapping from every streetlight. Farrah wasn't willing to make the leap from a single criminal act to blaming all the homeless people camped in the park. But the organizers of this meeting were jumping all the way to eliminating the gospel mission that had served the city for six decades.

Riley thought of director Russ Denton and Isaiah and all the folks who worked to get people like Caleb back on their feet. She was lucky that Mama and Daddy and even Cousin Mikala, uptight as she was, had been willing to take her in. *What must it be like to have no one?* She snatched the offending orange sheet from the lamppost and stomped into work.

Chapter 25

Riley

Later that week, Caleb and Isaiah came over to swim with Riley, an easy if unlikely routine they had fallen into. Caleb had turned out to be a halfway decent guy, practically the only person in Greenbrier whom Riley felt comfortable talking to. Besides Farrah, anyway. He'd heard enough from that asshole Rich at the restaurant to know that Riley was running from something, but he'd waited until she was ready to tell him about Silas and Dauphin Island. Most of it, at least. He showered in her pool house every night because the bathroom in his boarding house was on the fritz. It was fine with her if his landlord never fixed it.

Isaiah was a pleasant surprise. After his defense of the Gospel Mission at the neighborhood meeting, Caleb asked if they could invite him to the pool. Riley relayed the invitation to Cate, and the two of them showed up the next day. Isaiah had been coming alone ever since.

The boys were like the little brothers Riley had never had. Her *Old Testament* brothers, she teased them. Isaiah understood the reference. They had to explain it to Caleb. But that wasn't his fault. From what Caleb had told them about his mother, Riley was aware that church was not among the March family's priorities—unlike her parents, who were at Mobile's Calvary Baptist three times a week.

Isaiah executed his signature move—a cannonball off the diving board. Riley had positioned her lounge chair so the tidal wave of spray didn't reach her. His closely shaved head popped up in the shallow end, seeking her eyes, her approval. She understood that he had a slight crush on her, so she was careful to keep everything friendly and sisterly. Riley even gave up her bikini in favor of the worn red-and-white-striped tank suit left over from her swim-team days. Cate had been nervous at first about letting them become friends, but Riley could tell she'd relaxed.

Caleb waited until Isaiah grabbed a towel and hauled a chair over to join them. With his wet hair slicked away from his forehead, Caleb looked older—and more handsome—than when it was flopping everywhere. But he was still skinny, skinny, skinny, and those cutoff jeans did nothing to camouflage it. Isaiah, at sixteen, was already coming into his adult physique.

"So, Isaiah," Caleb asked, "I've been wanting to ask you more about your mom's work."

"Savannah Mom, I presume."

Caleb gave him a *duh* look. "Yeah, that one."

The friends had danced around this subject before. Isaiah was vocal in his anger at the neighbors who wanted to shut down the Gospel Mission but was understandably reticent about his family's involvement. Riley had no reason to push him. But Caleb was becoming increasingly interested in the neighborhood's history.

Caleb told them he had spent time on this very property back when his grandfather owned it. At first, he believed he had visited the old man from time to time. But lately he was convinced that he'd lived with his grandfather for a while. He couldn't remember his mother being here at all, just him and a man he called Granddaddy and three pit bulls.

"I finally remembered two of the dogs' names," he said. "King and Duke. But not the third."

"Queenie?" Riley suggested. "Duchess? Prince?"

He shook his head.

"When was this again?" she asked.

"When I was four or five or six?" Caleb glanced toward Mikala's house. "If I could go through the original house, I'm sure I'd remember more. But your cousins have erased every inch of the old place." He gestured to the far corner of the yard. "If it weren't for that sycamore, I wouldn't have recognized the site at all."

They knew that Isaiah's Savannah Mom had purchased Caleb's grandfather's house years before. The old man was dead, and the house was vacant and falling apart, according to Savannah. Isaiah, Cate, and Savannah hadn't been living next door at the time—another mill house had stood on that site—so Isaiah had nothing to share with Caleb.

"What do you want to know about my mom?" Isaiah asked.

"When did she start developing around Roosevelt Park?"

"I think the Hardys' house was her third. That's when she talked Cate Mom into building and moving here too. Before that, she'd worked mostly on the east side."

"And how many has she built here since then?"

Isaiah toweled off his face. "No telling. A lot."

Caleb's hair was drying, and it drooped into eyes. He brushed it away impatiently. "Have you ever met the people who lived in the houses before she bought them?"

Riley sat up. Caleb was entering new territory.

"No one besides you," Isaiah said, "who sort of lived here."

"Doesn't it bother you?"

Isaiah grew still and didn't respond.

"I mean," said Caleb, "like Earle Meadows said at the meeting, people have lived here for forty or fifty or sixty years, and now they have to move because their location has gotten so bougie. Rich people decide they want to live downtown, so the residents have to go."

"Your grandpa was already dead." Isaiah sounded unsure.

"Yeah, but other people aren't dead. They're pretty much thrown out."

"They don't have to sell."

"But your mom dangles fifty thousand or sixty thousand dollars in front of them, and it's more money than they've seen in their entire lives. They're not savvy enough to know it won't take them far house-wise."

"Wait a minute, Caleb," Riley interrupted. "Isaiah is not responsible for what his mom does."

"And aren't you being a little paternalistic?" Isaiah added. Riley thought he might be parroting something he'd heard Savannah say.

She recalled stories from the *Herald*'s archives. The city was concerned enough about its poorer residents that it had reached out, offering them financial counsel before they decided to sell. Affordable housing was part of the city's master plan for Roosevelt Park, but that effort was compromised when private developers snapped up old houses. Greenbrier's mayor was quoted often, urging residents to speak with city staffers before selling.

Caleb barreled on. "But a lot of these old mill houses are rentals. People have rented them for decades. If the owners sell, the renters have to leave."

Isaiah heaved a huge sigh and slumped forward. "Actually, I've made that same argument to my moms. Before and after that meeting."

Riley was surprised. "You have?"

He stretched out on his back, his long limbs melting into the lounge chair like a dog rolling over to present its stomach. "I have." He didn't say anything else.

Caleb looked from Riley to Isaiah. "You can't stop there, man."

"I'm kinda between a rock and a hard place," said Isaiah. "I have the same questions you have. But I'm also aware that it's our living." He pointed at the gleaming Charleston house next door. "I don't take that for granted, *man*."

There were undercurrents that Riley could only guess at. From what she'd learned that summer, both young men had been born into difficult, impoverished circumstances. Caleb had lived through his and had the scars to prove it. Isaiah had been miraculously whisked away from his.

She could tell Isaiah was contemplating whether to tell them something more. Riley signaled Caleb to wait, but there was no stopping him.

"Did you get in trouble after that meeting?" Caleb asked.

Isaiah spun over to face Caleb. "Not trouble exactly. But we had a family 'discussion.' I accused Savannah Mom of wanting to get rid of the Gospel Mission. It kinda went downhill from there." He paused. "But I've decided to make gentrification of this neighborhood my junior project."

Caleb eyed him suspiciously. "What does that mean?"

"At my school, we have to write a junior research paper. We do it junior year because we'll be traveling so much senior year. College visits." Caleb rolled his eyes, but Isaiah ignored him. "It doesn't have to be related to our volunteer projects, but it carries a bonus if it does." Isaiah swung his legs into a sitting position to face them. "My volunteer projects have been collecting food and building shelves for the Gospel Mission. This year, I'll be tutoring men to get their GEDs. So it makes sense to research why we need those things in the first place—how eviction and gentrification contribute to the problem of homelessness."

"Wow," Riley said. Even Caleb quieted.

"In fact," Isaiah continued, "I was going to ask if you could show me how to access those records you looked up about the sale of your grandpa's house. I can get current estimates off Zillow, and recent sales prices. But they don't always go back far enough."

"Sure," Caleb said. "Easy."

"Then, I'll need to find some people to interview. People who had to move out."

Caleb leaned back. "I don't know how to do that."

"I do," Riley said. The young men looked at her. "The *Greenbrier Herald* archives. They're full of stories about people who used to live here. I bet you can get contact information from the reporters."

Isaiah snapped his fingers. "Yeah, I've read some of those." He paused. "Savannah Mom complains about the *Herald* all the time."

"Well, there you go," she said.

Before Caleb could start in again, they were interrupted by the opening of Mikala's patio door. Even from a distance, Riley could see the perturbed look on her cousin's face.

Mikala smiled perfunctorily at Caleb and Isaiah before addressing Riley. "You have a guest." Riley squinted to make out the person in the doorway behind Mikala, but the interior was dim and the sun in her eyes too bright. "Or I guess *we* have a guest."

Riley heard a sharp intake of breath from Isaiah then "Holy shit!" from Caleb. She scrambled to her feet, straining to make out the figure emerging from the house.

"Hey, Riley."

Riley's heart plummeted, and she stumbled backward, nearly tripping over the chaise lounge. "Rayanne," she whispered.

Chapter 26

Cate

Savannah approached Cate from behind and nuzzled her neck. "What are you looking at?"

Cate didn't turn from their bedroom window. "Isaiah."

"Does he have a crush on Cousin Riley?"

"Probably. But look at this."

Savannah stabbed an earring through her lobe as she gazed at the small crowd on Mikala's terrace. "What am I looking at? Pool party?"

"Who is that with Mikala? She looks like Riley but with long hair."

Savannah secured her earring. "Boy, does she ever. Has to be a relative. Were Mikala and Luke expecting more of the Beverly hillbillies?"

Cate ignored Savannah's jibe. "Whoever she is, Mikala is not happy. Look at her."

Mikala had crossed her arms and was tapping a sandaled foot on her patio.

Savannah laughed. "I can see that famous scowl from here. Better get out of there, Isaiah. No lunch for you today."

"I think Riley's the one who feeds him," Cate said idly, "not Mikala."

Savannah hugged Cate. "Well, I'm off to the coal mines. What have you got on for today? Besides spying on the neighbors."

Cate whirled in a huff. "I am not!"

Savannah raised an eyebrow. "What do you call it?"

"Mothering." Cate pursed her lips stubbornly. "Attentive parenting."

"Whatever you say. *Dear.*"

Cate hated Savannah's condescension, and sudden anger prompted her to bring up something—one of several things—she'd been keeping to herself. She examined Savannah's beautiful face and wondered when they'd begun to keep secrets.

She strove to sound casual. "I almost forgot. Did you loan Mikala your copy of *The Empty Cell*?"

"No. I've been looking for it. I must have left it in someone's office. Why?"

"Our copy is in her pool house."

Savannah's eyes darted to the pool house. Her hesitation was so brief Cate wasn't sure it had actually happened. "Really? I must have left it when I was swimming. Good to know where it is."

"I didn't know you went swimming."

"Yeah. Sometime this summer. I can't even remember when." She turned hurriedly, her flowing mane flicking Cate's bare shoulder. "I'll see you tonight. Trivia Night, right?"

"Right," Cate said, returning her attention to the terrace and the pool house—and to a book inside it, signed *To Savannah and Cate.*

Chapter 27

Riley

Riley's heart was thudding. She hadn't seen her sister in a year and a half, not even at Christmas when Mama, her lower lip trembling, had asked if she knew why Rayanne wasn't coming home from Panama City. Riley lied and said she didn't know, and the three of them, Mama, Daddy and Riley, had their gloomiest holiday ever, tiptoeing around their missing member.

It hadn't occurred to Riley at first, not even when Silas's neighbor was so sure he had seen her late on the night of the murder. She'd thought the old man was confused, having seen her in and out of Silas's house so often that autumn. Shrimpers could be a rough bunch, and she figured Silas had gotten into an argument about fishing territory or his crew or any number of things.

That was because she didn't know about the money. Only during her last interrogation on Dauphin Island did the officers mention money that Silas's brother had belatedly realized never got deposited. Still, still, she didn't make the connection until she drove into her parents' driveway and saw Rayanne standing at the second-floor window of her childhood bedroom.

For Riley knew her sister was a thief. It had started small, as those things did, in middle school. Lipsticks from Walmart. Jewelry from the mall. Beer from the convenience store. Cash from Mama's purse and Daddy's wallet.

Riley would hear them murmuring in the kitchen—"I thought I had another twenty," or "How did I spend that much at the grocery store?" But they never asked outright, and she never told them.

Those thefts were larks for Rayanne, or so Riley imagined. She didn't need the money. It was the thrill she was after—Riley was sure of it. Even when Rayanne started drinking, that wouldn't have necessitated stealing on a major level. But as Riley watched her sister's drinking escalate, she witnessed the emergence of another addiction—gambling.

Casinos were rampant in Biloxi, Mississippi, an hour's drive from Mobile. With fake IDs, Rayanne and her friends began spending nights there the summer after high school, five or six of them piled into a hotel room. For most of them, it was a chance to drink, gorge at low-cost buffets, and lie by a pool. But not Rayanne. She never left the casino floor. Slots. Blackjack. Video poker. That was the big draw for her—the riotous gongs and whistles and lights and sirens of video poker. The noisy clamor filled something in her—or perhaps more accurately, distracted from the need-shaped hole inside her. Riley understood now that something had always been missing in Rayanne, even when she was a little girl.

With the discovery of video poker, Rayanne wanted to drive to Biloxi every weekend, and she wanted to take hundreds of dollars with her. Sometimes she'd win. More often, she'd lose.

Her friend Cheri finally became worried enough to recount their escapades. There was the time they'd rolled a rich drunk in a casino parking lot. Another time, they'd lifted a woman's credit card in a buffet line. And yet another time, Cheri and Rayanne had posed as hookers and fleeced a convention goer.

"Not much chance he was going to report anything," Cheri said wryly.

Then Cheri had fallen silent. Riley wondered if she and Rayanne were no longer posing as hookers but actually hooking. She hadn't really wanted to know.

By then, Riley had problems of her own. Dropping out of college. Drinking too much. Wondering what to do with her life. Around that time, she'd moved to Dauphin Island.

Rayanne squealed and ran to hug Riley. She looked pretty in red shorts, a tank top, and flip-flops, her long brown hair in a ponytail and sunglasses atop her head. Riley caught Mikala's steely eyes over her shoulder. She hadn't bargained on two guests. Maybe she would toss Riley out.

Riley had done everything for her sister, but their deal—at least, in Riley's mind—was that she wouldn't have to see Rayanne again. Riley squirmed in her embrace. She should have spelled out the phantom deal.

Riley was aware of all the listening ears—Mikala, Caleb, Isaiah. She was gritting her teeth, and her words came out in a hiss. "Rayanne, what are you doing here?"

"Serena moved." Rayanne spoke to Riley, but her eyes took in Caleb and Isaiah. She tossed her ponytail. "That's my friend in Panama City," she explained to them. "When I told Mama I was losing my place at Serena's, she said you'd left Mobile, so I decided to move home. I'd have the whole upstairs to myself."

"And yet you're not at home." Riley was too shocked to feign politeness. She glanced at Mikala and was surprised to see that she no longer appeared irritated. Instead, her brow was furrowed, and she was listening closely.

Rayanne twirled to address their cousin. "I'm on a road trip, Cousin Mikala. Can I stay in the pool house with Riley for one night?"

"One night?" Mikala's forehead cleared. "I suppose one night will be all right." She paused. "You can join us at Trivia Night and see where Riley works." She looked at Caleb and Isaiah, who hadn't said a word. "Do you boys want to help Rayanne with her luggage?"

Isaiah smiled eagerly and headed for the driveway. Caleb said "Okay" without enthusiasm. Riley felt a flare of gratitude that he had not been taken in by her sister's chirpiness. Rayanne must have sensed it too.

"Sorry, I haven't met you properly," she said, holding out a hand and dimpling. "I'm Rayanne, Riley's much younger sister." Grin, grin.

"Yeah, I got that." Caleb moved away. "I'll see if Isaiah needs help."

Rayanne arched an eyebrow at Riley. "Surly." She giggled.

Or maybe he's got your number. "Mikala," Riley announced, "Rayanne and I will catch up before I head to work. I'll see you tonight." She left Mikala standing on the patio and shoved her sister into the pool house.

Eighteen months earlier, when Riley had frantically urged Rayanne out of Mobile, all she could think was to get her out of sight before detectives realized how much they looked alike. Riley feared the connection they'd make. The pictures they'd seen in Mama's house hadn't revealed it. In most of those, Rayanne had been going through a bleached-blond phase and was younger, skinnier, gawkier. Riley was careful to remove the more recent ones that showed them together, looking almost like twins despite Rayanne's smiling face and Riley's solemn one. As for the Dauphin Island police, they didn't know Rayanne had ever set foot on their island. Only Silas's elderly neighbor had glimpsed her, and he'd mistaken her for Riley.

Why was I so hell-bent on protecting the person who killed Silas? Riley might never know the answer, but she suspected it had to do with the deep, dark bonds of blood and guilt, going back to when she was fourteen and realized that as much as she loved Mama and Daddy, she no longer felt the same about her broken, grasping sister. But Riley had spent eighteen months thinking and missing Silas and regretting the destruction she'd brought into his life.

She sank into a wing chair. "Why?"

"Why what?" Rayanne bounced on the sofa and looked around the pool house approvingly. "Cool digs."

Riley ignored her attempt at deflection. "About a million whys. But let's start with Silas." She choked the words out. "Why did you kill Silas?"

"Oh. Are we going there?" The smile left Rayanne's face. Riley stared at her, and Rayanne attempted a nonchalant reply. "You said he wasn't your boyfriend."

Riley clenched her fists, wondering how she had once shared a life with this girl and why they all—she, Mama, and Daddy—had refused to acknowledge the cracks and the demons inside Rayanne. They'd pretended her cruelties—breaking Riley's toys, spreading lies about schoolmates, trying to steal her boyfriend—were childish or teenage antics. They'd known something was wrong and, in that time-honored way of Southern denial, had refused to face it.

That time was over. *And yet... and yet...* Some small sliver of Riley's mind still hoped that Rayanne would deny it, that Riley had somehow gotten it wrong, that a member of Silas's crew had killed him over a pay dispute, over disrespect, over—*dear God,* anything at all.

Why did you kill Silas? The question hung in the air. Riley couldn't bear to repeat it.

"If you really think that," Rayanne continued, "why didn't you ask me before I left home?" She wriggled deeper into the couch. "You couldn't get me out of Mobile fast enough."

"I was trying to protect you, and I have no idea why. I assume you were after his money. To pay off a gambling debt." *Tell me I'm wrong. Tell me I'm wrong.*

She shrugged. "Then why ask?"

Riley's shoulders slumped. She was enraged, and she was bereft. She'd lost Silas, but somewhere along the way, she'd lost a sister, too, and never properly grieved the loss. "How did it happen?"

Rayanne eyed her warily as if unsure how honest to be. "After I saw him at your place that night, I realized I'd seen him before. It took me a while to place him, but it was on High's website. Mama and Daddy and I had gone for my birthday dinner, and Daddy and I looked up the menu ahead of time." She pulled her legs beneath her on the sofa. "So I knew he had money. Big money. Which I needed because me and Cheri had recently spent several nights in Biloxi. I lost on those damn machines. I borrowed from a guy to play some more. Lost that money, and he wanted it back. He *really* wanted it back, if you know what I mean."

She smiled tentatively as if she had explained everything. And Riley supposed that in her Rayanne-centric world, she had. Rayanne had needed, and that was all that mattered.

"But that night," Riley said, vaguely aware that tears had begun to flow down her face. "What happened that night?"

"I drove down to Dauphin by myself. I... I didn't want to get anyone else in trouble."

Riley locked her jaw and remained silent, suspecting that Rayanne hadn't wanted to split the money.

"I drove around the bars until I saw his truck, which I'd seen the night he came to your place. I followed you to his house, staying far enough behind so you never noticed. I parked on that sandy road about thirty yards past the inlet." She held up an admonishing finger. "I must say, you were stumbling pretty badly when you went in."

Riley closed her eyes, recalling her childlike tantrum. She tasted the salt of her tears and was reminded of the briny Gulf air. Her chest ached so hotly she wanted to scream and make Rayanne stop talking. But she had to know.

"About fifteen minutes later, you stormed out. I got back in my truck and waited to see if you were coming back. I think I fell asleep. When I woke up, his truck was still there, but your car wasn't. I figured he'd had a lot to drink, too, and was sleeping it off, so I sneaked up to his house." She cocked her head. "By the way, that house was pretty pitiful. Not what I'd expect for a Hightower." She gestured with a thumb toward Mikala's main house. "Nothing like this."

"That night," Riley repeated woodenly. "What happened that night?"

"Well, the door was unlocked."

Riley stopped her, blinking in confusion. "What?" Silas never left his door unlocked.

"Yeah, it was unlocked."

Her stomach heaved. He'd left it unlocked in case Riley returned.

"I... I walked in and took a look around the living room." Rayanne licked her lips. "No money. Same with the kitchen. Unfortunately, he heard me and came out, calling for you."

Riley hung her head and sobbed violently, no longer able to restrain her grief. Scenes of midnight shrimping and the secluded inlet house and Silas, smiling generously, flooded her mind. The memories swamped her, and she doubled over from the weight of them.

Rayanne quit talking. Riley couldn't lie to herself any longer, couldn't allow for the possibility that someone else had killed Silas. She raised half-blind eyes to Rayanne's face. She wanted to hit her perfect lips, break those perfect teeth, and Rayanne knew it.

Rayanne's eyes skittered around the room. "Maybe, um... maybe we should talk about this later."

"No! Go on."

She inhaled. "There was a... a knife on the kitchen table, and I grabbed it. I didn't plan it, Riley, I swear. More like an accident really." She glanced around the pool house again. "And... you know the rest."

"No, I don't!" Riley exploded. "I don't know at all! Why did you kill him?"

Rayanne cringed against the sofa arm. "I didn't mean to, Riley. I really didn't. But he kind of lunged at me. To take the knife, I guess. I just... dodged his arm, and the knife went in. To his stomach. It was an accident, I swear."

Once, Riley would have believed her or at least forced herself to. But no more. She wrapped her arms around her torso, rocking mindlessly. "Where did you find the money?"

"In his bedroom. Under the bed. In a shoebox."

"You left him lying in the kitchen and ransacked his bedroom?"

Rayanne gulped and held out her palms. "I know. I know. But he was already..." She didn't go on.

The guilt and sorrow washed over Riley in sickening waves, as much for her sister's callousness as for Silas. She tried to stop crying but couldn't, so she gave in to it. She grasped that the shame would never leave her, that it would define the rest of her life. She cried until her raw throat ached. Finally, she took a shuddering breath. She looked into the face so like her own and glimpsed the source of her self-loathing.

"Look, Rayanne," she managed, "we are square. I always felt bad about... the way your life turned out. About the way *you* turned out. Maybe because I'm older, I thought I was responsible somehow. But I didn't turn you in for murder, not even when they questioned me for more than a year."

Rayanne answered quickly. "If they'd arrested you, I would've confessed."

Riley's laugh was a mirthless bark. "Would you?"

"Of course, I would have, Riley. I never would have let you take the blame." She spread her arms expansively. "But it all worked out, didn't it? If they still suspected you, they wouldn't have let you leave Alabama."

"No, it didn't all work out." Riley leaned forward, spitting words past gritted teeth. "A good man lost his life so you could play video fucking poker. Do you not get that?"

Rayanne looked abashed. "But the debt, Riley. I... I didn't know what else I was supposed to do."

"You were supposed to take responsibility for your own damn life and not expect everybody else to bail you out. Not Mama or Daddy or drunks you rolled or old ladies you hustled or johns you suckered. Or me or Silas."

Rayanne's lips were quivering again, and Riley saw her as a six-year-old following her to the soccer field, where Riley shouted at her to go home. Her lips quaked exactly as they had then, and tears welled in her hazel eyes.

The familiar shame crept over Riley. She braced herself against the feelings that had ruined them both. "We are square," she repeated. "I think it's best if we stay apart."

A look she couldn't identify crossed Rayanne's face. Remorse... disbelief... or cunning?

"It's one night, Riley. One night. Then I'll be gone. I promise."

Chapter 28

Caleb

Riley and her lookalike sister weren't coming back outside as far as Caleb could tell, though Isaiah kept looking wistfully at the pool house. The young men gathered their towels.

"Can I come to your room tomorrow to start looking up real estate transactions?" Isaiah asked.

Caleb imagined welcoming Isaiah into the potting shed. Whenever they parted, he walked toward Montreat Avenue, carrying out the fiction that he still lived in the boarding house. "Nah. I can't always get on my buddy's laptop. How about your house?"

Isaiah hesitated, and Caleb wondered if he didn't want his moms to know about the project—or about Caleb. But then he said, "Okay, sure."

Caleb loped off toward the street to walk the long way around. The last thing he wanted to draw attention to was the thicket behind the boarding house, where his sleeping bag was stashed. As he approached the boarding house, a grizzled old man stood on the porch, flailing his arms. Freddy had mental disabilities, and Caleb didn't want to get drawn into a nonsensical conversation. But it was too late to pretend he hadn't seen him.

"Caleb!" Freddy shouted. "Caleb!"

Caleb sighed and opened the warped picket fence that fronted the house. Only when he was almost to the splintering wooden steps did he note that Freddy wasn't alone.

A figure stepped from the shade of the wisteria at the same moment that Freddy yelled happily, "Your mom, Caleb! It's your mom!"

Doreen March smiled, and Caleb could see the perfect, if oversized, teeth that indicated dentures. Better than the previous meth-rotted mouth, he supposed. He could not muster a smile in return but advanced silently, his eyes taking her in.

Her hair was still black and brittle, but a skunk-like stripe of gray marked the roots. Her face, chest, and arms were mottled beyond her fifty years. Clownish red lipstick was slashed across her mouth so that her smile was garish against the too-white dentures. A backpack and bedroll lay at her feet, sure signs she was living on the street. She was the woman he had glimpsed on the sidewalk outside Pizza by the Park and at the Gospel Mission thrift store. He imagined he looked about as happy to see her as Riley had been to see Rayanne.

"Caleb," she said, making an effort to keep her voice soft. "How you doing, son?"

"I'm okay," he mumbled.

"I been looking for you for days. Wanting to see you."

"Why?"

Her eyes narrowed. "I need a reason to see my son?"

Well, yeah, when you haven't wanted to in four years. "I went to the house. Saw that it was condemned."

"Yeah, I got behind on the rent, and the damn landlord wouldn't let me catch up."

"The bathtub fell through the floor," he said mildly.

A whine crept into her voice. "Yeah, he wouldn't fix nothing."

He motioned toward the boarding house. "Are you staying here?"

"Nah. Can't afford it." Her sunken eyes glittered. "I heard you were here. But Freddy says not anymore. That true?"

"That is, indeed, true." He got it, then—she'd hoped to crash with him. He tried to hide his relief that he was no longer a boarder.

"But where you staying?" she asked.

He gestured in a manner that could indicate anywhere or nowhere. "In the woods."

She sank into a rocking chair secured to the porch floor by a chain. "Yeah, I been camping too." Her interest in him had apparently waned since he couldn't provide what she wanted. She heaved an exhausted sigh.

Freddy didn't like being left out of the conversation. "But Caleb still visits 'round here, don't you, Caleb? And he works at the pizza place. In the park."

His mother sat up straighter. "You working?"

Shit. He didn't want his mother to know that. He adopted a dour expression. "Yeah, but it all goes to pay my probation officer. You know, for the registry."

He peeked at her out of the corner of his eye to make sure she believed him. He'd paid off that bill, but she had no way of knowing it. He upped the ante. "They take so much I couldn't keep my room here."

"But you always walking around here, Caleb."

Jeez, shut up, Freddy.

His mother eyed him with suspicion. "Why is that, son? Strange place to be walking."

"Right behind here," Caleb blurted. "It's where Granddaddy's house was, isn't it?"

Doreen blinked, and he thought of an alligator. A dangerous old alligator. She stood and walked down the stairs. He backed up, but he was not her target. She veered around the house then halted, hands on her narrow hips, surveying the Hardys' manicured property.

He joined her and pointed to the giant tree in the corner. "It was the sycamore that made me remember."

She nodded. "Is that Twenty-Six Gunter?"

"Yep."

"Well, then, yeah, it's Daddy's. Wow, who woulda thought?"

"I looked it up. Uncle Roger and Uncle Alan sold it. For sixty-one thousand dollars."

"Did they, now?"

"Why didn't you inherit too?"

"That's a good question, son. A real good question." Her shoulders curved in a posture of defeat. "And here we are living in the woods. Hardly seem fair, do it?"

He thought about his plan to drive to Raleigh to meet his uncles. *Should I take her?*

At that moment, she turned, her face filled with the want and greed he remembered so well. "When you gone get that registry paid off?"

Revulsion rose in him. She wanted his money, nothing else. No, he wouldn't share his travel plans with her.

Chapter 29

Mikala

Mikala was on the phone with her mother in Columbia. Learning what was going on with Aunt Crystal's girls was harder than rooting out routine family gossip.

"All I know," her mom said, "is those two have worn poor Crystal and Ed out. I think they both have drinking problems—the girls, that is—though Crystal has never come out and admitted it. You know, Ed did, too, when he and Crystal first got married. He carried on something awful. But he stopped. Now he's a deacon in that Baptist church down there."

Mikala mumbled assent to keep her mother talking. She was accustomed to pulling nuggets from repetitious monologues.

"Back when Rayanne was living at home," her mother continued, "it sounded like she was spending every weekend in those casinos in Biloxi. I hate to say it about my own blood"—her voice dropped to a whisper—"but she was acting trashy."

"Acting trashy" covered a multitude of sins for her mother. Drinking. Smoking. Drugs. Sex. Tattoos. Swearing. Gambling.

"But what happened?" Mikala pleaded. "I read about the murder of the restaurant owner. Riley was never charged, right?"

"Right. But he was a *married man* and a good bit older than Riley. She never denied having an affair with him. Can you imagine the scandal? His wife was all over the news, crying and carrying on."

Crying and carrying on. Also trashy.

"Anyway," her mother said, "the minute Riley got home from Dauphin Island—that must have been January a year ago—Rayanne up and leaves for Panama City. Crystal says the family hasn't been together in one place since. Not even this past Christmas."

"So Rayanne never visited Aunt Crystal and Uncle Ed and Riley that entire time."

"She did not."

"But now, two months after Riley moves in with us, here she comes. She says it's for one night, but, Mama, I don't trust that girl as far as I can throw her."

Her mother sighed. "Poor Crystal."

"Poor Crystal, nothing. Poor Mikala is the one who's got them both."

Her mother laughed. "And I bet you could knock better sense into them than Crystal ever did."

"I don't know about that."

Already, Mikala's mind was racing. Her plan required that Riley have privacy in the pool house. Rayanne would have to go. Unless... the ensuing bedlam of *two* houseguests could work to her advantage.

Mikala said goodbye to her mother, but her mind was elsewhere.

Chapter 30

Cate

The neighbors were gathered for Trivia Night at Pizza by the Park. Savannah looked particularly lovely in her business attire from work—black dress slacks, pumps, and a sleeveless silk blouse in forest green. Dark green was her color, bringing out the red streaks in her wild mane, the flirty freckles across her nose, and the emerald sparkle of her eyes. Cate watched her and watched the other patrons watching her, feeling simultaneously proud and threatened.

The furor over last month's Crescent Trail attack had waned somewhat, but people remained uneasy. The assault on Farrah had been vicious, and Cate noted that the girl had not returned to work. The ugly fissures revealed in the July meeting had made relationships feel fragile. Newcomers were aware of what the old-timers thought of them, and Isaiah reported that Gospel Mission administrators were still shocked by the vitriol. Savannah's strategy had been to work twice as hard.

Cate returned her attention to her wife. *Do I satisfy Savannah?* She watched Savannah lift her hair off her neck and whisper to a new homeowner on Parker. Savannah had bulldozed that deal start to finish—making multiple offers on a longtime rental, razing the house, building a forty-five-hundred-square-foot residence of stone and stucco. Hiring Cate to landscape. Selling the property to upstate New Yorkers who sought relief from the snow and ice—Cate had seen how Savannah became more charmingly Southern when dealing with buyers from the North. More Savannah-ish. More like her namesake town.

Cate had overheard Isaiah inquire about what had happened to the renters of the demolished mill house on the site. Savannah claimed not to know. Even in their household, ugly cracks had appeared that summer.

She gazed at her son, who was laughing with Luke and Mikala and Riley's mysteriously conjured sister. Isaiah had told her—with great enthusiasm—about how much the sister resembled Riley, and Cate agreed. *Great.* Just when she'd begun to trust Riley not to lead Isaiah astray, she had to contend with the twenty-four-year-old sister.

Cate realized that her instant dislike of Rayanne was unfair, but she couldn't help it. Rayanne was too old for Isaiah, yet she had her hand on his forearm and her head bent too close to his. Cate had known women like this. The flirting was instinctual, primal. The object of the flirting hardly mattered.

Riley came by to take their orders, and Savannah, busily networking, signaled for Cate to select dinner. After consulting with Isaiah, Cate chose a giant pepperoni and mushroom pizza and added a bottle of pinot grigio for her and Savannah. If they couldn't finish it, there were plenty of people at the table who would. Ordering done, she swiveled to join the Hardys and Isaiah. But Luke was nowhere in sight, and Isaiah and Rayanne rose to check out the old-fashioned jukebox Roman had moved to the patio.

Mikala leaned across the table, pouring more wine from a half-empty bottle. "How's it going? Is your summer as relaxing as you'd hoped?"

"Yes, thanks to your pool." Cate automatically looked around for Savannah, but she had disappeared too. "I really appreciate you sharing it."

Mikala waved away her thanks. "I'm glad to have someone use it. Luke and I can go weeks without going in."

"Where *is* Luke?"

"I'm not sure." Mikala appeared pensive. "But I'm pretty sure I'm not enough company for him."

Cate was startled. She'd never heard Mikala say anything about her marriage. She assumed everyone else was as happy as the front they projected, though common sense would indicate that wasn't true. A divorced client had once told her, "I'm bad about comparing my insides to your outside."

Cate lowered her voice. "I'm sorry. Anything you want to talk about?"

"Just the old marital cliché, I guess. I think Luke is cheating." Mikala cleared her throat and smiled brightly, artificially. "And I think it's a neighbor because he goes 'running' at night." She made air quotes. "But he's not sweaty when he gets back. I've seen him splash pool water on his shirt." She raised her eyes to Cate's face and whispered, "I know you're going to say maybe he's cooling off. But I don't think so. I think he's meeting someone."

"Sometimes I think the same thing about Savannah," Cate said impulsively. She was stunned by both of their candor. She and her neighbor were entering uncharted territory.

Mikala giggled, breaking the tension. "At least we know they're not cheating together."

Cate's face must have revealed something because Mikala stopped her glass halfway to her mouth. Cate looked down at the table, at the floor, and then, relieved, at Riley coming with her wine. She allowed Riley to pour a glass then gulped half of it.

Mikala was staring at her and finally demanded, "What?"

"Savannah is, um... S-Savannah is bisexual," Cate stammered. "She was married to a man before we met. Actually, *when* we met."

Mikala's face reddened as if she'd been slapped. Cate could almost see her mind whirring like an adding machine, switching thoughts, switching assumptions with a clack that was nearly audible.

"She left a man for you?" Mikala asked in a tone of disbelief and immediately recanted. "I'm sorry. I didn't mean it like that. I guess I didn't think about anyone changing in, um... midstream."

Cate smiled weakly. "Someone bisexual is attracted to the person, whatever the gender."

"But you... you're not?" Mikala asked hesitantly as if she feared giving offense.

"No, not me. It's always been women for me." Cate lowered her voice even further so that Mikala had to lean in to hear. Their foreheads almost touched. "I've been meaning to ask. Has Savannah used your pool this summer?"

"Not when I've been there. But Riley has folks over when I'm not home. I wouldn't necessarily know. Why?"

Cate's heart squeezed. To suspect a lie was so corrosive. *Should I tell her?*

"Why?" Mikala repeated.

"Savannah always keeps a book in her purse, in case she has to wait for someone at a house showing or something. About a month ago, I saw the one she's currently reading. It was in your pool house. She said she'd been swimming, but that was the first I'd heard of it."

"But Riley..."

"Riley works every night," Cate said.

Mikala shook her head as if too much information was flooding in. She started to speak, but Cate yanked her head to one side and reared back in her chair.

Luke slid into his seat. "Hello, ladies. How're we doing?"

Cate looked up to see Savannah standing at another table, chatting up yet another neighbor. She smiled at Luke. "Fine. Want to help me with this wine?"

Chapter 31

Caleb

Caleb and Isaiah huddled over the laptop in Isaiah's room. Caleb had gotten Isaiah started on the real estate transactions, and it would be a tedious process to go through the sales on West Roosevelt, Gunter, Parker, Montreat, Marigold, and other streets near Roosevelt Park.

"The trick," Caleb said, "will be setting boundaries so you don't get overwhelmed."

Isaiah didn't take his eyes off the screen. "I haven't been through many yet, but if your uncles got sixty-one thousand dollars, they did better than most. I wonder why."

"Being out of state, maybe they were savvier about what was happening." Caleb stood and stretched. "Okay if I use your bathroom?"

"Sure. Help yourself to anything in the fridge too."

Sweet. Caleb was dying to look around Isaiah's house but had been reluctant to ask. He used Isaiah's private bathroom—*Man, who has his own bathroom?*—then headed downstairs. He took a Dr. Pepper from the refrigerator, stopping to marvel at all the food. He grabbed a handful of Peanut M&M's and wondered if he dared take some of those tiny oranges for the shed. He was afraid to go near it in broad daylight. Maybe later.

He trekked through each room, staring at the gleaming hardwood, chandeliers, radiant paintings, and stark sculptures that fit so precisely against the broad expanse of walls. He peeked into an office, the formal living room, the dining room, and even a mirrored workout room complete with a weight machine, treadmill, and stationary bike. He pictured Savannah, Cate, and Isaiah working out together, laughing and enjoying each other's company. *What must it be like to be part of a normal family?*

As he rambled through the first floor, he was initially awed, but his awe soon gave way to another emotion—despair. He'd looked over Isaiah's shoulder at the sales price for the original mill house on this property—$46,500, paid by Savannah Darwin LLC. Now Zillow estimated the Charleston-style home's value at $915,000. That damn potting shed would probably go for $46,500.

Caleb felt helpless. He hated his addict mother for dooming him to a sorry life. But the other end of the spectrum was no better. People like Savannah Darwin—and by extension, her son, Isaiah—stacked the deck against people like him. Yeah, he'd screwed up by dropping out of high school and having an underage girlfriend, but damn if those things should ruin his life.

He hung his head, hearing his counselor's voice in his mind: "No doubt about it, you made mistakes. But now what? Gonna continue to make them? Or change the way you do life?"

Caleb did want to change, but he needed a boost. He needed to see his uncles—to threaten them, maybe, with legal action over his mom's share of their dad's inheritance. *Did Granddaddy leave a will?*

He thought about that upcoming encounter. His fair share could lead to a GED then college then a great job then a house like this. Caleb tipped back the Dr. Pepper for a swallow when he heard a shriek. His heart skipped, and he dropped the soda, watching in horror as brown fizz puddled on the hallway floor.

"What the hell are you doing in here?" shouted Savannah Darwin. She reached for her phone.

"I-I'm with Isaiah," Caleb stuttered. "I'm helping him. With his school project."

She lowered her phone, but her voice was disbelieving. "Where is Isaiah?"

"Upstairs. On his computer. He told me to get a drink." He pointed at the spill. "Do you... want me to clean it up?"

Savannah ignored his question and backed up to the bottom of the stairwell, never taking her eyes off him. She called for Isaiah. Within seconds, he joined them, taking in the situation.

"Mom, don't." His tone was icy. "This is my friend Caleb March. I invited him."

Caleb wished he were dressed in something besides cutoff jeans and a frayed T-shirt. Savannah's eyes found him wanting, but her manners kicked in, albeit stiffly. "I'm sorry I startled you, Caleb. Of course, Isaiah's friends are welcome. You, ah... you just frightened me."

Caleb doubted that very much. It would take more than a spindly dishwasher to scare Savannah Darwin. Isaiah emerged from the kitchen with a wet dish towel and went to work on the hardwood planks.

"Don't worry. Not the first or last spill in here." He paused in his wiping to address Savannah. "What are you doing home in the middle of the day?"

Caleb was surprised at the near rudeness of Isaiah's tone.

She smiled tightly. "I forgot something. For an appointment." She grabbed a sheaf of papers from the kitchen island. "It was nice to meet you, Caleb. I'm sorry about the circumstances. Isaiah, I'll see you tonight." She hurried out the front door.

Isaiah finished his scrubbing, balled up the towel, and walked toward a gigantic laundry room Caleb had missed. He arced it, basketball-like, from the doorway. Caleb wanted to ask Isaiah about the coldness between him and his Savannah mom. He wanted to know more about how all the money and grandeur and silly nicknames didn't add up to a loving relationship. But he didn't know how to ask, so he said nothing.

Chapter 32

Riley

She knew it. She knew it. She knew it.

Rayanne was still in Greenbrier. Two days after arriving, she'd packed, said goodbye to Riley, Mikala, and Luke, and marched to her truck in the driveway. Riley stood in the front yard, her fingers crossed behind her back like a five-year-old. *Go. Please go.*

As she'd half feared, half expected, the truck didn't start. Luke had it towed to a nearby repair shop. Rayanne walked to the shop every day to check on the mechanic's progress, and by the third day, it was ready. She packed, said goodbye to Riley, Mikala, and Luke, and marched again to her truck in the driveway. It didn't start.

At that point, Rayanne turned on the waterworks and fell into Mikala's rather unwilling arms. She sobbed and said the repair bills had used up all her money, and she'd need to work before she could move on. Mikala offered to pay her bus fare to Mobile, but Rayanne only cried harder.

Then Mikala had done something unexpected. Claiming that it was unfair for Riley to lose her privacy, she had moved Rayanne into a guest room in the main house. Riley wasn't sure who was more surprised, her or Rayanne. Or possibly Luke.

At any rate, Rayanne was now living in Mikala's house and working for a few end-of-summer weeks at Pizza by the Park. She claimed she would leave "next week, next week, next week." But who knew? Riley did not trust her sister.

Riley was lying in the shade of the pool house before work, listening to Motown on her cell phone and recalling how she and Silas had danced to this music. For the first time, she remembered him with melancholy instead of a gouging pain. Rayanne was out, and for an hour, Riley was reclaiming the feeling that she was at a luxurious resort. Mikala's pool and surroundings were as fine as those of any beachfront hotel. And her personal bar was only steps away.

Riley sipped a frozen piña colada she'd concocted after locating a blender in the cabinet above the refrigerator. She was sweating even in the shade, but she enjoyed the languor that overtook her limbs. Being wondrously alone made her realize how much her sister had infringed on her life. She half dozed.

"Ri-ley!"

Her sister's voice jerked her awake. Rayanne strode across the brick patio. Her white shorts showed off her shapely legs, and Riley knew if she were to see her from behind, they'd reveal butt cheeks. Riley was embarrassed for her because Greenbrier was a business community, not a beach town.

"Want to see what I got?" Rayanne teased.

Once she entered Riley's shade, it was clear that her left forearm was bandaged. Rayanne peeled away the gauze to reveal a brand-new tattoo, stark and raw against the creamy underside of her arm. It was a long-stemmed rose.

Rayanne nudged Riley's bare arm. "Like your lily! Because we're sisters."

Riley left for work in time to attend the neighborhood meeting that had been called for August 15. The orange fliers had done their job, and at least seventy-five residents milled around refreshment tables in the 200 block of Gunter Avenue. There was no beer or wine for this midafternoon gathering, only soft drinks and bottled water.

Riley recognized the police officers from the July meeting. The city practiced community-based policing, so presumably, these officers knew the park residents—those in mansions, mill houses, encampments, and the Gospel Mission.

She grabbed a Diet Coke and found some shade behind multiple rows of chairs. Mikala, Luke, Cate, and Savannah sat, fanning themselves, in the third row. Isaiah was in another section with Russ Denton—the mission director—and a group of shelter residents. A handsome man mounted the portable stage.

"That's the mayor," came a whisper behind Riley as Caleb slipped in. "Greenbrier's first Black mayor."

Mayor Mack Farnsworth introduced himself and talked about the years the city had worked toward establishing Roosevelt Park. "It's always been my vision for Roosevelt to be a place where all the citizens of Greenbrier—rich and poor, Black and white, Hispanic and Asian, all educational levels, all socioeconomic levels—come together. Because only when we know each other—care about each other as neighbors and as friends—can we tackle the issues of homelessness and lack of affordable housing. I am grateful to the citizens who organized this meeting today for allowing me to be part of it."

Caleb murmured, "I bet they didn't want to."

Even Riley recognized the mayor's intention to ratchet down the emotions behind the assembly. She suspected he'd invited himself.

The man who had been so vocal at the previous meeting leapt onto the stage. "Thank you, Mr. Mayor," he said, clapping him on the back. "Always glad to have you." He turned to the crowd. "Many of you know me. I am Randall Goldsmith, and I live at 101 Gunter Avenue. I appreciate our mayor's words. Nothing would please me more than for all of us to live in, ah... harmony."

A mutter rose from the Gospel Mission group.

"However, if we are honest, there is an element in this neighborhood that threatens the safety of everyone else. I'm talking about the homeless encampments and the Greenbrier Gospel Mission."

A boo erupted, and Russ Denton motioned for quiet.

Randall Goldsmith hurried on. "As you know, the police never made an arrest in the Crescent Trail attack on the young lady earlier this summer. It is unacceptable for us to pay as much as we do in property taxes and not to feel safe in our homes and neighborhood. With the increased traffic and recreational use of the park, it's only going to get worse. Visitors, as well as residents, will get robbed and hurt. We must act. I propose that we form a neighborhood committee to approach City Council about breaking up the encampments and moving the Gospel Mission out of this community."

Half the crowd burst into applause, and half sat back in shocked silence. Despite the fliers, they probably hadn't expected such a bold attack on the mission—especially with Russ Denton and Mayor Farnsworth present. An angry buzz emanated from Isaiah's section.

Russ Denton stood, his arm around a young man of about thirty, who was clean-shaven and smartly dressed in khakis and a dress shirt. Without waiting for an invitation, the two men climbed the shallow steps to the stage.

"You know my position," Russ Denton said. "The Greenbrier Gospel Mission has been serving homeless men in this city for sixty years. It breaks my heart that our *new* neighbors do not want us. I'd like for you to hear from Jason Barnes, a young man who has spent the past six months as our guest."

Russ Denton had chosen wisely. Jason Barnes could be a brother or a son of most of these folks. He described a normal childhood and teen years in a Greenbrier suburb, followed by a car wreck during college, excruciating back pain, and an ensuing opioid addiction. The addiction had precipitated a long, slow spiral into homelessness, spiked with moves back home and stealing from his parents. Two women started to cry, and Riley imagined they had lived through similar experiences.

Jason ended with a respectful nod to Denton and the mission counselors in the audience. "These folks saved my life. There are no two ways about it. If you close them down, you will prevent the saving of all the future Jasons."

Even Randall Goldsmith's supporters applauded the young man as he returned to his seat. Another man Riley recognized from July's meeting stood. "I wish Mr. Barnes the very best. He's a brave young man, and I have no doubt that the Gospel Mission helped him and helps many others like him. That's not the issue. The issue is that this community has more than its share of homeless people and agencies that help them. It's somebody else's turn to host them. We're simply asking that they set up somewhere else before another young lady ends up raped or even killed on the Crescent Trail."

Supportive whispers greeted his remarks. Riley wished the crowd could hear from Farrah. Hers might be the only voice that could turn this tide.

A woman raised her hand. "The fact is that Savannah Darwin promised us this was a safe place to raise our families. And with the Gospel Mission, it's not."

"How would you know?" shouted a man sitting next to Isaiah. "Have you ever visited us?"

Another man yelled, "You have no proof that any of our guys did anything!"

Six or seven people jumped to their feet and began talking and shouting. Within seconds, the meeting dissolved into small groups around the mayor, the police officers, and Russ Denton, as it had in July.

Savannah sat stiffly as people shoved aside chairs to reach her. A woman gripped her shoulder, and Savannah stood abruptly to face her accusers, an artificial smile plastered on her face.

Chapter 33

Caleb

Caleb was learning to play the game—that was what he thought in his more skeptical moments. Other times, he thought he was merely learning to do things right. He'd visited his old counselor at the Gospel Mission and showed him the thirteen hundred dollars he'd saved. He didn't mention that he was squatting in a potting shed, only that he was working more hours.

The counselor was impressed. He called his colleague at the mission's car lot, who let Caleb have the maroon Honda Accord for eight hundred dollars if he agreed to pay six months in insurance premiums up front. "A car can be a great tool," the counselor had explained, "but it can also trip you up faster than anything if you get hit with a repair bill."

Caleb was sure that was true—the counselor hadn't steered him wrong yet—but it was hard to worry about it in the flush of owning a car. *A car.* There was nothing flashy about the old Accord, but it was clean and reliable and had only a single tear in the upholstery. To Caleb, it might as well have been a brand-new Mustang.

On his way out of town he filled it with gas, another expense his counselor had warned about. The mid-August heat and humidity sent rivulets of sweat down his back, but nothing could ruin this day. He was headed to Raleigh to find his uncles. Isaiah had printed a copy of their $61,000 transaction on Twenty-Six Gunter Avenue. Caleb also knew that the current Zillow estimate of the Hardys' property was $995,000, though he doubted he would share that fact.

That number would make his uncles feel they'd gotten played, not more inclined to split the profit. Isaiah had also printed out instructions for the drive since Caleb didn't have a phone.

With the tank filled, Caleb followed West Roosevelt away from the park, crossing Greenbrier's central business district until the street became East Roosevelt. Within a half mile, it offered an exit onto Interstate 85. Caleb rolled down his window and turned up the radio as he cruised to Charlotte, North Carolina, the hot wind whooshing through the Honda's interior. It was the best feeling he'd ever had—this freedom, this independence.

The Honda was an automatic, so much easier to drive than Riley's stick-shift Beetle that he'd learned on. He grinned as he recalled the two of them lurching around an empty church parking lot, Riley laughing as he'd never heard her before.

"You're worse at this than I was!" she'd hooted.

He'd waited to take his driving test until he had the Accord, which was a breeze after maneuvering the balky Volkswagen. He and Riley had celebrated with frozen margaritas.

Zipping toward the North Carolina line, Caleb witnessed scenery much like that of Bender and Greenbrier, but he knew it was a landscape he'd never seen. In twenty-one years, he hadn't been more than twenty miles outside Greenbrier. His fifth-grade class had planned a trip to South Carolina's barrier islands, and he'd been so excited at the prospect of seeing the state's coast. His teacher, Mrs. Lynch, quietly pulled him aside to say the Parent Teacher Organization would pay for his trip, but she needed his mother's permission.

Doreen, on the heels of a breakup with her latest dealer-lover, wouldn't give it. Mrs. Lynch drove to his house to talk to his mother, which mortified Caleb. He met her at the door and begged her to leave. As Mrs. Lynch stood there, biting her lip, Doreen reeled to the door and screeched that her damn son wasn't going anywhere and to get the hell off her property. Caleb's teacher looked at him with pity and backed away.

Caleb stayed home from school for the two days of the trip, then the next two so he wouldn't hear his classmates talking about it. Doreen, sprawled in the living room, careening between crying jags and rage, hadn't even noticed. That was the thing about his mother—she'd been hateful even when she'd gotten nothing from it.

He circumvented Charlotte on I-485 before rejoining I-85 North for the long stretch to Greensboro. He was starving and eyed the billboards for a fast-food place that wouldn't take much of his money. He opted for a McDonalds, where he ordered two burgers, fries, and water. He ate while driving, merging onto I-40 for the hop to Raleigh.

His directions were for his Uncle Roger's address, or at least the address listed for him five years ago. Caleb hoped his uncle hadn't moved. He didn't have a plan B.

In late afternoon, Caleb arrived at Uncle Roger's place in one of Raleigh's endless suburbs. The house was a vinyl-sided ranch, blue with black shutters and white trim. The front yard was neatly cut, and one car sat in the carport. An SUV was parked behind it.

Caleb left the Honda on the street and, clasping his papers in a sweaty hand, walked up the driveway. He peered into the parked Nissan Xterra and noted an infant carrier in the rear seat. He was dressed for the occasion in new khaki slacks, a navy golf shirt, and black tennis shoes from Walmart. Riley had cut his hair.

"Much better," he could hear her saying, her soft hands brushing his neck. "Not so floppy."

He rang the doorbell and stepped back. A barefoot woman in knee-length shorts and a sleeveless blouse answered the door. She smiled pleasantly at Caleb. "May I help you?"

"I'm looking for Roger March."

"He should be home any minute. I'm his wife." She waited expectantly for him to state his business.

Caleb gulped. He hadn't prepared for this situation. "Is it okay if I wait out here for him?"

"Well, it's awful hot."

Suddenly a beautiful younger woman appeared behind her, chin-length blond hair framing a face free of makeup. An infant was hoisted on one shoulder. "Who is it, Mama?"

"I'm not sure."

Both women turned back to Caleb expectantly.

"I'm... I'm Roger March's nephew," he blurted.

The smile disappeared from the older woman's face. "Doreen's boy?" she asked incredulously.

"Yes, ma'am."

The younger woman reached over to push the door open. "Well, for heaven's sakes, Mama, let him in." She motioned Caleb in, and her mother stepped aside. "So, a cousin?" she said happily. "I'm glad to meet you. I'm Emma." She jostled the baby on her shoulder. "And this is Jackson." She raised an eyebrow at her mother, who was still silent. "And this uncharacteristically quiet woman is my mother, Carrie March."

Carrie gave him a pained smile. "I haven't seen you since you were four or five. It's Caleb, isn't it?"

"Yes, ma'am. I'm sorry, but I don't remember meeting you. Was it at the house in Bender?"

Carrie looked embarrassed. "No, you were staying with your grandfather. In Greenbrier." She clamped her lips as if to avoid saying anything further.

Caleb nodded then surveyed the formal living room, which looked too pristine for sitting.

"Come on back to the den," said Emma. "Can I get you a Coke or some lemonade? Have you driven all the way from Greenbrier? That's a haul."

Caleb didn't know which question to answer first. "Lemonade would be great. Thank you." He followed her into a more casually furnished room, which abutted a sunny yellow kitchen.

"I'll get it," murmured her mother. "And I'll call your father."

Caleb heard Carrie March on her cell phone, but her voice was too low to make out, especially given the fact that Emma was plying him with questions. He tried to answer but

stammered at her curiosity about his schooling, his job, his life, his friends. Somehow, in all the scenarios in his mind, he hadn't pictured chatting with a talkative cousin. He estimated that she was older than he, maybe in her thirties. When she caught him looking at her untucked shirt, she patted her stomach.

"Still got the mushy mommy tummy." She sighed. "Thanks to sweet pea, here." She kissed the baby's head.

Carrie March returned with a tall glass of lemonade. "Roger is on his way."

Caleb was glad Emma was present, because she talked nonstop about Jackson and even made her mother smile. Within five minutes, he heard two doors slam in the driveway. Caleb stood as a heavyset man in navy work clothes rushed through the kitchen door. *March Plumbing* was printed on an oval above his shirt pocket. His eyes shot over Carrie, Emma, and Jackson, and he seemed to relax before facing Caleb. Pushing through the doorway behind him was a second man, who wore dirty jeans and a flannel shirt despite the heat.

Carrie stiffened. "I... I didn't know Alan was with you."

"He was doing some work for me," said the first man.

So Caleb wasn't the only family surprise of the day.

The first man held out his hand. "I'm Roger March." He gestured over his shoulder. "And my brother, Alan."

"I'm Caleb March, sir. I wonder if I might talk to you for a few minutes."

Roger motioned toward the hallway. "Come back to my office."

"Formerly known as my bedroom," called Emma.

Caleb sat down on the edge of a daybed in the home office. Roger settled into a rolling desk chair, while Alan stood, fidgeting, by a window. It was clear that Roger was not only the older brother but the one in charge as well.

"It's good to see you, Caleb," Roger said. "Is it your mama? Did she die?"

"No, nothing like that." Caleb tried to remember the speech he'd rehearsed. "Actually, her house has been condemned, but that's not why I'm here."

"Condemned!" Alan spoke for the first time, and it was almost a shout. "Can't that damn Doreen do nothing for herself?"

Caleb looked at him in surprise, but Roger didn't react. "So why are you here?" Roger asked.

"I moved out of Bender four years ago. I've been working in a restaurant and living in a boarding house in the old Gunter Mill area." Caleb saw no need to tell his uncles about his meth addiction or the Sex Offender Registry or the Greenbrier Gospel Mission and certainly not his move to a potting shed. Let them think he'd been living in a boarding house for four years.

"Gunter Mill?" asked Roger.

"Yeah, and my boarding house is right behind number Twenty-Six Gunter Avenue. There's a mansion on it now, with a swimming pool and pool house. But I know it's where my granddaddy lived. I remember staying there with him."

Roger glanced at Alan. "Okay."

"I got interested in whatever happened to Granddaddy, so I looked it up and saw he died in 2010 and that you sold his house in

2016. For sixty-one thousand dollars." He held out the papers Isaiah had printed, damp and crumpled, and Roger skimmed them.

"Uh-huh."

Caleb swallowed nervously. "And I wondered why my mother didn't get a third of the sale price."

Alan unleashed a guttural sound and looked ready to explode again. Roger held up a hand and, without a word, swiveled in his chair. He reached into the bottom drawer of his desk and retrieved a hardback gray ledger. He flipped it open to the first page and spun it around so Caleb could see the neatly penned entries.

"See this?" His thick forefinger pointed to the first date, October 1, 2016.

The entry read *Paid $400 to TBS Properties*. Caleb recognized the name of the company that owned the house in Bender.

Roger ran his finger down both open pages then flipped it to show Caleb there were more. "Her $20,333 went to pay the rent on that house for four years and three months. We knew if we gave it to her all at once, she'd smoke it up."

Caleb's rigid spine collapsed, and he slumped forward. He should have known.

"I hope she at least lived there through December 2020," Roger said. "We paid through then."

"Probably," Caleb said, defeated. "I don't know."

"Why was it condemned?" Roger asked.

"From what I saw, the tub and toilet fell through the floor."

"TBS would've fixed that."

"She says not, but maybe." Caleb didn't really care. His mother had gotten her share of the inheritance, and it was gone.

"That damn Doreen," Alan said. "She don't wanna do nothing but drink and drug, and then she sends you to hustle us for more money."

"That's rich, coming from you," Roger said mildly.

Caleb saw the broken veins across his Uncle Alan's nose, the unkempt hair and nails. Maybe his mother wasn't the only druggie Uncle Roger had to deal with. He regretted that Roger and Carrie and Emma would never know him because they would assume he was his mother's son. But he wasn't—not in any way that mattered.

"Nah, she doesn't know I'm here," Caleb said. "I'm not defending her. But she didn't send me. I came on my own."

"Well, I'm sorry you made the trip for nothing," Roger said, rising to his feet. "But we split the sale price three ways. Fair and square."

They rejoined Carrie and Emma in the den.

"We got everything cleared up," Roger told his wife and daughter.

Emma was quiet, and Caleb wondered what Carrie had told her. He wished they would invite him for supper, but no one said anything. It was clear they were waiting for him to leave.

"One more thing," Caleb said. "That time I stayed with Granddaddy. I don't remember much, but it seems like I lived there for a while and wasn't just visiting."

"You did," Carrie said, friendlier now that he was about to go. "A whole year, I believe. Before you started school."

"But why?" Caleb asked.

Roger, Carrie, and Alan glanced at each other.

"Your mama lost her house for a while and was living on the street," Roger replied. "You must've been around four. Your grandfather took you in."

"But not her?"

"I don't remember the details, but he wouldn't have let her do drugs in his house. And she had a boyfriend, and Pop wouldn't have allowed that either."

"And she got her place back after a year?"

Roger shrugged. "Yeah, she straightened up for a little bit. Pop and I paid the deposit and a couple months' rent." He looked like he was going to say something else but stopped.

There was an uncomfortable silence. Caleb wanted so badly to stay with these people, to get to know them. Emma shot him a sympathetic glance, but she, too, appeared ill at ease.

He forced a smile. "Well, thank you for hearing me out. I'll be going now."

Roger led him through the kitchen and into the carport. There was a white van in the driveway, *March Plumbing* painted on its side. Caleb got it. His uncle had made a life for himself despite a difficult brother and sister. He feared that Caleb would make a claim on that life, just as Caleb feared Doreen would make a claim on his.

His uncle held out a hand again. "It was good to see you, Caleb. I'm sorry if we seem... harsh. But Doreen..." He shook his head and trailed off. "She caused us a lot of pain and a lot of distrust."

And you think she didn't do the same to me? Caleb wanted to yell at his uncle, to scream that he was a victim as much as they were. But he couldn't browbeat his family into accepting him.

"Yes, sir, I know. I lived with her."

Caleb imagined that his uncle's eyes reflected shame. *Good. Shame on you for leaving a four-year-old boy in her care.*

Chapter 34

Cate

Cate opened the mailbox as if she expected a snake to strike. She hated checking it these days and couldn't breathe easily until she'd collected the day's mail. Which was absurd because the dreaded letter, when it came, would not be from the postal service.

That day, it came. She knew as soon as she saw the dirty envelope crumpled in the back of the box. She whirled to inspect her surroundings. The mid-August humidity was keeping everyone indoors who had an indoors. Two T-shirted men with their sleeves torn off trudged toward the public library. In the next block of Gunter, a woman pushed a grocery cart loaded with everything she owned.

Could that be her? She was Black. The social worker had told them Isaiah's father was Black and his mother white, but maybe she'd gotten it backward.

Cate snatched the envelope and hurried into the house. She ripped it open and read.

I here your son is intersted in the poor people of this naborhood. Do you think he might want to know wher he comes from. This is your last chance to keep your secret. Put $5,000 under the center bush in your hege by Sundy at midnite. I am NOT kidding.

Cate clapped a hand over her mouth. *Oh, dear God.* This person heard Isaiah at the neighborhood meeting in July. Or she ate at the Gospel Mission. Or she went to the city pool where he worked. Or...

Cate realized the woman could have seen Isaiah anywhere and learned of his volunteer work and outspokenness on behalf of the shelter. She brushed a heavy drape aside and peeked through the plantation shutters onto the quiet street. Maybe she should set up a camera. But she wasn't sure what that would accomplish. *Do I want to know who this woman is, or is the whole point that I don't want to know?*

How could Savannah have been so careless in moving us to this neighborhood?

"Damn you, Savannah!" Cate whispered into the empty house.

Chapter 35

Mikala

Mikala read, in her glossy coastal magazines, that Charlestonians used to flee their humid, mosquito-ridden summers for the Upstate. She couldn't imagine why. August in Greenbrier was a baking oven when dry, a sauna when the storms rolled in. Walking out her front door was like hitting a physical wall, the air so heavy she could scarcely breathe.

The patio gatherings, galas, and street parties prevalent in May, June, and July had ground to a halt. Summer had worn out its welcome. Only Luke seemed unaffected. Long days in his air-conditioned office. Extended jogs in the evening. And apparently, there was no such thing as a Saturday too hot for golf.

Plus, this damn houseguest she'd never wanted. Unlike Riley, Rayanne was a tacky little thing. Mikala had known girls like her in high school, smoking and drinking behind the football stadium, letting boys have their way, not understanding the power of withholding sexual favors.

At first, she'd worried that Rayanne would ruin her plan. But then she realized that no, the more chaos in the household, the better. Her only concern was leaving the pool house free and clear. She'd accomplished that by bringing Rayanne into the main house. She didn't like having her underfoot, in her short shorts and tank tops and skanky tattoos. If she'd wanted to be around girls like her, she would have stayed in Mobile.

But Rayanne was a nuisance, not an obstacle. Savannah, now, that was another matter entirely. Cate's revelation that her stunning neighbor was bisexual had caused Mikala to rethink everything. She'd assumed the open friendship between Luke and Savannah was all about finance. Savannah the developer and Luke the banker had mutual interests in the success of Roosevelt Park. Now Mikala wasn't sure that was their only connection.

She had dangled Riley in front of her husband, given them every bit of privacy possible. But she honestly couldn't tell if anything was going on between them.

"Morning, Cousin Mikala!"

She jumped. Rayanne entered the kitchen in a yellow bikini and red flip-flops, a beach towel flung over one shoulder. Mikala had to admit she'd kill for her cousin's lithe figure.

Mikala gritted her teeth and turned on her pageant smile. "Good morning, Rayanne. How about some coffee? And fruit?"

Rayanne bounced onto an island stool and let Mikala wait on her.

Mikala reached for the coffee pot and grimaced. The moment she was a grieving widow, this chick would be history.

Chapter 36

Caleb

Caleb woke as the sun shone through the shed's east-facing window, then he startled because he'd overslept. He didn't like being in Isaiah's yard after daylight. Too risky. Cate could bring her coffee outside, as could the Hardys next door. Dawn was the only bearable time to be outdoors—though people like him bore it twenty-four hours a day.

He peered out the window. Nothing stirring. He crossed the shed to the west-facing window, all of four steps away. He gazed into the pool house, but Riley wasn't moving around either. He gathered his sleeping bag, granola wrappers, and water bottle, along with the clamshell that had held last night's calzone. Then he slunk from the shed. Another night's free shelter, another seventeen dollars saved. He ducked and ran to the tangled vegetation behind the boarding house, stuffing his sleeping bag under a ragged shrub.

No one was around, so he slid into the boarding-house kitchen through the rear door. There was so much coming and going in this house that he could brew a pot of coffee without anyone noticing. Once it was percolating, he rummaged through cabinets for a disposable cup that was sort of clean. He poured the first cup from the pot, inhaling its steamy warmth. He exited onto the front porch and claimed the rocking chair, leaning back to enjoy the morning's small successes.

Until he looked at the sidewalk. Trudging up Montreat, head down, shoulders hunched, was his mother. He scrambled to hide behind the thick patch of wisteria that cloaked one side of the porch, but she didn't even glance toward him. She was headed in the direction of the public library. Caleb wondered if that was where she'd spend her day.

Where did she say she was staying? He'd been more focused on keeping information from her than remembering what she told him. *Camping.* She'd said she was camping out. The woods around Roosevelt Park and the Crescent Trail held countless encampments of one to six people. Any group larger than six drew attention from the cops.

Curiosity got the better of him, and he slipped from the porch to follow, allowing her to get a block ahead. He didn't want her to associate him with this area of Montreat or Gunter. Otherwise, she'd try to join him in the shed.

But she was oblivious to her surroundings and didn't turn around. She swerved right onto Marigold Lane, a little through street that connected Montreat and Gunter, then turned right again onto Gunter. She was soon in front of Twenty-Four and Twenty-Six Gunter Avenue, where she halted. She stared at the houses for so long that he wondered if she was looking for something to steal. Or maybe she was contemplating the sale of her father's house. But his mother had gotten her share. She'd conveniently left out that part of the story.

Doreen started up again, and he followed at a distance. She continued on Gunter until she reached West Roosevelt. Several men standing in front of the post office greeted her, and she stopped to talk. One man handed her a wrapped biscuit. Caleb's stomach growled—he should have gone by Trinity Faith Center for breakfast. He dropped into the shade of a pink-blooming crepe myrtle on a hillock beside the post office. He could watch her and find a sandwich later.

The men left, but his mother remained in front of the post office. A woman in yoga pants and sunglasses approached, holding a toddler by one hand and a large yellow mailer in the other. His mother spoke to her, and the woman listened momentarily then shook her head and dragged her child into the building. Doreen tried panhandling a few more times with no success. People on West Roosevelt were savvier than those on Main Street and knew the services available to the homeless. Caleb could have told her that.

After a half hour, she gave up and crossed West Roosevelt to the far side of Gunter. He followed as she passed the Gospel Mission then Pizza by the Park then a gated community of attached brick town houses. That was where Farrah lived. In front of the pristine development, the street was broad and tree-lined. He was deep into Roosevelt Park.

His mother stepped off the street to walk through a trimmed buffer, cross the parallel Crescent Trail, then enter an expanse of untouched woodland. Caleb moved from tree to tree to track her descent into the thick, snarled woods, briars ripping at his pants. Down by a thinly trickling stream—almost dry this time of summer—were three tents. She entered the middle one, and all was silent but the morning buzz of insects.

Caleb turned to leave the woods, slapping at mosquitoes and remembering a time when he, too, was at their mercy. He'd come a long way. It didn't always seem that way, but he had. He headed up the trail to Pizza by the Park, where he had left the Honda the day before. Roman had said it was all right for one night, but Caleb didn't want to press his luck.

He clambered inside the stifling car, the thrill of ownership sharp as ever. As Caleb drove slowly up Gunter and out Roosevelt to Main Street, he turned up the radio's volume and opened the window, splurging on a little gas to feel the freedom the Honda gave him. He didn't try to wipe the smile from his face.

After a short wheel around downtown, he reluctantly swung toward the public library and parked the Accord at the very end of the last row. He hoped that if he moved the car daily, no one would get aggravated enough to have it towed. *So far, so good.* He slapped the maroon hood, promising to return the next day.

Chapter 37

Cate

Cate was paralyzed. Another deadline from Isaiah's alleged mother had come and gone, and she'd done nothing because she could never decide the right thing to do. She wanted to tell Savannah, but she hadn't. She couldn't recall a time in her life when she'd felt more conflicted.

The one thing she was sure of was that Isaiah's biological mother didn't want anything to do with Isaiah. She simply wanted money. Cate's indecision had served her well.

Or so she thought until she opened the mailbox and saw the crumpled envelope. *The woman won't give up.* Cate pounded the box in frustration, but fearing someone might be watching, she stopped. She hurried into the house, slamming the red door behind her, and tore into the dirt-streaked envelope.

Time is up. If the money isnt under the hege by tonite, I talk to Isiah.

"You can't even spell his name!" Cate cried.

"Whose name?"

Cate reeled to find Isaiah standing on the staircase. She'd thought he was at the Hardys' pool.

"Mom? Why are you crying?" Isaiah strode toward her and took the letter from her shaking hand. He read it and frowned. "What is this?"

Cate closed her eyes and slumped onto an ottoman off the foyer. "I've been getting letters from someone claiming to be your birth mother. She wants money not to tell you."

Isaiah laughed in disbelief. "You're kidding."

Cate shook her head.

"How many have you gotten?"

"Three."

"And how much does she want?"

"Five thousand dollars."

"Is that all I'm worth?" Isaiah saw the distress on Cate's face. "Sorry. Bad joke." He paused. "So she doesn't want to meet me. She wants money to scare you into *ensuring* that she doesn't meet me. Class act."

"Isaiah, I am so sorry." Cate put a hand on his arm, and when he didn't shake it off, she stood and pulled him in for a hug. He was six inches taller than her, but he moved in willingly.

"Does Savannah Mom know?" He spoke into the top of her head. "I figure she'd have killed somebody by now."

He pulled away, and Cate tried to smile. "No, I didn't tell her."

"Why not? Why didn't you tell us both? You're always saying that we're family."

Cate shrugged. "I don't even know. Things have been so, I don't know... *tense* this summer. With the neighbors and the homeless and whatever." She didn't mention her suspicions about Savannah's unfaithfulness. That was off-limits for any family discussion.

"Well, don't pay up." He smiled mischievously. "Unless you want to pay *me* not to go live with this person who can't spell my name. Or spell much of anything else."

Cate laughed as she wiped the tears from her face. *What a dear boy.* "Yeah, I guess there isn't much danger of that, is there?"

"Mom, seriously, even if it weren't about living in a real house and having nice things and going to college, I'd never leave you." Isaiah sat heavily on the bottom step of the staircase so that he faced Cate. His voice dropped. "Maybe Savannah Mom, but not you."

Cate wasn't sure she'd heard him correctly. She sagged onto the ottoman, putting them at the same level. "What do you mean?"

"I know she's ferocious, and I wish she'd gotten these letters instead of you. Totally. But she doesn't care about the things I care about, you know? The things you and I care about. I mean, I know she supports us and all that..." His eyes explored the ceiling as if he might find the right words there. "And I'm grateful. I really am." He hesitated again. "But, Mom, she is forcing people out of their homes. Remember how you always told me, 'If you're not part of the solution, you're part of the problem'?"

Cate nodded.

"Well, she's a serious part of the problem, isn't she? She's the one Matthew Desmond was talking about in *Evicted.* She's making poverty worse. She may even be making people homeless."

Cate knew that her horror must show on her face. She'd had these same fears, but somehow, in her son's voice, they were heightened. They had talked *around* these issues in family discussions, but she and Isaiah had never laid the blame at Savannah's feet.

Isaiah was speaking faster, as if he wanted to clear his mind of thoughts he'd been fighting. "You know, this junior project I'm working on? I'm meeting real people whose lives she could mess up. You remember the older man who spoke at that meeting in July?"

Cate nodded, dreading what she was about to hear.

"His name is Earle Meadows. He worked at Gunter Mill as a loom fixer, right out of high school. Well, right out of tenth grade. He and his wife, Reba, have lived on Parker Street all that time. He told me how proud he was to be able to buy their house from the mill."

"You've been to their house?"

"Yeah. That's where I did the interview. They were really nice once they got talking. Mrs. Meadows served me coconut cake. She showed me pictures of their daughter and grandchildren."

"Did they know you're Savannah's son?"

He looked sheepish. "No. I told them my last name is Rosemond. Which it is. I just left off the 'hyphen Darwin.'" Watching her face, Isaiah scrambled to explain. "Mom, they wouldn't have let me in if they'd known."

"Okay. Go on."

"Anyway, Savannah Mom—and other developers—started their offers on the house at twenty-five thousand and are up to sixty-eight thousand. Plus, he owns that old boarding house behind the Hardys' where Caleb lives. That's where he grew up. Mr. Meadows says he's 'ornery' enough not to take the money on principle. And where would they go? It's all the things you and I have talked about. He provides a human face for my paper. He told me all about playing for the Gunter Mill baseball team and having a garden and knowing all their neighbors back in the day."

Cate waited for what she feared was coming.

"They plan to leave both houses to their daughter. But she lives out of state, and they figure she'll sell. But get this—they made a list of developers they recommend their daughter deal with instead of Savannah Mom." He looked at her imploringly, and his voice lowered. "Because they hate her. They really hate her. It doesn't seem... I don't know, just a professional thing, if you know what I mean. It's personal. They talk about her like she spews toxic chemicals. Mr. Meadows called her 'a machine of greed.' Those were his exact words."

Cate was stunned. "I hardly know... I can't..."

Isaiah leaned forward, speaking so softly that his words were nearly lost in the cavernous stairwell. "Mom, sometimes I think we shouldn't be living here."

Cate stayed silent because she thought Isaiah might be right. And not only because living here violated their shared sense of right and wrong but also because it was dangerous to provoke that kind of hatred. She feared she'd let her obsession with her wife put her son in danger. And she could not allow that.

Chapter 38

Mikala

Mikala slithered into a sleeveless black cocktail dress in a size 10—down two sizes since June. She had clothes in sizes 14, 12, 10, and even 8, if they were expensive, well-cut 8s. She was honest enough to acknowledge that her weight fluctuated wildly. She was not one of those women who got rid of the large sizes when she was down a notch or two.

This dress, for instance. She had purchased the wrap style for stomach camouflage, but there was almost too much fabric now. She bunched it in one hand, turned sideways to the mirror, and let it fall. The dress was still flattering and without the tight, chafing fit it had once had. She gazed at her shiny hair with satisfaction. *Does Luke see the difference?* When other men started ogling her, as they had in her pageant days, maybe he would regret straying.

She selected dangling earrings of onyx and walked to the bedroom window as she slipped them on. The pool and terrace were empty that evening. *Blessedly empty*. This summer had been stressful and irritating with two guests and a pool full of their visitors. Ordinarily, she wouldn't have put up with it, but it was a means to an end. *A means to an end.*

She pulled out the drawer of her bedside table, checking, as she did at least once a week, that her revolver was there. Her daddy had given it to her when she graduated from Auburn, for those nights when Luke was away on business. Satisfied, she slid the drawer shut.

She slipped her feet into strappy black sandals and took a last look in the mirror. She smiled, her fire-engine-red lipstick dramatic against her white teeth and pale skin. The art museum was unveiling the new Ringgold that night. It was purely a celebration—she wouldn't be trying to twist arms or dazzle anyone to raise money, so the event was more muted than a fundraiser. A friend-raiser, she called it. Luke planned to come directly from the bank.

She passed Rayanne's room and nudged the door open. Both sisters were at work, so Mikala didn't have to worry about them embarrassing her at the party. Riley, at least, knew how to dress modestly, if cheaply. But Rayanne—the girl looked like a streetwalker. There was a yellow thong lying on her bed. A *thong. How skinny do you have to be to wear a thong?* Mikala sighed, not feeling quite as good about her appearance as she had a minute before.

Mikala drove her BMW into the museum parking lot. The night's event was for donors only—those who made the Ringgold purchase possible and those who donated to the general fund at a significant level. She parked next to a Subaru, where fellow committee member Suzie Westover was checking her makeup. Mikala got out of her car and waited.

"You look great," Suzie said, giving her a side hug.

"So do you. That blue brings out your eyes."

The women walked around to the front of the museum, chatting easily, and mounted the steep stairs to the oversized doors. They'd lobbied to have at least one of the doors stand open, but the curator—eyes bulging, Mikala recalled—had insisted that the artworks must have a controlled temperature.

Mikala and Suzie walked to the textile gallery, where the Ringgold was hung but covered with a black cloth. They were early, but everything seemed well in hand. They helped themselves to white wine as they awaited their guests.

By seven fifteen, the gallery was full, and the murmur of voices had risen in volume. As expected, the weeknight gathering had caught a fair number of people on their way home from work. It was time for the unveiling. The director and curator stood in front of the piece, prepared to speak about its place in art history and in the museum's collection specifically. But the honor of pulling off the black cover fell to Mikala.

She took her place, smiling, and at the director's nod, she yanked the gold cord. The vibrant Faith Ringgold piece appeared—looking like nothing so much as her grandmother's quilts, Mikala thought—and the crowd burst into excited applause. Donors raised glasses of champagne as the director and curator beamed.

As they started to speak, Mikala stole away. She had spoken to Luke when he came in around six o'clock and to Savannah, Cate, and Isaiah shortly afterward. Looking around, she saw Isaiah headed for the front exit and Cate listening intently to the mini lecture. But she didn't spot Luke or Savannah.

She passed Suzie Westover, who raised her glass in a silent salute to their success. Mikala smiled and headed for the restroom. As she approached, she heard low-pitched voices coming from the hallway that made a sharp right a few feet past the bathroom. She paused in front of the door, and the voices halted. Had they heard her footsteps? No—the conversation had given way to soft moans.

Glancing around to make sure no one had followed her, she slid to the end of the wall and sneaked a look. Luke had Savannah pressed against the wall, and she had one muscular leg raised to draw him closer. They were locked in a kiss so passionate that Mikala couldn't help but watch. She tried to remember if Luke had ever kissed her like that. His hands were entangled in Savannah's lush curls. She had one hand around his neck and one edging toward his crotch.

It was everything Mikala had suspected all summer, so she was surprised at the bile that rose in her throat and the anvil that banged against her chest. She pulled herself back and leaned against the museum wall, silently screaming.

Chapter 39

Caleb

Caleb left work promptly at eleven o'clock. Riley didn't invite him over for a shower, and he didn't ask. She'd been quieter lately, and Caleb suspected it was because of Rayanne. The younger sister was flirty and vivacious—annoyingly so, in his view, but male customers gravitated to her. Riley, on the other hand, appeared to be shrinking. Physically and emotionally.

Caleb dragged up Montreat, wondering if he could get into the potting shed early. He usually waited until Isaiah's house was dark. He sneaked through the side yard of his old boarding house and saw a light in the kitchen. He wanted a quick drink of water, so he mounted the rickety back steps and entered the worn room stained with a century of grease. Freddy was sitting at the kitchen table, and another man sat facing away from Caleb. Noting the man's unruly gray hair, Caleb took a step back.

But it was too late. The man turned with an effort, and Caleb's stomach dropped. It was the house's owner, Earle Meadows.

"What are you doing here, Caleb?" Mr. Meadows was dressed in the faded green work clothes Caleb figured he'd been wearing for decades.

"Just stopped by to say hi to Freddy," he lied. He didn't want his former landlord to know how freely he still used his kitchen and porch.

Freddy beamed. "Hi, Caleb!" He addressed Mr. Meadows in his near shout. "Caleb doesn't live here anymore, but he visits us a lot. Don't you, Caleb?"

No, Freddy. Be quiet, please.

"He does, does he?"

"N-Not a lot," Caleb stammered. "Occasionally. How are you, Mr. Meadows?"

The old man narrowed his eyes at Caleb but didn't answer. Freddy was glad to fill the silence. "Me and Mr. Meadows have been talking about property," he said importantly. "About the woman who buys all the houses. She lives through there." Freddy pointed diagonally toward Isaiah's house. "And she visits next door. There." He pointed at the Hardys'.

Now it was Mr. Meadows who seemed ready for Freddy to stop talking. He scraped his chair abruptly on the peeling linoleum. "Well, okay, Freddy. I best be going."

But Freddy was not to be silenced. "I'm going to keep an eye out, aren't I, Mr. Meadows? To see where that woman with the red hair goes." He grinned widely, glad to be tasked with such important work.

Mr. Meadows ignored him. "Caleb, if you want to move back in, let me know."

"Okay." Something occurred to Caleb, and he blurted, "Mr. Meadows, did you know my grandfather?"

Mr. Meadows looked at him blankly. "Your grandfather?"

"Henry March. He used to live where the Hardys live now."

"Henry? Henry was your grandfather?" Mr. Meadows smiled for the first time. "Caleb March. I never made the connection. You don't look much like ol' Henry. But yeah, we were neighbors all my life. He sold me my first fishing rod. And lures. And a couple of knives. Quite the collector, your grandpa." Mr. Meadows peered at him more closely. "You told me you were from Bender."

"I was. But just this summer, I remembered I lived with Granddaddy for a year. When I was four or five."

"Well, what do you know? I was living over to Parker Street by then. I never knew Henry had a grandson." He nodded, a little more friendly than before. "Well, I'll have to tell Reba."

Caleb expected him to exit through the house's living room and front porch, but instead, he went out the kitchen door to the backyard. Caleb would need to be vigilant. He didn't want Mr. Meadows to know he'd left the boarding house for a neighbor's potting shed.

With the house's owner safely gone, Caleb scooted over to Isaiah's unfenced yard. The rear windows were dark, but Caleb knew from experience that if anyone was watching, they'd do so from an unlighted window. He waited by the hedge for several minutes, his eyes adjusting to the dark, his ears straining to hear movement.

When it came, it was a surprise, for the voice swelled from behind him, hoarse and familiar. A hated voice.

"What are you doing out here?" His mother didn't even try to keep quiet.

Caleb panicked. *Did she follow me? Does she know about the shed?* He rifled in his mind for a reason that he might be there. "Sometimes I... swim at that house." He pointed to the Hardys' pool. "A girl I work with lives there." He hoped that would be enough for her.

"You ain't swimming this time a night." It was a statement, not a question.

"Nah, just walking around." The lie sounded weak even to his ears.

"Oughta be our pool anyway," Doreen said. "That was my daddy's property they stole out from under us."

Caleb was tempted to tell her what he'd learned—that her brothers had given her a fair share of the sale price. But he didn't want her to know he'd met them. He secretly hoped they would reach out and invite him into the family. He knew it was unlikely, but it would be impossible if he was tied to her.

Doreen spit then kicked at the hedge. Caleb could smell stale alcohol emanating from her pores. It was a smell from his childhood, a sickly odor he loathed. She walked along the shrubbery line, kicking and mumbling. She reached the end of the clipped hedge, where it bumped against the jumble of vines and undergrowth behind the boarding house.

"Looks like a sleeping bag under there," she rasped.

Caleb cringed. He could see her too-large white teeth in the dark.

"Guess I'll take it if it don't belong to nobody."

He swallowed. The shed floor was going to be hard without that sleeping bag. But he couldn't have her knowing he slept nearby. She hoisted the bedroll to her back, cackling.

Does she know it's mine and that I live in the potting shed? Maybe. But if there was a chance she didn't, he wanted to keep his secret for a while longer.

Chapter 40

Riley

Riley had hoped to stay in Greenbrier through the fall and winter, but she no longer thought it possible. Rayanne had been at Mikala's house for three weeks and showed no sign of leaving. Having her around had triggered memories of Silas and Dauphin Island, and Riley was having trouble eating and sleeping. She didn't bother with mixed drinks anymore, going straight to tequila shots. She needed to quit drinking—she knew she did—but she was too anxious. She was in a bad place and didn't know how to get out.

She sometimes caught Mikala studying Rayanne when her sister showed up with a new bikini or a new tattoo instead of saving for truck repairs. Mikala held her tongue, though Riley couldn't imagine why. Her cousin didn't strike her as the type to let manners override her annoyance.

As Riley's restaurant shift ended one night in late August, she tried to slip out without her sister, but Rayanne saw her and ran to catch up. "Why can't we drive your Beetle to work?" she whined.

"I need the exercise," Riley said, though she'd lost three pounds since Rayanne arrived.

Rayanne harrumphed. "It's spooky walking by that mission place. And who knows what's going on in those woods? All those homeless guys have box cutters, you know." Riley said nothing, and her sister's complaints continued. "Roman was on my case tonight. Claimed I talked too long to a customer. But I mean, he was totally hot, and he bought another couple of drinks because of me. What is Roman's problem, anyway?"

Riley whirled to face her. "If you dislike everything so much, why are you still here?"

"I've told you. I'm saving to fix the truck."

"No, you're not. You've bought a new bathing suit and that tattoo. And probably other things I don't know about."

Rayanne's eyebrows shot up. "I need those things."

"Oh, yeah. We all *need* tattoos."

"You have one!"

"But I could afford it. You're supposed to be working to fix your truck so you can leave."

They passed under a streetlight, and Riley saw a look of craftiness cross Rayanne's face. "Well, maybe *you* want me to leave, but you don't own the house, do you? I'm not so sure our hosts want me to go."

"I can assure you Mikala does."

"Who's talking about Mikala?" Rayanne's smirk was so condescending Riley wanted to smack it off her face. But her words sent a chill down Riley's spine.

"No, no, no, no. Rayanne, you are not messing around with Luke. Please tell me you're not."

"Okay, I'm not." She lifted her arms and twirled around like a little girl. "I guess you're the only one who can mess around with a married man."

Riley felt her face flush. "That was a mistake. A huge mistake."

Rayanne continued to spin. "Yeah, whatever. But just let me say that Cousin Mikala isn't very eager to keep her man. In three weeks, I haven't heard a single bedspring squeak, if you know what I mean."

Riley was disgusted by her sister's immaturity, but the comment registered. Hadn't she felt the same prickly notion about Mikala and Luke? She recalled Mikala asking if Riley and Luke wanted to walk to the museum while she drove and Luke asking if he could take Riley home. Maybe innocent, maybe not. They seemed to have everything, but were they happy?

Rayanne stopped pirouetting and staggered dizzily, laughing. If she was flirting—or worse—with Luke, it was bound to blow up in her face. And if she got tossed out of Greenbrier, Riley wouldn't be far behind.

"So, can I come to the pool house for a drink?" Rayanne asked.

"No. I'm going straight to bed." That wasn't true. Riley was suddenly and desperately thirsty for the tequila on her kitchen counter.

"Please, Riley? Just one?"

She faked a yawn. "No. I'm really tired."

Rayanne pouted the rest of the way home. Riley just wanted to get away from her. She needed to be alone to think about where she could go after Greenbrier.

Chapter 41

The Day Of
Caleb

Caleb woke from another painful night on the shed's wooden floor. His knobby hips and knees ached, and he regretted that he had no fat to pad them. He'd tried sleeping one night in the Honda, parking it on the dim side of a giant twenty-four-hour grocery store. No one disturbed him, but the car's cramped quarters were worse than the shed's unyielding floor.

He thought about concocting another boarding-house fiasco and asking Riley if he could sleep on her couch. But since Rayanne's arrival, Riley had been on edge. He didn't want to endanger her accommodations.

He hadn't been able to score a sleeping bag anywhere, though he'd asked at the Gospel Mission, Trinity Faith Center, and even the mission thrift store. He was twenty-one years old, and his mother was still ruining his life. He made up his mind to get his sleeping bag back. *Today.*

The sky showed the first streak of gray. With the summer equinox more than two months past, he could remain safely in the shed a few minutes longer each morning. However, it was the first day of September, and while that was truly a summer month in South Carolina, the fall landscaping season was coming. He worried that Cate would rummage through the shed before long.

He gathered his clothes, food wrappers, and water bottles and peered out the door. He could see no movement, so he glided through Isaiah's yard, thinking of his young friend sleeping soundly—and comfortably—in a room all his own. He had nothing against Isaiah, but shit, life wasn't fair.

He brewed coffee in the empty boarding house kitchen and sipped it on the shady front porch, wondering if he should go to his mother's campsite right away or wait until later in the day. He decided there was nothing to be gained by waiting. If she was not *in* the sleeping bag, maybe he could sneak it from her tent.

The early-morning streets were busy. The Gospel Mission sent overnight guests out the door at six o'clock in the morning. Other guests were signing in. Homeless residents of nearby encampments lined up for breakfast sandwiches in the cafeteria. Caleb kept an eye out for his mother but didn't see her. She was probably sleeping off the previous night's crack.

A few blocks past the mission, there were no people, just the twitter of birds greeting the day. He stepped off the street, crossed the Crescent Trail, and ducked into the woods. Squirrels chittered madly as he passed.

One of the three creek-side tents in Doreen's camp was gone, and he heard loud snores from the faded green one. He stole toward the brown tent that he'd seen his mother enter two weeks earlier. He waited by the front flap, expecting to hear snores. But he heard another noise—a snort followed by a wet gurgle.

Caleb slowly lifted the flap and was assailed by the acrid smell of vomit. He slapped a hand over his nose and mouth and peered inside. His mother was lying on her back, pink-and-red-speckled vomit smeared over her face and pooled beneath her encrusted hair. Her mouth was strangely sunken, and he realized she'd removed her dentures. His eyes swept the tent, taking in two empty gin bottles and too many beer cans to count. She snorted again, and it hit him that she was breathing in vomit.

He knew he should flip her on her side, put his fingers in her mouth to clear her airway. He'd done that once when he was a boy, and she'd awakened and slapped him before staggering to the bathroom.

It was not a young boy's fear that filled him now but a lifetime of disgust and loathing. He wouldn't force himself to touch her. He watched for so long that he had to remove his hand to take a fetid breath. He clapped it over his nose again.

He observed the hateful, bloated face and the pink bubbles foaming at her lips. Her snorts turned to croaks and then burbles. Her body bucked and ceased, spasmed and ceased. She was not taking in enough air, and he could hear the rattle in her lungs. Her muscles seized once more, and her back arched. But she didn't have the consciousness or the strength to flip onto her side, and she sucked more vomit into an airway. He watched as she gagged a last time, loud and raspy. Then all fell silent.

He waited to feel something, but nothing came. He was numb. His eyes skimmed over his sleeping bag, which was spattered with vomit and wet splotches of alcohol or urine, and he gave up on it. But a corner of a dirty envelope peeked from beneath Doreen's body. Could there be money in it?

He turned his face to inhale fresh air and plunged his arm into the tent. Doreen's body was dead weight, and the envelope didn't budge. He twisted and thrust his entire torso into the tent. He shoved her awkwardly onto her side, yanking at the envelope as she teetered. The irony was not lost on Caleb that such a movement a minute earlier would have saved her life. He didn't care. He tugged the envelope free, and her body thumped to its original position.

He wriggled out, lowered the tent flap, and expelled his held breath. He glanced toward the green tent, afraid he'd made too much of a ruckus. But the snores continued, smooth and soothing. A horsefly landed on his arm and bit viciously. He slapped it and backed away. Its brethren would descend on his mother's tent shortly.

Caleb wanted to run, but he knew that stealth was more important than speed. He crept from the camp site, careful not to step on a dry branch. Once on the Crescent Trail, he shuddered in relief and revulsion and something else. Surely not grief.

He pulled a piece of wrinkled notebook paper from the smudged envelope, wondering for a split second if his mother had written to him. Of course not—but the message was puzzling.

Too bad Isiah has to fin out. I gave you ever chance.

Chapter 42

Riley

Riley, Caleb, and Isaiah were enjoying Isaiah's last morning before school resumed. Well, perhaps *enjoying* was too strong a word, at least as far as Caleb was concerned. Within minutes of arriving, he'd fallen asleep on a chaise lounge in the shade. He'd been weirdly crabby all week, so Riley let him sleep, hoping he'd wake up in a better mood.

The news reports promised a storm, and it did feel like this heat couldn't continue. Something had to break. Riley was headed to work at two o'clock, but it was nice to swim first, and she and Isaiah leapt in every few minutes to cool off.

"Are you looking forward to school?" she asked him.

"Yeah. I'm anxious to talk to my advisor about my project. And to start mentoring at the Gospel Mission. That'll be cool."

Riley smiled. Isaiah made her wish she had a brother. He jumped into the pool, splashing noisily. Sometimes he seemed twenty-five, other times twelve. She dashed into the pool house to get him a Dr. Pepper and sneak a shot of tequila. Since Rayanne had been here, Riley had fought to keep herself on an even keel, and the tequila helped. A little.

"What've you got going this week?" Isaiah inquired when she handed him his soda.

"Just work. Roman keeps saying we're going to slow down with school starting, but I haven't seen it. Plus, we've lost two waiters. And he never replaced Farrah."

"School sounds more fun than that." Isaiah grinned and ran to perform a backflip off the diving board.

An hour later, Caleb woke, staggered groggily to the pool, and jumped in.

"Whew!" he said when he climbed out. "That's better. This pool is the bomb." He glanced at Isaiah and stretched. "I guess you'll buy a place like this when you get out of college."

Isaiah looked surprised. "I doubt it. As you'll notice, we don't have a pool now. I'm using the Hardys', just like you."

"Well, hardly just like me. I couldn't afford your potting shed."

Riley laughed, but Isaiah appeared uncomfortable. "Actually," he said, "I had an idea, but I don't know if it'll make you mad."

"What is it?

"You know how you said employers look at you funny because you don't have a high school diploma? I thought you might join my tutoring sessions at the mission. Get your GED. I bet we could have you ready for the test in no time."

"That's a great idea," Riley said.

But Caleb glared at Isaiah, and several emotions crossed his face. His lip curled into an ugly sneer. "Oh, so it's *tutoring* I need?" he said with exaggerated courtesy. "Not twenty-one years of food and shelter and family and private school and my own bedroom and bathroom and two-hundred-dollar sneakers? How could I lack such insight? Thank you, Isaiah, for enlightening me."

Isaiah and Riley gaped at him.

"What the hell, Caleb?" she asked. "How is this Isaiah's fault?"

"Yeah, how is anything Isaiah's fault?" His voice dripped sarcasm. "Precious little Isaiah. Nothing can possibly be his fault." Caleb's voice cracked, and Riley realized he was close to crying. "He sure didn't do anything wrong. He didn't do anything at all. He didn't do one damn thing to have everything handed to him on a silver platter." He threw his towel at her and stalked off.

Mystified, she turned to Isaiah. But instead of the anger she expected on his face, she saw him squinting in thought, his eyes roving to the open patio door of his house next door. Cate was standing in the doorway, and Riley wondered how much she'd overheard.

Chapter 43

Mikala

Mikala felt like a prisoner in her own home. She didn't want to sit by the pool because Riley, Isaiah, and their sleazy friend were out there. Trampy Rayanne would be up soon and wandering around in her silky boxers or bikini.

Mikala was nervy and addled and needed something to distract her from the thought that this might be the night. The local news channels were filled with speculation about an impending storm. That sounded good to her. Maybe it would break this endless heat wave.

She called Cate. "Any chance you have time for coffee? Downtown maybe?"

"I've just made a fresh pot," Cate replied. "Come help me drink it."

"Are you sure it's convenient?"

"I'd love the company," Cate said.

Mikala exited by her patio, waving to Riley and Isaiah and noting that their hanger-on was gone. Isaiah was certainly a handsome boy. Cate and Savannah would have their hands full with girls throwing themselves at him.

Mikala knocked and let herself into Cate's kitchen. Cate was at the counter, pouring coffee into oversized aqua mugs with *Life's a Beach!* scripted in gold. Mikala remembered how many beach-themed gifts the couple had received at their housewarming. People assumed the Charleston house reflected a love for the coast, but Savannah and Cate's taste was more formal. A stark Japanese-looking painting in teal and black anchored one wall of the kitchen. Their artwork was as puzzling as the museum's.

"Can you believe this heat?" Mikala said, having broken a sweat simply walking next door.

"It's keeping me from planting, that's for sure."

Mikala cocked her thumb toward Cate's glass doors, through which they could see a corner of the Hardys' pool. "Isaiah has become such a good-looking boy. Seems like he grew up overnight."

Cate looked stricken for a moment but then smiled. "We appreciate you letting him use your pool this summer. He has really enjoyed Riley."

Mikala wondered about the look and was determined to discover whether Riley was its cause. She noted that Cate hadn't mentioned that Caleb boy. "Isaiah starts school tomorrow, right?"

Cate nodded and took a seat at the huge island, which was painted black and topped with black-and-white marble. Mikala climbed onto a high-backed stool across from her.

"Yes, and I'm looking forward to getting back to normal. This summer has been..."

"Has been what?" Mikala asked.

Cate smiled, and Mikala thought it was a sad smile. "I'm not sure. I think I may be doing some preliminary grieving before Isaiah leaves for college."

"But that's two years away."

"I know. Silly of me." She shrugged. "But it's been a weird time. Isaiah growing up. That sweet girl, Farrah, getting attacked. They never caught the guy who did it."

"Not to mention people blaming Savannah for it." Mikala paused, hoping she hadn't overstepped.

But Cate nodded. "Well, yes, that. And the whole ugliness it revealed about homeless people versus homeowners, you know? Didn't that bother you?"

It hadn't bothered Mikala. She'd have been happy to have every old mill house flattened, every campsite razed, and the Gospel Mission shoved out to Bender. But she understood that Cate and Isaiah were big mission supporters. Savannah, she wasn't sure about anymore. Mikala wondered if that was behind Cate's unease.

"It's never good to have the neighbors at each other's throats," Mikala responded diplomatically.

"It's more than that, though, isn't it?" said Cate. "It's a clash of socioeconomic classes. The people who were here before resent us, and a lot of the newcomers have misplaced anger toward them. And yes, before you say it, I know that Savannah brought the newcomers here."

"I wasn't going to say that."

Cate's eyes filled with tears. "You might as well."

"She's not the only developer working around the park. If she hadn't built our houses, someone else would have."

Cate remained silent.

"And for that matter," Mikala continued, "Luke is financing a lot of them. So he's as much to blame as she is."

Cate looked up sharply. Mikala wondered if she knew their suspicions of Luke and Savannah were correct.

"I'm sure you and I have differing politics," Cate said slowly. "But it does matter how we make our living, how we live in the world. I'm wrestling with what's going on in this neighborhood—who lived on our property before and where they're able to live now." She lowered her voice, and Mikala could hear the anguish. "Instead of taking part, of *benefiting* from gentrification, should I be setting an example for Isaiah by protesting it?"

She compressed her lips as if she'd said too much. Or more likely, Mikala thought, as if she was afraid her words would make their way to Savannah. Cate sipped her coffee and looked away. Mikala had heard this argument before, primarily at museum board meetings as art lovers tended to be a liberal bunch. It struck her that people moved into the neighborhood and then worried that it was changing—at least, those who were not intent on changing it to begin with. Luke had prepared her for the tension that would exist until all the mill house residents and homeless people were gone. She tried to remember some of his arguments.

"Cate, this is happening in every desirable city in the nation. It's a sign that a city is coming back to life." Mikala recalled one of Luke's more convincing claims and suspected it would resonate with Cate. "Plus, I know you're concerned about the environment and urban sprawl. This neighborhood is a perfect solution. If not here, these houses would have been built eight miles east, out in cow pastures."

Cate smiled weakly. "You sound like Savannah."

"You know I'm right."

Cate's smile disappeared, and her voice took on an edge. "Well, no, sorry, but I don't agree. I think there must be another solution, something between protecting the environment and displacing people."

"That's going to take someone smarter than us."

"Not really." Cate had taken on a dogged look that Mikala didn't find attractive. "The city is preserving the park as green space *and* trying to buy up land to build affordable housing. The Gospel Mission is trying to put people on their feet, not simply shunting them to another place. Same with Trinity Faith Center." She paused. "My fear is that people like us are part of the problem, not the solution." She glanced out the window. "Isaiah reminded me of that recently."

Mikala was losing interest in this conversation and welcomed the chance to redirect it. "Have you heard anything more about Farrah Newell?"

"Only that she is traumatized, as you'd expect. But she left for college, and her parents have listed their town house, so she won't have to return to this area. Police interviewed everybody in those trailside camps and anybody who wasn't in the mission that night. But they suspect whoever it was hopped a bus and left town." Cate's eyes filled with tears again.

What the hell is wrong with her? Mikala adjusted her voice to indicate concern rather than aggravation. "Cate, is something the matter? It's not about Isaiah, is it?"

"No. Yes. Partly." Cate shook her head and began to cry in earnest. "I don't even know anymore."

Mikala wondered again if Cate knew about Luke and Savannah. She would not ask, because she didn't want to reveal her own certainty. Knowing was one thing. Having other people know was another thing entirely. *Especially after tonight.* She looked around the kitchen and spied a copy of *The Empty Cell* on the desk below a shelf of cookbooks.

She trod carefully. "I see you got your book from the pool house. That was the one you mentioned, right?"

"Yeah, Isaiah brought it back."

"So maybe he's the one who left it."

"No, Savannah did." Cate wiped her eyes and stared at Mikala over the rim of her coffee mug. "She runs sometimes. In the evenings."

She said nothing more. Neither did Mikala. The air was thick with things unsaid.

Chapter 44

The Night Of

The past few weeks of worrying about Rayanne and sleeping poorly had caught up with Riley. Because the restaurant was shorthanded, her shift started at two o'clock. She yawned through a steady afternoon, a raucous happy hour, and a busy dinner.

When business slowed around eight forty-five, Roman sent her home. "You're dead on your feet. Go home and get some sleep."

She didn't wait for him to offer twice. It was fully dark by the time she left, with heavy clouds eliminating any stars or moon. The streets were deserted, probably due to the looming storm. A cool gust ruffled her hair, reminding her of the breeze off Dauphin Island.

She entered Mikala's hushed backyard and glanced through her cousin's patio doors. The kitchen and sunroom glowed, but she didn't see Mikala or Luke. Or Rayanne, thank goodness, who hadn't been at work.

When she entered the pool house, she headed for the tequila. Then she hesitated. Summer was ending. Maybe it was time to cut back on her drinking. She thought about lying in bed, exhausted but unable to sleep, and reached for a glass. Just one. Just enough to put her under.

As Riley padded through the living room, she stopped at the rear window and brushed aside the sheers. The window opened easily, and the wind blew through with a satisfying chill. The impending storm had dropped the temperature by fifteen degrees or more. The overhang should prevent rain from coming in, and even if it didn't, water wouldn't hurt the tile floor.

Riley carried the glass and bottle into the bedroom, stripped to a T-shirt and panties, and propped herself against the headboard. Thunder rumbled menacingly above, but she was snug inside. She'd skipped dinner and was hungry, but she was too tired to fix anything.

She leaned her head back and took stock. Thanks to Mikala's hospitality and the generous tips at Pizza by the Park, she'd saved forty-eight hundred dollars this summer, spending money only on gas, groceries, and a few clothes. Well, and alcohol. But if she'd been paying rent, that money would be gone. She thought about fall and next year and the year after. She didn't want to be tending bar or waiting tables at age thirty. It was time to decide what she did want to do.

Riley sipped the tequila. Maybe return to college. Maybe return to AA. Attending meetings was the only way she'd ever racked up sober time. *Maybe turn Rayanne in.* She sat up straight, shocked. *Where did that come from?*

She'd spent the past year and a half covering for her sister. *Did I honestly think there was a chance in hell Rayanne didn't kill Silas?* It occurred to her how insidious—how mindless, really—her protection of Rayanne had been. She supposed part of it was trying to protect Mama and Daddy. But it wasn't possible to protect people from someone else's hurtful actions. She could be the best daughter she could be—and so far, that had been piss-poor—but she had no control over her sister.

She pictured Detective Miller Washburn and those interminable interviews in Mama's living room and in the airless rooms of the Mobile County Sheriff's Office. Perhaps her stubbornness had kicked in because he was such a bully. But that didn't make her actions right. She had a lot of thinking to do but yawned ferociously. She was simply too tired to think anymore.

Riley finished the tequila and didn't even contemplate pouring another. Instead, she switched the light off, wriggled beneath the covers, and slid into what she hoped would be a dreamless sleep.

Mikala had waited for this evening for three months, watching Luke, watching Riley, watching Savannah, watching the weather. Earlier in the week, when she'd heard about the storm, she'd worried that it might halt Luke's "run." It didn't. When Rayanne announced that she had a date, Mikala knew it was the night to act.

Waving Luke off for his alleged run, she hurriedly dressed in black jeans and a turtleneck then drove to the oldies movie theater on Calhoun Boulevard. She tossed her lustrous hair while chatting to the ticket clerk about *Fried Green Tomatoes.* Inside, she bestowed a brilliant smile on the bored teen taking tickets and commented on how excited she was to see the beloved movie.

"Yeah, my mom likes it too," the teen said.

Twerp. She wasn't his mom's age. Mikala tucked the torn ticket in her wallet and walked to the restroom. She entered a stall and stuffed her hair under a faded gray baseball cap. She waited until no one was around, which was easy because this was the day's last showing, and oldies fans preferred matinees. She slipped past the theater, where she'd refamiliarized herself with Fannie Flagg's tale a few days earlier, and jogged through a side door, confident that no one saw her leave.

She drove to Sarah Steinberg's house on upper Montreat Avenue, where a raucous wine-fueled book club would go until midnight. Mikala parked her BMW behind ten other vehicles lining the street, pulled her hat low over her eyes, and speed-walked, head down, through Marigold Lane and onto Gunter Avenue.

The sky was inky, and thunder growled. She saw the first streak of lightning in the distance. Keeping to the shadows, Mikala crept past Savannah and Cate's house and entered the dark stretch of their adjacent yards.

She paused, secure in the blackness that surrounded her, then peered through the kitchen window of the pool house and saw Luke leaning against the sink, his back to her. Like every other night, he'd left the interior lights off, but from this close, she could see him in the reflected lights of the pool. He was talking to Savannah, though his body blocked her from Mikala's view.

Rage built in her chest, urging her on. It was the unfairness she couldn't tolerate. He'd sworn to be faithful *to her.* Thunder grumbled again, growing closer, and Luke glanced out the window. She ducked, though she knew he couldn't see her in the dark.

Mikala slipped on plastic gloves from her jeans pocket. She reached behind the air-conditioning unit and groped for Riley's gun, which she'd retrieved from the Beetle earlier that day. She crouched in the bushes to wait.

Savannah headed out for a run, though a storm was brewing. "I can beat it," she called to Cate as she closed the front door behind her.

Though Savannah wore running clothes, Cate noticed that she had freshened her makeup and crimped the waves in her luxurious hair. Cate slumped onto the living room sofa, wondering how much abuse she was supposed to take. She'd moved to this neighborhood despite her misgivings, all to keep peace in their marriage. But apparently, she was the only one honoring the commitment.

From the living room window, she viewed the stretch of night where Savannah had disappeared. Cate was sure her wife would circle back to the Hardys' pool house. Mikala hadn't come out and said it that morning, but it was clear that she believed what Cate had feared all summer—that Savannah and Luke were having an affair.

Worse, they were having it in the pool house, right under their spouses' noses. Somehow, the fact that they didn't try any harder to conceal it made the betrayal crueler.

She suddenly recalled Savannah's first marriage, when Cate herself had been the secret lover. *Were we so reckless, so unconcerned with anyone else's feelings? Possibly.* She'd been manically high, untouchable. She pushed the thought away. Cate was sickened—by her own former behavior and by this new treachery. She couldn't live like this.

She climbed the stairs to her bedroom and, through the window, scrutinized the tidy brick structure in the Hardys' yard. No lights were on, but in the reflected gleam from the pool, a figure passed before the kitchen window. Tall, a man obviously. *Luke.* Though she'd expected to see him, her chest ached as if from a blow. He was waiting for Savannah.

Cate chewed her lip as her thoughts boomeranged. Obviously, confrontation was not her strength, but she felt an unaccustomed emotion rising, not her usual trepidation or worry but anger—a feeling born of resentment and betrayal. *What kind of role model am I for Isaiah if I allow Savannah to walk all over me?*

She sat on their king-sized bed, hurt and smoldering. Tears of frustration leaked down her face. Then she walked resolutely to her closet and spun the dial on the floor safe left, right, left, using Isaiah's birthdate. Cate pulled out her pearl-handled copperhead killer. Tucking it in the back of her pants, she ran barefoot down the stairs and through the side porch.

Without a sound, Cate stepped onto the dry grass. Her mind ricocheted, thinking how nice it would be to get rain for her flowers. *Focus, Cate.* She found the gate to the Hardys' yard standing open and slithered through it.

The pool lights didn't reach the rear of the structure, so she made her way with caution, placing one foot tentatively in front of the other to avoid banging a bare toe. She reached a window at chest height. Through filmy sheers, she could see the living room sofa and, beyond it, French doors and the reflection of underwater lights. In their glimmer, she observed Luke's lean torso rising above the sofa's back, arching in ecstasy. Even from this angle, she could tell his eyes were closed and his head thrown back.

Rage boiled through her. *How can Savannah do this to me, to Isaiah, to our family?* She was furious at Savannah but at herself, too—at her complacency, at her willingness to bend. Then her shame hardened, leaving only fury.

Riley wasn't sure what woke her. A giggle, a sigh, a moan… someone else was in the pool house. She slipped from the bed, clutching its lightweight comforter as a shield, and tiptoed to the closed bedroom door.

Another giggle and a responding murmur. Two people, and they weren't trying to be quiet. *Don't they know I'm here?*

She paused. She wasn't supposed to be there. For the first time that summer, she'd left the restaurant early. Her mind whirred over the evening, recalling her exhaustion and how Roman had sent her home more than two hours before her shift ended. Until that night, her schedule had been like clockwork, her arrival home at 11:20 p.m. unerring.

She whirled to look at the red 10:38 on her alarm clock. *Has this been going on every night I've been at work?*

She reached the bedroom door and, holding her breath, turned the knob slowly. It was noiseless, and she nudged the door open. From the gleam of the pool lights, she made out two figures entangled on the couch. She identified Luke's lean form, muscled back, and black hair. She couldn't see who was under him but recalled the red-gold hairs left on the sofa and Savannah's surprise visit the afternoon Riley was supposed to be out. She knew who the second figure was.

Mikala rose from the bushes outside the pool house, shaking off the numbness in her legs. She slid a key from her pocket and eased it into the kitchen's doorknob, but the lock didn't click. She gripped the knob and discovered the door wasn't locked. Odd, but she was in.

She inched to the doorway between the kitchen and living room. The pool lights glowed brightly enough that she could see a couple on the sofa, writhing with a passion she could scarcely remember. She couldn't see Savannah, but Luke hovered above her, torso naked, head up, eyes closed. It was a sight she'd once relished from Savannah's vantage beneath him. How had things gone so wrong?

He moaned, yanking Mikala out of her reverie. She wanted him to open his eyes and see, in his last seconds, what he'd made her do. She raised the gun to be ready when he did.

She waited. And waited. *Why won't he open his eyes?*

Her heart pounded and her arm trembled, and she couldn't wait another second. A streak of lightning washed the room in white light, and a clap of thunder crashed directly overhead, shaking the pool house. And then came the unleashing of rain, heavy as machine-gun fire on the roof. Luke turned his head to the glass doors, but still, he didn't look at her. Suddenly, thunder roared again, but no, this roar was *inside* the pool house.

Luke's eyes flew open, and for a moment, he looked directly at Mikala. In shock. In pain. His eyes fluttered to the red-and-black hole ripped into his side.

Mikala recoiled and whipped her head around in bewilderment. She heard another explosion as she stumbled backward and all but fell through the kitchen door and into the driving rain. Despite her confusion, she kept an unyielding grip on one thought—she had to get back to the movie theater in time for the end of *Fried Green Tomatoes*.

Riley stood frozen in her bedroom doorway. The ear-splitting blasts assaulted her from all sides, inside and outside the pool house. She saw Luke's body buck, heard his cry. Then came another burst, and tufts of fabric and stuffing flew through the air.

She staggered back inside her bedroom, her mind whisked to a murder scene she'd never witnessed—Silas lying on his kitchen floor, his green eyes wide and disbelieving, groaning as Luke was groaning now. She sank to the floor, pulling the comforter over her head. A door slammed.

This couldn't be happening again. It simply couldn't. She closed her eyes and rocked and rocked and rocked.

Riley didn't know how long she crouched under the comforter, her mind bouncing between Dauphin Island and Greenbrier, between a dead Silas and an injured or dead couple in the next room. She seized upon the hope that she was dreaming. Yes, surely she'd moved on from death by shark to a menacing shadow to a new nightmare. She knocked her head against the wall hard, and the immediate pain told her no, this was not a dream.

A whimper resumed in the living room, rising unsteadily above the pounding rain, but she didn't dare go in. *Why not? Didn't I hear the shooter leave?*

She tried to force herself to stand, to walk into the living room, to call 9-1-1.

But she couldn't. She recalled the hard face of Detective Miller Washburn. *You're not a suspect, Miss Masterson, only a person of inter-*

est. That was what he'd said. But his face, the way he swaggered, the way he sneered—they had indicated something else entirely.

Riley's mind and body were at war. Her mind was telling her to go in and see what had happened—that anything would be better than not knowing. Her body was telling her to run—that the Greenbrier police would never believe her presence was a coincidence.

But her muscles were locked. There was no going anywhere—not to the living room, not to her car. She gasped even to breathe, and a new panic arose. She hurled the comforter off her head and gulped in the black air.

Then another thought skidded to the surface. Her rigid muscles were taking their cue from something her mind was trying to work out. She thought back to the figure in the kitchen doorway raising an arm, followed by the explosion of light and sound. Suddenly, she got it. The gunshot flash had not come from the doorway but from somewhere else. *But where? The shadowy rear of the living room? The bathroom?* She'd heard one door slam, but there might be a second person still here. The shooter.

Again, she shut her eyes and heard a whimper. But this time, it was coming from her.

A flash of lightning brightened the potting shed momentarily, giving Caleb a chance to read the note from his mother's tent for the twentieth time: *Too bad Isiah has to fin out. I gave you ever chance.*

Isaiah had told him about his mom receiving a blackmail note from his biological mother. *Was Doreen blackmailing Cate and Savannah? Could she be Isaiah's mother?* He remembered the day she'd taken his sleeping bag after kicking around Isaiah's hedge and another day when she'd stood in front of Twenty-Four Gunter Avenue, watching. He'd assumed she was looking at her father's former property next door or seeking something to steal. But her presence in front of Isaiah's house had been no coincidence.

All day, his emotions had been banging from guilt to elation to fear to horror. His mother was dead. *Isn't that what I always wanted?*

Word had rocketed around the homeless community about the choking death of a woman in the park. He'd heard about it while eating a sandwich at the Gospel Mission and again while getting an afternoon water bottle at Trinity Faith Center. Police were searching for her next of kin, but he figured it wasn't high on their priority list.

He couldn't identify her. Not yet, anyway. He had no poker face, and he could picture an officer frowning and leaning closer. *Something you not telling us, son?*

Caleb wondered if it was a crime to stand by while someone died—failure to intervene or something like that. He didn't know and didn't intend to find out. Let them locate Uncle Roger or Uncle Alan. Or did it matter if they never identified her at all? It wasn't like there was an inheritance at stake. Let them throw her ass into a potter's field.

There was only one thing Caleb needed to know. He picked up the cell phone that Trinity Faith Center had given him the previous week. It had limited minutes, but it was free. He'd never made a call from the potting shed—never done more than hum to himself while here. But rain and thunder were making an unholy racket above his head, and no one could hear him.

Uncle Roger answered. "March Plumbing."

He stuck a finger in one ear. "Uncle Roger, this is Caleb March. Your nephew." The pause reminded him of his family's reluctance to accept him. "I don't want anything," he added, angry that he had to voice such a thing to his own family.

"Yes, Caleb. What is it?"

"That time I lived with my granddaddy for a year. Did my mo... did Doreen have a baby? A baby she gave up?"

Another pause. "Yes, she did."

"Do you know why? I mean, if Granddaddy took me in, wouldn't he have taken in a baby too? At least for a while?"

"No. Pop's health wasn't good enough to take care of a baby." He hesitated then sighed. "He wouldn't have anyway."

"Why?"

"Because the baby was Black."

Caleb pictured that grim mill house and the old man who'd been a textile worker in 1950s and '60s South Carolina. Volunteering to raise a biracial child? Wasn't going to happen.

He waited for another thunderclap to recede, glad to have a moment before he spoke. "So why didn't Doreen keep it? I mean, she kept me." *Why was I the only one who had to grow up with that sociopathic, uncaring bitch?*

"From my understanding, that wasn't an option. She tested positive for cocaine in the hospital, *and* she was homeless. There was no way your county authorities were going to let her keep that baby boy."

His chest tightened. "And it *was* a boy?"

"Yeah." Uncle Roger went quiet again. "Caleb, why are you asking this?"

He thought quickly. "No reason really. I remembered Doreen saying something about a brother one time. I thought she was talking about her brother. You. Or Alan." The lies rolled off his tongue as his mind gained clarity. "But as I was remembering more, I decided maybe she was talking about *my* brother. I was curious."

"Are you going to try to find him, anything like that?"

"Nah. Like I said, just curious." Caleb was eager to get off the phone before he said something incriminating—something Uncle Roger would remember if he was contacted about his sister's death. He attempted a breezy tone. "Well, I'd better go. Thank you, Uncle Roger." He hung up.

Caleb dropped to his knees, flinching as they banged on the shed's hard floor. *Isaiah is my brother. Half brother.* He needed to verify that Cate and Savannah's blackmail notes had indeed come from Doreen. But he was sure of it.

So, what now—should I even tell them? He sincerely doubted that Isaiah's moms would open their home to him. He didn't want to be rejected by another family. This would take some thought.

And Savannah—she provided Isaiah with every material advantage, true. *But look what she did to the people who formerly lived on this property. Where are they now? Doubled up with their children? In a homeless camp?* There was no way to know, but one thing was sure—they didn't reside in anything like the mansion where Savannah, Cate, and Isaiah lived.

Another thunderclap boomed in his ears, this one juddering the shed. He stood and peered out his window toward the pool house. He ducked quickly. Someone was standing ten feet away in the drenching rain, staring into Riley's living room window.

He slowly raised his head because the peeper's attention was not on his shed. He saw a gleam of silvery hair, wet and glistening. Cate. *What is she doing? Is that a gun in her hand? Is she threatening Riley?*

Caleb searched frantically for the gun he'd taken from his mother's abandoned house in Bender. It was under a flowerpot, and as he fumbled to lift it, he dropped the pot, shattering clay shards across the floor. Gripping Doreen's gun, he clambered from the shed, his knees and elbows whacking the doorjamb in his haste. He fell against a metal milk can, sending dirt and geraniums flying across the tiny porch.

He had never made so much noise, and he hoped the storm would cover him. Finally gaining his balance, he dashed toward the Hardys' yard in the downpour.

Riley clapped her hand over her mouth to stifle the whimper that escaped involuntarily. Thunder reverberated again, but it wasn't the bone-rattling crash of a few moments before. She crawled to the doorway of her bedroom and saw movement on her left—the sheers on the living room's rear window billowing into the room on a draft of wind and rain.

Over the torrent on the roof, she heard a croak.

"Are you... hit?" The voice strangled into a gasping breath followed by a jerky exhalation. Then silence.

Oh my God. He's dead. Luke is dead.

Riley had to go in there. She rolled onto her knees and used the doorjamb to scramble up on wobbly legs. The swirling sheers caught her eye again just as another flash of lightning threw the yard into relief. A face appeared at the window.

Her shock was reflected on the narrow face. They stared at each other, fearful, calculating. *What is he doing here? Is he the shooter?*

Then he disappeared. Riley closed her eyes, any thought of running away moot. She couldn't pretend she wasn't here. Even if Caleb tried to protect her, the police would sense his lies. And if he was the shooter, protecting Riley would be the last thing on his mind.

She lurched to the sofa, clutching her phone like a lifeline. She approached the end, where Luke's head hung lifelessly. He so completely covered the figure beneath him that his was the only body she saw. If she hadn't known better, she'd have thought he was alone.

She bent to look for a tousle of strawberry blonde hair. But that wasn't what she saw. A slender arm dangled from the sofa—a stark white arm with a rose tattoo.

"No, no, no, no," she stuttered. She backed away in horror until she crashed into the patio doors, as paralyzed as she'd been in the bedroom. Her heart seized, and she gulped several deep breaths, growing dizzy.

She had to be sure. Her legs were rubbery and didn't want to respond, but she forced them to take her to the couch. She clenched her teeth and tugged on Luke's shoulder to uncover the body he was hiding—slight, dark haired, covered in blood. Weirdly, a pillow concealed her face, but it could be only one person. Rayanne.

There was so much blood that Riley couldn't tell what was Rayanne's and what was Luke's. *And why is that pillow between them?* She dropped Luke's shoulder, frightened that she might have left fingerprints on his body, though she had no idea if fingerprints could be lifted from clothing or flesh.

Riley felt an absurd urge to laugh and recognized that she was edging toward hysteria. She looked around the room, trying to discern what had happened and what would happen next. Her mind fragmented, leaping to Silas's kitchen and the scene that she'd heard about over and over and over until she felt like she *was* standing above him, watching him bleed out from stab wounds.

Now she would hear about this murder scene over and over and over. And it was all because of the person lying beneath Luke. She wasn't sure she could face that again. Her mind might truly snap.

Riley looked at what she could see of her sister, the rose tattoo, the dark hair spilling over the sofa's edge, and she raged inwardly. "It's all your fault," she hissed.

She spun and returned to the only solace she knew—the bottle of tequila on her bedside table. Several minutes passed before she could make herself call 9-1-1.

Chapter 45

After
Patrick

Homicide Detective Patrick Marconi left his wife and son sleeping in their modest brick ranch house six miles from downtown Greenbrier. He scribbled a note for his boy, apologizing that he wouldn't be able to drive him for his first day of elementary school. His wife would read it to him. There would be disappointment but no anger or hurt feelings. They knew the drill when there was a murder in the city of Greenbrier. Or in this case, two murders.

Patrick was running on two hours of sleep because the incident at Twenty-Six Gunter Avenue hadn't been the normal drug deal gone wrong or hit-and-run on the side of the interstate. Those were the deaths he and partner Javon Hortense usually worked.

No, these deaths were something altogether different and not just because of the ritzy address. A prominent bank president and his wife's cousin had been caught in the act. *Juic-eee*, as Patrick's wife would say.

That was why the detectives stayed up speculating until four o'clock in the morning and agreed to meet again at the Law Enforcement Center at seven. They wanted to be back on Gunter Avenue by eight. They would have liked to be there earlier, but they were trying to be respectful in these early stages. They'd already had *the* conversation with their chief about who these players were and what kind of influence they wielded at City Hall.

"Not an issue," the chief told them. "Follow the evidence."

They'd see how long that lasted when the chief's bosses on City Council started getting calls from irate bank execs and developers.

Javon, tall and rangy and looking every bit the high school basketball player he'd once been, waited in the squad room with sausage biscuits and coffee. Patrick gratefully nicked a biscuit, knowing his diet for the next few days would consist entirely of caffeine and fast food. His waistline would reflect it, while Javon would eat triple the amount and drop weight.

Javon was leaning back in his desk chair, beaming. His shaved head gleamed darkly, though there was stubble around his jaw. "You are not going to believe the hit we got from NCIC." He looked supremely pleased with himself for the quick response from the National Crime Information Center.

His mouth full, Patrick raised an eyebrow.

"Riley Masterson?" Javon said. "The little cutie staying in the pool house? She was a suspect in a murder on the Gulf Coast a year and a half ago."

Patrick nearly choked and gulped from his coffee cup. "No way." He recalled Riley's demeanor from the night before. Nearly catatonic. Javon's news explained a lot.

Javon rotated his laptop around, and Patrick could see the masthead of the *Mobile Press-Register.* "I called up the news reports. Looks like she was having an affair with a restaurant owner from Mobile. He was down shrimping on Dauphin Island and turned up dead in his kitchen, stabbed with his fishing knife. A neighbor swears he saw this Riley Masterson through the kitchen window. She denied it. The only reason they never arrested her is that her fingerprints were *not* on the knife, while plenty of other people's were."

"Huh."

"I've already put in calls to the Dauphin Island PD and the Mobile County Sheriff."

"Damn. What time did you get in?"

Javon looked sheepish. "I never left." He nodded in the direction of a former storage room that now held bunk beds.

Patrick wiped his hands on a napkin and finished his coffee. "Looks like I've got some catching up to do. Let's ride."

The detectives arrived at the Hardys' house to find Riley Masterson and Mikala Hardy bundled in blankets and sitting at the kitchen island with coffee. Mikala poured the detectives two cups without asking. Her eyes were red rimmed but dry.

"We want to do anything we can to help," she said.

Riley would not meet their eyes.

Patrick asked Mikala to join him in the living room, while Javon remained in the kitchen with Riley. He had earned the right to question their most interesting suspect. Meanwhile, Patrick turned his attention to Mikala, who sat on one end of a creamy ivory sofa, a rich red blanket draped around her. He'd always wondered who lived in these houses.

He studied her with interest. Mikala was pretty, even with her hair knotted and her face puffy from a lack of sleep. She was wearing sweatpants and an Auburn sweatshirt and was barefoot, her toenails shiny with bloodred polish.

She tugged the blanket more tightly around her shoulders. "I can't get warm."

Patrick nodded, though he could see through the window that steam was rising from the grass. The storm had left behind a greenish light that was spookily beautiful.

"It's the shock." He opened a notebook. "I know we talked last night, but I'd like to go over your movements once more." He'd also collected her gun from a bedside table. It hadn't been fired.

"Luke and I had an early dinner. Just the two of us."

"Is that normal? I know you have some houseguests. Your cousins, I believe."

"Yes, but they don't eat with us because they work. They're waitresses at Pizza by the Park. But last night Rayanne had a date." Mikala corrected herself. "Or she *said* she had a date. I guess she did. With Luke." She lifted her chin.

Patrick strove for a neutral expression. "Go on."

"Luke often ran in the evenings. I knew he was going to, so I went to a movie. The place on Calhoun that shows oldies."

"What did you see?"

Mikala smiled sadly. "My favorite. *Fried Green Tomatoes*."

"Do you have your receipt? Or ticket stub?"

Mikala looked around vacantly. "Do I? Maybe." She retrieved her purse from a table by the front door and fumbled through her wallet. She held up a torn blue ticket. "Here it is."

Patrick studied it. "There's no date stamped on it. Did you speak to anyone? See anyone you knew?"

Mikala shrugged. "Just the girl at the ticket booth and the boy taking tickets. Maybe they'll remember me? I don't know."

"We'll ask." He waited a beat, wishing he knew the plot to the movie so he could casually reference it. He was sure his wife would know. "And you arrived home when?"

"The movie let out about eleven thirty. I was home by eleven forty-five. And I found all you guys here." She shivered and pulled the blanket more tightly around her shoulders.

Patrick switched gears. "How were things between you and Mr. Hardy?"

Mikala's eyes welled with tears. They appeared genuine to Patrick. "I would've said they were great. We moved into this house three years ago. Our dream house. Luke worked more than I liked, but... he was conscientious about providing for us." Tears streamed down her cheeks. "Clearly, I did not understand what was going on."

"Tell me about your cousins and why they were staying with you."

Mikala dabbed her eyes. "I hadn't seen either of them for years, more than a decade. But my mother stays in close touch with my aunt Crystal—she's their mom—down in Mobile. That's where we're all from." She swallowed. "I knew Riley had run into some trouble and was having a hard time. I never learned the details. Something about an affair with a married man who was killed. Mother asked if she might spend some time up here, get back on her feet. Luke and I said yes."

"So it was your mother's idea."

Mikala looked at him blankly. "Why, yes, as near as I can recall."

Patrick hesitated before asking his next question. "I don't want to be... indelicate. But were you concerned about your husband? Since your cousin had had an affair with a married man in the past?"

Mikala looked horrified. "No! She wouldn't. I mean, we're family! That's completely different."

Patrick was silent, watching. "Is it?"

"Yes! I mean, Riley used to watch me prepare for pageants. She was my little cousin."

"And Rayanne?" Patrick asked, and he sensed Mikala growing more rigid.

"That was a surprise to us all, Riley included. All I agreed to was that Rayanne could stay one night. Then her truck broke down, and one thing led to another, and she ended up staying too." Mikala's voice had hardened.

"Why was she staying in the main house rather than the pool house?"

"Well, I'd already promised the pool house to Riley, and it has only one bed. It made more sense for Rayanne to use one of our guest rooms." She flung an arm out to indicate the upstairs. "As you can see, we have several."

"Mrs. Hardy, did you have any idea that Rayanne was sleeping with your husband?"

Mikala hung her head and took a moment to respond. "No. I was stunned. Still am." It was, Patrick thought, the most honest thing she'd said. He waited for more.

"Rayanne, ah... I wouldn't have thought..."

Patrick sat back. "You wouldn't have thought what?"

She raised her head and looked him in the eye. "I wouldn't have thought she was my husband's type."

"And why is that?"

"I hate to be unkind, especially now. But my husband was a smart man. I'm a little surprised that he was interested in someone like Rayanne. She wasn't particularly intelligent. Or interesting. Or classy." She gave a pained smile. "But obviously, that wasn't what he was looking for, was it?"

Patrick recrossed his legs. "Mrs. Hardy, can you think of anyone who would want to harm your husband?"

She bowed her head. "No, and a robbery in a pool house would be kind of odd, wouldn't it?"

"Yes, it would." He reframed his question. "Do you think this affair with your cousin led to his death?" Her head came up at that. "Is there anyone—besides you—who would be upset by it?"

"I... don't know. Would Ri...?" She shook her head. Patrick wasn't able to get another word out of her.

Chapter 46

Riley

Detective Javon Hortense had to be the good cop. He and Riley were in Mikala's kitchen, and he was trying to come across as Riley's best friend. Or therapist.

She struggled to concentrate on his questions, saying no more and no less than he asked. She knew she was not the one he was seeking. But she'd known that once before, hadn't she?

"Miss Masterson, now that you've had time to rest, let's go over the events of the evening again."

She hadn't slept, but she didn't contradict him. "Okay."

"Tell me about your entire day yesterday."

"I'd had trouble sleeping the night before, so I got up around six a.m. or so." She didn't tell him about the nightmare that woke her—a bloody Silas staggering around his boat, with Rayanne stretched on the deck in a bikini, laughing. "Had breakfast." She didn't mention that breakfast was a string of tequila shots. "Swam with our neighbor, Isaiah Rosemond-Darwin, and my work friend, Caleb March. Had lunch. Then I started my shift at Pizza by the Park at two."

"You worked how late?"

"It was supposed to be until eleven. But we weren't too busy. Roman sent me home before nine."

"Roman Baxter will verify that?"

"Yes."

"Then what happened?" he asked.

"I went to bed."

"Do you usually go to bed that early?"

"No. I usually work until eleven then come home and stay up another couple of hours. I guess that schedule finally caught up with me. I was beat last night."

"What happened next?"

"Something woke me—sounds from the living room. What turned out to be Luke and my sister, though I didn't know it then."

Detective Hortense nodded encouragingly. He had kind eyes, but Riley wouldn't drop her guard.

"They must not have known I was there. As I said, I wasn't supposed to be. I got up to see what was happening." Riley paused. She'd thought a hundred times about what to say and had decided to stick as close to the truth as possible. "I opened my bedroom door and saw them. Uhm, having sex."

"You could see clearly who it was?"

"No. Not at first. I could see Luke—because of the pool lights—but I couldn't see Rayanne. He was completely hiding her."

He must have sensed something in Riley's voice because he cocked his head. "And were you surprised that your sister was, ah... having sex with Mr. Hardy?"

Was I? Riley remembered her sister's silly prattling about Luke and Mikala as they'd walked home from work the week before. *Did I believe her?* "Yes, I was surprised. I had no idea."

"Then no idea how long it had been going on?"

"No."

He hesitated. "Miss Masterson, I don't want to make you uncomfortable, but did Mr. Hardy ever attempt to initiate a relationship with you? I mean, you were here for several weeks before your sister arrived, right?"

How to answer? Luke had never done anything improper that Riley could point to. She'd probably conjured those queasy feelings on her own. "No. He was a perfect gentleman."

Detective Hortense waited. It was an old trick, luring people to fill the void. Riley had fallen into that trap with Mobile County Detective Miller Washburn before she'd learned she didn't have to do his job for him. She remained silent.

"Last night," Detective Hortense finally said, "when you saw a couple on the sofa and couldn't see it was your sister, who did you think it was with Mr. Hardy?"

Riley widened her eyes. She needed more coffee, but hers was cold. She needed toast to settle her stomach. Or a drink. "I'm not sure I should say. I was obviously wrong."

"Miss Masterson." The detective leaned in, gazing at her intently. "Sometimes we know things that we don't even know we know. Subtle things that may have built up over days, weeks, months. Our brains are amazing sorting-and-cataloging machines. We are not going to arrest someone based on a feeling you had. But we do need to gather all the thoughts of those around the deceased—no matter how tangential." He rocked back. "So. You thought you knew who Mr. Hardy was with. Who was it?"

She fidgeted and sighed but ultimately answered. "His next-door neighbor. *Their* neighbor. Savannah Darwin."

He didn't react. "Okay. Why?"

Damn, he isn't going to give up. "Cate—that's Savannah's wife—found a book in the pool house that Savannah had left. And I found some long red hairs on a sofa cushion. I knew she'd been in the pool house when I was out." Riley shrugged. "But lots of people came over to swim. It's not like the pool house was mine."

Detective Hortense flipped through a stack of papers. "Cate Rosemond and Savannah Darwin," he said almost to himself. "Officers talked to them last night." He looked at Riley, frowning. "Ms. Darwin is not a lesbian?"

"I assume bisexual," she said, holding up her palms. "But I have no idea. That's why I didn't want to guess."

"Fair enough." He slapped the papers onto the island and wrote in his notebook. "Okay, back to last night. Please continue with what happened after you were awakened by sounds from the living room."

"May I... is it okay if I get more coffee?"

"Of course."

He watched as Riley reheated her mug in the microwave then added more from Mikala's pot. She felt dizzy so she popped two pieces of wheat bread into her toaster.

"Can I get you anything?" she asked.

He shook his head. She returned to her stool with steaming coffee and two pieces of dry toast on a paper towel. Her hands were shaking as she bit voraciously into the toast.

"Last night," he prompted. "After you were awakened...?"

She finished chewing and guzzled the hot coffee. "I got out of bed and opened my bedroom door. I was still trying to make sense of it, I guess, and then I saw a figure in the kitchen doorway. He, or she, started to raise an arm, and there was a gunshot." She paused, remembering. "But I'm not sure the gunshot came from the kitchen doorway. Or if it did, that it was the only gunshot. It sounded like it came from a different direction." She threw up her hands again. "Or I could be mixing the whole thing up with thunder. And lightning flashes. The storm was going on at the same time." She looked him in the eye. "I'm sorry."

"Nothing to be sorry about. You're doing fine." He crossed his legs. "Miss Masterson, do you own a gun?"

That surprised her. "What? Well, yes."

"And where it is?"

"In the glove compartment of my car."

"Do you mind if we take a look?"

Riley felt the hairs bristle on the back of her neck. *Does he know something I don't?* "I... I guess not."

He smiled. "Let's go, then. Got your keys?"

She shoved a hand into her backpack and pulled them out. Detective Hortense opened the patio door, and they walked by the pool and around to the driveway without speaking. She unlocked the Beetle's passenger-side door. An uneasy feeling churned through her stomach, and it was hard to tell what was a hangover and what was trepidation. She opened the glove compartment. The gun was not there.

She whirled on Detective Hortense. "Did you take it?"

He looked at her curiously. "Your car door was locked."

"But I did not move my gun!" She heard her voice escalating. Things were spinning out of control again. *Rayanne.* Rayanne must have taken it. But she hadn't used it.

Riley half expected Detective Hortense to slap handcuffs on her, but his tone remained conversational. He walked her toward the backyard as her mind buzzed, trying to figure out what Rayanne had done. They were silent until they reentered the kitchen and settled onto their island stools.

"Last night, your cousin Mikala mentioned that all Alabama girls own guns," he said. "She does. That's why I thought you might too."

"Y-Yeah, she's right," Riley stammered. "My dad gave me one when I started college. But I've never used it except on a range." He said nothing, and this time she did rush to fill the silence. "Detective, I swear I did not move that gun. I carried it more to appease my dad than because I wanted it."

"Speaking of your family in Alabama..."

Oh no, here it comes. He'd found out about Silas. She hoped her face reflected calm, but her stomach cramped painfully. She shoved the toast aside.

"We read about your relationship with a murder victim in Alabama a year and a half ago. A Mr. Silas Hightower." He left the statement dangling.

She took a deep breath and forced herself to calm down. She had learned a few things from Detective Washburn. *Don't speak until you're ready*.

She breathed again and sipped from her coffee cup. "Then you know I wasn't charged with anything."

"That's right. But a funny thing struck me as I read the news accounts last night."

She cut her eyes to his. "Funny?"

"Not funny, ha ha. Funny, odd." He paused. "I didn't read anything about a sister who looks so much like you. Not one word."

Riley didn't trust herself to speak. There was no Rayanne to protect anymore, though she supposed she would like to protect her memory for Mama and Daddy. But not at her own expense. Not anymore.

"Can you explain that?" Detective Hortense asked.

"No." She swallowed convulsively. "I guess you'd need to ask the police down there."

"Well, now is your chance." The voice boomed as the patio door flew open. A huge figure loomed there, all shoulders and muscle blocking the morning light. A figure from Riley's nightmares.

Javon Hortense twirled on his stool and stood.

"Detective Hortense, I presume," said the familiar Alabama drawl—the hated Alabama drawl. "Your office sent me over. I'm Detective Miller Washburn of the Mobile County Sheriff's Office."

Chapter 47

Patrick

Patrick entered the kitchen in time to see Riley Masterson's face go completely white. Javon had his back to her, so Patrick rushed over in case she toppled off her stool. She glanced at Patrick, and he saw her strain to regain her composure. He almost felt sorry for her.

Javon introduced him to the hulking man in the doorway, and the man thanked Javon for last night's call. Everything about Miller Washburn screamed law enforcement—bristle haircut, bulging muscles that had known a steroid or two, curled lip. The Greenbrier police had his type, and Javon and Patrick had run afoul of them more than once. Washburn stuck out a giant hand and shook Patrick's with a hard grip. Unnecessarily hard.

Patrick's eyes darted to Riley, who was not even half Washburn's size, and he battled a smile. She'd beat Washburn once, and the Mobile detective was aching to get another shot at her. Javon offered the visitor a seat then coolly repeated the question Patrick had overheard him pose to Riley.

"Detective Washburn, why was there no mention of Rayanne Masterson in the coverage of the Silas Hightower case? There was so much about Riley Masterson and your witness who saw her. I find it odd that the entire case depended on an eyewitness account, and there was a virtual twin to your suspect who was never mentioned." Javon's expression was open and relaxed. He might have been inquiring about the weather.

Washburn flushed an unhealthy red. "That's what I'd like to know." He stared at Riley. "Miss Masterson, was there a reason you never mentioned that your sister looked so much like you?"

"You never asked," she said. "I guess I thought you knew. There were pictures at Mama's house. You were there quite often."

"As I recall, those pictures showed a scraggly little blond kid."

"She grew up."

"You led us to believe she lived in Panama City, Florida."

"Sh-She did," Riley stammered. "Back then, she did."

"But you neglected to say she'd recently been in Mobile. And I presume on Dauphin Island."

Riley didn't respond.

Washburn turned to Javon and Patrick. "Entirely my fault. I was so focused on this one that I didn't think she might have been covering for someone." He slapped his thighs with his meaty palms. "Well, I've already stopped by your coroner's office and obtained Rayanne Masterson's fingerprints and sent them to Mobile. My colleague there will compare them with the unidentified print we have on the murder weapon."

Patrick saw Riley's shoulders sag. *Has she been protecting her sister all this time?*

"A fish knife, right?" asked Javon.

"Right." Washburn glared at Riley. "But even if there's a match, I'll still have lots of questions about how the Misses Masterson ended up at another murder scene."

Javon and Patrick looked at each other. Patrick knew that his partner didn't like the bullying Miller Washburn any more than he did. But Washburn had a point. There were too many coincidences for Patrick's taste too.

Chapter 48

Cate

Cate was drinking her fourth cup of coffee in her palatial kitchen, drumming her fingers on the marble-topped island and mindlessly jiggling a bare leg. Police officers had spoken to her briefly the night before, gathering preliminary information. She claimed she'd been alone, watching television, and heard only thunder, no gunshots. Though no one had asked yet, she decided she'd been viewing cable news. She caught up that morning—an approaching hurricane in the Gulf, a mass shooting at a warehouse in Colorado, a sexual harassment charge by a Congressional aide.

She assumed that no one had seen her behind the Hardys' pool house and that her bare footprints hadn't survived the downpour. But she couldn't make sense of Savannah's behavior. A minute after Cate had ducked through the patio door, frantically drying her gun, Savannah had burst through the front door. She was drenched, her long red-gold hair as wet as if she'd stepped from the shower, her clothes sticking to every part of her body. She and a similarly sodden Cate stared at each other, wordless, until Savannah whirled and ran up the stairs.

When police arrived, Savannah was in the shower, and all their wet clothes were in the washing machine. Cate was in her pajamas, her dripping hair combed to look freshly washed. The scene in their household, she hoped, had looked like a normal weeknight for night owls.

But Cate's mind was running in circles. *Where was Savannah last night?* Cate had been so sure she was with Luke. But Savannah claimed she'd been caught under an awning for half an hour, waiting out the worst of the storm. *Did I get everything wrong?*

Isaiah entered the kitchen, stretching and yawning.

Oh my gosh, she thought with a jolt. *The first day of school. Did I let him oversleep?* No, it was only seven o'clock.

"Good morning." Her voice came out as a squeak, and she cleared her throat. "Would you like bacon and eggs?"

"Sure."

"Honey? Did you hear the sirens last night?" She'd found him in bed with his headphones on. Hoping he was asleep, she'd closed his door.

"Sirens? On our street?"

"Yes. I have some bad news. Luke and Rayanne were shot and killed last night. In the pool house."

Isaiah gawped at her then began firing questions. "Rayanne? What do you mean? Why would she be in the pool house?" He strode to the patio door and squinted into the Hardys' yard, mumbling, "I thought..." Then he went still. "So what happened exactly?"

Cate paused from scrambling eggs to hold up her wooden spoon. "Riley and Mikala are all right. I saw them walk across their yard this morning. The police canvassed the neighbors last night and said detectives may come back to see us today."

Isaiah whirled around, searching the downstairs. "Where's Savannah Mom?"

"Still sleeping, I guess. We were up late. Obviously." They heard a bump upstairs, and Cate gave him a weak smile. "Well, no, she's up."

"I can't believe this. Luke and *Rayanne*? I mean, had they been swimming?" He interrupted himself. "No, there was a storm. What were they doing?"

Cate didn't answer, and the truth apparently dawned on Isaiah.

"Oh." He murmured again in disbelief, "Luke and *Rayanne*? Then they shot each other?"

Cate handed him a filled plate. "I don't think so. The police are looking for an intruder. They asked if we'd seen anyone."

She recalled the two officers eyeing their pajamas and wet hair once Savannah had gotten out of the shower. They didn't seem surprised that the women had heard nothing because of the storm. But then, they didn't show surprise at anything.

She perched on a stool to watch Isaiah eat. "We'll probably know more by the time you get home from school."

He nodded, his mouth full, then swallowed. "It's so weird. I mean, Luke and Rayanne. I wonder if Riley knew about them." He paused. "Wait a minute. Was Riley there? I thought she was working last night."

Cate shook her head. "I don't know."

He finished eating and carried his empty plate to the sink. "I'll come straight home," he said, gazing at the pool.

Yellow and green leaves clogged its surface as well as the surrounding patio. The storm had left a mess. In front of their potting shed, a milk can lay on its side, spilling geraniums across the miniature porch.

"Storm got your flowers," he pointed out.

Savannah waited until Isaiah had retreated to his bedroom before she appeared downstairs, dressed for work. "Were you able to sleep?" Cate asked.

Savannah poured a glass of orange juice. "Some. How about you?"

"Not at all."

Savannah enveloped Cate in her arms and pulled her close. "I'm so sorry."

Cate tensed. "For what?"

"That this... intruder has *intruded* on our lives. Made us feel unsafe in our own home."

Cate stared at her. Savannah continued. "First, that attack on the Crescent Trail. Now this. The neighbors will be up in arms about the homeless. No doubt, there will be another neighborhood meeting this weekend."

Cate was speechless. Then she found her voice. "You think a homeless person killed Luke and Rayanne?"

"Don't you?"

"I guess... I guess I thought it might be personal."

"Personal? Luke, maybe. But Rayanne hasn't been here long enough for anybody to hate her." She chuckled. "Well, except Mikala."

Cate was confounded. She thought suddenly of the notes she'd received and knew she would have to share them with police. "Um, Savannah, there's something I need to tell you."

She led the way to their formal living room and pulled down a leatherbound copy of the collected works of Shakespeare. No danger of Savannah stumbling across the messages there. Cate handed over the wrinkled notebook pages and watched as Savannah read them, her face flushing.

"When did you get these? Why didn't you tell me? Do you know who they're from?" Savannah narrowed her eyes. "You didn't give her money, did you?"

"No, no." Cate shook her head. "I didn't pay her. I didn't call the police. I didn't do anything."

Savannah waved the pages angrily. "Cate! What were you thinking?"

She bowed her head. "Isaiah knows."

"You told Isaiah and not me?"

"Not exactly. He overheard me yelling about them."

Savannah tried not to smile but couldn't help it. "Well, that's more like it." She hugged Cate again. "I can't believe you kept this to yourself. But you have to tell the police. Who knows what this insane person could have done? I mean, maybe she was coming after us and got the wrong house."

Cate looked up in alarm. She recognized that the police would want to know about anything out of the ordinary, but she hadn't considered that their blackmailer could be a murderer. *Could she?*

Maybe Cate had been naïve about the threat the homeless encampments posed and that so many of their neighbors feared. Maybe a stranger *had* targeted Cate's wife, assuming—as Cate had—that Savannah would be in the pool house.

"I'll tell them." Cate looked out the living room window and saw three men in plain clothes leaving Mikala's house and heading toward their front door. "Here they come now."

Chapter 49

Patrick

On the way to the Rosemond-Darwin house, Javon filled Patrick in on what Riley had said—that she'd expected to find Savannah Darwin, not Rayanne, on the couch beneath Luke Hardy.

Patrick stopped abruptly. "Savannah Darwin, the developer?" he asked, pointing to the resplendent white house with Charleston porches. "*This* developer?"

"Yep."

"Curiouser and curiouser," Patrick murmured. "You want to get Ms. Darwin alone and ask about it?"

"Yep."

"What are you ladies gabbing about?" called Miller Washburn from behind them.

Javon shot a look over his shoulder. "Lord, put him on a bus back to 'Bama," he muttered.

The women were waiting for the detectives and escorted them into the living room. Patrick noted that the heavy draperies, thick rugs, and steel sculptures were formal in a way that many homeowners had moved away from, especially those with teenagers. But it looked like this house was big enough to include seldom-used rooms.

"Can your son join us?" Patrick asked.

"He slept through the whole thing," said Cate. "He didn't learn about it until this morning."

"I'd still like to hear from him."

"Very well."

Very well? He supposed she spoke this way because they were in the formal living room—or maybe they called it the drawing room.

Instead of calling up the stairs, Cate climbed them and returned moments later with a good-looking young man carrying a backpack.

"Oh, right," Patrick said. "First day of school, right? I'm missing that with my six-year-old."

"I'm sorry," said Savannah. "That's something you'll never get back, Detective."

Patrick noted Savannah's sunny smile and over-the-top glamor. He'd heard from the community officers that she had charisma. Isaiah sat close to his other mother and didn't glance at Savannah. *What is going on here?*

Savannah spoke again. "My wife has something to tell you."

All three men swung their eyes to Cate. She retrieved some pages from the coffee table and handed them to Javon. He scanned them and passed them to Patrick, who read the misspelled letters demanding money for the writer's silence concerning "Isiah." Patrick paused before showing them to Miller Washburn.

"Where did you get these?" Patrick asked.

Cate's hands were shaking. "I got the first one on the third of July. I remember because there was a block party going on right out front."

"And it was left where?" he repeated.

"In our mailbox."

"Did you call the police?" Patrick was fairly sure of the answer.

"No. I probably should have, but I didn't."

"And I take it from the subsequent letters that you didn't leave five thousand dollars in your hedge either?"

"That's right. I didn't."

"And when did you receive the other letters?" Patrick asked.

"I'm not sure of the specific dates, but maybe three weeks apart? The last one was a week ago. Then Isaiah... learned about them, so there was no need to pay her off." She gripped her son's leg.

"Ms. Rosemond, did you think the letters were really from your son's biological mother?"

"I guess I did."

"Can you tell me why? It seems quite a stretch."

She glanced at Isaiah, who was studying the floor. "Well, when we adopted Isaiah, the Department of Social Services told us he was born to a Black father and a white mother who were homeless. In Greenbrier. It seems like a good many of Greenbrier's homeless live in this area. I guess it's something..." She raised her head and looked from Javon to Patrick. "It's something I've feared since moving here."

"Cate!" Savannah interrupted. "You never told me that."

"Actually, I did. You thought I was being ridiculous." She recoiled at the hurt in Savannah's eyes. "I wanted to believe you were right. You were so passionate about this neighborhood."

"And you too! You have so many design jobs here."

When Cate spoke again, her voice was so low the detectives had a hard time making it out. "I should have spoken up more clearly."

Patrick and Javon exchanged looks. There would be a discussion in this house tonight—that was for sure.

Isaiah and Cate left for school. Isaiah protested that he could drive alone, but his mother claimed the principal wanted to speak to her about a landscaping project. It was clear that she wanted to calm her son's fears before his school day. Patrick dispatched Detective Washburn to the Law Enforcement Center since their conversation with Savannah would have nothing to do with Riley's earlier case. Then Patrick and Javon trailed her into the kitchen, where she offered them coffee. They accepted, not because they wanted it but to put Savannah at ease.

She dimpled. "Clearly, gentlemen, you want to speak to me alone. What can I help you with?"

"We want to know about your affair with Luke Hardy," said Javon. Savannah tensed and fiddled with the coffee maker, taking her time to fill three mugs. They waited her out, knowing that she was calculating how much they knew.

"Can we keep this between us?" she finally asked. "I'd prefer that Cate and Mikala not know."

"If we can," Javon answered. "But in a murder investigation, that's not always possible."

Savannah closed her eyes and joined the detectives at the island. "All right. Yes, we were having an affair."

"When did it begin?" Javon asked.

"This spring."

"Where did you get together?"

"The first time was in his office. I was in and out of there quite often on business. That first time, we were celebrating a large sale. It... just happened and surprised us both, I think."

"And you continued to meet in his office?"

"A few times. But it was too dangerous. We started meeting in his pool house. After dark, there was no chance of Mikala going in there. And even after Riley moved in, she worked nights."

"Where did you tell Ms. Rosemond that you were?" Javon asked.

Looking miserable, Savannah shifted on her high-backed stool. "Sometimes, I said I was working late. I'd park near the post office on West Roosevelt and go straight to the pool house. Other times, I'd go out for a run and circle back."

"That strikes me as more dangerous than meeting in Mr. Hardy's office," Javon said.

Savannah shrugged. "You may be right. But of course, it wasn't all that often." She paused. "How did you know?"

"We are not at liberty to say. But you can see the implications."

Savannah frowned. "What do you mean?"

"Well, you and Luke Hardy were having an affair. Someone killed Luke and, ah... a sexual partner in the pool house, where you usually met."

Savannah gaped at the men. "Are you saying someone was trying to kill *me*?"

"We're asking you. Is that possible? People might have seen you walking from the post office to the pool house or pretending to jog and circling back to the pool house."

Savannah shook her head in confusion.

"Ms. Darwin," said Javon, leaning forward, "we've heard that some of the neighbors are quite angry with you. The older residents think you are taking advantage of them. The newer residents accuse you of lying about the neighborhood's safety. One of them may have tracked your movements."

"No, that's crazy! Every developer in the city goes through this." She pointed a finger at them. "As soon as you make an arrest in that damn Crescent Trail attack, this will blow over."

"Will it?" Javon asked. "Or will it escalate because of Luke Hardy and Rayanne Masterson's murders?"

Savannah's hostility fell away. "I have to admit that I thought a transient might have killed them. But I was thinking drugs. Or robbery. I had no idea it had anything to do with me." She furrowed her brow and tossed her curls behind one shoulder. "In fact, I *don't* believe it has anything to do with me."

Patrick and Javon watched her in silence. She met their eyes.

Javon spoke softly. "Tell us, Ms. Darwin. What did you think when you learned Luke Hardy was with Rayanne Masterson?"

Her face reddened. She straightened her back and raised her chin. "I was shocked."

"Last night, you told us you went out for a run and got caught in the storm."

"Yes. Luke and I hadn't made plans to see each other. Clearly, he had other plans, as it turned out." She drew her shoulders back. "Anyway, I spent close to thirty minutes under the overhang at the post office. That lightning scared me."

"Did anyone see you?" Javon asked.

Savannah stared at him then smiled self-deprecatingly. "No. Everybody else had more sense than to be out in the storm."

When she didn't continue, Javon changed tacks. "Back to Rayanne Masterson. You have no idea how long Mr. Hardy had been seeing her?"

"How could I?" she snapped. "I didn't know he was seeing her at all." She paused, visibly checking her anger. "I mean the girl was living in his house. It could have started anytime, I suppose."

"What did you think of Rayanne Masterson?"

She snorted. "I didn't think of her at all. My son, Isaiah, is a friend of Riley, but I'd hardly seen her sister." Her eyes narrowed and she leaned back. "I don't mind telling you I wouldn't have thought she was in Luke's league. I guess I've learned my lesson." Savannah blinked and stared at Javon and Patrick. Her shoulders slumped. "Look, I've been silly. And wrong. I'm embarrassed by this whole debacle, and I would very much appreciate it if Cate and Mikala didn't find out."

Javon rose, so Patrick did the same. "We can try, Ms. Darwin," Javon repeated. "But we can't promise anything."

At the door, Patrick turned as if he'd thought of something. "Is there a gun in the house, Ms. Darwin?"

"Yes, two. I have one beside our bed, and Cate has one for work. For snakes. She keeps it in an upstairs safe."

"Could we see them, please?" Patrick asked.

"I suppose."

The men followed Savannah up the stairs and into an expansive master suite decorated in cool gray and white. She opened a bedside table drawer and showed him the revolver inside. Javon placed it inside a plastic evidence bag. She then knelt in front of a safe in the closet and spun the dial. She reached for a pearl-handled pistol, what Patrick would call a peashooter, but he stopped her.

"Don't touch it!" He pulled out another evidence bag and used a pen to convey the pistol from the safe into the bag. From what he could smell, neither gun had been fired recently.

Chapter 50

Mikala

Mikala flung herself face down on the comforter in her master bedroom. She was trembling. Though she had plotted it for so long, nothing about Luke's murder had gone as planned. First, her husband had been with Rayanne, not Savannah.

The little tramp. What did Luke see in her? And is that how Rayanne repaid my hospitality?

Savannah had hijacked her original plan of dangling the compromised Riley in front of her husband, but even that could have worked—until Rayanne showed up. Mikala thought she'd handled it by hustling Rayanne away from the lovers' rendezvous and into the main house. She'd never dreamed Luke would be attracted to the common little minx.

Second, Riley was supposed to be finishing her shift and walking home from Pizza by the Park with no alibi. Instead, she was in her bedroom. That was a shock, but it could have worked to Mikala's advantage—if Riley hadn't recognized her in the kitchen doorway. *Or did she?*

Third—and this was the biggie—someone else had fired two shots. *Who was it? Riley?* Now, that would be truly ironic. Or maybe it was a bona fide intruder, targeting Savannah. Mikala thought of the angry faces at the last neighborhood meeting, the drawing of Farrah Newell's rapist on the orange fliers, and the old mill-village resident who'd accused Savannah of carpetbagging. Mikala shuddered. She could have been killed herself.

Mikala was quite sure her alibi would hold up. She'd tossed her head and chatted enough with the theater employees to establish her presence during the movie showing. The wild card was Riley, who might have recognized Mikala in the kitchen doorway. But maybe the pool house had been dusky enough to obscure her.

If Mikala's initial narrative took root, it wouldn't matter. Riley would be labeled a twice-suspected murderer, and no one would believe it was coincidence. No one would believe that Mikala had been there.

Mikala was gratified to hear that the big lunk had arrived from the Mobile County Sheriff's Office. Greenbrier officers had made the connection to the Dauphin Island murder more quickly than she would have thought. All she needed to do now was lie low and let the investigation proceed.

She crossed to her walk-in closet and began pulling together black ensembles. After all, she was a widow. Not a black widow, exactly, since her plan had gone awry. More like a shimmering-silver widow.

Chapter 51

Caleb

Caleb woke up wet and miserable on the porch of the boarding house. His muscles ached from the plank floor, and a splinter had made its way into one palm. He stumbled into the kitchen to make coffee.

Between the previous night's unnerving gunshots and people scrambling through the darkness, he hadn't dared return to the potting shed. It was the first time he'd departed without cleaning up, and he worried about what he'd left behind.

After witnessing the blood-bath scene through the rear window of the pool house, Caleb had dashed to the boarding house and mingled with his ex-roommates as sirens wailed. He listened to their absurd theories, which circulated along with a whiskey bottle.

"Luke Hardy was Mafia."

"No, he was an undercover DEA agent."

"No, the Hardys were in Witness Protection, and they were discovered."

Unfortunately, Freddy had joined the midnight festivities. "Hey, Caleb, that's where you swim, ain't it?" he proclaimed loudly. "Caleb's girlfriend lives there."

Six faces swiveled to study him. "So that's where you got to, is it?" said a middle-aged man whose mouth was filled with rotted black stumps. "Not bad."

"She's not my girlfriend. I work with her—that's all." Caleb sized up the room then added, "I wish."

The men laughed. "Where you been livin', then, Caleb?" asked one.

The lie came easily. "Camping out beyond the mission."

Nods all around. They'd been there. No one asked why he continued to hang around the boarding house. The whiskey was more interesting.

Seeking Caleb's attention, Freddy pulled on his sleeve. "It's been busy tonight. Even Mr. Meadows was here."

"He was?" Caleb was getting ready to ask why the landlord was out so late, but through the kitchen window, he saw police officers fanning out to the potting shed and to the houses on Montreat.

Afraid to wait another minute, he slipped to the front porch then took off running to the yard across the street. He passed alongside a house, tripping in the dark, then crossed another yard to emerge onto an artery that took him to Calhoun Boulevard. He walked for three miles to an apartment complex built around an old swimming lake. He'd hurled his mother's gun into its depths. He was a homeless man with a sex conviction who lived within ten feet of the site of a double homicide. Possession of an unregistered gun would only have meant trouble.

Back in the boarding house kitchen, coffee in hand, Caleb swung open the door and peered through the eerie green light left by the storm. Limbs and twigs littered the Hardys' yard, and bright-yellow police tape crisscrossed the pool-house doorway. In the distance, through the space between Isaiah's house and the Hardys', he could see a black Ford SUV—the choice of Greenbrier plainclothes officers—parked on Gunter.

Caleb shivered, though the air was moist and warm. They would come for him soon. He'd spent too much time at the Hardys' pool to avoid being questioned. He'd gotten rid of his mother's gun just in time.

Chapter 52

Patrick

It didn't take Patrick and Javon long to track down Caleb March. His employer, the same Roman Baxter who employed Riley Masterson, had his address listed as a boarding house on Montreat Avenue. But the residents assured the detectives that while Caleb hung out frequently, he hadn't lived there since June.

Patrick left word at the Greenbrier Gospel Mission and Trinity Faith Center. He contacted their colleague Jeff Jordan, the neighborhood's uniformed community officer. Officer Jordan located Caleb moving his Honda across the lot at the public library and offered to drive him to the Law Enforcement Center to meet the detectives.

Patrick greeted Caleb, who was a lanky beanpole with short blond hair. He was rumpled and sported a stale scent that Patrick associated with people who slept outside. He also looked scarcely out of his teens. Patrick was surprised that he and the luminous Riley Masterson were friends.

The name Caleb March niggled at Patrick's memory, and it hit him when the young man walked in. "Jeff," he called before the officer exited the lobby. "Wait up." He continued once they were out of Caleb's hearing. "Wasn't March the name Rathsburg was looking for? Next of kin on that dead homeless woman off the trail?"

"Yeah, I think so. I'll find him and send him in."

Patrick and Javon settled Caleb in a small room and gave him a Pepsi and a large Snickers bar. In their experience, young men his age were bottomless pits of hunger. Patrick could tell that Caleb was nervous but trying to hide it.

"So, Caleb," Javon began. "Where are you living?"

"I was at the mission for a year then a boarding house on Montreat another year. And now... now, I'm camping out, you know? Saving money."

"Camping where?"

"Way out in the woods on the far side of Roosevelt Park."

"You live near anybody we might know?" Javon asked.

"No, by myself."

"In a tent?"

"I wish, man. Just a blanket."

A sharp rap on the door made Caleb jump. Officer Oliver Rathsburg passed a note to Patrick, eyeing Caleb as he did so. Patrick read the name on the paper but allowed Javon to continue his questions.

"You work at Pizza by the Park with Riley and Rayanne Masterson?"

Caleb twisted the Pepsi can nervously. "Yeah. But I was there a long time before they came."

"Roman Baxter speaks highly of you," interjected Patrick.

"That's good to know."

"And you spent a lot of time this summer with Riley? At her pool house?" Patrick continued, smoothly taking over.

Caleb was sweating. "Yeah. She's real nice. She says me and Isaiah—he lives next door to her—are like her brothers."

"Is that right?" Patrick leaned across the table. "You realize that Riley thinks you still live in the boarding house on Montreat."

Caleb's response was barely a murmur. "Yeah."

"So you lied to her?"

"Well, I *was* living in the boarding house when I met her. I never told her I moved out. But I needed to save money. I was afraid it might freak her out if she knew I was sleeping in the woods."

"I see." Patrick shifted in his seat. "Did you ever spend the night in the pool house? On the couch maybe?"

"What? No! No."

Patrick observed his vehemence and decided he was telling the truth. "What we are curious about, Caleb, is who could have known that Luke Hardy and Rayanne Masterson would be at the pool house last night."

"I don't know."

"Did you know they were seeing each other?"

"No."

"You never saw Mr. Hardy pick up Rayanne at Pizza by the Park, anything like that?" Patrick asked.

"No."

Patrick changed directions. "Did you like Rayanne, Caleb?"

He squirmed in his seat. "She was okay, I guess. But not really."

"Why not?"

"I think she made Riley unhappy. She kind of barged in where Riley was trying to make a new life for herself, you know?"

"A new life?"

"Yeah, after..." Caleb hesitated.

"We know about the incident on Dauphin Island," Patrick said.

"Yeah, okay, after that. Riley was trying to get over her grief, I guess, and here comes her sister, shoving her way in."

Javon took over. "We know you are a good friend to Riley. But we need to understand the dynamics of the Hardy household. You probably spent more time there than anyone but family. What can you tell us?"

Caleb looked startled. "I was never in the big house."

"But you saw Mr. and Mrs. Hardy at the pool?" Javon asked.

"Mrs. Hardy a few times. Mr. Hardy was always at work."

"You saw Riley and Rayanne interact with Mrs. Hardy. You saw their neighbors come and go. Let's see, Cate Rosemond and Savannah Darwin. You spent considerable time with their son, Isaiah."

Caleb swallowed as if his throat hurt. "You think one of them did it?" His voice was squeaky.

"We are exploring every option."

"I guess I assumed it was someone mad about Mr. Hardy pushing poor people out of the neighborhood. Because of his bank and everything."

The detectives exchanged glances.

Caleb twirled the candy bar on the table. "You know, because of all those neighborhood meetings. Feelings were running pretty high. Even that house he lives in, it was once..." He halted.

"It was once what?" asked Patrick.

Caleb ducked his head, visibly berating himself for bringing it up.

"Caleb?"

"It was once my grandfather's property," he said miserably. "I looked it up and found out my uncles sold it." Caleb raised his eyes and plowed ahead. "I was helping Isaiah on a school project. About gentrification. I showed him how to look up the sale prices of the old mill houses and compare them to values now."

"Speaking of family," Patrick said, waving the paper the officer gave him. "Do you know a woman named Doreen March? We've been looking for next of kin."

Caleb's eyes widened. Clearly, he wasn't expecting the question. "She's... my mother. She lives in Bender."

The detectives remained quiet.

"I left home when I was seventeen." He closed his lips tightly as if willing no more words to emerge.

Patrick and Javon glanced at each other again. Caleb was hiding something. But what? The woman had choked on her own vomit. No foul play was suspected.

"We are sorry to inform you that your mother died," said Javon.

"Died? In Bender?"

"No, she was living in a tent off the Crescent Trail," Patrick said.

"A tent? Huh." Caleb studied his shoes. "Okay."

"You never ran into her? At a Gospel Mission breakfast or something like that?" Patrick asked.

"No. Like I said, I thought she was in Bender."

"We'd like for you to identify the body, and then we can give you her belongings," said Patrick.

"No! No, I don't want anything. We... we weren't close."

"Are there other siblings?"

Caleb appeared confused for a moment. "No. Just me."

Javon scribbled something. "Another thing, Caleb," he said, pulling a sheet from his burnt-orange notebook, which was pebbled like a basketball. "We see here that you're on the registry."

Caleb's shoulders drooped. "Yeah," he said, refusing to meet their eyes.

"Want to tell us how that came about?"

Caleb looked up.

"We know, for instance, it can encompass anything from urinating in public to child molestation."

"Not that! I'm no pedophile." Caleb met Javon's eyes. "I swear. I had an underage girlfriend. I was eighteen, and she was sixteen. But it was consensual. I swear it."

"That's what your mission counselor said too."

Caleb looked startled that the detectives had made the connection to the mission so quickly. They were purposely keeping him off-balance.

"One last question," said Patrick. "Getting back to what you said about Luke Hardy's murder and how some of his neighbors were angry at him. I assume you mean the neighborhood's original residents. Did you hear anyone threaten Mr. Hardy at those meetings? Or anywhere else, for that matter?"

Caleb seemed to relax as the focus shifted off him. "No, his name didn't come up at those meetings."

"So why would you think people were mad at him?"

"Everybody knows he's head of the bank that finances a lot of these houses." Caleb tore the wrapper off the Snickers bar. "But you're right. He's not the one I would've expected to get offed."

Patrick raised his eyebrows. "Is there someone you would have expected?"

"His next-door neighbor. Savannah Darwin is the one everyone is mad at."

After meeting with officers who had canvassed the Hardys' neighborhood the night before, Javon and Patrick retired to a small office to talk.

"That block of Gunter is like *Gunfight at the O.K. Corral*," said Patrick. "Was there anybody we talked to who didn't own a gun?"

"Caleb. Or so he says. But I don't trust that boy. Something twitchy."

Patrick ticked items off with his fingers. "Okay, we've got Mikala Hardy's gun, found in her bedside table. Not fired. Savannah Darwin's gun, found in *her* bedside table. Not fired. Cate Rosemond's gun, found in her home safe. Not fired. And Riley Masterson's gun is missing. Presumably, it was the murder weapon. But where is it? A huge hole in Luke Hardy wants to know."

"As well as a gusher of a femoral artery in Rayanne Masterson," added Javon. "But if you could have seen Riley's face when she opened her glove compartment, you'd not assume that she knows where it is. She seemed genuinely surprised that it was missing. All but accused me of taking it."

Patrick twirled a pencil through his fingers. "But you know, that's not even taking into account how many other gun owners live around the park. That could take weeks to find out."

"That's what our highly paid colleagues are for," Javon said. "We'll send the unis out."

"Then we have the question of intended target. Was someone trying to kill Luke Hardy?" Patrick shuffled some papers. "His wife inherits, but you'd expect that. It looks like he has a substantial life insurance policy and substantial savings. Not to mention that house. He was having an affair, possibly two, but his wife swears she didn't know. And her alibi checks out." He waved a police report from their colleagues. "Two theater employees remember her."

Javon took over. "Riley at least—and maybe others—expected Savannah Darwin to be with Luke. Was *Savannah* the intended target? She was having an affair with Luke Hardy, and I'd bet Cate knew it. But she also angered her neighbors. *And* she and Cate had a blackmailer they refused to pay. Lots of potential shooters could have been after her."

Patrick thought for a moment. "But Savannah had been thwarted too. Replaced by a much younger woman. So she had motive—*if* she knew about Rayanne, that is." He paused. "You know what's tricky about this? Figuring out whether the murders were personal or a result of the tensions in this neighborhood. I mean, look at the meetings they've held this summer. Savannah Darwin and Luke Hardy represent the newcomers who want to get rid of the Gospel Mission and homeless people in general. That could have provoked someone."

Javon smiled. "So Russ Denton?"

"Well, probably not Saint Russ, but yeah, somebody who saw Luke and Savannah as threats to the mission work that has gone on for a long time. Or as a threat to the original residents of this neighborhood." Patrick snapped his fingers. "And there's that boarding house right behind the Hardys'. The people who live there are a half step from being homeless. I bet anybody in there has lived in the woods or at the mission at some point. And they have eyes on the pool house."

"Still. Still," said Javon slowly, "the person who *was* killed was not Savannah but Rayanne Masterson. A visitor to Greenbrier. Not a developer or a banker or even a resident."

Patrick tapped his teeth with his pencil. "According to our friends in Mobile, she may have been a killer herself. Could someone from Silas Hightower's past have arranged this? Is that too far-fetched?"

"Anything's possible, I guess."

The two went quiet, running over the events of the night, letting their minds roam, and making connections.

"You know," said Patrick, "everyone has talked about how Rayanne was not in Luke Hardy's league. Is something there?" He swiveled idly in his chair. "Could she have been running a scheme? Seducing him then threatening to tell Mikala?"

Javon leaned back in his chair, staring at the ceiling. "I like that. Yeah, I like that a lot." He slammed his feet on the floor and stood. "Let's find out all we can about Rayanne Masterson. Was she in debt? Does she have previous arrests? And is that her fingerprint on the knife that killed Silas Hightower on that island off Mobile?"

Patrick smiled. "I say we let Detective Washburn do something useful."

Chapter 53

Riley

Riley barely made it to Mikala's upstairs bathroom before she threw up. It felt like a gallon of acidic coffee gushed from her stomach, but she hoped she was getting rid of last night's tequila too. Her stomach cramped and cramped, and she grasped the pristine toilet, heaving until there was nothing left.

Seeing Miller Washburn in the flesh—as opposed to her nightmares—had sent her reeling. She hadn't shot Luke or Rayanne, she kept reminding herself. But she hadn't stabbed Silas either, and that hadn't prevented eighteen months of harassment. *Am I in for that again?* Her stomach seized at the thought, and she gagged once more over the toilet.

The detectives had instructed her to move into a guest room in Mikala's house because the pool house was a crime scene. She didn't want to be here, and surely, Mikala didn't want her either. But if jail was the alternative, she would gladly choose these lavish digs.

Riley rose shakily to her feet and entered the bedroom Mikala had pointed out. She tossed her backpack onto a floral seafoam-and-taupe comforter. A police officer had watched her pack the night before. Riley had included her black-on-black work uniforms among other random items. But she wasn't sure she still had a job. With Miller Washburn blabbing away, it wouldn't take long for her previous life to become common knowledge in Greenbrier. Would Roman react the way Dino had, with a quick firing?

Riley crawled between the cool, clean sheets of the queen-sized bed, her head pounding. She needed to call Mama and Daddy, but she had to lie down for a moment first. She was sure she wouldn't sleep, but fatigue overwhelmed her. She was too exhausted to wake when the dreams started, so the horrors that usually roused her went on and on. Silas and shrimp boats and sharks. Rayanne and fish knives and blood-soaked couches. Luke and Mikala, thunder and lightning, pool lights and gunshots.

She thrashed and woke but fell back into the dreams then thrashed and woke again. At last, she dragged herself from the lurid sounds and pictures. She lay under Mikala's tray ceiling, panting and sweating as she focused on the thing that had bothered her most during the past twenty-four hours—the moment Detective Hortense had her open the Beetle's glove compartment.

Some parents gave their child a set of luggage or a trip to Europe for high school graduation. Daddy had given her a lightweight Sig Sauer P238. He was proud of the costly pistol.

"I know you can't take it to college," he said, "but when you're living on your own, you'll need it."

She kept it on the top shelf of her childhood closet while commuting to the University of South Alabama. When she moved to Dauphin Island, it went with her, unloaded, in the glove compartment of the Beetle. The magazine rode in the trunk. Obviously, she was conflicted about having a gun at all.

Riley strained to think of the last time she'd seen it. The handgun was as much a part of that cluttered glove compartment as the five-year-old pack of Rolaids, but surely she would have noticed if it *wasn't* there.

She recalled packing for the move from her parents' house to Cousin Mikala's. *Was that only three months ago?* It seemed like a lifetime. She tried to picture herself glancing into the glove compartment. Yes—Daddy had asked if she had her auto insurance card, and she'd checked for it. The gun was inside, nestled in its blue velvet Crown Royal bag. The pistol had made it to Greenbrier.

Only Rayanne could have known that. She'd been up to something. Riley suspected that her endless truck repairs had been a ploy to stay in Greenbrier. *Did it have to do with Luke?*

Riley swung her feet onto the carpeted floor. She was wobbly and needed to eat. She grabbed her phone and saw four missed calls from Mama. Guilt washed over her. The Mobile police would have sent officers to tell her and Daddy about Rayanne. Riley's heart squeezed when she thought of their pain. There was no excuse for not calling them. But dread flooded over her, and she put it off a minute longer.

She exited the guest room onto a gargantuan landing furnished with wing chairs, bookshelves, tables, and wall art, like it was a real room. Next door to her room was Rayanne's, decorated in delicate pink and white like the inside of a conch shell. The police had gone through it, but they didn't know her sister like Riley did.

She surveyed the layout from the doorway. The double bed was sloppily made, and an overflowing suitcase on the floor revealed that Rayanne had never unpacked. A bikini hung from a hook on the closet door.

Ever since she was a little girl, Rayanne's favorite hiding place had been her shoes. Riley had found rocks there as well as seashells and bits of colored glass. Then Mama's earrings, dollars from Riley's babysitting money, and unopened eyeshadow from Walmart.

She bent to search the closet floor. Flip-flops. Sandals. And there—tennis shoes. She reached into the toe of one but found nothing. She tried the other one, and it was empty. Riley sat back on her heels. She'd been so sure.

Her eyes roamed around the closet. A blanket was folded in one corner, and she lifted it to reveal a shoebox. Inside were new purple-and-black tennis shoes, and she wondered if Rayanne had shoplifted them. She reached inside the toe and felt paper—probably the crumpled paper found inside new shoes. But no. She pulled it out and discovered a roll of bills. She snapped off the rubber band and saw that they were hundreds. Dozens of hundred-dollar bills. Her breath quickened.

She fumbled in the toe of the other shoe and found more of the same. She lurched to her feet, livid at Rayanne but also livid at herself for not paying more attention. She'd been trying so hard to stay away from Rayanne that she'd allowed Luke and Mikala to veer into her destructive path.

The money was far more than Rayanne had earned at Pizza by the Park—that was for sure. And it was more than enough to pay for the truck repairs. *What was she up to?*

Riley looked over the room again, breathing heavily, trying to see it through her sister's eyes. She opened the drawer of the bedside table, peered under the bed, and dumped the clothes out of her suitcase. Under the suitcase was a business card, Nichols Auto Repair. She called the number, and when a man answered, she asked about Rayanne Masterson's truck.

"Yeah, the white Ford," he said. "It's been ready. We parked it out front for you to pick up today. Like you said."

"Oh yeah," she stammered. "Thank you."

So Rayanne had planned to leave Greenbrier that day. With thousands of dollars, just as she'd left Dauphin Island. Riley suspected she'd lured Luke into an affair and taken money from him, maybe as a gift but more likely as extortion. Her heart pinched. Luke and Mikala had welcomed Riley into their home, and when Rayanne followed, Riley hadn't remained vigilant.

What did I allow her to do? Riley tried to calm down in order to think. If Rayanne had been extorting money from Luke, he might have wanted to kill her. *But that wasn't what happened, was it?* Rayanne could have taken Riley's gun and precipitated a series of events that led to her own shooting. Or she could have angered someone who then stole Riley's gun to put a stop to her games.

Surrounded by her sister's clothes, Riley dropped onto Mikala's thick carpet. She waited another minute until she'd gained control of her fury and her grief, then she dialed Mama's number. As soon as her mama answered, Riley began to cry.

For Silas. For Luke. For Rayanne. For herself.

Chapter 54

Mikala

Mikala was asleep on the sunroom couch when the doorbell rang. She leapt up, disoriented, and swiped at the drool on the side of her face. She hadn't made it to bed yet, and her body ached with tiredness.

The doorbell rang again, and she shuffled to the front door. Sunlight pierced her eyes, and she frowned.

"I'm so sorry!" exclaimed Joanna Hastings from next door. "Did I wake you?"

Joanna sported a casserole dish in her hands and an expectant look on her face. Beyond her, Mikala saw Margaret Tremont coming up the sidewalk with her famous banana bread. Of course—the food brigade was descending on her. Luke's death would be a huge event, and Mikala hadn't even thought about calling her housekeeper for an emergency cleaning.

She pulled Joanna into the foyer and gestured for Margaret to hurry then flapped her hands to indicate her snarled hair and sweatpants. "Can you two hold down the fort while I shower? Detectives have been here all morning."

"Sure, hon," said Margaret. "You go right on up, and we'll make coffee and iced tea."

Mikala had miscalculated. She'd pictured herself gliding around the funeral home and the Episcopal church, beautifully bereaved, bowing her head, accepting condolences. She'd neglected to plan for the hordes that would descend on her house with food and questions: "How could this happen? And with the cousin you took in? How dare she? But the intruder"—voice lowered to a whisper—"was it one of those homeless people?"

She ran up the stairs and slammed her bedroom door.

Freshly showered, with her face made up and hair pulled into a becoming bun, Mikala felt more human. She selected flowing black trousers and a sleeveless black silk blouse with the tiniest white polka dots. As she slid into the heels the pants demanded, she heard a knock on her bedroom door. She opened it to Riley.

"What's going on downstairs?" Riley whispered.

"The neighbors are bringing food."

"Oh, I guess I forgot about that since it was, you know..." *Murder*, Riley finished, but she couldn't say it out loud.

"Yeah, me too," Mikala said. "But Southern funerals must go on, I suppose." She looked at her cousin's pajama pants and T-shirt. "You may want to put on a dress or something."

"Yeah, right." Riley headed for her room before apparently realizing she hadn't brought anything appropriate from the pool house. Mikala pointed to Rayanne's room. "Borrow hers."

Mikala paused, wondering if she was being too abrupt with Riley. The poor girl had gone through that horrible time in Mobile and now had lost her sister. But what a worthless sister. Riley would be better off in the long run. Besides, Mikala might still need her cousin to take the blame.

Mikala steeled herself and walked down the staircase, a handkerchief in one hand in case she was able to muster tears. She paused at her living room, where a stricken silence fell, and five faces turned to her. Then came a crescendo.

"Mikala, I am so sorry for your loss."

"Luke was such a great guy."

"How can we help?"

Her neighbors surged forward, enveloping her in hugs and perfume. She could feel their kindness but also their curiosity. They were not leaving until they heard some dirt.

She thanked them and headed to the kitchen, hearing whispers in her wake. "Homeless... affair... robbery... drugs."

Joanna and Margaret had been hard at work. Mikala's counters were filled with cakes, pies, cookies, vegetable trays, and plates of sliced bagels. "There's a roast chicken in the fridge," said Joanna. "And yummy pimento cheese. We're freezing the casseroles for now. We didn't know how many of your family are coming."

My family? Dear God. That was another thing she hadn't thought of—Mama and Daddy, of course, but also Luke's sister and brother-in-law and nephews. *And what about Aunt Crystal and Uncle Ed?* She would get Riley to put the kibosh on that by offering to ship Rayanne's body to Mobile. She dropped wearily onto an island stool.

Joanna plopped next to her. "The priest from All Saints called and asked that you call back when you're ready to talk." Mikala looked at her blankly. "About a service," Joanna added.

"He called on my phone?"

"Yes. You left it down here, so I've been taking messages."

"Oh. Thank you." Her brain was sluggish. "Anybody else call?"

Joanna made a face. "It might be easier to tell you who didn't."

"Oh."

"I've written them down. You don't have to return them all. Some even said that. They just wanted you to know they're thinking of you."

Mikala looked helplessly at her neighbor. "I wasn't expecting... I guess I thought all this"—she waved around the kitchen—"would be put off until after the police finish. I don't think they'll release Luke's body for a while."

The doorbell rang. Margaret returned to the kitchen with a young woman carrying a briefcase-sized shoulder bag. Before Margaret could introduce her, the woman offered her hand to Mikala. She said her name, but Mikala heard only "*Greenbrier Herald*."

"There's a TV truck out front too," Margaret whispered.

It turned out Mikala did need the handkerchief, not for grief so much but to hide her horror.

Chapter 55

Cate

Cate steered Isaiah's old Volvo onto Gunter Avenue. He wasn't happy about not keeping his car at school, but she'd assured him she would return to pick him up. She also couldn't face talking to the principal about landscaping, so it was still early when she reentered their neighborhood. Unfamiliar cars were parked in front of Mikala's house.

Her eyes scanned the street and the hundred-year-old oaks and sycamores towering above the homes. If this had ever felt like a peaceful place, it didn't anymore. She wondered about the people behind those windows—what they watched, what they thought. What they knew.

She knew that a malevolent woman had approached their house at least three times, leaving hateful, threatening notes. And that a person with a gun had possibly crossed her side yard to access the Hardys' pool house. The burning question for Cate was whether that person was a stranger or a friend.

She pushed away the memory of her own presence during the evening's violence. Already, she questioned what she'd done and doubted what she'd seen. She would have sworn it was Savannah on the couch beneath Luke when clearly it was not. She'd crammed puzzle pieces into a picture in ways they didn't fit.

Who else might have assumed Savannah would be in the pool house? She thought back to the cryptic conversation—*Was that only yesterday?*—when Mikala, too, had appeared to suspect Luke and Savannah's dalliance. And those critics from the neighborhood meetings. Feelings against Savannah ran high.

Despite her efforts to drag her mind from the image, Cate saw Isaiah's horror-stricken face when Savannah had distanced herself from his Gospel Mission friends. She recalled his growing unease with Savannah's part in the gentrification of their neighborhood and his murmured response that morning: "But I thought..." Like Cate, Isaiah could have suspected Savannah's affair with Luke.

No, no, I won't go there. But could Savannah have been the target?

She pulled the Volvo into the three-car garage and tripped as she got out, her heart pounding at the ugly pictures in her mind. Cate tripped again on the mat in front of the steps to the kitchen. She was exhausted.

Thinking that green space might derail her mind from this relentless loop, she walked through the kitchen into the backyard. On the potting-shed porch, she picked up the milk can the storm had knocked over and carefully patted the geraniums back into place. The blooms should last another two months.

She entered the shed to find a broom to sweep the remaining dirt off the porch. She stood for a moment, puzzled. A flowerpot lay broken in one corner. Her first thought was the cat that stalked their yard. *But how would he have gotten in?*

Her eyes landed on two empty water bottles and several orange granola bar wrappers. Surely, the police hadn't left them. She turned to the miniature porch and considered the antique milk can once more. Perhaps it hadn't been the storm that upended it.

Cate had heard about neighbors who discovered homeless men sleeping in their garages or storage units. This could change everything. Perhaps Luke and Rayanne had been killed by an irate—even mentally ill—homeless person who'd been staying in her potting shed. As frightening as the thought was, it was better than thinking

Savannah had been targeted by an enraged neighbor or by Isaiah's biological mother.

Cate tugged Detective Patrick Marconi's card from her jeans pocket and dialed his number, unsure of what to make of the relief flooding through her.

Chapter 56

Caleb

Caleb was hidden in a thicket beside the boarding house, watching officers descend on the potting shed in Isaiah's yard. This couldn't be good. He saw a uniformed woman carry a suitcase-like apparatus, and he feared it was a fingerprint kit.

He could get into his car and flee. But his savings wouldn't take him far. He thought of driving to Raleigh and cringed. He wouldn't be welcome, especially with the police on his heels.

If the officers determined he had been sleeping in the potting shed, what was the worst he could be charged with—trespassing?

The detectives who'd questioned him downtown emerged from the shed to make room for the fingerprint lady. Both ducked to get out, and he remembered all the mornings he'd crept from the shed, bent double. He inched to the farthermost edge of the tree line, almost into the yard next door, to see what they were doing. To his amazement, they pointed to the milk cans, and a gloved officer carefully upended one, pouring the dirt onto the tiny porch. Isaiah's Cate Mom wouldn't like that. But wait—there she was, arms folded, watching without expression.

Two more officers began walking methodically around Isaiah's yard, poking into the shrubbery with long pointed sticks. *What are they looking for?*

Back at the shed, the officer finished going through the geraniums and dirt from the first can and tipped over the second. Almost immediately, a shout went up, and Detectives Hortense and Marconi rushed over. Caleb leaned away from his tree cover as far as he dared. *What could be in there?* Suddenly Detective Marconi was racing across the yard, headed directly for him. Caleb crouched behind a giant oak, but he'd been spotted.

"Caleb March!" the detective called. "We'd like to speak to you."

Caleb leapt to his feet, wondering if he could outrun him and make it to his Honda parked at the library. Adrenaline surged through him, and he pushed off the tree trunk—and smashed into the chest of Detective Hortense.

"Going somewhere, buddy?" the detective asked.

Back in the same Law Enforcement Center room he had been in that morning, Caleb frantically went over his situation. There was no way the police could connect him to his mother's gun. It was deep in a lake off Calhoun Boulevard. They couldn't know it existed.

Nor was there any way the police could connect him to something in the geranium planters. He'd never touched them until he barreled into one on his way to the pool house last night.

Nor was there any way he could be connected to his mother's tent—at least, he didn't think so.

There was, however, every possibility he could be connected to the potting shed. But it wasn't breaking and entering if a door was unlocked. So again, the only charge would be trespassing. *Right?*

He'd been waiting in the room quite a while. Caleb wiped sweat off his forehead with the bottom of his T-shirt. *What are they doing?* He consciously slowed his breathing.

The door opened, and Detectives Hortense and Marconi entered. They did not offer food or drink this time. He wondered if that was a bad sign. They settled into the chairs across the table from him.

"Afraid we've got bad news for you, Caleb," Detective Marconi said.

He stiffened.

"We've got your fingerprints all over that shed behind the Rosemond-Darwin house. Looks like you've been living there."

Caleb hung his head.

"Want to explain, son?" Detective Hortense said.

"Yeah. I do." Caleb swallowed. "I wanted to save money. That's all. I'd been staying in the boarding house on Montreat for a year, and it was taking all my pay. I needed a car to find my uncles in North Carolina."

Detective Hortense looked interested but said nothing.

"I could see from my bedroom window that no one was using that shed during the summer. So yeah, I sneaked in and slept at night. I'm sorry, but I didn't think I was hurting anything."

"Did Isaiah know?"

"No. No one did."

"When did this start?"

"Maybe the middle of June? I kept almost every penny I would've spent on rent, and I bought a car. A Honda Accord. From the Gospel Mission lot. Your officers have seen it." Caleb knew he sounded desperate.

"Okay, son, I believe you," Detective Hortense said. "But that's two and a half months in a shed in the Rosemond-Darwin backyard. How did you keep from being discovered?"

"I didn't go in until midnight or later, when everyone in Isaiah's house was asleep. And I left before dawn each morning. I was careful to clean up in case Isaiah's mom—the landscaping one—went in."

"But here's the thing," Detective Marconi jumped in. "For some reason, you didn't clean up last night. That's how Ms. Rosemond knew someone had been in there."

Caleb dropped his head again.

"Caleb, what was different about last night?"

He hesitated. Isaiah's Cate Mom, unlike the other one, had always been nice to him. She hadn't made him feel like a piece of gum on her shoe. But he was in trouble.

"I saw something," he whispered.

"What did you see?"

"I saw Isaiah's mom outside the pool-house window."

The detectives glanced at each other in surprise. "Which mom?" asked Detective Hortense.

"The landscaper. With the silver hair."

"What about her being there made you rush from the shed? I assume it was you who knocked over that big can of flowers on the porch?"

Caleb nodded. "I was afraid... she was going to hurt Riley."

Detective Marconi appeared genuinely perplexed. "Hurt Riley? Why would you think that?"

"Well, I didn't think it before or anything. But it was storming, and I looked out the window and saw Ms. Rosemond looking in Riley's window. It looked like she had a gun. I... I was just scared for Riley, and I ran out to help."

The detectives looked skeptical. "So, what happened?" asked Detective Marconi. "Did you confront Ms. Rosemond?"

"She was gone by the time I got there."

The detectives stared at Caleb for a long time. "Why didn't you tell us this when we talked earlier?"

Caleb's voice escalated. "Because I didn't want anyone to know I was staying in the shed!"

Detective Marconi sighed. "Well, Caleb, we might believe you except for a few items we found in the shed."

Caleb's head jerked up. "No, there's nothing in there. What?"

Detective Hortense opened a folder. As soon as Caleb saw the dirty notebook paper, he froze.

The detective pushed it toward him. Caleb didn't need to read it. He could recite it by heart: *Too bad Isiah has to fin out. I gave you ever chance.*

"It looks like you were trying to extort money from Isaiah's mothers," Detective Hortense said.

Caleb shook his head, wondering how much he could say without revealing that he'd been at Doreen's tent. He couldn't think fast enough, and he started to hyperventilate. "No, no, it's not what it looks like. That wasn't me. I swear."

Detective Marconi stretched. "Well, Caleb, here's what we think. We think you became friends with Isaiah during your time at the Hardys' pool. You found out that he was born in Greenbrier to a homeless couple. You saw a chance to add a little to your savings by threatening his mothers. You even told them to put the money under their backyard hedge because you were nearby and could easily pick it up."

Caleb was wagging his head like a metronome. "No, no, no. I know how it looks, but that's not what happened. I'd never do that to Isaiah."

Detective Hortense leaned back in his chair and watched Caleb through slitted eyes.

Detective Marconi pressed on as if Caleb hadn't spoken. "If that's not enough, there is one more thing. We found a gun hidden under the flowers in that can on the shed's porch. Want to guess who it's registered to?"

Caleb sagged with relief. He was safe after all. "I know it's not me."

"No," Detective Marconi agreed. "But just about as good. It's registered to one Henry March. Your late grandfather, I believe?"

Caleb's mouth opened and closed, but he didn't make a sound.

Detective Marconi remained conversational. "Preliminary ballistics show it's the gun that killed Luke Hardy and Rayanne Masterson. You shot them through the living room window."

Chapter 57

Patrick

Patrick and Javon retired to their cubicles, accepting high fives from colleagues who whistled and catcalled in appreciation of an arrest less than twenty-four hours into their case. The two mugged and bowed. But as they huddled over the paperwork, they grew quiet. Caleb had shut down after hearing that his grandfather's gun had been used in the murders, so their questions about motive went unanswered. He was currently being booked.

Patrick sank into his chair. "Obviously, I like Caleb for this. No question. But do you get why he'd kill those two?"

Javon shook his head. "No, I don't. I assume he was targeting Savannah Darwin, maybe for not paying the extortion? But it's a big leap from a five-thousand-dollar extortion to double homicide." He locked his huge hands behind his head. "Maybe rage? Savannah Darwin bought his grandfather's house for pennies, and now the Hardy property is worth—what? Close to a mil? Meanwhile, he's living in a potting shed with no electricity, no AC, no bed even. He saw Luke and Savannah meeting repeatedly in the pool house. And he figured he'd take out the banker and the developer with one blow. Make sense?"

Patrick wagged his hand to indicate *maybe.*

Javon continued. "But he's still hiding something, and for the life of me, I can't imagine what. What is so important that he's willing to go down for two murders?"

"Did you believe him about seeing Cate Rosemond outside the pool house?" Patrick asked.

"Yeah, maybe. If so, she lied to us. We need to circle back to her. Also, we need to find out who removed the window screen. It was propped against the pool house. Had it been like that for a long time? Or did Cate or Caleb remove it that night before he shot through the window?"

Patrick shuffled some papers on his desk. "Here's the info from Miller Washburn we asked for. About Rayanne Masterson." He scanned the sheets. "Woo-eee. This little filly was trouble." He passed the top sheet to Javon. "Gambling debts. A prostitution charge but no conviction. Credit card theft. Conviction but community service. Aggravated assault. Sounds like a cat fight." He read on silently. "Charges in Biloxi, Mobile, and Panama City. That's how she avoided serving time—by spreading out the mayhem."

He smacked the last sheet on his desk. "And the fingerprint on Silas Hightower's knife was hers. Wow. Egg on Washburn's face."

Javon took his time to read through the arrest records then raised his head. "Riley Masterson was protecting her sister that whole time they were leaning on her? Unbelievable."

"And from the looks of it," said Patrick, "a sister who wasn't worth protecting."

The men paused, contemplating the previous investigation, wondering if they would have discovered Rayanne living in Panama City. It was hard to say.

"Okay, loose ends," said Patrick. "What else?"

"I'd like to compare the handwriting on that extortion note we found in the shed. To Caleb's."

"Yeah. And you know what? It seemed to me that Caleb got squirrely—even more than usual—when talking about his mother. Let's look into the death of Doreen March. Maybe she was the link for getting her father's gun into Caleb's possession. And then there's..."

The phone on Javon's desk rang. He seized it and listened closely. "Medical examiner," he mouthed to Patrick. "Are you sure? Hundred percent?" He listened some more. "All right. Thanks for the rush."

Javon swiveled to his partner, shock showing on his face. "You are not going to believe this. The lovely Rayanne didn't bleed out from that bullet to the femoral artery. She was asphyxiated."

Patrick went still, remembering the blood that covered both bodies and a bloody pillow they'd assumed Luke had used in an attempt to staunch their wounds. "That sofa cushion?"

"Yeah, there were traces of her saliva and mucus in addition to all the blood."

They stared at each other. "Luke *smothered* her before they were shot?"

Javon completed a rotation in his chair, taking in this new information. "Could be. Or he was trying to stop the bleeding and passed out and accidentally smothered her before she bled out. He was considerably bigger and heavier than her."

"Given Rayanne's history, I think he did it before." Patrick's eyes widened. "Damn. What was going on with these people?"

Javon reached for the reports from Mobile. "And what was Rayanne up to that finally got her killed?"

Chapter 58

Riley

The news that Caleb was in jail flew through the neighborhood and beat Riley to Pizza by the Park. She reported for work in the late afternoon, not at all sure she still had a job. But Roman greeted her solemnly, even patted her shoulder.

"How're you holding up?" he asked.

Maybe with Caleb's arrest, the attention was off her. For the moment, anyway. "Okay," she told him.

But then he leaned in. "There's an out-of-town police officer to see you. I put him in a rear booth so you can have some privacy."

Riley twisted to see Detective Miller Washburn working on a pepperoni pizza. Her stomach, finally settled after a Coke and a turkey sandwich at Mikala's, convulsed again.

"Take your time," said Roman.

Her hands balled into fists, and she breathed to calm down. The sight of Miller Washburn triggered every horror of the past year and a half. Riley had been convinced she was going to prison, because—despite what her sister had said—Rayanne would not have stepped forward to prevent it.

Filled with dread, Riley approached Detective Washburn's booth. He motioned toward the vinyl-coated bench across from him and wiped his mouth with a napkin. "Please sit."

She slid in, wondering what was coming—an apology or more harassment.

He eyed her over his draft beer. "First of all, we are closing the Silas Hightower case, with your sister, Rayanne, named as the perpetrator. And we *could* pursue a charge of obstruction against you." He waited. When he got no reaction, he sighed. "But none of us really has the stomach for it."

"Will you release the story to the media at home?" She was afraid of what the news would do to her parents.

"Reporters in Mobile already got hold of it. The sheriff has planned a press conference for the minute I get back. And I'm sure reporters up here are trading information with them."

It was Riley's turn to sigh. She supposed there was no getting around it. Silas's murder had been a big story, and Rayanne's murder had raised the stakes. The fact that she'd been killed during a tryst with another murder victim boosted the prurience level. Riley's parents might have to leave Mobile.

"Miss Masterson..." Detective Washburn's voice was gentler than she'd ever heard it. "I'm to blame for not connecting the dots about an out-of-town sister who looked so much like you. That's on me. But I'd like to understand why you were willing to take the heat for her. Her rap sheet indicates she has stolen and hustled for quite some time."

Riley contemplated his question. "It's not that clear-cut," she said slowly. "For one thing, I wasn't sure it was her. Who killed Silas, I mean."

That wasn't true, and he knew it. She wagged her head as if to clear it of lies and started over. It was hard to give him a true answer when she didn't know it herself.

"I guess... I felt responsible even if I didn't do it. I knew Silas was married. And I knew, or should have known, what Rayanne was capable of. It was because of me that he crossed paths with her." Riley raised her palms. "I can't explain it very well."

"It may be inexplicable," he agreed. "Guilt and family and all that." He stared at her. "I still wish you'd been honest with us. When I think of all that wasted time..."

She saw a flash of his old anger. He brought it under control and finished his beer, but he couldn't resist a parting shot. "If we'd stopped Rayanne back then, Luke Hardy might still be alive."

Riley could no longer meet his gaze. It was not lost on her that her silence had allowed Rayanne to spread her poison. Without Riley, Rayanne would never have come to Greenbrier, and Mikala would still have her husband. Luke might have been a cheater, but he'd been kind to Riley. There was no end to her guilt.

"Well, I've got to get on the road," Detective Washburn said with a rap on the table. "I'll leave you to the Greenbrier Police. I hope you'll be more forthcoming with them about what your sister was doing here. But it looks like her lifestyle caught up with her, doesn't it?"

Riley gulped past the lump in her throat. He pulled out his wallet.

"You can pay at the register," she told him then slid from the booth without saying goodbye.

Isaiah came in during her eight thirty break that evening. He filled Riley in on what had led to Caleb's arrest—Cate's discovery that someone was living in their potting shed.

"And the detectives found a letter like the ones left in our mailbox," Isaiah whispered, his voice strangled. "Caleb was the one trying to get money from my moms."

"By claiming to be your birth mother? That doesn't sound like him at all."

"I know."

Isaiah was focused on Caleb's letter writing, but Riley was bothered by another aspect of his stay in the shed. *Was he watching me through the rear window of the pool house?* After she'd ascertained that it faced an empty shed, she hadn't worried about it—until last night, when she saw Caleb's ghostly face. From the shed's darkened interior, he could have watched her every night that summer. She shivered.

"Creepy, I know," Isaiah said, misinterpreting her discomfort.

"Do you think he shot Luke and my sister?" she asked. "I wouldn't have guessed that in a million years."

Isaiah shrugged. "Me either. I overheard my moms talking. They think he was after Savannah Mom. Because of her buying his granddad's property."

Riley looked at Isaiah without speaking. So he knew that Caleb had expected Luke to be with Savannah.

"Yeah, I've heard the rumors," he affirmed with a grimace.

She thought about Caleb targeting Savannah. It made sense, she supposed. Especially if it turned out that Caleb was trying to blackmail Savannah and she wasn't paying.

But it's Caleb. Aside from Farrah, he was her only real friend in Greenbrier. The one she'd taught to drive. The one who had her back at the restaurant. The one who spent all summer by the pool, talking about buying a car, getting a GED, and working his way out of the boarding house.

Well, that turned out to be a lie, didn't it? He didn't even live in the boarding house.

Isaiah looked pensive. "I wonder if it was because of my project. Seeing all those old sale prices for the mill houses and their current values."

"He was looking into that before you started your project," she pointed out. "It was Caleb who got *you* interested."

"Anyway, there's *another* neighborhood meeting tomorrow. The fact that Caleb was homeless has everyone up in arms about the

Gospel Mission again. Channel 5 led with it. 'Homeless man arrested in killing of Roosevelt Park banker and guest.'"

"I'm sorry." Riley didn't know what else to say. She was sorry for drawing Luke into Rayanne's destructive orbit. Sorry for introducing her to Caleb. Sorry for introducing her to Silas. Sorry she hadn't intervened when Rayanne started stealing. Sorry she hadn't confided her suspicions to Mama and Daddy. Sorry she hadn't loved her sister.

"I gotta get home," Isaiah said.

Roman and Gus offered to walk Riley home at the end of her shift, but she told them no. Ironically, the person who used to accompany her was the one charged with double homicide. She couldn't believe Caleb had done it. She *didn't* believe it.

Now that her shift was over, she drooped with fatigue. She'd gotten no sleep the night before. She walked slowly toward Mikala's house, her sweat cooling in the September night, which had been swept free of humidity. She stopped under a streetlight and thumbed open the *Greenbrier Herald* website on her phone. A story posted twenty minutes earlier had pushed Caleb's arrest to second place.

Second murder victim was smothered, coroner says. She read the story then read it again. And again. Rayanne had been killed by asphyxiation, not the gunshot. The story didn't say so but strongly hinted that Luke had done it. Police had been confounded by a bloody sofa pillow between the victims, and they'd originally speculated that Luke had used it to stem the blood flow from their wounds.

She thought back to Detective Washburn's last words and wondered if she should tell the Greenbrier police about the money she'd found in Rayanne's closet. It would explain Luke's motive, though she wasn't sure Mama and Daddy could take the added smear of Rayanne's name.

Riley pulled up the *Mobile Press-Register*'s website and scanned the stories about Rayanne and Silas. She saw his face, and for a moment, her heart faltered. She saw her own face side by side with Rayanne's, and read Detective Washburn's admission that Mobile officers hadn't understood there was a lookalike sister who lived in Florida. Reporters had also uncovered Rayanne's arrest record. There was nothing Riley could do to make things worse.

She paced beneath the streetlight then came to a decision. It was time to look after Riley. She pulled Detective Hortense's card from her jeans pocket and called his cell phone.

"I have something you need to see," she said. "About my sister... I wasn't sure before. But I think it will explain things."

"What is it?" he asked. She heard knocks and bumps and suspected she had awakened him.

"Money. Hidden in her closet. Thousands of dollars."

"I'll be right over."

As Riley hurried to Mikala's house, she thought about her sister's death. It made sense that her stealing and greed had finally caught up with her. Silas had been blindsided, but this time, Rayanne had crossed the wrong person.

But what about Luke's murder? Riley had seen Caleb's face in the window, and she understood that he was incensed about his grandfather's property. He could have shot through the pool house's rear window. But there was another person in the kitchen doorway. *Who was it?*

Despite the neighbors' fears, Riley wasn't at all sure Luke's murder could be attributed to the anger of a young homeless man.

Chapter 59

Mikala

Mikala fell asleep once more on the sunroom sofa, exhaustion overtaking her anxiety. She'd been checking news sites compulsively, mystified by the arrest of Caleb March, a boy Luke barely knew existed.

Plus, she'd been on the phone nonstop, trying to persuade family members not to come to town. The coroner wouldn't release Luke's body anytime soon. She hoped her family would stay away until she needed them for optics.

If she could just put off all decisions for twenty-four hours—if she could eat and sleep and stay in her pajamas for one full day—she could regroup and face this mess. But no one wanted to grant her such a reprieve—not the neighbors with their sympathy and casseroles or the media with their fake empathy and questions. Not even her mother, who protested that she hadn't suggested inviting Riley to Greenbrier.

"Mama, I'm sure you did," she'd told her that afternoon. "At least, that's what I thought you said."

"Why, no, Mikala. I thought you were asking for trouble."

"Well, it doesn't really matter whose idea it was," Mikala said through a pounding headache. "But since I thought that's what you said, could you tell the police you did? In case they ask, which they probably won't."

"My goodness, Mikala, what in the world?"

"And, Mama, can you make sure Aunt Crystal and Uncle Ed don't come to Greenbrier? I cannot handle having Rayanne's parents here. That lying slut." Mikala had to raise her voice to override her mother's objections to her language. "Having Riley here is bad enough," she rushed on. "I'll have Rayanne's body shipped to Mobile when the coroner releases it."

Her mother had abruptly stopped trying to reason with her. "All right, but are you sure Dad and I can't come now to help you with arrangements?"

"I'm sure. Just give me two more days to pull myself together. I am exhausted and cannot face seeing anyone yet."

That was one conversation. There were others with Luke's sister in New Orleans, a cousin in Mobile, a First State Bank executive, their priest, a funeral director, the coroner, the art museum director, two of Luke's golfing buddies, three of her volunteer acquaintances, untold numbers of neighbors, and most distressingly, Aunt Crystal. It had been an unending nightmare.

Mikala was asleep for only minutes when the front door opened. It was Riley, she knew, but she heard a second voice too. She stood unsteadily and was surprised to see Detective Javon Hortense.

Her face must have shown her displeasure because he held up his hands. "This won't take long. Miss Masterson and I need to see Rayanne's room."

They didn't wait for a response but bounded up the stairs. Mikala followed. She peered through the bedroom doorway to see Riley pulling wads of cash from a shoebox on the closet floor. Detective Hortense asked how much there was.

"Fifteen thousand, if I counted correctly," Riley answered.

Mikala was stunned. Rayanne had whined that she didn't have enough money to repair her truck. *What is this?*

Riley glanced up, and for a moment, her eyes reflected surprise, as if Mikala's stance in the doorway had triggered a memory. Mikala quickly stooped to join Riley on the floor. Riley's expression had closed again, and Mikala hoped she'd imagined the look of recognition. The detective couldn't know she'd been in the pool house.

"I'm so sorry, Mikala," Riley said. "Do you think Rayanne could've been getting money from Luke?"

"I… I don't know. I never looked at his bank accounts."

Detective Hortense spoke gently. "You might want to go online. The *Herald* doesn't know about the money, but it's reporting a new finding from the coroner."

Mikala struggled to her feet and ran downstairs to find her phone. When Riley and Detective Hortense joined her, she was slumped on the sunroom couch.

"Luke killed Rayanne?" she whispered, wondering how things had progressed so fast without her getting a whiff of what was happening under her own roof.

Riley, as if she knew what Mikala was thinking, shifted uneasily. "I swear I didn't know. Any of it."

"Then how did you know about the money?"

Detective Hortense pivoted to hear Riley's answer.

"I found it this morning. I do know—did know—Rayanne. I was looking for something, anything, she might have hidden. Notes. A diary. She's hidden things in her shoes since she was a little girl." She dropped into a wicker chair. "I also called about her truck. They were expecting her to pick it up today. Apparently, she was leaving town."

Mikala didn't have to feign her astonishment. But there was another emotion pushing its way to the surface—a helpful emotion, actually, as her lower lip began to tremble. Humiliation. She placed her hands over her face and allowed the tears to come. *How could I have been so deceived? What did I do to deserve this treatment?*

She was aware of Detective Hortense writing out a receipt and bagging the cash to take with him. She peeked between wet fingers and watched Riley walk him to the door. If she'd had any remorse about wanting Luke dead, it was gone. He'd let himself get extorted by that sleazy little whore. He was even worse than she'd suspected. She was only sorry she hadn't gotten a shot in.

And if Caleb March was blamed, that was as good as pinning it on Riley. Kinder, really, for poor Aunt Crystal. It was strange how things had worked out, as if the universe was finally on Mikala's side.

Chapter 60

Cate

Cate and Isaiah searched for a seat inside the sanctuary of Trinity Faith Center. The church's pews were packed for this meeting about the shooting in the Hardys' pool house. Savannah was in the front row, but they would have to stand in the rear.

Cate recognized the usual suspects—Mayor Mack Farnsworth, Gospel Mission Director Russ Denton, the Greenbrier Police information officer, loudmouth neighbor Randall Goldsmith, and reporters from the *Herald* and Channel 5. But there were new faces as well—Detectives Hortense and Marconi along with their boss, Police Chief Mary Claire Riddle. Since their arrest of Caleb March had triggered this meeting, the detectives probably wanted to gather more information.

The organizers allowed the mayor to start off, and he spent five minutes lauding Chief Riddle's department for the quick arrest and appealing to the community's sense of fairness regarding the Gospel Mission.

Randall Goldsmith approached the microphone next. "I appreciate your position, Mayor Farnsworth. But the fact is, we've had two violent incidents in or near Roosevelt Park this summer—a rape and at least one shooting death, possibly two, depending on the coroner's finding du jour." No one laughed. "In both cases, the perpetrator was homeless." Randall Goldsmith held his palms up. "Are we going to sit back and wait for a third attack? Frankly, I don't understand why we're even talking about it. It's clear that the neighborhood needs to be rid of this dangerous element."

Applause broke out. Cate noted that some of the people clapping had seemed undecided at earlier meetings. Sentiment had turned with the murder of their popular neighbor. Cate envied them their certainty. As much as she wanted to think that Luke had been shot by a homeless intruder, she wasn't convinced that pitiful Caleb March was the culprit.

She studied Isaiah's profile. They'd talked at length about both murders—the bewildering fact that Rayanne had died before she bled out from a gun wound to the thigh and also the fact that the shooter had been willing to kill two people. Cate was aware that she'd pointed police to the homeless person living in her shed. But she'd had no idea it was Caleb. Her elation over the discovery had dimmed when she realized it was her son's mild-mannered friend who had been sleeping in their yard. She was sad that the young man had no family and no friends, really, other than Isaiah and Riley. And they were hardly able to offer him help.

Isaiah didn't believe that Caleb was guilty. Cate didn't know what she believed. The gun that had belonged to Caleb's grandfather—the gun buried under her geraniums—was the murder weapon. The detectives were sure of that damning fact. But Caleb and Isaiah had spent almost every day that summer together. *Could Caleb have shown Isaiah the gun?*

Cate shoved the thought away. She watched Savannah smooth her skirt as she prepared to speak. She hadn't heard her wife and son exchange a word since the shooting. She sneaked another look at Isaiah. He was staring at Savannah blankly.

When did this distance between them develop?

There was something she hadn't told Savannah and certainly not the detectives—when she'd checked to see if Isaiah was asleep on the night of the murders, his hair had been wet. *Could he, assuming Sa-*

vannah would meet Luke in the pool house, have stolen over during the storm? Perhaps he'd planned to confront one mother about her disrespect of the other. Agitated that her mind kept going places she didn't want it to, Cate blew out a noisy breath. Isaiah frowned at her as Savannah began to speak.

"My family and I have been longtime supporters of the Gospel Mission. My wife and I support it financially. Our son has volunteered there for years." Savannah's gaze swept the audience, meeting eyes, garnering approval. "One of the reasons we moved here was to be good citizens, to rebuild a strong community for all of Greenbrier. However, I must admit the shooting of our next-door neighbor has shaken me. The fact that a homeless man was living in our backyard shed has shaken me."

Next to Cate, Isaiah groaned.

Savannah addressed the officials in the front row. "I'm afraid, Mayor Farnsworth, Police Chief Riddle, that the city must do something about the homeless people in this neighborhood. At the very least, you need to shut down the camps around the park. And you need to look at moving the Gospel Mission out of the city."

The majority of attendees clapped and cheered, while the men surrounding Russ Denton buzzed angrily. Russ Denton stood to rebut Savannah, but he sounded overwhelmed and defeated.

Isaiah gripped Cate's arm. "Did you know she was going to say that?"

Cate shook her head at her son's ravaged face. She was torn. Savannah could well have been the intended victim, and Cate could now be a bereaved widow alongside Mikala. She loved Savannah. She truly did.

But do I love Isaiah more? She closed her eyes and crossed into the mental territory she had avoided all day. *Did Savannah's endless redevelopment of this neighborhood provoke the ire of a young homeless man? And was Isaiah aware of it?*

Chapter 61

Patrick

Detective Patrick Marconi scrutinized Cate and Isaiah from a back corner of the church. Something was going on between those two. The teen looked ready to detonate, and his mother appeared haggard and worried.

Patrick had caught Cate at home earlier and told her that Caleb March had seen her behind the pool house around the time Luke and Rayanne were shot. She didn't seem surprised, only exhausted. She admitted that she'd gone behind the pool house, seeking proof that her wife was having an affair with Luke Hardy.

"But Caleb saw your gun," Patrick said.

She stared at him, her chin quivering. "Yes," she whispered. "God help me, I carried my gun over there. But I didn't shoot anyone."

Patrick believed she hadn't shot anyone with *her* little pearl-handled gun, which hadn't been fired. But the murder weapon had been found under her flowers. Cate Rosemond still had a lot more explaining to do.

It was clear that something was bothering her. And clearly, these two, mother and son, had a tight bond. But what about the other mother? Patrick hadn't witnessed a single interaction between Savannah and Isaiah, not even when they were in the same room.

Patrick and Javon were at the neighborhood meeting because they were not entirely persuaded of Caleb March's guilt. Sure, he looked good for the shooting. The fact that the murder weapon had belonged to his grandfather pretty much sealed it. *Still...*

Could Henry March have given or sold the gun to a neighbor? Or for that matter, could it have been stolen? Patrick surveyed the people packed into the pews. Several original residents were present, graying men and women angry at the moneyed newcomers who had rendered Gunter Mill unrecognizable. Patrick knew from his own grandparents how tight-knit these mill villages had once been, with their company stores and chummy front porches and mill-centered ball teams.

Patrick had learned that wild-haired Earle Meadows, who was sitting with his wife, had grown up in—and now owned—the decrepit three-story house behind Henry March's former property. The detective could picture a scenario in which a gun might make its way from one neighbor to another. Of course, that same scenario could also lead to Caleb, who had lived in the Meadowses' boarding house.

But there was something peculiar about the kid—and despite his twenty-one years, Caleb appeared very much a kid to Patrick. That wasn't surprising, considering that Caleb had raised himself. Aside from his counselors at the Gospel Mission, he hadn't had any role models for appropriate adult behavior.

Patrick glanced at his watch, thinking the meeting was about to break up. He wanted to grab Cate and Isaiah before they got away. But a hum was spreading through the first rows of the sanctuary. Patrick stretched to see what was happening but was blocked by the crowd.

"Can you see anything?" he asked the taller Javon.

"Holy shit," Javon said. "It's our Crescent Trail vic."

Patrick pushed through the throng, flashing his badge when anyone resisted. He reached a side aisle where he could watch as a young blond girl mounted the stairs to the stage, a man hovering protectively on her left, an older woman on her right. He recognized Farrah Newell and her father from their visits to the Law Enforcement Center. The woman was the pastor of Bethel United Methodist Church.

The pastor approached the pulpit and introduced herself. "I'd like for you to meet one of my parishioners, a very brave young woman, Farrah Newell. She has come home from the University of South Carolina this evening to address us."

The church fell silent. Though the media had not announced Farrah's name in the July 3 rape and assault, many in the neighborhood knew her or her parents. The pastor ushered Farrah into place behind the slender podium. Even from a distance, Patrick could see her nervousness. Her hands trembled, and she gripped the pulpit to steady them.

"Good evening," Farrah began, her voice wavering. She cleared her throat and tried again. "Good evening. I'm really nervous, so please bear with me." She attempted a smile, but it didn't quite come off.

Patrick was glad to see many in the audience respond to her genuineness, leaning forward to encourage her.

"Take your time, honey," a voice called.

"As Pastor Audrey said, my name is Farrah Newell. I was the victim of an attack this summer on the Crescent Trail." There were gasps from a few people who hadn't recognized her, but she plunged on. "It's been really hard. I quit my job and didn't leave my house for over a month. I wasn't sure I'd be able to return to school. But I did. Last week."

She took a shaky breath. "You probably saw in the *Greenbrier Herald* and on some fliers an artist's sketch of the man whom police believe is responsible. They—and I—think there's a good chance he lived in an encampment beside the trail."

A voice yelled, "That's what we've been saying!"

"No," said Farrah firmly. "Please let me finish." Silence returned to the sanctuary. "Homeless or not, that man is responsible for his actions. Of course, I'd like to see him arrested. I'd like to know he's in prison." She raised her head and met the eyes of person after person.

"But it is not right to brand an entire community of homeless people or Gospel Mission residents with the actions of one. That is not how our criminal justice system works."

She glanced toward her pastor. "That's not how our faith works. Rather than pushing the Greenbrier Gospel Mission out of this neighborhood, we should be expanding it so it has room for all the homeless people who want to change their lives."

Patrick searched for Russ Denton, who appeared stunned.

"Rather than busting up the encampments," Farrah continued, "we should be sending outreach teams to encourage people to seek help. Losing your home has nothing to do with being a criminal." She halted and looked to her pastor, who joined her at the pulpit mic.

"Farrah is too humble to say this, so I will," Pastor Audrey said. "If anyone has reason to be angry or to hate or to seek revenge, it is she. But she isn't doing that. Instead, she is following the teachings of our Lord Jesus Christ. She is following the teachings of the church. May we all do the same."

The pastor took Farrah's elbow, allowing her father to envelope her in a hug before the trio started down the steps. The sound of a single person clapping broke the shocked silence, and Patrick turned to find the source. To his surprise, it was Riley Masterson. The next moment, Isaiah Rosemond-Darwin leapt to his feet, then a woman in tears, then the men from the mission.

Soon, a third of the crowd was clapping and stomping and cheering for Farrah. She darted a look back, surprise apparent on her face. Then she ducked her head and exited the church through a side door.

As the meeting dissolved on its unexpected note, Patrick pushed through the crowd to catch Cate and Isaiah. "I take it that's not how the other meetings turned out."

"No," said Isaiah. "Wasn't she great?"

Even Cate was smiling through tears. "Quite a young lady."

Patrick got to his point. "Isaiah, you said Caleb March was helping you on your school project, didn't you?"

"Yeah, he was."

"Do you have any samples of his handwriting? Did he write anything down for you?"

"Yeah, I'm sure he did." Isaiah turned to Cate. "Have you emptied the trash in my room? I haven't."

Cate shook her head.

"Then yeah," Isaiah said, "there should be samples, even if they're in my trash can." His face brightened. "It's the extortion notes, right? You want to compare his handwriting to the notes."

Patrick nodded. There was no reason to keep his hunch from them. "Can I come home with you and get them now?"

"Sure!" Isaiah was excited. "We walked, but we can ride with you if you want."

"Come on."

Minutes later, Patrick, Cate, and Isaiah were in Isaiah's bedroom, digging through the trash can beside his desk. Isaiah identified three different papers that bore Caleb's scribbles. Patrick folded them carefully and promised to let them know what he found.

He returned to the church where Javon and Police Chief Riddle, a stout woman with spiky ash-blond hair, were talking about Farrah's unexpected appearance. The chief was furious that a suspect hadn't been arrested in Farrah's assault. Patrick was glad it wasn't his case.

"From what I hear from the mayor, Miss Newell may have changed some minds. Incredible." Chief Riddle lowered her voice and muttered, "Doesn't mean we're doing our job, though."

Patrick showed Javon the crumpled papers. "I'm no handwriting expert, but these don't look anything like the writing on that note we found in the shed."

Javon agreed.

Chief Riddle asked, "What are you thinking?"

"Not sure," said Patrick. "But I think it's time we looked into Caleb March's family."

"Starting with the mom," Javon added.

"You don't think you got this wrong, do you?" Chief Riddle's gray eyes narrowed at her detectives. Javon studied his feet.

"No. It's not that." Patrick wasn't ready to admit his doubts to their boss. "The murder weapon is pretty damning. But the kid's lying about something."

"Yeah, he is," Javon said. "It may mean nothing. But we want to dot our i's and cross our t's, as you always say."

Chief Riddle frowned and grunted. "Make it stick." She climbed into her car.

Chapter 62

Caleb

Caleb thought he would be awake all night, but the jail's iron bed and thin mattress were a vast improvement over his recent lodgings, and he slept soundly. He'd heard older men on the street admit to deliberately shoplifting or trespassing to get arrested, especially during brutal winter months. Jail offered a bed and three meals—not awful when compared to the alternatives.

Within seconds of waking, however, Caleb's terror returned. He'd been accused of murder. Two nights in jail were one thing, but he couldn't face a prison cell for the rest of his life.

Rested at last, he realized that his thinking had been muddled. He'd been trying so hard to hide his connection to Doreen that he'd worsened his predicament. Standing by while his mother choked to death was nothing compared to the crime he was accused of—shooting Luke and Rayanne. He didn't give a damn about either of them, much less hate them enough to shoot them. That was true, as well, of Savannah Darwin, whom police seemed to think had been his real target.

And his grandfather's gun, an old Colt .38, according to the detectives—he'd never seen it in his life. *Where did it come from?* His mind leapt to Doreen. If she'd had it, that would explain why she'd left her own pistol under the mattress in Bender—the pistol that was now at the bottom of a lake.

The detectives insisted that his grandfather's Colt was the murder weapon. They showed him a picture of a revolver with a weirdly curved grip. But he couldn't see how it had gotten from Doreen to the milk can in Isaiah's backyard. One possible link could be Doreen's neighbors in the tent encampment. A homeless man or woman could have lifted the revolver from Doreen's tent, shot Luke and Rayanne, then hurriedly buried it next door.

How else could it have ended up in the makeshift planter on the shed's porch? Caleb's frenzied mind halted. *Wait a minute.* His grandfather's gun had once been on the very property on which Luke and Rayanne were killed. *What if it never left?*

Caleb recalled something he'd seen the night of the murders and withheld because he couldn't admit his own presence. He was past that—he had to tell the detectives. *Today.*

Caleb settled into his familiar seat across from Detectives Marconi and Hortense. His court-appointed attorney, whom he'd met for the first time a half hour earlier, was glad for him to explain his self-destructive behavior to the police.

"I don't know where to start," he told them.

Detective Hortense leaned back and stretched his legs. "We've got all the time in the world, son. Don't hurry. Tell us everything. We'll decide what's relevant."

"Okay. I'll start with my mother. Doreen March. She was, um... a terrible mother. A meth addict. An alcoholic. Mean. You can ask my old teachers or principals if you don't believe me."

"We already have," Detective Hortense assured him. "So far, so good."

"Oh." Caleb was surprised. "Okay. Well, as I told you earlier, I left home when I was seventeen. Stupidly, just a few months before graduating."

"Where did you go?" asked Detective Marconi.

"I lived in abandoned trailers around Bender. Empty warehouses. That's when I got into trouble with Becca Ragsdale's dad. He made sure I got on the registry." He looked directly at the two men. "But I've never been a pedophile. That stuff makes me sick."

Caleb waited until the detectives acknowledged his statement. "Kept sleeping rough around Bender," he continued, "but outside the schools, no one up there served hot meals. Or any meals. So I made my way to downtown Greenbrier, basically to eat. I lived in the woods near Roosevelt Park for a long time and ate at the mission, Trinity Faith Center, all those places. Worked enough odd jobs to keep myself in drugs."

The detectives exchanged glances, and he hoped they were impressed by his honesty.

"Then some social workers invited me into the Gospel Mission. I wasn't sure at first, but I accepted their help. That's the point you gotta get to, you know? Admitting you've screwed up and you need help. At least, that's what the mission guys say. Anyway, I got off the drugs and got the job at Pizza by the Park. Then my counselor recommended me for a room at the boarding house on Montreat Avenue, where I lived for another year. That's kind of where this whole thing started."

Detective Marconi didn't change his expression, but Detective Hortense smiled encouragement.

Caleb let out a long sigh that sounded like a whistle. "I had a bedroom on the third floor and could look out and see the Hardys' backyard. I recognized their sycamore tree and eventually remembered staying there a long time ago. Turns out it was my grandfather's place. I got in touch with my uncles in Raleigh, and they told me I had lived there for a whole year when I was four or five. Doreen had been homeless and pregnant that year, and my granddad took me in."

"But not her?" Detective Hortense asked.

"No, not her." Caleb paused. "But I haven't been back in that house again that I know of. And I never saw my granddad's gun. I swear to you I never laid eyes on the gun you pulled from under those flowers."

"Go on," said Detective Marconi.

"Well, from my boarding house window, I could also see the empty shed in Isaiah's yard. From what I could tell, his mom, Cate, stopped going in it around the first of June. I was trying to save money for a car but was paying a hundred twenty-five dollars a week for that crappy room. I couldn't save enough money. So I started sleeping in that shed. I told you all this earlier."

"Yeah, you did," said Detective Hortense. "We'll come back to your last night in the shed in a minute. But is there more you wanted to tell us about your mother? Did you know she had moved to Greenbrier?"

Caleb hung his head. "Yeah." He inhaled slowly. "It's all kind of mixed up, but I'll tell it as clear as I can. I saw her one day at the mission thrift store out on Calhoun. I couldn't believe she would leave Bender, so I took a bus out there to look around. Our old house was condemned, tape over the door, floor busted. So I knew it really *was* her in Greenbrier.

"One day, I followed her to a tent off the Crescent Trail beside the park. Like I told you, she was never much of a mother. I didn't want her to know where I was or that I had a job and a car. I knew she'd hit me up for money. But then she tracked me down to the boarding house. I wasn't living there anymore, and I sure as hell didn't want her barging in on my shed, so I didn't tell her about it. But she found my sleeping bag stuffed under some bushes behind the boarding house, and she took it. That's why I went back to her tent a few days later—to get my sleeping bag." He halted for so long the detectives wondered if he was finished.

"You went to get your sleeping bag," prompted Detective Hortense.

"And I found her... choking," Caleb said in a barely audible voice. "On her own vomit. Beer and gin bottles were everywhere. Just like she'd done when I was growing up."

"You let her choke?" Detective Hortense asked.

"Yeah. Yeah, I did. I, um... I'd tried to help her once when that happened in Bender. When I was a kid. She... slapped me."

Detective Hortense didn't speak but squinted at his partner. Caleb fervently hoped his story rang true for them. "Anything else?"

Caleb raised his eyes. "Yeah. After she was dead, I saw an envelope. I thought it might be... I don't know what I thought, but I took it."

"And what was in it?"

"That note you found in the shed about Isaiah."

The detectives sat up straighter, taking in this new information. Detective Marconi was the first to speak. "Are you saying that Doreen March was Isaiah's mother? That you are his—what? Half brother?"

"I think so. Those same uncles I told you about, the ones in Raleigh? I called my uncle Roger, and he said Isaiah's father was a Black man, and he and my mother were homeless that year I lived with my grandfather. Doreen had a baby, and DSS took it away because it tested positive for drugs." Caleb met the detectives' eyes. "The timing works out. My uncle said Doreen then got clean for a while and he and my grandfather paid for her to get into the house in Bender. She took me with her. Lucky me."

"Your mother was trying to extort money from Isaiah's mothers?" Detective Hortense asked.

"That's my guess."

The officers looked at each other. "We need to get samples of her handwriting," Detective Marconi murmured. "Motor Vehicles or Caleb's schools or maybe even a sign-in sheet for food at Trinity Faith Center. That may be the easiest." He turned to Caleb. "And give us your uncles' names, addresses, and phone numbers."

Detective Marconi drummed his fingers on the table. "All of this is very interesting. But it doesn't absolve you from shooting Luke Hardy and Rayanne Masterson. Did you find your grandfather's gun in Doreen's tent?"

"No!" he cried. "I told you. I'd never seen that gun before you showed me the picture. I didn't even know Granddaddy had a gun. I swear!"

"Would your uncles know about it?"

"I don't know. Maybe." He shifted in his seat. "But think about it. Isn't it possible it never left the property—that it's been at Twenty-Six Gunter Avenue all these years?" Something else occurred to Caleb. "There is no way my fingerprints are on that gun. Can you not tell whose fingerprints are on it?"

"We couldn't lift discernible prints," Detective Marconi admitted.

"There! Doesn't that mean anything?"

"It means you could've worn gloves. Or that the dirt and rain rubbed them off."

Caleb wagged his head wearily. "No, no, no." He straightened. "But I still haven't told you one more thing. It might make a difference."

"Go on."

"On the night of the shootings, I had gone into the shed early because of the storm. I told you I saw Cate Rosemond standing outside the pool house, looking in at Riley. Or whoever was in there."

"Yeah."

He needed to be careful here, omitting that he took his mother's pistol when he ran to the pool house. No reason to bring that up. "When I got there, Cate Rosemund was gone. I looked through the window, too, but I couldn't see anything over the top of that living room sofa."

"So you didn't witness the shooting?"

"No. I must have been too late. But I did see something."

The detectives waited.

"I heard the pool house's side door open, the one off the kitchen. I ran toward it along the rear of the house. I saw someone with a ball cap and blond hair run across the patio."

"Are you saying—" Detective Marconi started.

"Yes," Caleb said. "She ran into her own house. It was Mikala Hardy."

Chapter 63

Mikala

Mikala hadn't thought it would come to this. The detectives were waiting in her foyer to take her to the Law Enforcement Center for further questioning. They mentioned she might want a lawyer. Her mind was whirling.

"Wait," she said. "Wait. Maybe that's not necessary. Come in."

She led them into the living room. She folded her hands in her lap and gazed at them with the wide eyes that had played well for a lifetime. "What's changed?"

Detective Marconi took the lead. "We have a witness who saw you running from the pool house on the night of the murder. We revisited your alibi at the movie theater. Employees saw you enter and leave, as you undoubtedly planned. But there's no one to verify that you actually stayed in the theater during the whole two hours."

"You have a witness?"

"Yes."

"Can you tell me who it is?" Mikala asked.

"Not at this time."

"It has to be Riley, then, doesn't it?"

The detectives remained quiet. This was exactly what she'd feared when she learned that during the murder, Riley had been in the pool house, not walking back from her restaurant shift as Mikala had so meticulously planned.

"All right." At this point, the truth might be the only way to go. "All right," she repeated. "I did plan to kill Luke. I went to the pool house to do it." She remembered waiting, waiting in the kitchen doorway for Luke to look up and see her. "But somebody else beat me to it."

Detective Hortense looked skeptical. "Somebody else."

She nodded vigorously. "I know it sounds crazy. But you can ask Riley—if she didn't do it, that is. You said Luke was shot in the side and Rayanne was shot in the leg through the back of the sofa, right? Well, I never fired a shot. I never left the kitchen doorway. Ask her. Ask Riley!"

"Do you really think she'll be inclined to help you?" Detective Hortense asked.

Mikala was silent.

"Did you take Riley Masterson's gun from the glove compartment of her car?" he continued.

Mikala shuddered, and her shoulders slouched. She didn't speak.

"Okay," said Detective Marconi. "Let's go."

"No, wait." Mikala didn't want the neighbors to witness the detectives placing her in their vehicle. And they'd be watching. They were probably watching at that very moment.

"Yes. I did take Riley's gun. But I never fired it. You'll see."

"Where is it?"

"Back in her glove compartment."

"So you planned this whole thing how long ago—when you invited Miss Masterton to stay with you?"

She didn't answer.

"We've talked to your mother, by the way," said Detective Hortense. "We know it wasn't her idea for Riley to come here."

Mikala looked up. "I'm not proud of this, any of it," she said, wiping the tears from her face. "But I swear to you I didn't shoot Luke." She gulped, attempting to gather herself. "He had been unfaithful. Serially unfaithful, as it turns out. In fact, I thought—no, I knew—he was having an affair with Savannah Darwin next door. I saw them at the art museum. That's who I thought he was with that night." She laughed bitterly. "Imagine my surprise when I discovered he had yet another girlfriend. My own cheap, tacky cousin." She cried harder, her humiliation complete.

Detective Marconi waited until her sobs quietened. "We will certainly check out Riley's car in a moment. But we don't think that's the gun you used."

Mikala's head jerked up. "Wha... what? You already looked at the gun in my bedroom. You know it wasn't fired."

"Oh, we have the murder weapon. Coincidentally, it belonged to Henry March, the man who lived on this property before you. We think you discovered it on the site, cleaned it up, and used it to shoot your husband and Rayanne Masterson."

Mikala's face twisted in horror. "No, that never happened! I never found a gun! What are you talking about?"

Detective Marconi rose decisively. "You can tell us all about it at the LEC," he said, placing her in handcuffs.

Chapter 64

Riley

Riley watched from the landing as Detectives Hortense and Marconi carted Mikala away. She'd overheard everything—how Mikala had tried to set her up and how she'd intended to use Riley's gun then presumably plant it for police to find. Scenes from earlier in the summer began to make sense. Installing Riley in the pool house. Throwing her and Luke together. Whisking Rayanne into the main house, out of the way. Well, that one had backfired.

Obviously, a few things had thwarted Mikala's plan. For one, Savannah and Luke had already been involved by the time Riley arrived. Also, Luke had probably never been interested in Riley, but even if he had, she would have been too wary after her experience with Silas.

Her breath caught. *Silas.* That was what this was about. Mikala thought Riley had killed Silas and could be manipulated into an affair with Luke and then blamed for his murder. *My God, the deviousness. She must have planned this for months.*

She collapsed into a wing chair. What Mikala could not have predicted was Rayanne—the unexpected appearance of a deviousness to match her own. Rayanne had introduced a whole new wrinkle—she'd wriggled her way into an affair with Luke then blackmailed him. Or so Riley assumed from the cash in her bedroom. *Unbelievable.*

Mikala had almost pulled it off. She'd adapted her plan when Savannah entered the picture and it was clear that Luke and Riley were not involved. If Riley had been walking home from Pizza by the Park with no witnesses, Mikala would have used her gun to kill them both. Who knew what tale she would have then spun. Riley shuddered to think what Miller Washburn would have made of it.

But something, or someone, had stopped Mikala. The fatal shots had not come from the kitchen. Riley was fairly sure of that. They'd come from the rear of the pool house—through that open window—or from someone inside, hidden in the shadows.

She wondered if Mikala's arrest meant Caleb would be released. The detectives had never said that. And the gun they'd accused Mikala of using had belonged to Caleb's grandfather.

Riley suddenly realized the detectives would be back. They'd ask more questions about the money she'd found in Rayanne's room. They would want to know if she'd seen Caleb that night.

And they would press harder about what—and who—she'd seen in the kitchen doorway. They would know that a bullet had hit Luke in his side and another had pierced the back of the sofa before hitting Rayanne in the thigh. The shots could not have come from the kitchen. Riley could back up her cousin's story and say Mikala had never moved from the doorway.

Or not. Riley was shocked when the thought slithered into her mind. But Mikala's scheme to kill her husband and blame it on Riley was nothing short of wicked. It preyed on Riley's isolation, her grief, her vulnerability.

So who was to say that Mikala hadn't walked to the rear of the living room before shooting, a short walk of a dozen feet or so? *Yes, it could've happened like that. Exactly like that.*

Chapter 65

Cate

Cate watched from the window in Isaiah's bedroom as Mikala was escorted to the detectives' black SUV. Isaiah came up behind her.

"She's in handcuffs!" he said in disbelief.

"Yes."

"I'm gonna call Riley."

Cate thought about stopping him, but her curiosity was too great. Isaiah called and invited himself over. Police had blocked off the pool house but didn't say anything about staying out of the pool. She heard Riley acquiesce.

It hit Cate that the poor girl was alone in the cavernous Hardy house. Luke was dead, her sister was dead, and Mikala was at the Law Enforcement Center. "I'm coming with you," she said.

Cate packed some grapes, apples, bananas, and granola in a tote. She doubted Riley had been eating from the food brigade's offerings. She waited for Isaiah to change into swim trunks, but she stayed in her shorts and T-shirt.

Mother and son walked barefoot across their yard to the Hardys' patio. The bricks were hot where the sun scorched them. Except for the yellow tape across the pool-house doors, the scene appeared much as it had all summer.

Riley couldn't quite manage a full smile. *Well, how could she?* Her life and her temporary home were in ruins.

Isaiah hesitantly hugged her then pulled away. "We saw Mikala leave with the police. What's going on?"

Riley tugged her hair away from her neck, already sweating. "I'm not sure I understand everything. But I overheard the officers say she wasn't at the movie like she said. They think she could have found Caleb's grandfather's gun." She glanced around the yard. "Somewhere around here, I guess."

"They think *Mikala* shot Luke and Rayanne with an old gun owned by Caleb's grandfather?" Cate wanted to be sure she comprehended. "The same gun that led them to arrest Caleb?"

"Yeah."

"So will they let Caleb go?" asked Isaiah.

Riley shrugged. "I'm not sure. I think they may be questioning both of them."

Cate cleared her throat. She didn't want to ask, but she needed to know. "Did Mikala admit she shot them?"

"No, she denied it." Riley was clearly holding something back. Cate wondered if she didn't want to say anything about Savannah in front of Isaiah.

"You can be honest with us," said Cate. "I don't think much can surprise us at this point."

Riley's eyes flicked between them. "Mikala said she knew Luke was, um... seeing Savannah. That's who she expected to find. Not Rayanne."

No surprise there. "But I'm not sure I understand," Cate said. "She admits she was in the pool house but *didn't* shoot them?"

"Right. She says someone else shot them before she had a chance."

Isaiah made a sound that started as a scoff and ended as a bark. Both women stared at him. "What?" he said. "Don't you think that's lame?"

It was Cate's turn to hedge. If Mikala had done this, what a relief it would be. But Riley wasn't telling them everything. *Is she protecting someone? Bless this girl—is she protecting Isaiah?*

Cate smiled and passed her fruit-filled tote to Riley. "You probably need to eat. I'll leave you two to your swim." She walked back to her house, her thoughts swirling.

Chapter 66

Patrick

Patrick and Javon met in the break room, carrying Pepsis and packs of peanut butter crackers for lunch.

Patrick opened the conversation. "Do you believe her?"

Javon ripped open a packet. "All that hysteria is persuasive. I'll give her that." He thumped the top of the can before popping the top. "But the fact that she planned the murder months in advance, stole a gun, set up an alibi, arranged for Riley to take the fall, and *then didn't do it?* I'm not buying it."

"But when we introduced Henry March's gun, she seemed truly mystified, didn't you think?"

"Yeah," Javon said. "And why would she not use Riley's gun after going to the trouble to take it from her car?"

The men stared at the ceiling as if it might offer a solution.

"Okay, one possibility," Patrick said. "Mikala intended to kill Luke and the woman she thought was Savannah Darwin. Then Caleb swooped in with his grandfather's gun and shot them through the window before she had a chance. That would fit."

They had conferred with the officers who'd responded to Doreen March's death and interviewed the man in the tent beside hers. They'd contacted Caleb's uncle Roger and verified Doreen's history of drug and alcohol abuse. They'd checked her handwriting and were confident she was the one attempting to extort Isaiah's mothers. As a result, no one wanted to bring charges against Caleb in his mother's death.

"It would fit," Javon agreed, "but my gut says no. I could see him panicking during a robbery and killing someone maybe. Maybe. But out of anger over his granddad's old property? Seems a stretch."

The two were silent again, thinking about the young man who had faced so much adversity in their city. "He's a good argument for the Gospel Mission," Patrick murmured. "They're the only ones who have helped him."

Javon nodded. "You don't think Cate is involved? She could've found Henry March's gun while she was landscaping the Hardys' yard. She could've shot Luke Hardy and the woman she *thought* was her cheating wife through the window before Caleb arrived. Then she could've hidden the gun under her flowers and pointed us to Caleb living in her shed."

Patrick considered the scenario. "Yeah, it's possible. Ditto for Savannah. She could've found Henry March's gun and shot them both because she was being cheated on. Though no one reports seeing her at the pool house." He finished a pack of crackers and opened another. "Are you as struck as I am by the sheer number of gun owners on those two plots of Gunter Avenue? We're lucky we haven't had a mass shooting over there."

Javon grinned. "I blame all those Alabama girls bringing their crazy asses to South Cackalacky."

Patrick burst into laughter. "Which brings us to..."

"I almost hate to go there."

"We can't eliminate her."

Javon sighed. "I don't want to do a repeat of Miller Washburn." He paused. "Well, we have to question Riley about Caleb and Mikala anyway. Maybe she won't know she's a suspect herself."

Patrick laughed. "I'm not sure we're that skilled."

Javon tossed his empty soda can at the trash bin across the room. "Speak for yourself, my man."

Chapter 67

Cate

When Isaiah came home from the Hardys' pool, Cate was waiting with a late-afternoon snack of a grilled cheese sandwich, potato chips, and milk.

"Thanks," he said. "I'm starving."

"You always are after swimming. Have been since you were a little boy."

"Where's Savannah Mom?"

"At work."

"On a Saturday?"

Cate shrugged because she had no answer. "It gives us a chance to talk."

He raised his head from his sandwich. "About what?"

"What else? About the murders." She watched her son take a huge gulp of milk. "Isaiah, I don't think you've told me everything about that night."

He looked startled. Her son could not hide his emotions. "Why would you say that?"

"Your hair was wet. When I came in to see if the sirens had woken you, you seemed to be asleep with the headphones. But your hair was wet."

Isaiah didn't speak.

"You'd been out in the storm, hadn't you?"

He stared at her then almost imperceptibly nodded.

She spoke carefully, wanting him to trust her. "You were outside." She waited a moment. "Were you with Riley? In the pool house?"

He jerked upright. "In the pool house? No!" He glared at her. "Wait a minute. Do you think I shot Luke and Rayanne?" His voice cracked on the last words.

Cate's stomach was churning, but she continued to look at him, clear-eyed. "No, no. Not that. But you may know something. About one of your friends. Did you see Riley or Caleb that night?"

When he didn't respond, she forged on. "I know Savannah Mom has... disappointed you. Maybe your loyalties are divided, and I would understand."

His brown eyes flared with anger. She recalled him telling her how the old mill couple he'd interviewed hated Savannah, calling her a "machine of greed," and forbade their daughter to sell their two houses to her. She was sure Isaiah agreed with them.

Cate spoke words that cost her with every syllable. "I don't think you knew it was Rayanne. You thought Savannah Mom was with Luke."

His face was anguished. "I'm so sorry, Mom. For how she's treated you."

"It's okay, Isaiah," she whispered. "Whatever you saw or did, we'll fix it. But I have to know exactly what happened if I'm going to help you."

Chapter 68

Riley

The detectives were back a half hour before Riley needed to leave for work. She wished she'd left earlier, but then they probably would have shown up at the restaurant. She met them at the front door and led them into the kitchen. Mikala's other rooms were too fancy for her. She was rattling around this house and was tempted to ask Mama, Daddy, and Mikala's parents to come. But if they arrived and Mikala was released from jail, Mikala would kill her for real.

"Have you let Caleb go?" Riley asked as they settled on the tall stools at the island.

"No, he remains a suspect," Detective Marconi answered formally.

"Him *and* Mikala?"

"We believe both could have had access to Henry March's gun, so we are continuing to question them. And others."

"Miss Masterson," Detective Hortense started. "We need for you to try to remember what you saw on the night of the murder. When you came out of your bedroom, you had a vantage point between the open rear window and the kitchen doorway. We'd like to take you over there and see if we can jog your memory."

She recoiled. "Go inside the pool house?"

"Yes, if that's all right."

Both men were studying her. It wasn't really a request.

"I... I guess so."

She fumbled for the keys on a hook beside the door and led them across the patio. Riley was shaking, so she gave the keys to Detective Hortense. His large hands dwarfed them, but he delicately slid one into the front door as his partner ripped off the police tape.

Riley's breathing accelerated as they entered the dim coolness. No one had turned off the air conditioner. A few sofa cushions were missing, but the massive frame remained in the living room, its floral fabric permanently marred by pools of rust brown. Luke's lifeblood. And her sister's. Riley reached for a chair to steady herself.

"You can sit if you need to," said Detective Marconi.

She shook her head.

"Well, if you don't mind, then," said Detective Hortense, "walk us through that night."

Riley went into the bedroom and closed her eyes then repeated the story of waking to the sounds of Luke and Rayanne. She shared how she'd stumbled to the living room to discover someone in the kitchen doorway.

"Could you tell if it was a man or woman?" Detective Hortense asked.

Could I? "I think the person was dressed in black, because I couldn't tell anything about the clothes. She had a ball cap pulled low. But I don't think I could have said man or woman if I hadn't heard Cousin Mikala tell you it was her."

"So you heard that?"

"Sound travels up that stairwell."

"Miss Masterson, had you been drinking the night of the murders?"

They'd found the tequila by her bed, so there was no use in lying. "Yes."

"Do you know how much?" he asked.

"Not really. But as you probably know, I had tequila before I went to bed. It wasn't a full bottle. It was already open." That part was true. She didn't admit to gulping more of it *after* finding the bodies.

"Okay, so what can you tell us about the figure in the kitchen doorway?"

"Nothing more than I said. I'm sorry I wasn't more observant, but I was kind of groggy, waking up like that."

"Quite all right. We don't want you telling us more than you actually remember." Detective Hortense made a show of flipping through his notebook, though she imagined he'd memorized his notes. "Now, in your original statement, you said you didn't think the shots had come from the kitchen doorway."

Trick question. He knew they hadn't. "That's right."

"Is that still your memory?"

"Yeah, but..." she began. Both men looked up expectantly. "I don't think the shots came from the doorway. But like I said, I was groggy. I couldn't swear that the figure in the doorway didn't move."

Riley saw their interest flare as they considered the possibility that Mikala had stepped to the rear of the living room before firing. That would fit with the shots fired into Luke's side and Rayanne's leg.

"Think hard, Miss Masterson," Detective Hortense said. "Did you see the figure in the doorway move?"

She didn't want to oversell it. "I'm sorry. I can't say for sure."

"This is important," Detective Marconi inserted. "Try to remember. Did the figure in the doorway leave the kitchen?"

Detective Hortense gave him a look that warned *Back off.* He probably feared some future accusation of leading Riley into a false memory. "Okay, let's move on to the window at the rear of the living room. The screen was removed. Do you know when?"

"No. I opened that window earlier to get a breeze from the storm. There was no screen then, but I wasn't worried about mosquitoes because of the storm." She paused. "That was the first time I'd opened it all summer. The screen could've been down for months."

"And did you see anyone at the window?"

They already knew this from the first night's questioning. She trusted that Caleb had told them the truth and that she wasn't contradicting anything he'd said.

"Yes, I saw my friend Caleb. I assume he heard the shots and came over to check on me. We got to be good friends this summer."

"You saw Caleb *after* the shots were fired."

"Yes."

The men smiled encouragingly. "It sounds like you don't think Caleb fired those shots," Detective Hortense said.

"No, I don't. Caleb had no reason to. Not like... well, not like other people did."

"What other people, Miss Masterson?"

"Well, like, I thought Cousin Mikala admitted she had a reason."

The officers sat back. "Can you tell us what you think happened, Miss Masterson?" Detective Hortense asked.

Careful, careful. "You never think it could be someone you know, right? I guess at first, I thought it was a local resident who was mad at Savannah. Some of those neighborhood meetings got pretty heated." She halted as if she was considering her words, but she already knew what she was going to say. "But then I heard Mikala talking to you. I suppose the most logical thing is that she carried out her original plan. To kill Luke and blame me."

"And your sister?"

Tears sprang inexplicably to Riley's eyes, and she wasn't pretending anymore. "She was in the wrong place at the wrong time. I honestly don't think Mikala could have known. I think she expected Savannah to be with Luke."

"That is certainly a possible scenario." Detective Hortense sat down and stretched his back. He was trying to look casual, but Riley didn't buy it. "But you see, Miss Masterson, there is one other possibility that concerns us."

She tensed. *Where did I make a mistake?*

"If Mrs. Hardy is telling the truth—if she *didn't* move from the kitchen doorway—there was another shooter. Coulda been from the rear window. Coulda been from the powder room. Coulda been from a dark corner of the living room."

Riley listened to him carefully because she knew, in fact, that was what had happened.He stopped and stared at her. Maybe he knew she'd skewed the story to implicate Mikala.

"Do you see where I'm going?" he asked.

She blinked. Suddenly, she did. She hadn't seen the shooter, but the shooter had seen her.

Detective Hortense leaned forward. "Miss Masterson, we are worried that you might be in danger."

Chapter 69

Cate

Isaiah stopped eating his grilled cheese sandwich and stared at Cate. She wasn't sure her words had registered, so she repeated them. "Whatever you saw or did, we'll fix it. But I have to know exactly what happened if I'm going to help you."

He shook his head. "No, this isn't on you." He pushed his plate away, his gaze boring into Cate's eyes. "You know I love you, right?"

"Yes. Me too."

"Right." Then he sprinted upstairs to his room.

Cate numbly cleared away his half-eaten snack. She heard thumps from his room and wondered what he was doing. There had to be a way she could protect him, but she wasn't sure exactly what had happened and how deep his involvement reached.

Could he have found Henry March's gun—maybe in the pool house, maybe in the Hardys' garage or yard—and shared it with Caleb or Riley? She could have kicked herself for leading police to the potting shed. If not for that, the dirt-filled milk can would continue to harbor its secret.

Cate thought back over the previous year, trying to find the point when the relationship between Savannah and Isaiah began to splinter. The trigger must have been more than Savannah's betrayal of the Gospel Mission, but who knew what went on in the mind of a sixteen-year-old boy? The male brain didn't fully mature until the mid to late twenties. Perhaps the knowledge that his Savannah Mom was cheating on his Cate Mom, combined with Savannah's disloyalty to the Gospel Mission, had been enough to curdle Isaiah's respect.

And there was a murkier concern, one that any adoptive mother carried in the deepest recesses of her soul—no matter how good the nurturing was, would nature eventually assert itself? The last she'd heard, the police thought Caleb had written those threatening notes, and maybe he had. But what kind of genes might Isaiah have inherited from his birth mother? Her mind jumped to the fat woman in front of the post office, the one who had played such a vivid role in her imagination. Cate envisioned her creeping to their mailbox and watching their house like an avenging hawk.

Cate's breath faltered, and she wondered if she was on the verge of a nervous breakdown.Presumably, Riley was the one who had put the detectives onto Mikala. Her heart skittered out of rhythm. *What else did Riley see that night? What did she do?*

She heard Isaiah's heavy steps rushing down the staircase, and then the front door slammed. *Where is he going?* She peered through the shutters and saw him pounding on the Hardys' front door. An idea occurred to her. A terrible idea.

Her legs felt like lead as she ran to the kitchen and yanked open the drawer where she kept the keys of three neighbors. When they traveled, she fed one's dog, checked on another's cat, and watered the Hardys' plants. She was not surprised to find that the Hardys' key was missing.

Chapter 70

Riley

Isaiah had never come to the front door before. Riley opened it, and he tumbled in.

"You just left." She laughed, remembering their morning at the pool.

He looked sheepish, as if embarrassed over his eager entrance. "I thought I'd walk you to work."

"Why?"

"It's getting dark earlier."

She pointed to the window, where the sun was shining brightly. "Yeah, but I start work at four o'clock. It's not going to be dark by then."

"I know. But like that man said at the meeting, there have been two murders and a rape right around us. All unsolved. It's too dangerous for you to be out alone."

Riley recalled another warning about her safety, this one from Detective Hortense. She didn't know if the detective was really concerned about her or thought she was withholding information about what she had seen in the pool house. Miller Washburn had succeeded in sowing distrust, and she couldn't blame the Greenbrier detectives for doubting her. But none of that explained Isaiah's behavior.

"What is up with you?" she asked.

Isaiah didn't answer but went to the patio door and bolted it. He did the same at the door to the garage. "Only three entrances to this house?"

She was mystified and becoming a little edgy. *Is he locking us in?* She inched toward the front door. "I don't know what you're doing, but I have to go to work, Isaiah." Stepping onto the front porch, in view of all the neighbors, she felt better. She considered leaving him inside, but that made no sense. "Come on!" she called.

From the porch, Isaiah looked over at his house as Cate stepped into their front yard. As Riley and Isaiah were leaving, she called, "Isaiah, you need to come home!"

"No!" he yelled. "I'm walking Riley to work then spending the night at Matt's. He's picking me up at the restaurant."

Cate paused, looking uncertain. Then she went inside. Isaiah shoved his hands into his pockets, and they walked without speaking all the way to the Gospel Mission. Several men called out to him. He waved but didn't smile.

"Are you all right?" Riley finally asked.

He cocked his head to indicate the mission. "This place is the best thing in Greenbrier," he said softly. "How does she not realize that?"

"Who? Your mom?"

"She's not my mom," he said flatly. "I think we've established that much this summer."

She was taken aback by the turmoil in his voice. It reminded her of how Caleb spoke about his mother. Riley thought again of how surprised she'd been to find Rayanne instead of Savannah on the sofa with Luke, and she wondered if Isaiah would have been similarly surprised. *Could he have been there?*

The idea startled her, and she tripped on a raised lip where an ancient oak had buckled the sidewalk. Isaiah caught her roughly before her knees could crack on the concrete.

She gained her balance and twisted out of his grip then dashed for the welcoming terrace of Pizza by the Park. "Bye!" she yelled over her shoulder. "Thanks for walking me."

She rushed inside the restaurant, dizzy with the notion that was bouncing around her brain. *For Pete's sake, it's just Isaiah,* she told herself. *It's Isaiah.*

Chapter 71

Cate

Cate yanked the kitchen drawer completely out of its cabinet and flipped it upside down. Pens, paper clips, a screwdriver, and nails clattered to the floor. The other two neighbors' keys were there. But not the Hardys'.

Cate longed to talk to Savannah. That was what she'd always done, at least until this summer. But if she released her unspeakable suspicion into the universe—that Isaiah might be protecting someone who had targeted Savannah—those words could never be taken back. And a part of her refused to believe it was a possibility.

He was spending the night at Matt's, she assured herself. If Caleb or Riley revealed anything about Isaiah's knowledge or involvement in the shooting, the police would come here. She'd have a heads-up.

She punched her wife's name on her cell phone, and Savannah picked up immediately. "Hi," said Cate. "Where are you?"

"At a showing. What's up?"

"Not a thing. Just wondering when you'll be home and what you want to do for dinner."

"Surprise me. In or out is fine with me."

"Well, you're easy," Cate said. Silence followed.

"Anything else?" Savannah asked.

"Mikala has been arrested."

"What?" Savannah was plainly shocked. "Wait. Let me get somewhere more private." Cate heard her murmuring to someone then heels clicking before she came back on the line. "They think Mikala killed Luke?"

"I don't know any details, just that those two detectives took her away in handcuffs."

"When was this?"

"Earlier today. This morning."

"Damn. Where's the grapevine when you need it?" Savannah paused. "Any idea what led to that?"

"Isaiah said they'd talked to Riley for a long time. Maybe she told them something."

"Wow. Interesting. I have another hour and a half here, then I'll be home. How about piña coladas on the porch?"

Cate relaxed for the first time all day. "You got it. I'll have them waiting."

"Where's Isaiah tonight? Working?"

"No, he's spending the night with Matt."

"Ah, the house to ourselves. Sounds wonderful."

Cate hung up with a slight release of tension. Maybe she'd been worried for nothing. Maybe the murders were all about Luke, and Mikala and hadn't touched her family. She and Savannah would have an evening together, talking about what had gone on with Luke and getting everything out in the open.

She felt bad about the dissolution of the family next door. But maybe it would be the salvation of her own.

Chapter 72

Riley

Isaiah hung around Pizza by the Park for most of Riley's shift, drinking Dr. Pepper and talking to Gus. Twice, he disappeared for an hour, but apparently, he'd just walked around Roosevelt Park. On her break, she'd asked him what he was doing.

"Waiting to walk you home," he responded.

"Why? If I need an escort, I can ask Gus or Roman."

"But you won't."

The kid knew her better than she'd thought. "Seriously, Isaiah, this is ridiculous. You can't be hanging around my workplace all the time. You've got your own friends, your own life."

"Once you're safe at home, I'll leave you alone."

"You told Cate your friend Matt was picking you up."

He grimaced. "I know."

"You lied to her?"

"I guess I did."

Riley had thrown up her hands and returned to work. At almost eleven o'clock, Isaiah was seated on the patio, watching her. For some reason, her aggravation turned to anxiety. *What is up with him?*

She considered asking Gus to walk her home, but he was busy with a bachelorette party that had gotten rowdy. She asked Roman if he needed her to stay, but he said they could handle it. His hands were full, and he didn't offer to accompany her.

Riley pictured herself walking home with Isaiah and couldn't shake her apprehension. Maybe Detective Hortense was right, and she'd seen something—or someone—she hadn't realized she'd seen.

Finally, rather than pass Isaiah to exit through the patio, she sneaked through the kitchen door and emerged onto the Crescent Trail. The asphalt path was lit only sporadically, so there were inky stretches of blackness between streetlights. She shuffled, hoping not to trip over a fallen branch or a darting possum. With trees crowding in on either side, she questioned her decision to duck Isaiah. She slunk behind the Gospel Mission, and almost ran into a man whose cigarette glowed red-orange in the dark. He grabbed her shoulders, and she screamed.

"Hey, steady, steady," he said, releasing her. "You were about to run me over."

"Sorry," she mumbled. "So sorry."

She needed to get off the trail, so she cut across the Gospel Mission parking lot, glancing down Gunter to make sure Isaiah wasn't following. Just in case, she crossed the street and headed to Mikala's house by a circuitous route, walking up Parker past the mill house that belonged to the Meadowses. A red-orange dot like the one she'd just seen glimmered from their porch, and Riley guessed Mr. Meadows was outside for a smoke. But then the glimmer rose, and she could tell he was standing. The glow zigzagged and disappeared, and she wondered uneasily if it was because he'd seen her. She sped up, irritated at Isaiah for making her so edgy.

She passed the vacant house next door that looked like Silas's. It had been a while since she'd walked this way, but the squat house hit her all over again. The thought that Silas's murder had led Mikala to invite her to Greenbrier sickened her. Even if Mikala hadn't killed Luke, she'd intended to. If Riley had been lonely enough to start something with Luke, she would be in jail right now, facing decades in prison.

She shivered. *How could Mikala do that to me—and to Rayanne, who's dead because of the actions Mikala set in motion?*

Riley wrenched herself away from the orange brick house and circled onto Montreat. Passing Caleb's old boarding house, she heard footsteps and a banging door. She twirled, scanning nervously for Isaiah, for a stranger, for anyone. She heard bushes rustling but could make out nothing.

She began running, turning onto Marigold, then Gunter, sweeping her eyes along the yards and front porches that lined the grand avenue. She'd neglected to turn on the front-porch lights, so Mikala's house loomed dim and foreboding. Gasping for breath, all she could think about was getting inside and locking up tight. Once she was settled, she'd call Mama. She was ready to leave Greenbrier as soon as the police would allow it. Riley didn't want to be in this house, in this town, another minute.

She sprinted up the front steps and slid her key into the lock then slammed and bolted the door behind her. Double-checking the doors to the patio and garage, she found them bolted as Isaiah had left them. As her breathing slowed, she puzzled again over his strange behavior and wondered if he would pound on the door soon. *If he does, should I answer or call Detective Hortense?*

Sighing, she fetched an open bottle of Mikala's chardonnay from the refrigerator and emptied it into an oversized wineglass. Tired and anxious, she trudged up the stairs and reached for the wall switch as she entered her bedroom.

The neighbor seated on her bed blinked. Riley saw the latex gloves and the oddly notched knife. Still, it took several seconds for her brain to catch up to what her eyes were telling her.

"Oh," she finally said. "It was you."

Chapter 73

Riley

Riley was unable to tear her eyes from the wood-handled knife in her neighbor's hand. Somehow, those latex gloves signaled that she intended to use it. "I thought you were the target," Riley said. "Everyone was so mad at you."

"I'm sure they were," Savannah answered. "Your whore of a sister surprised us all."

Riley started to shudder. "But... why are you here? Why are you telling me?"

"Since you ratted out Mikala, I figured I was next."

"I didn't tell the police about Mikala! I didn't know it was her!" She was practically wailing. "And I never saw you!"

"No? Too bad, then. I was afraid you had."

Riley thought back to the moment she'd stumbled from her bedroom in the pool house, wakened by the noise Luke and Rayanne were making. She'd seen the figure in the kitchen doorway, who turned out to be Mikala. She'd seen a burst of gunfire. She'd seen Caleb at the rear window. But she'd never seen Savannah.

Her legs started to quiver, and the wine splashed out of her glass. She wanted to sink to the floor, but she couldn't defend herself from there. She needed to run—to get far, far away from that blade.

Her mind flashed to Silas and his electrifying green eyes and the way they softened when he looked at her. His life had ended with a ripping blade. And it was all her fault. Maybe it was appropriate that her life would end the same way.

"I... I thought it was you on the sofa," she said, edging backward, one hand feeling for the doorjamb. "With Luke. I'd seen your hair on the pillows. Earlier, I mean."

Riley was babbling, and Savannah looked uninterested. She touched a finger to the point of her knife. "Luke told me he was working late. And it wasn't the first time. When I started hearing him make the same excuses to me that he'd made to Mikala, I got suspicious. With good reason, it turns out." She shook her head in disgust. "Because of that little guttersnipe."

Despite everything, Riley was incensed at hearing Rayanne scorned by this woman who'd grown up in no grander circumstances than they had. How dare she speak so dismissively of her sister? Of both of them?

"You can't get away with this." Riley tried to speak firmly, but it came out more a squawk. "Detective Hortense will know it was you."

"Ah, but will he?" Savannah displayed the knife as if she was selling it. "This is a Bowie, a favorite of collectors. Earle Meadows bought it from Henry March, and I, um... borrowed it during one of my visits. It won't take much convincing for the police to think resentful old Earle Meadows purchased Mr. March's gun as well. Completes a circle, don't you think?"

Riley's eyes searched the room for a weapon. A lamp, maybe. Across from her was the closet. Maybe she could jab Savannah's eyes with a metal hanger. As she stared, a hanging shirt sleeve fluttered.

Her eyes flicked to Savannah, who was advancing. Riley hurled her wineglass and hit Savannah's forehead. Savannah cried out, but Riley knew the pain wouldn't last, and she ran onto the landing to find a lamp. She tripped over an ottoman and fell sprawling.

Savannah was on her in an instant, and Riley could feel the cold wine dripping from her face and hair. Savannah was enraged and swung the knife wildly. Riley tried to seize her hand but missed and felt the blade slice into her upper arm.

Her screams joined with an unearthly squeal of metal on metal from the bedroom. Blindly, frantically, Riley pushed at her, cringing against the stabbing sensation she knew was coming. Savannah was a whirling dervish of weight and motion, elbows and knees, and another slash caught the same arm. Riley screamed again and tried to shove her off.

Over her shoulder, the incongruous sight of clothes flying added to the surreal scene. As her mind clamored to understand, Isaiah burst through the bedroom doorway, tears streaming down his face, brandishing his cell phone.

"Mom, stop!" he shouted, dropping the phone to grab Savannah around the shoulders and throat and yank her off Riley.

Savannah choked and coughed and swiped recklessly with the knife. A shiny red line erupted on Isaiah's forearm. His expression was incredulous, and he flung her away. She rolled, hit the wall, and scrambled to her feet, pointing the knife at him, then at Riley, then back at him.

"Isaiah!" she cried. "No... what? No!"

"I've got Detective Hortense on the line. He heard everything."

"No, Isaiah, you've got it all wrong," she pleaded, approaching him with open arms. "Where is your phone? Give it to me."

"No!" he shouted. "It's too late, you lying, greedy..." He burst into sobs.

They heard a splintering roar from downstairs, as if an entire wall was collapsing, then the hammering of officers' footsteps seconds before Detectives Hortense and Marconi surged onto the landing. While Detective Marconi trained his gun on Savannah, Detective Hortense jerked Savannah's arms behind her and snapped on handcuffs.

Riley stood on shaking legs and hurled herself into Isaiah's arms. He held her awkwardly, his tears wetting her hair, the blood from their arms dousing their shirts and dripping onto Mikala's carpet.

"I'm so sorry, Riley," he said. "I'm so sorry."

Riley was crying, too, out of relief and shame. "Me too," she managed. "I'm sorry I doubted you."

They remained like that for several minutes, even as police officers applied pressure to their wounds with T-shirts they found on the floor of Riley's bedroom. She pulled away, curious about what had gone on in there. The closet rod was down, and her clothes were scattered in heaps as if a tornado had roared through.

"You were hiding in the closet?" she asked Isaiah. "Before she got here?"

He nodded. "I took the house key Mikala gave to Cate Mom. And Luke gave Savannah Mom pool-house keys that included the patio door to the main house."

"But you were at the restaurant, waiting to walk me home."

"Yeah. I knew if I came in with you, nothing could happen." He looked at her sadly. "When I realized you'd ditched me, I ran all the way here. I was coming through the front door when I heard Savannah Mom coming in from the patio."

"How long have you known?" Detective Marconi asked Isaiah. "We were still looking at your mother as a possible target."

"I was, too, at first," he said. "But I saw her that night on the porch of the potting shed. I didn't understand what she was doing. When you found Mr. March's gun in the planter, I realized she must have hidden it there."

"What were you doing outside in the storm?" the detective asked.

"The thunder woke me up. It shook the house, and I was afraid lightning had struck a tree in the backyard. So I went outside. And saw her." Isaiah hung his head.

"But we found the gun two days ago, Isaiah. Why didn't you say something then?"

Mother and son gazed at each other. Savannah remained unblinking, but Isaiah's face was anguished. His voice was barely a whisper.

"She's my mother. I didn't want to believe... I tried to..." He wiped his face with his hands.

"Everything changed when you believed she was a threat to Riley," Detective Hortense said.

Isaiah nodded.

Savannah shot him a look of pure contempt. "I want my lawyer," she demanded.

Chapter 74

Cate

Cate bolted upright, ripped from a troubled sleep by what sounded like an explosion next door. Savannah was not in bed, so she raced to Isaiah's room to peer out his window. He was not in bed either.

That's right—he's at his friend Matt's. Calm down, Cate.

Her mind was muddled. Savannah hadn't drunk her share of piña coladas earlier, and Cate had imbibed one too many. She saw police SUVs parked crookedly on the street and officers streaming into the Hardy residence.

Her heart accelerated, beating so fast and so loud that she couldn't think. *Did Isaiah lie? Could he be next door?*

Cate jerked the window-blind cord so hard the blinds snapped from their frame and toppled onto her feet. She kicked them aside and pressed her face to the windowpane. The familiar figures of Detectives Hortense and Marconi emerged from the hole where the Hardys' door had once stood. Between them was not the tall, beloved figure of Isaiah but the smaller, voluptuous redhead who was her wife.

Cate sagged against the wall. Somehow, she'd gotten it all wrong, and she was bewildered. But already, she was aware of the tiniest sliver of relief creeping in. As she dashed from the room, barefoot, unheeding of her camisole and pajama pants, she didn't understand what was happening. All she knew was that her son would need her.

Chapter 75

Riley

Riley met Isaiah and Caleb on a bench in Roosevelt Park after school. Isaiah had invited them to his house, but Riley was afraid her presence might be too hard on Cate. She passed out the chilled cans of Dr. Pepper she'd bought after saying goodbye to Roman and Gus.

The Beetle was packed and ready for the trip to Mobile, where she and her parents would hold Rayanne's funeral. It would be small and private after all the horrors of the news coverage. Then Riley wanted to stop drinking, return to college, and become a person she could respect. Who knew if she had the strength to follow through with any of it?

She'd left Mikala's house without seeing her again and spent two nights in a hotel at the request of the police as they wrapped up their investigation. Detective Marconi helped load her car as he explained how Savannah had found Henry March's gun when she bought his vacant mill house. She'd put it in storage, where it remained until she decided to shoot Luke Hardy and the woman he'd chosen to replace her. It was a happy coincidence that Henry March's grandson was living in their potting shed to take the blame.

"Did she love Luke that much?" Riley asked.

"Who knows with someone like her?" Detective Marconi said. "I think it was more that she was furious to think he would discard her."

"But that old knife—how long had she planned to kill me?"

"That was spur-of-the-moment. Cate told her that afternoon that Mikala had been arrested. Savannah assumed you had told us that Mikala was in the pool house and that you knew she was there as well."

"Right. Savannah told me that much."

"She headed straight to Earle Meadows's house. Luckily for her, he wasn't home, and his wife let her in, ostensibly to hear yet another offer on their house. Then Savannah asked to use the bathroom and stole the knife from Mr. Meadows's display of collectibles. He'd shown it to her years ago, before he grew to distrust her." Detective Marconi slammed the Beetle's trunk. "She hoped to plant the narrative that *you* had recognized Mr. Meadows as the shooter and he had to get rid of you."

Riley exhaled shakily. Savannah's violent plan had come close to materializing.

The boys wanted to tell Riley something, so she leaned back, lazy in the afternoon heat.

"Go ahead." Caleb punched Isaiah's arm. "You start."

Isaiah could hardly contain his grin. "We're brothers!"

"Well, half brothers," Caleb said.

She stared at them, her mind leaping to make the connection. "The extortion notes?"

"Yeah," said Caleb. "It was my mother, Doreen, who was trying to get money from Isaiah's mothers. I found a letter in her tent after she died and asked my uncle Roger. Around the time Isaiah was born, she was living on the street. That was the year I was with my granddad. Doreen was doing drugs, and DSS took the baby. Detective Hortense helped us get the DNA test to confirm it."

"The best part," said Isaiah, "is that when Cate Mom found out, she offered to let Caleb live with us as long as he enrolls in college or Greenbrier Tech. He and I are working on getting his GED right now."

"But not on Gunter Avenue, right? I saw your For Sale sign."

"Yeah, Cate Mom and I want something smaller, less pretentious," Isaiah said. "As long as it has three bedrooms. We were never comfortable living here, as you know. And moving away from Mikala, well, that's a no-brainer."

"Wow," Riley said. "That's incredible. I'm really happy for both of you." She turned to Caleb. "You gonna keep working at Pizza by the Park?"

"Oh yeah." He dipped his head in a way that was both dear and familiar. "Roman gave me your old job."

"You're going to be a waiter? That's terrific. Better tips!"

She pointed across the street to the Greenbrier Rescue Mission, where homeless folks were lining up to get sandwiches and bottled water. "What do you hear about the shelter?"

Isaiah shrugged. "It's not going anywhere for now. Farrah Newell bought us some time." He looked at the ground. "And of course, no homeless person was responsible for Luke and Rayanne's deaths." They were silent for a moment, allowing him to bring up Savannah's name—or not. He did. "But Savannah Mom wasn't the only developer. Gentrification will always be an issue, don't you think?"

"I suppose." Riley looked at these two young men, related by blood but raised so differently. "You know, though, you two would make quite a team, fighting for the mission. Caleb has the personal experience. You have the money and connections."

"Could be," Caleb said. "We've got time to figure it out."

"Make me a promise," she said, standing to leave. "Let me know how it goes."

Isaiah peeled away to teach his GED class while Caleb followed Riley to her car, chattering about his promotion at Pizza by the Park and the courses he hoped to take at Greenbrier Tech. He opened the door of the old Beetle and helped her inside. *My little brother*, she thought fondly. She would miss him.

He closed the door. "Oh, and Riley," he said, glancing around to make sure he wasn't overheard. "One last thing. Be careful. I saw you, you know."

Her mind was already on the long drive ahead. She stowed her purse in the floorboard of the passenger seat. "Saw me?"

"That night. Through the window. I saw you."

Chapter 76

The Night Of
Riley

The discovery that the body beneath Luke was Rayanne, not Savannah, shook Riley to her core. She whirled and sprinted to the bedroom, grasping the tequila bottle on her bedside table. Ignoring the glass beside it, she chugged from the bottle. The slippery liquid burned as it hit her esophagus. Her stomach revolted, and it almost came back up, but she swallowed convulsively and kept it down. She drank some more. She had to regain her calm.

Her mind churned at what she'd seen. *Rayanne.* Her sister was dead. Her sister was dead. She waited for grief to wash over her, but that wasn't what happened. Her mind was a whiteboard with block letters in black marker: *She got what she deserved.*

Rayanne had killed Silas, whom Riley genuinely loved. And somehow, after all this time, Rayanne had gotten what she deserved. Riley replaced the tequila on the table, and a thought occurred to her—maybe it had always lurked, but she hadn't allowed her mind to explore it. *Did Rayanne kill Silas for the money or because I loved him?*

Riley stood motionless beneath the ceiling fan and considered this possibility for the first time—consciously, at least. It had prowled through her subconscious all along. She recalled her sister's glee in showing her friends how alike they looked. She recalled the rose tattoo Rayanne had gotten that summer. On the underside of her forearm, so like Riley's lily.

And earlier, how she'd appropriated Riley's clothes, jewelry, friends, and boyfriend. How Mama, so often, had come into her bedroom and said, "Riley, please talk to your sister. You're the only one she'll listen to." *But did she listen for my counsel or only for clues as to what was important to me—what she could take, what she could destroy?*

Out of the corner of her eye, Riley had watched Rayanne's face as they threw suitcases and cardboard boxes into her truck bed so she could flee to Panama City. The expression was excitement, which Riley had attributed to fright. But maybe it had been excitement, pure and simple—excitement over killing someone Riley had loved.

Her heart felt like a concrete block, hardened and numb. She picked up her cell phone. It was clear that the shooter was no longer in the pool house, and she needed to call 9-1-1.

But first, like an automaton, she returned to the living room. Rayanne's arm dangled from the sofa, slender, lifeless, the rose tattoo in stark relief against the white of her arm. Blood loss, Riley guessed, had made it whiter than normal. The arm was so small, so girlish. She could still be a teen.

Riley stared at her sister's arm until it moved. She wrenched her eyes away, blinking. No, that couldn't be right. She was hallucinating from the stress.

Filled with dread, she dragged her eyes back to Rayanne's arm... and saw the pinkie quiver. Death throes, surely. Maybe both bodies were settling.

Riley watched, her breathing shallow. No movement. She felt dizzy and bent to regain her equilibrium, but the motion sent the tequila sloshing in her stomach. Still queasy, she raised her head...and saw the tremor of a finger.

Rayanne was alive. All other thoughts fled. Riley rushed to the sofa and lifted the bloodied cushion from her sister's face. Rayanne's eyes fluttered open, and relief flooded them.

"Riley," she croaked. "Help me."

She knew that Riley would help her because Riley always had. Rayanne knew that she could lie and steal and cheat and even kill with impunity because Riley had allowed it. She knew that whatever this was, Riley would fix it.

"All right," Riley whispered. "All right. Everything is all right." She gently replaced the cushion over her sister's face. And pressed. And pressed. And pressed. Until she was no longer moving.

Then she called 9-1-1.

After

Caleb stood by Riley's car door, smiling. But everything had changed in an instant. It was eighty-five degrees, but suddenly, Riley was freezing. She stared into Caleb's face, at the blond bangs that were growing out floppy again, and at the skinny frame that made him look younger than he was.

He had seen her through the rear window of the pool house. She knew he'd been there earlier—she'd seen his face in the drenching rain. But it seemed like hours had passed since Rayanne's death. It must have been minutes, perhaps even seconds. He must have stayed, watching.

Will I never learn? Images of Detectives Washburn, Hortense, and Marconi flashed before her eyes, marching toward her like a TV police squad, smiling victoriously. But no, Caleb was the one smiling, nodding, encouraging her. He'd waited until Isaiah left to say what he had to say.

He rapped the car roof in a gesture of goodbye. He was letting her know he had her back.

Riley put the old Beetle into first gear, which took a couple of tries because her hands were trembling. He hadn't told the police, and he wouldn't.

She breathed deeply and pulled onto Gunter Avenue. She was free to drive to Mobile or anywhere else. She turned onto West Roosevelt, heading across town for the interstate.

Riley had relived every minute of that night. Incessantly. She saw Rayanne lying on the pool-house sofa, bleeding copiously from her upper thigh, her skin white beyond white. Over and over, she assured herself that Savannah was the shooter, Savannah was the guilty one. Rayanne would have bled out from her gunshot wound eventually. Justice had been served.

Sometimes she even believed it.

Acknowledgments

This is my first book with Red Adept Publishing, so my heartfelt gratitude goes out to owner Lynn McNamee and her team, including editors Sara Gardiner and Sarah Carleton. You have made it a pleasure.

My previous work as a pastor to homeless parishioners wouldn't have been possible if Reid Lehman, Ryan Duerk, Lauren Stephens, Jeremy Huff, David Hanna, and their colleagues hadn't managed nearby shelters, much like Greenbrier Gospel Mission presented here. Thank you, friends.

Thanks to the staffs and participants of Triune Mercy Center, United Ministries, United Housing Connections, Greater Greenville Mental Health, Greenville Homeless Alliance, Gateway, New Horizon Family Health Services, Miracle Hill, Salvation Army, Jumpstart, and Soteria, who soldier on. You make our community stronger.

As always, my writers group of Wanda Owings, Susan Clary Simmons, Jeanne Brooks, and Allison Green were ever willing to read and re-read.

Thanks to other early readers: Elaine Nocks, Madison Moore, Anne Spence, Lynne Lucas and Toni Masters.

Most beach mates would gripe if you holed up in a bedroom to finish an edit. So thanks to Bryant and Gayle Brown, Owen and Mary Beth McFadden, and Steve and Debbie Dawes for understanding—and entertaining the dolphins in my absence.

To all my readers, I am most grateful to you for sticking with me through this, my sixth book. I promise to keep writing if you'll keep reading! All reviews are helpful—on BookBub, Shepherd, Amazon, Goodreads, or wherever.

Big thanks to my late mom, Doris Richardson, who was always my biggest book pusher; to Lori, Robert, Rick, Candace, and Maggie, who are quick to help with a launch party, and to Sam, Ryan, Bennie, Robin, and Tyler, who spread the word beyond the Carolinas.

As always, my greatest thanks go to Vince, Dustin, Taylor, and Madison, my constants. And a huge welcome to Michael, our newest family member.

Lastly, I love book clubs, book luncheons, book dinners, book coffees—you get the picture. If you'd like to have me speak at yours, contact me at richardsonmoored@gmail.com.

About the Author

Deb Richardson-Moore has worked as an award-winning newspaper journalist and as a pastor to homeless congregants. Her murder mysteries fall somewhere between cozies and gritty psychological thrillers and have twice been named finalists in Killer Nashville competitions.

Deb and her husband live in upstate South Carolina, where she enjoys gardening, volunteering, public speaking, and watching TV thrillers adapted from favorite books. She travels frequently to the beach and to visit their three adult children, who are spread from South Carolina to southern California to Southeast Asia.

Read more at debrichardsonmoore.com.

About the Publisher

Dear Reader,

We hope you enjoyed this book. Please consider leaving a review on your favorite book site.

Visit https://RedAdeptPublishing.com to see our entire catalogue.

Check out our app for short stories, articles, and interviews. You'll also be notified of future releases and special sales.

Made in the USA
Columbia, SC
23 June 2024

37421689R00209